Walt Whitman

From a daguerreotype of about 1854
by Gabriel Harrison

PLATE I

WALT
WHITMAN

an American

~~~~~~~~~

A STUDY IN BIOGRAPHY

BY HENRY SEIDEL CANBY

'Walt Whitman, an American, . . .
. . . of mighty Manhattan the son.'

WITH ILLUSTRATIONS

1943

HOUGHTON MIFFLIN COMPANY · BOSTON

The Riverside Press Cambridge

The Riverside Press
CAMBRIDGE · MASSACHUSETTS
PRINTED IN THE U.S.A.

Acknowledgments

∿∿∿∿

1

For suggestions, criticism, and permissions in the preparation of this book I am indebted to many students of Whitman, to publishers of books about him, and to friendly advisers. I wish to name here particularly Professor Emory Holloway, to whose extensive studies and discoveries I owe much; Mr. Clifton J. Furness, another Whitman scholar; Mr. Alfred F. Goldsmith, expert in Whitmaniana and friend of all lovers of Whitman; Miss Bertha Johnston, daughter of Whitman's friend; Mrs. Martha L. Davis, custodian of the Whitman House in Camden; Professors Robert E. Spiller and Townsend Scudder III of Swarthmore College; Mr. Christopher Morley, a connoisseur in Whitman; Mr. Gilbert Troxell of the Yale Library; Mr. Herbert Bolton, librarian of *The Century Club;* and the librarians of the Library of Congress. Also my wife and my publishers, who have been most helpful in criticism of details. I wish especially to acknowledge the help as secretary and assistant of Mrs. Burton W. Benjamin of New York, who has prepared the selective bibliography, and worked with me upon every chapter of the book.

But my indebtedness is more extensive than these references would indicate. To my predecessors in the field of Whitman biography, particularly to Horace Traubel, to Henry Bryant Binns, to Bliss Perry, to Emory Holloway, to Jean Catel, and to Clifton Furness, I owe much, and have not hesitated to contract debts and fully acknowledge them. Now, when it is so necessary for Americans to feel the strength and continuity of their own traditions, a new life of Whitman should be not so much a final mopping up of unpublished letters and fragments, as an attempt to set in order and make use of all pertinent information. I have included in this book not a little unpublished writing of Whitman, but I have made no attempt to do so where the texts and facts already printed by my predecessors are more enlightening than fresh (and usually repetitive) sources.

2

I thank, particularly, Doubleday, Doran and Company, custodians of the Whitman text, for their general permission to quote from books noted in my bibliography, especially 'The Gathering of the Forces,' 'New York Dissected,' 'I Sit and Look Out,' and 'The Complete Writings of Walt Whitman,' published by G. P. Putnam's Sons. Also Houghton Mifflin Company, for some quotations from Bliss Perry's biography; E. P. Dutton and Company, for their courteous permission to avail myself of pictures in Binns's biography; Dodd, Mead and Company and Sir Max Beerbohm for the use of his cartoon; Harper and Brothers, and John A. Kouwenhoven, for two pictures reprinted from *Harper's Weekly* in his 'Adventures of America'; and the Horace Traubel family for quotations from 'Walt Whitman in Camden.' Where possible, I have recorded indebtedness for Walt Whitman's pictures used in this book. For the Camden etching and the Gilchrist painting I thank Mrs. Frank J. Sprague. Doctor Bucke's biography of 1883, in which Whitman was a collaborator, has been of great value; also the two volumes by John Burroughs, in the first of which he had a hand, and Clara Barrus's 'Whitman and Burroughs, Comrades.' The Nonesuch Press (and the Limited Editions Club) and the editor, Emory Holloway, have allowed me to quote from their admirable edition of all the poetry and the best of the prose of Whitman. I thank also the Yale Library and the Library of Congress for unpublished documents used by permission in this book. Other references to special works will be found in the Notes.

3

There will presumably never be a final book on Whitman,

because the 'Leaves of Grass,' which was, essentially, his most important life, will have new aspects and therefore new interpretations for every generation. New facts as to his personal life may of course be discovered, but it seems most improbable that anything new can be learned about Whitman which will change the estimate of his character and achievements that can now be formed. Reticent as to his private affairs, he was self-revealing beyond all of his contemporaries in his poetry, and that must always control any biography which deals, as a good biography must, with his inner life. An assemblage, for the benefit of scholars, of all known information about his friends, his family, and his daily doings, is much needed, and such an assemblage is soon to be made readily accessible in a book by my friend, Mr. Furness. But the searcher through Whitmaniana, in print or unpublished, whose purpose it is to write of Whitman himself and of the 'Leaves of Grass,' finds himself choked with duplicating material in which the law of diminishing returns quickly begins to operate.

Whitman's sources were extensive, often amorphous, and so rapidly assimilated into his metabolism that only the most general reference and description seem useful in a biography. A book on these sources should be written, and will be a contribution to the intellectual history of the United States, though I doubt whether it will much affect our estimates of the value of Whitman's poetry. There should also be a special study of Whitman's extraordinary influence abroad and here, and his parallels, particularly in Europe in the revolutionary movements of the nineteenth century. Though I have devoted much attention to the spiritual, intellectual, and national climate of his mind, and have mentioned, where relevant, his extensions abroad, I have not felt these special studies in detail lay within the limits of a book in which the history is essentially of the man himself.

Also, Walt Whitman's America was not a real America, though the real America was his background and a source of his inspiration. It was a symbolic America, existing in his own mind, and always pointed toward a future of which he was prophetic. No sociological, political, economic, or psychological history of the

United States in which Whitman lived, will, in itself, interpret and explain the poet Whitman. One must first make intelligible Whitman himself and his 'Leaves.' While I have by no means neglected his American background, it has been a study of Whitman the man, and Whitman the poet, and his symbolic autobiography in the 'Leaves of Grass,' which has been the purpose of this book.

KILLINGWORTH, CONNECTICUT
June 5, 1943

CONTENTS

ILLUSTRATIONS

CHAPTER I

Preface on the importance

of the subject

WALT WHITMAN is destined to become — perhaps has already become — a legend in American history. Like one of his heroes, George Washington, the poet of democracy has assumed some of the qualities of myth. His ample figure and tumultuously bearded face are more familiar than his writing, which is more quoted from than read in its entirety; and indeed his face, which he put on view at every opportunity, has the symbolic and representative character of the statues of Alexander, the powerfully jawed portraits of Washington, the brooding photographs of Lincoln in his later years.

For this legend of a representative man of heroic stature, neither the earlier worshipful studies nor the later factual, and far more accurate, biographies of Whitman give an adequate explanation. There was only one brief period of his external life which could be called even mildly heroic, and he himself so frequently and reverentially celebrated his services in the hospitals of the Civil War, that more than one misguided enemy has charged him with creating a legend which had little basis in fact.

There is not only a Whitman legend, but also many quite unheroic facts and a good deal of innuendo in the many books about Whitman. Readers of some of these books retain a picture which is superficial, though it has much truth. They remember best Whitman as he was in his maturity, a rubicund bearded man, egotistical, idolized by a circle of friends which contained no great names, slandered or misunderstood by most of the intellectuals of his own country, unknown to the masses of which he professed to write, a prophet without honor except among a few, and too many of that few outside of the United States. They recall that, when pursuing the great career which Emerson prophesied, he used (with pathetic unsuccess) every means of publicity, fair and dubious, from pose to self-glorification. They think of an old man, paralyzed, sitting in an untidy room among drifts of letters and manuscripts, scratching out with his cane documents of long-dead controversies and tributes to his genius, in order to help his disciples build up a legend of greatness in which the plain facts of an uneventful life would be obscured or forgotten. That is how he is remembered by many who do know his history — and it is all true, but only part of the truth.

For the truth of the matter is that a satisfactory biography of Whitman must be essentially a biography of an inner life and of the mysterious creative processes of poetry. It was in Whitman's inner life that the great things, some of them heroic, happened. It is his inner life that infused into the 'Leaves of Grass' such greatness as it possesses, which is far more than his contemporaries guessed. When the middle-aged poet wrote of the 'Leaves,' 'Who touches this touches a man,' he was telling the literal truth. We all distrust interpretive biographies, but the biography of Whitman has to be interpretive, because the sources for an account of what is really significant in his life are in his writings. Walt's visible life in the theatres of New York, on the streets of Brooklyn, in the hospitals of Washington, and in his room at Camden is a by-product of that inner life, which itself was conditioned by influences as much spiritual as physical. And the American that he created in his poems, out of what his eyes saw and his ears heard, was meant from the beginning to be a symbol of a faith and a dream.

So here we have the problem child of American literature — a just term, for in some respects Whitman never outgrew his adolescence. And here also the prophet — or better the seer — of American democracy — a just term also, for no other poet, and no other prose writer but Lincoln, made its ideals entirely articulate. The problem child constantly reached for what he could not grasp, and left much of his work in confusion — a confusion which unfortunately has been reflected in many of the early books about him. The seer, with one of the most perceptive and prophetic minds in modern history, dealt in dreams and faiths with a realism which shocked and an egotism that repelled his contemporaries. The poet — the very great poet — like a young trotting horse of native strain, broke constantly into uneven and irregular gaits, and was seldom at his best for more than a score of lines at a time; nor did he try to keep to poetry when prose would serve his ends.

The solvent of these seeming contradictions and confusions is not to be found in a pedestrian chronicle of Walt's daily doings. This biographer and that, using hints or boastings, or the dubious evidence of poems, has endeavored to spice this daily life with hypothetical journeys, unverified quadroon lovers, illegitimate children, and dark suggestions of vice and degeneracy. Yet even if all these stories about Whitman's hidden activities were true, they would not account for a passionate fervor that has deeper and more burning sources. They would not, most emphatically, account for his slow emergence as the great poet of democracy and one of the great poets of love. The clues to the so-called mystery of Walt Whitman are not to be found in unrevealed scraps of personal experience, but in the unique history of the electric America in which he matured, an America charged with spiritual idealism, double-charged with intellectual and physical energy; and in his inner life, as conditioned by his youth in that America. Also, of course, in his psychology and physiology, both of which were unusual. They will not be easy to follow, nor are the results easy to describe with both a just appreciation and a critical detachment. But it can be done.

And is worth doing, for though a poseur sometimes, and often a careless carpenter of words, seven great achievements, of which any literature might be proud, can now be safely credited to Walt Whitman. He made articulate and gave an enduring life in the imagination to the American dream of a continent where the people should escape from the injustices of the past and establish a new and better life in which everyone would share. He made articulate and best defined for the imagination the democratic faith which was and is the only binding national force in the United States. He established an ideal for international democracy which has proved to be as prophetic of danger as it is shrewd and noble in its ideas. Next, speaking for hearty physical man, workers, lovers, eaters, and drinkers, he burst through the inhibitions of the genteel age and put sex back into literature as a partner with spirit. Also, he broke with the timidities of the intellectuals of the Eastern seaboard, who were still colonial and imitative of England in their culture, and tried to speak for a new and still inarticulate America. Furthermore, he is the pivot in American history on which we swing from the sectional and the provincial to the national and continental in our literature. And he did what only really great writers have done, he made a great style to express himself and his country in poetry — although, unfortunately, he by no means always used it.

Many still think of Walt Whitman as a crank, a freak, or a barbarian. For their benefit, let me set down in advance the factors of this man's life which any biography must narrate and explain. Self-educated, though more widely educated than is commonly supposed, a poet certainly from the beginning, but curiously inarticulate, imitative, or vacuous in the usual literary forms of his youth, Walt Whitman made himself a skilful and influential political journalist, conventional and conformist except in a strong bent toward liberal humanitarianism. At the beginning of what could have been a great editorial success, the controversies preceding the Civil War left him without a party. But before that had happened, an intense perceptiveness, working like yeast in his inner life, had reached his consciousness and powerfully stirred the imagination. His interest shifted from the respectable bourgeois reader of his editorials to the plain unreading man, the toiler, the pioneer, the common person, man or woman, set free to rise in a new continent of unexampled freedom and richness. His emotions warmed with ideas of the common gift to all mankind of physical and spiritual passion.

Guessing rightly that from these plain people and from this common ground the new America, and perhaps the new world, would be made, he believed with all his strength that a fresh culture must be made for democracy, based, of course, upon the past, but rich and broad and simple and hearty enough to civilize the

American breed. This culture was already present, but inarticulate except for its crudest wants, and inarticulate particularly in its loves, its faiths, and its dreams. He determined to learn how to speak for it, and painfully, crudely set to work, with too little taste to know when, or even how, he failed, and too great a passion to be discouraged by what, for years, was an almost complete unsuccess with the general reader. Yet he did make himself the mouthpiece of a new language about, if not for, the common man, finding subject matter new to literature in the full-blooded, largely illiterate, yet intensely ambitious masses of America.

The man, indeed, was like a radio in the making, whose aerial was catching waves not yet registered by polite literature. And it was his good fortune that the attempt was made in precisely the period in which the unprivileged man of the masses was given his widest opportunities in history, and socially and politically came of age. This will be a theme of this book, but its story will deal essentially with how and what Whitman himself learned about America, democracy, love, and death — and of how he became a poet and what he did with poetry.

CHAPTER II

Paumanok

I T MAY or may not be true that the locomotive in Whitman's
To a Locomotive in Winter, with its fierce beauty and irresistible energy, devouring distance, cars trailing behind it, was a
symbol for the high-pressured, the spiritually and physically
burning Mrs. Gilchrist, who came from London to marry him.
The guess is not out of the way, for Whitman was a symbolist
long before this poem was written, a symbolist, indeed, before
symbolism. As soon as he found his own kind of poetry, he began
to write, as he said, 'indirectly,' by which he usually meant in
symbols. Manhattan was not the same thing in his imagination
as the physical New York. It was symbolic New York. And
Paumanok, the Indian name for fish-shaped Long Island, was a
symbolic word which stood for youth as well as geography. He
was born in its hills, and while most of his childhood and young
manhood was spent in towns, he went back to rural Long Island
constantly to visit his parents or his grandparents, to teach
school, to ramble, to loaf (which with him meant to meditate and
absorb), and to be near the beaches and the ocean.

The Walt Whitman country in rural Long Island is west of the
middle, beginning twenty to thirty miles from New York and
extending from Long Island Sound to the Atlantic Ocean, which
are so close together that the booming surf of an ocean storm
could be heard on the low hills above the Sound where he was
born. Eastern Long Island, the Great South Bay, and the Greenport and Montauk regions are not in his earliest childhood. This
was his vacation country, where, when he left, or lost, or took
time off from, a job, he pushed on from his own neighborhood into

pleasant places of which as a small child he must constantly have heard.

The Whitman land — once a tract of five hundred good acres with a great orchard of twenty — was on the North Shore at West Hills in Suffolk County, sloping south and east, and about three or four miles south of Huntington harbor. The Van Velsors, his mother's family, lived on their land two or three miles off, at Cold Spring, about a mile from the harbor. This North Shore country is really an extension of Connecticut. The intervening waters of Long Island Sound, only about ten miles across, separate hilly, glacier-scoured Connecticut from the great terminal moraine which became Long Island. It is also hilly but not, like Connecticut, rocky. Its soil is richer, its trees heavier, its inlets longer and sandier, and bluer because deeper, its aspects more friendly.

And when the first of the Long Island Whitmans, about 1660, crossed from Stratford to settle on West Hills, they were pioneers extending New England, and particularly Connecticut, southward. Middle and eastern Long Island, up to the vague line that separated the Dutch of New York from the New Englanders, and which ran near Walt's birthplace, was not only a Connecticut extension, it was actually, about 1660, under the protection of Connecticut. But in 1674 Charles II punished the stiff-necked, sectarian, republican Yankees for their Puritan sympathies by assigning all Long Island to New York.

And yet the New England settlements in Long Island, while keeping their New England concern for education, seem to have left behind them not only the strict ecclesiasticism of Connecticut, but also some of the Puritan concern for the intellect, and for blue-law morals. In the Whitman region, the pioneers from across the Sound or from Massachusetts found themselves mingled with equally tenacious but more full-blooded, more easy-going Dutch from New York. Quakers, persecuted or harshly rebuked in New England, settled comfortably in this more tolerant region, which still has its meeting-houses. New York, a cosmopolitan seaport, generally regarded as irreligious and iniquitous from a very early period, was the market for this country, easily accessible by water or by land. By the eighteenth century, the New England families of Long Island had rubbed off the angles of extreme Puritanism, if, indeed, they had ever possessed them, had become part of a society of mixed faiths and races, and more resembled, in their modes of life and thinking, the tolerant worldliness of the Middle Colonies than the self-convinced orthodoxy and the Yankee singularity of Connecticut. It is noteworthy that Whitman's family, for a generation or two at least, had belonged to no church. The Whitmans, he told Doctor Bucke, were always of 'democratic and heretical tendencies.'[1] And it was the New York Dutch that he celebrated as his most vital progenitors. His English ancestry was also often on his lips, but about Connecticut, which was their stepping stone to Long Island, he was incurious.

The villages of the hill country of Long Island still have a New England look to them, although the old houses on the streets and in the countryside, with shingled walls and sideward stretch, would be more at home in Cape Cod than in Connecticut. The land, however, in this region, much more resembles than does most of New England, the kind of hill country which American pioneers ploughed for agriculture from the Hudson west to Wisconsin and south into Virginia. This North Shore country is a narrow strip with deep sea entrances, and amphibious in its pursuits. South of it lay the inner plains of Long Island, flat, seemingly interminable, some of it cultivated, much of it grazed, a vast prairie where one could easily imagine oneself on the great plains of the corn belt, or the grazing lands beyond the Mississippi. Beyond this plain were the lagoons and beaches of the southern shore, then barrier islands, and the open ocean. And back from this South Shore and stretching eastward to the dunes and downs of Montauk were pine forests, like those of the seaboard of our South; and, where the land was fertile, plantations of the Southern type, run by slave labor, with a manor house at the centre, suggesting in many ways the rich plantations of South Carolina.

I am trying to suggest, and with justice, I think, that the Long Island of Whitman's youth might very well be regarded as a very representative sample of America from the seaboard to the Great Plains. The 'Leaves of Grass' was in his intention a representative book of America. There are no mountains in Long Island and none in the typical background of the 'Leaves of Grass.' The chief geography of the imagined America in that great symbolic poem is curiously represented in this youth land of Whitman's memories. His Long Island had, as I have said, sea and sea life, small harbors with local trade, plains for herding and grazing, a slice of that Eastern tidewater country in which so much of our civilization had its birth, a rich rural suburban area, a typical big city in New York, over two hundred thousand in population by 1835, a characteristic small town of America in Brooklyn, and villages of the New England type. It would have been possible for a poet of imagination such as Whitman to build upon the vivid memories of his youth a United States minus its Far West and sub-tropical South. And, in fact, that is very much what he did in many and many a poem of the 'Leaves of Grass.' He wrote of the Okonee, Koosa, Ottawa, Chattahoochee, Sauk, Oronoco,[2] which he probably never saw, because the names suggest the breadth of a continent. He urged us to

See, on the one side the Western sea and on the other the Eastern sea, ...
See, pastures and forests in my poems — see, animals wild and tame ...
See, mechanics busy at their benches with tools ...
See, lounging through the shops and fields of the States, me well-belov'd, close-held by day and night.[3]

But at the core of many of these vivid descriptions of cities, towns, and lands he had passed through once, or not at all, could well have been his youthful memories of Paumanok, its country, its villages, its big town, its great city. Since it is not the accuracy so much as the symbolic and ideal value of Walt Whitman's America which is significant, this theory of a transference from the subconscious stored in his youth to the representative has its importance. It accounts, I think, for the warmth with which he embraces a continent of which, actually, he had seen so little while he was writing his best poetry.

2

The Whitmans seem to be descended from John Whitman, who came to Massachusetts in 1640 on board the *True Love*. His brother, Zechariah, who had arrived in 1635, was an Independent clergyman at Milford, Connecticut, and is the only recorded intellectual of the family; but he left no descendants. Walt's first Long Island ancestor was Joseph Whitman, who was in Stratford, Connecticut, by 1653, and who seems to have crossed the Sound about 1660 when middle Long Island was, politically, Connecticut. He was constable in Huntington in 1665, and he and his descendants prospered. Whitman's great-grandfather, Nehemiah, cultivated his five hundred acres with slaves, who, after his death, were directed by his great-grandmother, Sarah White Whitman, a 'large, swarthy woman,' who smoked, chewed, rode horseback, used opium like so many pioneer women, swore, and petted her slaves.[4] Walt's grandfather, Jesse, lived on the same land, and Walt could 'almost remember' this grandfather's slaves, and the pickaninnies squatting on the kitchen floor waiting for their mush. One of the liberated West Hills slaves was a friend of his youth. He did not experience Negro slavery, but had been told about it until it seemed real.

Whitman went back to the old place in 1881, to see: 'The broad and beautiful farm lands of my grandfather, (1780,) and my father. There was the new house, (1810) [where he was born] the big oak a hundred and fifty or two hundred years old; there the well, the sloping kitchen-garden, and a little way off even the well-kept remains of the dwelling of my great-grandfather (1750–'60) still standing, with its mighty timbers and low ceilings.'[5]

Walter Whitman (1789–1855), Whitman's father, was the son of Jesse Whitman and of Hannah Brush, who had been a school-teacher and was generally regarded as 'superior.' This Walter Whitman, senior, was both superior and frustrated. He had character and a mind, admired Thomas Paine, whom his father and perhaps he himself had known, subscribed to the somewhat revolutionary journal of Fanny Wright, *The Free Inquirer*, and took in a Brooklyn paper when he went to live there. He had been apprenticed to a carpenter — a 'framer' — in New York when he was fifteen, and from him and from his great-uncles, Isaac and Jacob, learned the trade.[6] Later, he became a builder, an indication that his share of the Whitman land was no longer able to support the Whitman family. It was, to be sure, an era of extensive building in the expanding, growing republic, and to get rich by a trade already in the family may have been his object. Nevertheless, by Walt Whitman's early youth, his father seems to have been landless. And if Walter senior never quite went under in the many busts that followed the booms, he never succeeded. He had, or developed, a temper:

> The father, strong, self-sufficient, manly, mean, anger'd, unjust,
> The blow, the quick loud word, the tight bargain, the crafty lure, ...[7]

But in spite of this unflattering description, Walt respected him, though he did not love him, and the man seems to have been honest, and easily swindled. He was as independent as Walt himself. 'My old daddy used to say,' he told Horace Traubel, 'it's some comfort to a man if he must be an ass anyhow to be his own kind of an ass.' [8]

Walt Whitman himself, named Walter, but called Walt from an early period, was born with hair that became black as tar, in the 'new house' at West Hills, on May 31, 1819. In the child's fifth year, his father followed his trade to Brooklyn, then a thriving town, and thirty miles away. Thus, though born on a farm, Walt knew little of farming life as a farmer's son sees it. After this early childhood, he was a visitor, an observer, a very casual worker, if a worker at all, on the land. The country for him in his youth was where his grandmothers lived. When Doctor Bucke wrote his life, Whitman added this to the proof of the book: 'Both grandmothers, who were very fond of him, (and he was with one or the other of them part of every year, until he was quite a big lad) appear to have been noble and endearing characters. At the death of his own mother he spoke of her and his sister Martha, and the two grandmothers alluded to, as "the best and sweetest women I ever saw, or ever expect to see."' [9]

Transcending everything else in the influence of his family were

his love for his mother and hers for him. She was the steady adoration and comfort of his life. It is hard to reconstruct her personality from her letters, which are cramped and difficult, yet it is
clear that she was one of those ample women, wise and of great
heart, who powerfully hold together families and succeed by character and love. She was a notable story-teller. Walt throughout
his life reports to her like a schoolboy. She is his rock of confidence and affection in a world where he found adjustment difficult
and love an irritant more often than a happiness. She backed him
always, everywhere, with a faith unshaken by her complete ignorance of what he meant by his work. It was an extraordinary relationship, never once shaken. What he missed in marriage, which
he regarded always as the only ideal state for man and woman, he
found, as far as it could be found, in her. And it was his emotional dependence upon his mother which, more than his sexual
singularities or his poverty, may be presumed to account for his
bachelor life.

The Whitman women, Walt thought, were superior to the men.
But then good women (by which he did not always mean 'respectable women, so-called')[10] were always, so he said, a great
influence upon his life; no one could have been more fortunate in
friendships with them, a statement which will seem increasingly
curious and significant as we follow his biography.

Rural Paumanok was for him a place to ramble, to teach in
country schools, to experiment with country journalism, but most
of all vividly to remember. These earliest memories seem to be
much more colorful of his mother's than of his father's family.
Major Cornelius Van Velsor, his maternal grandfather, was pure
New York Dutch, a ruddy, hearty man, a horse-breeder, with
other members of his family. The title, which Whitman puts in
quotation marks, was of the militia, if, indeed, it was military at
all.[11] He was the third or fourth generation from the original
Holland immigrants and his father, Garret Van Velsor, had been
a weaver.

The Van Velsor place at Cold Spring, as Whitman described it
when recording his memories, was 'a long rambling, dark-gray,
shingle-sided house, with sheds, pens, a great barn, and much open

road-space.... The vast kitchen and ample fireplace ... the house full of merry people, my grandmother Amy's sweet old face in its Quaker cap, my grandfather, "the Major," jovial, red, stout, with sonorous voice and characteristic physiognomy,...' [12] From 1825 to 1840 Walt was a familiar at this house.

These Van Velsors were noted for fine horses, bred and trained from blooded stock. The 'Major's' other occupation, however, at least during Walt's boyhood, was the less romantic one of driver of a stage and transport wagon. For over forty years he drove to Brooklyn ferry hauling produce for sale, the boy sometimes as his companion. Walt's beloved mother was a daring rider in her youth.

Amy (Naomi) Williams, his grandmother, was a Quaker and both she and her daughter, Louisa, Walt's mother, used the plain language, at least in the family. Amy came from a seafaring race. Her father was Captain John Williams, all of whose sons followed the sea.[13] Her mother, Mary Woolley, it is interesting to note, was described as shiftless.

Lest the reader fall into the error of Whitman's sister, Mrs. Heyde, who, in her neurotic moods, used to boast of the family's wealth and distinction, it should be made plain that these Whitmans and Van Velsors were in no sense county gentry. They were, like most Americans above the bond-servant or hired classes, substantial, hard-working people, ready to turn a penny in any available way. Whitman's mother was as near illiterate as one can be who can read and write, her grammar and spelling being equally uncertain. They were representative 'farming folk,' changing, with Walt's father, into representative mechanics, on their own, but frequently paying heavily for their independence. Nor, of course, were they peasants, as is stated by H. B. Binns, the usually excellent English biographer of Whitman. There were no real peasants on Long Island, and, if there had been, they would have been hired folk to the Whitmans and Van Velsors. Yet there is not one trace of the aristocratic, and only a trace of the intellectual, in Walt Whitman's family tradition.

Where Walt's hair, which he told Mrs. O'Connor was 'black as tar' when he was a child, came from, I am not sure. It was streaked with iron gray very early, and soon turned white. But his ruddy skin (the reddest man, Thoreau said, he had ever seen) was surely inherited from the rubicund Major, and probably his fleshy muscles [14] and full lips and impression of weight and solidity, all Dutch traits, if one may judge from Dutch portraiture. The resemblance to his beloved mother, in a picture of her taken in old age, is strong.

Walt never forgave Washington Irving for his satire on the New York Dutch. They were practical, he wrote to William Kennedy, yet 'terribly transcendental and cloudy, too,' and the 'Leaves,' he thought, came from his 'Hollandesque interior of history and personality,' [15] a curious remark, probably meaning nothing except that he felt more tolerant Dutch than stiff New Englander. Walt on the influence of his heredity is not to be taken too seriously. It is his mixed environment, as I have described and shall continue to describe it, which is significant and certainly subject to analysis. However, that his lifelong heartiness was good Dutch Van Velsor I have no doubt, nor that his dangerous obstinacy was New England, or at least paternal, in its origin. And even more important in heredity would be his mother's nature, which he describes in the same additions to Doctor Bucke's proofs as '*markedly spiritual and intuitive.*' That he started 'from fish-shaped Paumanok where I was born,' and became a 'lover of populous pavements' in his city of the imagination, New York, is quite as important as his ancestral strains.

CHAPTER III

~~~~~~

Brooklyn Ferry

Brooklyn was the ferry on which the child crossed into a more representative world. I know the danger of dividing a great man's life into periods, but if there ever was a justification, Walt Whitman supplies it. His whole life, with the exception of his activities as printer, carpenter, political worker, and hospital visitor, may be summed up in two functions: absorption and communication. Communication began in Brooklyn, but this chapter on his boyhood and early youth is concerned almost exclusively with absorption.

Whitman's own reminiscences of his childhood are records of absorption, with very little really about the boy who did the absorbing. There will be very little about Walt as a personality in this chapter, because there is so little evidence. In his poems, however, he wrote much that is poignant, though it is maturity looking back and making its own pictures. A legend spread by his early biographers of Walt as quite an ordinary youth who in his late twenties or early thirties went through some mystical experience which made him a prophet and a poet, is just the reverential guess of his admirers. Knowing of his uneventful life, they thought that the perilous stuff of the imagination which suddenly burst forth in the 'Leaves,' and resembled nothing he had written before, came from some blinding inspiration, like Paul's on the road to Damascus. Yet this black-haired boy was certainly intuitive, like his mother, from first consciousness, a poet in his absorptive stage:

There was a child went forth every day,
And the first object he look'd upon, that object he became,

And that object became part of him for the day or a certain part of the day,
Or for many years or stretching cycles of years.

The early lilacs became part of this child,
And grass and white and red morning-glories, and white and red clover, and
    the song of the phoebe-bird, . . .
And all the changes of city and country wherever he went. . . .

The doubts of day-time and the doubts of night-time, the curious whether and
    how,
Whether that which appears so is so, or is it all flashes and specks? . . .
The village on the highland seen from afar at sunset, the river between, . . .
The schooner near by sleepily dropping down the tide, the little boat slack-
    tow'd astern, . . .
These became part of that child.[1]

Unless we take every introspective youth in Walt's trite and
sentimental stories to be Walt himself, a very dubious procedure,
we must admit that we know from his own mouth or from testimony of others only that the child was sensitive and absorptive,
that he showed aptitude for the printing and publishing trade,
took with passion to books and the theatre, was extraordinarily
independent in his life, and soon made a reputation for the indolence of meditation, which is not the same thing as laziness,
though some thought so. Of what went on inside his mind, his
own reminiscences tell us little. I suspect it was neither thought
nor analyzed feeling, but extraordinary absorption, such as is
described in the quotation above. He seemed (except for this absorptive capacity) a quite ordinary boy, for whom nobody could
have prophesied anything — not even his successful editorial
career.

I wish there were more to write about in his childhood. The
youth of Shelley or the youth of Poe gives the biographer a chance
to compose short stories of stormy temperaments beating through
the winds of circumstance. But to fictionize the young Whitman,
to give him the dramatic poses which, later, he provided for himself, is impossible for an honest chronicler. This Whitman family
was Quaker-like in its emotional reticence, as the family letters
(except Hannah's) show. When they lived intensely, they seemed
to live deep. One should not be deceived by the reticence of these

depths, nor by the fact that Walt seemed unremarkable to his companions. When he comes to write of his boyhood he has not forgotten the passionate yearnings of the child who listened to the mockingbird mourning for its dead mate by the ocean shore:

The boy ecstatic, with his bare feet the waves, with his hair the atmosphere dallying,
The love in the heart long pent, now loose, now at last tumultuously bursting, ...
The unknown want, the destiny of me.[2]

Yet from the Whitmans there are few self-revelations. What they felt they kept to themselves, or showed it in affection and concern as did Louisa for all of her children. Young Walt, overgrown and thrust out to earn his living when he was only a child, has never a word of complaint. He suffered no opposition, no frustrations from his family that we know of. His imagination was busy with pleasant things; even death, as his early stories show, was friendly. There is a revealing line or two in a poem which, eventually, he attached to the preludes of the 'Leaves':

Beginning my studies the first step pleas'd me so much, ...
I have hardly gone and hardly wish'd to go any farther,
But stop and loiter all the time to sing it in ecstatic songs.[3]

Myself, I get from this a likely picture of the gawky youth, so slow and meditative, so eager within as he drinks from books or any deep or trivial experience. It takes a long while to make a poet who is going to write about himself, and love, and his country.

2

When the family moved to Brooklyn, on May 27 of 1823, it was to profit by the building boom under way in all the area adjacent to the bay of New York, that harbor which was already clearly destined to be the great port of entry to the United States. 'The middle range of the nineteenth century in the New World; a strange, unloosen'd, wondrous time'[4] was beginning. Its vibrations were already exciting to a child, and one result was that

Walt himself was very early unloosened from the bonds of a pro-
tected life.

Walter Whitman came to the cities of the bay too soon, or too
ill prepared. His Brooklyn houses, two of which, at least, he built
for himself (loving as he did to sleep on floors of his own making),
were mortgaged and lost. The building trade, as usual, suffered
from boom-and-bust. This tall (taller than Walt), heavy, satur-
nine man seems to have had Walt's optimism, but directed toward material success which he never achieved. His daguerreotype, taken in old age, shows a bitter, disappointed face. While
there is no record of poverty in these years of Whitman's early
childhood, and nothing to show that the boy had reason to complain of his world, yet these constant movings under stress, constant childbirths in a family of nine children, constant sense of
failure, and the sickness of his mother must have had their reper-
cussions on the family circle.

Until 1831, when Walt was eleven, he was still in this family
circle. We know that he went to elementary school — which was
all the schooling he was ever to get. We know that he rambled the
shaded streets of Brooklyn and the near-by marshes, fishing for
killy-fish — those tiny fish that were later to make so much
trouble when they got into the new water pipes. We know that he
must have watched the old horse-driven ferry to New York. But
as to what happened at home, in the family circle, his memoirs are
singularly reticent. At school, he was described as good-natured,
slovenly, and not otherwise remarkable.[5]

When he was ten he left school, and at eleven was employed
(probably as errand boy) by the Clarkes, father and son, and law-
yers. They gave him a seat by a window in their office on Fulton
Street, Edward C. Clarke helped him with his handwriting and
composition, and he was given a subscription to a circulating
library: 'the signal event of my life up to that time,' as he says in
'Specimen Days.'[6] Here he acquired that habit of romantic reading which was to be a lifetime indulgence, devouring the 'Arabian
Nights,' and Scott's novels, one after the other, and his poetry.
Scott and especially his ballads are deep in the source of the
'Leaves of Grass.'[7] No one else in the Whitman family, except

Hannah Heyde, seems ever to have read literature for pleasure.

This hunger for books must have been a factor, and possibly a cause, in his next and really decisive step toward a career. At the age of twelve, Walt left home and was apprenticed in a newspaper and printing office 'to learn the trade.' It was printing, publishing, editing which was chosen by him, or more probably, for him, not carpentering, though he added carpentering later. *The Long Island Patriot* was owned by Samuel E. Clements, a Quaker from the South, who had left strict Quakerism far enough behind to wear a blue waistcoat with brass buttons, and take his apprentices on Sundays to the Dutch Reformed Church on Joralemon Street. In the summer, this Brooklyn character wore an enormous straw hat, which flapped as he delivered his paper to his five hundred subscribers from horseback. Walter Whitman was one of them.[8] *The Patriot* was Democratic in politics, as were the Whitmans. The boy Walt was printer's devil, having learned to set type from an old printer named William Hartshorne, and boarding with his granddaughter. This Hartshorne was also a character, an eighteenth-century man, precise in manner, who had seen both Washington and Jefferson, and told the boy about them. It seems to have been a happy and fortunate experience. In 1832, Walt worked for *The Long Island Star* of Alden Spooner, a veteran Brooklyn journalist, founder of the free school system in Brooklyn and of the Natural History Museum.[9] Ink was trickling into Whitman's blood.

So far it was mostly on his fingers. These local papers, with their tiny circulations, had little general news, and their energy was largely political. To edit them, one had to know the town, and how to abuse the mouthpieces of the other party. Walt was a compositor, not a reporter, but he was living away from home at a centre of local gossip, and was free to ramble out of hours. Already he felt himself on his own and independent, and must have looked it, for at fifteen he was as large as a man. Physically, Whitman throughout his life looked older than his age. Mentally, there was always, even in his seventies, something still adolescent about him.

These apprenticeships are the beginning of the small-town

phase of the experience which helped to make the 'Leaves of Grass' representative. Brooklyn in 1830 to 1840 was a town of from fifteen to thirty-six thousand inhabitants, in no real sense suburban to New York, though, of course, in active touch with the metropolis. Whitman learned to know it so well that a journalistic history of the town which he wrote for *The Brooklyn Standard* in 1861 and 1862 is vivid with youthful, nostalgic memories of streets, old houses, people, and amusements. It was a neat town, with plenty of civic pride, though, to judge from Walt's history, the pride was in the rapidity of its growth in population and prosperity. He seems to have approved, in spite of very different conceptions of civic greatness in the 'Leaves.' He could take, when he wished, the typical attitude of the booming American town, in the unloosened nineteenth century.

Brooklyn of the thirties, when he was an apprentice to his trade, and Brooklyn of the forties, when he was a smart young editor, remained in his imagination, with New Orleans and Washington, as one of his three cities of romance. It is hard at first to see why, for the truth is that this community seems to have been unrelieved in its typical quality of a very ordinary American town. The answer must be that the boy was happy there. This youth, who everywhere else was a transient, a lone soul observing and criticizing and idealizing, in Brooklyn became an integral and accepted part of a society which he seems to have adopted as a family circle in place of his own, from which he was so consistently absent. The deep divergences which were to set him in constant spiritual and psychological, yes, and physiological, conflict with the public opinion of his age, had not yet become marked. And as New York was port of entry to the great West, so Brooklyn, for him, was port of entry to Paumanok, land of his youth, where he was always happy. Happiness as a theme with Whitman has a way of always sliding back to his youth. If it is hard to keep one's finger on the early history of this boy, it is because he is always skipping off from a job, or between jobs, to rural Long Island. In Brooklyn and Paumanok generally his associations were prevailingly with quiet and pleasant men and women whom he liked.

And Brooklyn had a past which appealed to Whitman's imagination, as much as did its present to his liking for kindly, unpretentious people. It is impossible to exaggerate his veneration for the heroes and heroics of the American Revolution. The Williams family, on his mother's side, had two representatives in the war, and some of the Whitmans were there also, though not Walt's direct ancestors. All of the Whitmans and the Van Velsors were close to scenes of actual conflict.[10] It may have been the 'Major' who told him stories of Washington's great retreat from Brooklyn. Certainly Hartshorne must have done so, and his father also, whose admiration for Tom Paine indicates his sympathies for liberalism. Walt's young mind was indoctrinated with the passion for freedom — quite unanalyzed, but still a passion. He seldom recalls Washington's forces, which were in such danger on Long Island, and suffered so heavily at Brooklyn, without calling them the 'sacred army.' He returns again and again, in both prose and verse, to this battle at Brooklyn. As a young editor, he began the movement which later resulted in a monument at Fort Greene. Here, where he wandered, was part of the consecrated ground. It was in Brooklyn, in 1824 as a child of five or six, when Lafayette was presiding at the dedication of the site of a library, that he was taken in arms by the old hero, and set in a safe place where he could watch the ceremony. This was an accolade.

And, of course, from Brooklyn, a small town figuratively as well as literally, he could look across, and soon was taken, to New York. At thirteen, he saw old John Jacob Astor in his ermine cap, being tucked into his sleigh.[11] New York after 1825, when the Erie Canal had been opened, was the focus of American energy, the new metropolis that had outdistanced Philadelphia, the harbor of the great West, the open door for the European immigrant. And from Brooklyn on the heights, better than from New York, he could view the ships of the world sailing up the bay, could see the first Vanderbilt periaugs tacking across to New Jersey with passengers and freight for Philadelphia and all the South, could look at the New England schooners coming down the East River, the Hudson River steamboats on their way to the North;

could guess, as the ocean ships came in, at the thousands of settlers pushing toward the rich central lands of New York State,
where the landowners had at last relaxed their grip, and on to the
Great Lakes and the illimitable West. The boy began with a
sense of the opening of a continent to which few American writers
were to attain for half a century.

3

By 1834 and 1835, still unsettled in a lasting job, Walt was a
big fellow, probably already six feet, heavy, but not athletic, a
rambler on beaches, farms, city streets. He played no games
except tossing ball, was hearty, healthy, a swimmer, a dreamer,
somewhat of a solitary (since he mentions no youthful friends),
yet with a passion for people and events. He has not yet, so far
as we know, got the reputation for laziness which clung to him
through life, but he says of himself that he spoke and thought
slowly from an early age. He has been well treated so far by life,
for it is clear that he did not ask of it, as most do, family companionship and sheltering love. Aside from his trade and his restless
ramblings, there is nothing so far to mark him as destined for a
literary career. But some significant interests are indicated in
the scanty records. As early as age sixteen or seventeen (so he
says), he had become interested in debating societies, and by his
fifteenth year, certainly, had acquired a passion for the theatre.[12]
I do not believe that an inability or unwillingness to hold a paying
job, or even to stick to an assigned task, is a sign of literary promise, but these traits are very characteristic of men whose inner life
is active and demands nourishment. Already one can say that
Walt was practising, what later he preached, as did Thoreau, that
living is more important than making a living. 'Some men lead
professional lives — some men just live,' he said to Traubel years
later. 'I prefer to just live.' [13]

In 1833 (the year of the great meteor shower), when the youth
was still at Alden Spooner's, the family moved back into the
country. Walt's mother had been wretchedly ill. It was between
1834 and 1836 that Whitman had his first experience of life in

New York. He says himself that he went there on May 12, 1835, and left in May of 1836; [14] and in another place that he was a compositor in New York in 1836–1837, an error as to dates, but certainly not as to occupation. Probably, both in New York and Brooklyn, he worked long enough to save money for the Paumanok vacations.

The facts, such as they are, of these years are of some importance, since Jean Catel, one of his most intelligent biographers, has built up in his 'Walt Whitman: La Naissance de Poète' an edifice of theory based on references to vile boarding-houses, poverty, prostitution, and drunkenness amidst which an unhappy youthful adventurer lives in New York, and all drawn from Whitman's later temperance novel, 'Franklin Evans.' This youthful vagabondage, he thinks, left scars on the poet's mind. There are terrible scenes of a great city recorded in the 'Leaves of Grass,' but they sound like adult, not youthful memories. Actually, the story of these so-called lost years of Whitman's boyhood is, like so many Whitman mysteries, probably no mystery at all. All that he says is, that he set type and went happily again and again to the theatre.[15]

We can check on that. There was acting in Brooklyn, and it is most probable that he went to one or the other of the theatres there very young. He was on a 'free list,' so he says, for 'many seasons,' 'writing for papers even as quite a youth.' [16] There are always free seats for the theatre in a newspaper office, and while the printer's devil at Clements' and Spooner's certainly did not review plays, he must have had his chance at a performance. In New York, it would have been the same story, except that he was older, and could get more opportunities. He remembers Fanny Kemble, 'perhaps the greatest' of the long list of great ones he had seen at the old Park Theatre in New York. 'Nothing finer did ever stage exhibit' than her rendering of Bianca in *Fazio*.[17] That could have been in 1832, as Margaret Armstrong, the biographer of Fanny Kemble, thinks; though an improbable opportunity for the Brooklyn apprentice of age thirteen. But Fanny played *Fazio* again in the summer of 1834, just before her marriage and first retirement from the stage. It was presumably then that young

Walt had left Brooklyn for a while and was composing in some newspaper office in New York. 'It must have been about 1834 or '35,' he says in 'November Boughs,' that he saw the great Booth, arriving late, capture the audience in 'one of the most marvellous pieces of histrionism ever known.' [18] I submit that what record we have of Walt's first venture into New York is of privileged opportunity to study a great art (very close to what his own was to become) rather than of unrelieved hardship and the fright of a small-town boy in a great city alone.

There was a great fire in New York in 1835 and unemployment afterward; [19] the panic year of 1837 was approaching. This time, when he lost or left his job in the spring of 1836 and headed for Long Island to join his family at Hampstead, it may be that he did not expect to go back. Or was he lonely, and nostalgic for Paumanok? Whatever the cause, the boy made again one of those sudden shifts of occupation so characteristic of minds not set in the career by which they earn their living. By June, he had begun to teach school in Norwich. In the autumn he went to a country school west of Babylon. Between 1836 and 1841 he had taught in seven Long Island rural schools with intervals of writing and editing — probably one term only in most of them.[20] As was the custom, he boarded 'round' with the families of his scholars. He was probably paid about forty to fifty dollars for each term of about three months, and, with free board, could have saved most of the money.[21]

Thoreau, in the same years, with a Harvard degree, was beginning in the public school of Concord. He did not need his B.A. degree for the job. Teaching was the obvious thing for youngsters professionally inclined, who needed some means of subsistence while they got under way. The surprising parallel between the two youths is the similarity and (for that day) originality of their methods. Thoreau would not strap his pupils, and so lost his first position. Whitman, under no influence of which we are aware, also managed his classes without physical punishment, read poetry to them instead of sermonizing, and, in that easy-going community, seems not to have been rebuked. Henry and John Thoreau, likewise, when they opened their academy, sub-

stituted interesting talks on nature and science for the moral lecturing regarded as indispensable. Deep influences of a new individualism, far deeper than personal taste, were at work upon
these pioneers of the nineteenth century.

In the long time spaces between school terms, there was abundant opportunity for Whitman to extend his country recreations
beyond the possibilities of his childhood. It was probably in these
years that he went eeling on the ice of Great South Bay, met the
Paumanokers, the half-wild herding and fishing folk, once called
Creoles, and fished and sailed.[22] And, more important, now he
lived as an adult, not as a child, with the farming people — 'One
of my best experiences and deepest lessons in human nature behind the scenes and in the masses.'[23]

It was, as I have said, the absorptive period of a man who was
to declare again and again later that his purpose was to make
himself representative of America. He wanted now simple country folk, country pleasures, time for meditation — and country
teaching opened the door. We are told that in these days he was
lazy and liked to lie under the apple trees watching the sky; that
he sat around in his shirt sleeves, was none too well-mannered,
kept to himself: 'a dreamy, quiet, morose young man,' who spent
most of his spare time in winter reading by the fire.[24]

For 'morose' substitute self-centred, with the faraway look in
his eyes evident in all his earlier portraits (and in few of his later
ones), and this becomes a fair description of Walt in his earliest
manhood. He was absorbing passionately human nature behind
the scenes and 'in the masses,' though what he meant by the
'masses' in rural Long Island I do not know; also scenes of nature,
and books. Not, however, the ill-assorted masterpieces of literature which his notebooks later record as his self-education. He
had no access to them probably, except for the Bible. Rather, to
judge from his first imaginative writings in the forties, he was
reading Scott still, and whatever of magazine and newspaper
sentimental romance he could lay his hands upon. When Walt
began to create in the years preceding and succeeding his school
experience, he produced bad copies of what is perhaps the worst
popular writing in the history of literature.

We know of his membership in at least two debating societies in rural Long Island. Katherine Molinoff has described from manuscript records what went on in the Smithtown group of serious rural thinkers. They debated morals or politics chiefly, both infused with a strongly felt liberalism. Walt was secretary of the Smithtown Society, which shows that he took the arguing seriously.[25] With his previous interest in debate in Brooklyn, and his passion for declamation already aroused in the theatre, here is an early indication of the desire and the will to communicate. The 'Leaves of Grass' was once planned as a lecture series. It became elocution and oratory in verse. More of this later.

Emerson, in his famous letter acknowledging the receipt of the first edition of the 'Leaves of Grass,' said the book 'must have had a long foreground somewhere, for such a start.' That foreground of experience, of course, stretches back through this chapter into Whitman's earliest youth. But the foreground of conscious purpose is not in sight. It is tempting to guess at what was going on in the mind of the indolent youth, stretched on the turf between spells of work; but it is safer, and probably truer, to believe that his friends were right when they said he was dreaming, wrong when they called him slothful and lazy. His slow mind was certainly still soft, like his muscles; soft, like a sponge absorbing. It was formless as yet, its inner recesses afloat with the vague romanticisms which first appear when he begins to write, and with the idealisms he had absorbed from his earliest environment. At nineteen, he returned again to his trade, this time as an editor, though he did not then finally give up teaching. It will be approximately ten years before a creative will begins to squeeze the sponge, and prophecy and poetry appear.

4

One more biographical item must be evident already. It was surely not only a liking for independence which took Walt so early out of the family and kept him there, except for brief periods, throughout his life. There is no more consistent record of devotion to a family than Walt's — it is probably unique among poets, who do not usually like their families.[26] Yet his close relatives, with the exception of his sister, Hannah, understood nothing of his life work. 'I saw the book,' said brother George of the 'Leaves,' 'didn't read it at all — didn't think it worth reading. . . . Mother thought as I did.' [27] And Whitman clearly, while loving them, felt no passion for living at home. He came, he went. His visits must have been like his meal-time habits, when he was staying with them in Brooklyn. He would come in hours too late, or leave with his food just ready to set on the table.

This escape from family life, when he loved the family and his mother above all living things, he seems to have regarded as an accident of apprenticeship, of jobs that took him away. But no job ever kept Whitman from doing what he wanted. It is necessary to suggest that it could not in his youth have been a very pleasant family. Walter Whitman was truly morose, a frustrated man, with a temper. Whitman's mother, the best of his companions, who cherished and adored him, was often sick, and usually overworked. Edward, the youngest, born in 1835, was mentally always a child, though able to help with the simple household jobs. He was much loved by Walt, but a constant worry and care through the poet's life. One of his sisters was normal enough, but Hannah, in her later life, was clearly neurotic, a slattern, a boaster, who fought, to the scandal of neighbors, with her equally pathological painter husband. Jeff (Walt's frequent companion) and George were right enough, George in his literal-minded way a superior man. But Andrew had a bad career and died leaving a wife of dubious morality and destitute children; and Jesse, the oldest, was syphilitic and ended his life insane in an institution. It was probably better for a boy to be much away from the home as it was in the years of his father's struggle to keep afloat. For there were bad genes as well as good ones in the stock, and it was not Edward only who was difficult.[28]

CHAPTER IV

Spiritual climate

Mr. Emory Holloway, who has been for many years a devoted student of Whitman, describes him, in no flattering terms, as he emerges from his casual pedagogy into what was, at first, almost equally casual journalism. The boy, he intimates, was not only unformed, but without resolution or any clarity of ideas as to where he was going. He is wilfully irresponsible, a dilettante in everything except loafing. His earliest picture, in a newspaper clipping of 1840, shows in his features that 'want of energy and resolution' which Whitman himself ascribes to Archie Dean in a biographical story he wrote in 1848.

Mr. Holloway sees too much, I think, in this photograph of a dandyish young man, freshly bearded, his cane hung over his shoulder, trying obviously to look like a real editor and literary man-about-town. The rest of his charges are unquestionably true; yet, of course, they in no way contradict the description above of a meditative mind in its absorptive period. And they suggest a preconception, for which Doctor Bucke was originally responsible, that because Whitman was to write only good editorials and literary trash for the ten years after he passed out of boyhood, therefore nothing of importance was going on in his unformed mind. Doubtless nothing clear, nothing resolute was there; but poets are born, not made, though they have to do a good deal of making also. And Walt was not lying under apple trees or getting down on his stomach in the fields because he was too lazy to stand up. It will soon be seen that he was one of the hard workers, as well as the best loafer, of his age. A great difficulty in considering Whitman's life is to remember these curious contradictions, which yet are always facets of the same personality. 'Do I contradict myself? Very well then I contradict myself,' [1] he was to write later, which was quite as much a loose-geared mind's apology for weaknesses of which it was clearly aware, as a confident statement that he was too wide in his sympathies to be entirely consistent.

At age twenty-one, in 1840, Whitman did not yet know where he wanted to go, because he was not ready to begin going. He could speak in this very year, of a wonderful book he would like to write,[2] about the nature of man and government, upon the danger of riches, upon pretty much everything human except women, of whom, he said, he knew as yet nothing. But the publisher who had contracted with the stripling editor for his book would have got a mass of bad rhetoric, and wide generalities, signifying only a precociously ambitious mind. Whitman's mind, to quote Mr. Holloway again, was still a chaos, not a cosmos. But his imagination was like a battery charging.

Remembering these early years in *A Backward Glance O'er Travel'd Roads,* he says that he entered unsuccessfully into competition for the usual rewards, business, political, literary, only to find himself, at age thirty-one to thirty-three, unplaced and with a very different ambition. For once, Walt was too modest. He had become by his thirtieth year, as we shall see, a really successful editor. Yet that he wanted none of these rewards was true. Like Thoreau, again, in these same thirties and forties, he sought vaguely a different kind of success, but knew even less than Thoreau just what it was, or how to attain it. In the interim (and here he differed from Thoreau) he was quite willing to adopt a congenial occupation which kept him afloat and did not interfere with the ferments under way in his half-conscious depths.

2

This book, also, may be allowed to drift from chronological narrative for a few pages. My purpose is not to analyze in guesses this slow and absorptive and intensely sensitive mind of a boy and youth, but rather to describe the spiritual climate in which young

Walt lived in the twenties and thirties of the century. I say spiritual, because to call the influence of this climate of opinion and belief intellectual would be to confuse the record. Walt's spongy mind in his early youth was not, I am sure, doing much thinking. When it was most active, it was feeling, and what he absorbed were emotions and emotional attitudes, rather than ideas with sharp edges and clear definitions. An excellent example is to be found in another poem of childish reminiscence, written in 1865, *A Child's Amaze*:

> Silent and amazed even when a little boy,
> I remember I heard the preacher every Sunday put God in his statements,
> As contending against some being or influence.[3]

Walt's climate of opinion was suffused and highly charged with the peculiarly American variety of eighteenth-century liberalism. The rights of man, the importance of the individual, the sacredness of revolution, the evils of privilege and the absurdity of rank, were all in this tradition which Whitman later used to call 'the good old cause.' And an emotional sanction and an appeal to the ego of a young American was given to these principles by the still recent triumphs of our Revolution and the founding of the Republic, and the widespread conviction among such patriots and liberals as Walt's father that the New World and especially the United States was the seed ground of future liberties. So the Jeffersonians and the Jacksonians believed; and so did the Whitmans. The Declaration of Independence was their gospel, and it may be assumed that these friends and followers of Thomas Paine were already democrats in an American period when the country at large was still definitely not a democracy. This concern for freedom and this faith in a democratic future, Whitman of course absorbed from his family, from old Hartshorne, and from the political newspapers on which he worked, at least one of which was thoroughly Democratic. That it went deep with him is to be explained by his own nature, which was emotional, expansive, intensely responsive to whatever liberated passion, love, freedom, and nobility.

Democratic liberalism in the United States of these decades was still revolutionary in its fervor, and vitalized by conscious success. Our country in those days, as described in patriotic speeches by the Democrats particularly, who had defeated reaction, and as it was dramatized in the boy's imagination, was the bearer of the torch by which Europe was to be enlightened. Our principles were dynamic against a reactionary Europe and an unawakened world. We were the people who knew how to succeed! The memory of a Washington, the principles of a Jefferson, were blended, a little incongruously, into a formula for success. There was a naïve confidence in the young country, and especially in the Democratic Party, to which the Whitmans belonged, that became the basis of the optimism which was usually the last word in Whitman's poetry. He was born in an atmosphere of successful revolution, and unhesitatingly proclaimed himself a revolutionist throughout his life.

With this vague but dynamic liberalism was mixed, in his youth, an influence by no means so general in the early nineteenth century, a strong humanitarianism. The young Longfellow, some ten years older than Whitman, had watched bullfights in Spain in 1827, with no comment except that many horses were killed; and had seen in the ragged misery of the Peninsula only the picturesque. Whitman, as soon as he begins to write, shows a Quaker concern for every instance of cruelty, greed, or injustice. Brutal whippings in school stir him to anger; hunger, struggles with debt, the misery of prostitutes and prisoners, terror as an instrument to stop wrongdoing — he is far better as an editorial writer on these themes than in his would-be elegant or humorous moods. It is true that humanitarianism by the thirties and forties had become fashionable, yet Whitman was certainly moved beyond current fashions, and we have to account for the passionate sympathies, the fanatical extensions of love and pity, of that greatest of humanitarian poems, the 'Leaves of Grass.'

It is probable that the Quaker environment of his youth is responsible for this bent as for other traits that go back to his childhood. The Van Velsors and the Whitmans, who venerated the great Quaker Elias Hicks, and were half Quaker themselves, must have made the boy feel, if they did not teach him, the second of the great lessons of Quakerism — love and respect for the individual in whom God moved and spoke. Even children in school, said Whitman, were reasoning beings with souls, and should be treated as such, a remark which would have found little sympathy in early Connecticut. The Quakers had long been testifying against the abuses which aroused in Whitman his first humanitarian interests. For a parallel to his concern for the miseries of war as he saw them from Washington in the 1860's, one has to go back to the Journal of the great eighteenth century Quaker, John Woolman. However, all I wish to suggest is that humanitarianism of a practical, principled, passionate kind was part of the spiritual climate in which his happy early days on Long Island were spent.

These influences came from the past. Yet if it was an old country with a sacred history into which Walt was born, it was also, and much more impressively as we look back from today, a new, young nation, displaying already the extraordinary mobility of the American nineteenth century. The aristocratic republic which most of the Founders intended to set up had already broken down politically with the triumph of Jefferson, and was disintegrating. The Federalist Party that had given it leadership had disappeared. The new power was democracy which the old men had feared — democracy and the West. It was an age of booms and busts, of recurrent depressions. Class consciousness was weakening since, except for Negroes and recent immigrants, it was becoming difficult to find a class with an established consciousness of itself, unless among the planters of the old South, and even there cotton had created a new frontier where anyone with a little capital might quickly get rich. John Jacob Astor, an immigrant, was called the landlord of New York, because he owned so much of it. In the cities, the extremes of poverty and wealth were great, but individuals by thousands were in constant shift up or down. In the country, especially in the North and West, but, more than is remembered, also in the old South, the landholders and speculators were letting go. The stablest class was the simple farmer, such as those Walt boarded round with in his teaching days. But these were mobile too. Walter Whitman had become a carpenter; the Major was trucking; some, even from Long Island, were moving West. There was as yet no proletariat, no labor class, except the slaves, and soon the Irish who gave Thoreau so much to think about.

Therefore, if you believed, as did the young Whitman, and probably most of the active minds with which he came in contact, that the United States was the destined great nation of the future, then it was natural to see in the undifferentiated masses, on the move up, or on and beyond with the rich and undeveloped West before them, the hope and reliance of that future. These masses were not the unprivileged or dispossessed to whom we apply the name today. There was a sad abundance of social injustice, exploitation, slums, and frontier misery, but all this was felt to be temporary, accidental, and, potentially, it was. The America to come was to be found in the undifferentiated people as Whitman saw them — not in the well-to-do, or in the patricians reflecting what he regarded as European decadence, or in the riffraff of city morals, but in the mechanic, the tradesman, the sailor, most of all in the farmer, with leaders to arise from among themselves. By a natural translation, the noble savage of Rousseau whom we were all to approximate in virtue had become, in the minds of this democratic environment, the honest, healthy, full-blooded, unspoiled worker of our America. All this was in Whitman's air, though much of it was made articulate only when he became truly articulate himself. Son of a carpenter, apprenticed to a mechanical trade, living with farmer folk, he could not miss it, being the sponge and dreamer that he was.[4]

3

There was also a more personal, more truly spiritual element in this climate of environment in which he passed his boyhood — the influence of the Society of Friends, called Quakers. I am well aware, of course, that Whitman was never a Quaker, never could have been a good Quaker in the full sense of the term, and that he became, later, a bad Quaker by any strict definition. His voluptuous senses were definitely not Quaker from the beginning, and became less and less so. He was never, as he said later, made to live inside a fence. It was his mental habits, his mysticism, his spiritual attitudes, and some of his moral principles, that were always of a Quakerish cast.[5] The evolution of democracy, as he saw and tried to lead it, took him farther and farther away from the Quaker discipline, yet not only his belief in the Inner Light, but also the modes of his inner life, were, and remained, curiously Quaker. Like many another, he learned more of his religion at home than at the Dutch Reformed Sunday School.

The indirect influence of the great Quaker rebel, Elias Hicks, was undoubtedly powerful with Walt. To the end of his life he spoke of him constantly, and one of his last literary tasks was to prepare, too late, a study of his character and spirit. I am far, of course, from suggesting that this man — or for that matter Quakerism in general — was a dominant influence, or more than an element in Walt's 'kosmos.' Whitman had heard his powerful oratory once in early youth. He had heard about him again and again from his mother.[6] Walt's grandfather Whitman had been his friend and neighbor from boyhood; his father knew and admired him.[7] It was Hicks who caused the great split in Quakerism, which only now begins to be healed.[8] Technically, this rupture, which broke up families and destroyed institutions, was over dogma. For Hicks, God was in us all, speaking with inner voice in any man, and Christ was his mouthpiece, and not in any historical or doctrinal sense the only Son of God. Yet actually the violent dissensions which arose came from deeper causes. Hicks, a deeply religious man, as indeed was Whitman, had carried the theory of George Fox to its logical conclusion. Not the Bible, not any doctrine, but only the voice of God felt through the Inner Light was the guide and reliance and faith of man. It was individualism, personalism in religion, carried to the farthest extreme, for every man was his own temple and priest. Yet, though individualism, it was not separatism. The Inner Light, Hicks maintained, brought men who shared it in common into a union, giving them a social consciousness, like the social consciousness derived from partaking of the Sacraments, the validity of which he denied — a consciousness supernatural in origin, but intensely democratic in its results. And this democratic mysticism which Hicks preached was certainly Whitman's religion through life.

Neither Whitman nor his father belonged to nor, so far as I know, ever went to the meeting. But this close familiarity with Hicks and his message, so often testified to in the family, must have carried with it more than a superficial acquaintance with the beliefs and practices of Quakerism in general. And this knowledge was surely given life and meaning in young Whitman's frequent visits to the Van Velsors, and by his love for his Quaker-trained mother who addressed him as 'thee,' and his affection for his 'sweet-faced' Quaker grandmother.

The essence of the Quaker mode lies not in simplicity or non-resistance or in protest against worldliness, but in quiet — the seeking of the Inner Light, the search for a 'concern' by which life shall be governed and given meaning. This habit of retirement to the inner springs of being, this periodic escape from the world, this indolence of the body while the soul is questing, was clearly Whitman's habit from early youth. I am far from meaning that Walt, spreading his bulky limbs on the turf under an apple tree, or wandering off his job to reflect and meditate, was always, or often, or more than occasionally, concerned with religion. I suspect, rather, that his youthful dreaming was usually of such romantic and sentimental stuff as comes out in his early poems and stories. But this was certainly not true later, nor always true in youth,[9] where by his own frequent testimony he was trying to find his true self. His employers and casual acquaintances called this withdrawal and meditation laziness. But the point as regards Quakerism is that he had lived at home, and with his grandparents, and very probably in more than one farmhouse afterward, with people who took meditation seriously, who believed that God and the answers to the great questions lay within. What the Quakers found there was precious, and even the least articulate, worst educated among them was listened to, when his time for testimony at meeting came. This Walt certainly believed of himself. In a hundred poems he speaks as one not removed except by intuition and intensity from the common ground and the common man, but empowered to speak because of the voice within him. What it was (he calls it soul) he was much too unmetaphysical to analyze into a definition.

—The faculty of absorption was peculiarly Whitman's own, and a part of his genius. It was his weakness too, for excessive absorption like his is uncritical, and leads to contradiction and an amorphous philosophy. Yet it cannot be doubted that what I call his Quaker habit of retirement within himself, and his Quakerish faith that anyone may be a mouthpiece for spirit, gave to this native absorptiveness a spiritual significance, and later a spiritual direction, which Walt often asserted was the ultimate purpose of the 'Leaves of Grass.' It is most certainly not a Quaker book, but there is more of George Fox and Elias Hicks in its background than has been supposed. I wish they might have read it. They would have been, I suspect, less shocked than were the readers of the genteel age, though presumably in violent opposition to Whitman's inclusion of the functions of the body in a spiritual democracy! Yet much of the 'Leaves' they would have understood far better than a generation trained, like ours, in materialism.

CHAPTER V

〰〰〰

'What do you hear Walt Whitman? . . . What do you see Walt Whitman?'

W E RETURN to Walt himself again (Walter still when he
signs his name). We return to him in what would be an
overstatement to call his career, in 1838, a year or so before the
fretting Mrs. Benton, wife of his employer on *The Long Island
Democrat*, complained of falling over his big feet in her dining-
room. His activities as printer, journalist, and free-lance writer
were, however, soon to become a real career, and make him a
fluent and influential editor, and a contributor to magazines that
sold current imitations of foreign models and current fashions in
literary tripe.

Though still sailing without a true-north compass, he was not
lazy. In the early eighties, he told Doctor Bucke, his biographer,
that from thirteen years of age onward until he was past fifty, he
had worked at 'regular labor' on the average of from six to seven
hours a day — not much for a printer, but plenty for an editor,
who has to get around. Nor did this include his own studies and
free-lance writings, which were extensive; nor his loafing, lounging, and rambling, which got him his reputation for indolence,
but whose amazing fruits are to be found in his notebooks long
before the publication of 'Leaves of Grass.' In the ten years
from, say, 1838 to 1848, when his country was dizzy with its
period of most rapid expansion, Whitman himself was expanding
with equal rapidity — and deepening also.

Since it is obvious what Walt was headed for in these years,
it is not right to call him a drifter. He wanted to be an editor —
later, a political editor — and he succeeded. He wanted also to
be what he would have called a 'literatus' — a writer like Haw-

thorne or Longfellow or the successful popular-story writers who
filled the magazines and reviews. Unfortunately, he was trying
to be the wrong kind of writer for the imagination which was
forming deep within him. When he found that out, he seems to
have begun all over again in his attempts to make poetry, while
keeping journalism as a trade.

Even as a boy of nineteen on Long Island, Walt must have had
more initiative and ambition than Mrs. Benton's estimate indicates, for he got, somehow or another, type and equipment
from New York,[1] and in the pleasant town of Huntington published his own weekly paper, *The Long Islander*, for which he was
editor, printer, and delivery boy on his horse 'Nina.' Perhaps he
had saved a little from teaching for a down payment, but someone must have thought well enough of his abilities to sponsor him.[2]
We know nothing of this paper except for unimportant quotations in other journals, and the tradition that it died from its
editor's neglect. John Burroughs reports an old man who remembered Walt telling stories to the youth of the village, and
reading poems which he called 'yawps' — a word that was to
have a history:

> I too am not a bit tamed, I too am untranslatable,
> I sound my barbaric yawp over the roofs of the world,

he was to write in *Song of Myself*. But by this time 'yawp' was
certainly not apologetic. It had been transferred to the cry of
'the spotted hawk,' the night hawk which is not a hawk at all,
screaming at dusk over the flat roofs of New York or Brooklyn,
as many must have heard it not so long ago, a wild raucous cry
like the occasional stridency of the *Song of Myself*.

When *The Long Islander* died of lack of attention or (and much
more probably) cash, Whitman began to alternate teaching with
work on Mr. Benton's *Long Island Democrat* in Jamaica. His
writing was valued but he was probably regarded as a printer by
trade. As late as 1849 he still calls himself a printer — a printer,
incidentally, badly in need of cash.[3] It may be suggested here
that if some adjective has to be used with his name by writers of
introductions, 'printer-poet' is much more accurate for Whitman

than 'carpenter-poet.' Printing was important in his career.
It was a trade, like Thoreau's pencil making, by which he could
turn a penny when he needed it; his carpentering was an episode
only. The first edition of the 'Leaves' was, in all probability,
printed only because Whitman was a fellow workman and could
help.

2

But livelihood aside, the evidence seems to show that Walt's
first interest in the newspapers, where for twenty years now he is
to be either editorial and feature writer, or printer, or both, was
in his chance to break into periodical literature. *The Long Island
Democrat* published some of his poems, and pseudo-philosophic
ramblings in the manner of Irving called *Sun-Down Papers*. He
is contributing by 1841 to *The Democratic Review*, where his
name appears on a list which was to include Bryant, Whittier,
Longfellow, Hawthorne, Thoreau. This monthly, 'of a pro-
founder quality of talent than any since,' as Whitman said in
1858,[4] was 'impressing the public, especially the young men.'
To write for it, as Whitman did at twenty-two, was equivalent
to breaking into *The Atlantic Monthly* or *The Century* in the
1890's. The young man was getting on. Two of the earliest
letters of his which have been preserved are directed to the
editor of *The Boston Miscellany*, offering him in 1842 *The Angel of Tears*, for eight dollars, and citing his story, *Death in the
Schoolroom*, in *The Democratic Review*, which, with others, had
received 'public favor' and been 'pretty popular.'[5]

'Pretty terrible' would be a more accurate term. Many of
these early attempts to be literary have been reprinted by Whitman's editors — and some by himself, in spite of his reported
remark that he hoped to God that his friends would not find a
copy of his own novel (but they did), and his statement to
Traubel [6] that he once was full of unexecuted designs, 'even
stories . . . God help me!'

The poetry he wrote in these early forties was better, but only
a little better. Here is Whitman the would-be poet in 1843:

> Not in a gorgeous hall of pride
> Where tears fall thick, and loved ones sigh,

> Wisht he, when the dark hour approached,
> To drop his veil of flesh and die,

which shows that he could write empty verse in passable metre.
And here is his literary prose of the time, by no means at its
worst: [7] 'High, high in space floated the angel Alza.' (He had
been reading Poe.) This was the article offered for eight dollars.
And from the opening of *Death in the Schoolroom*: 'Ting-a-ling-
ling-ling went the little bell on the teacher's desk of a village-
school one morning, when the studies of the earlier part of the
day were about half completed.'

His prose and verse is conventional or imitative, with a superficial sophistication and the bluff of being wise and literary so
characteristic of half-educated youth. At any moment it may
break into crude coltishness, as for example in his Indian stories
written in a kind of post-Cooperian jargon that is distressing.
Whitman's work of this kind contains some foreshadowings of
his obsession with death, a strong charge of humanitarianism,
and some vague autobiographical references out of which biographers have probably made too much. Saying that, one says
all.

I shall dwell a moment more on Walt the would-be popular
writer, because, to a literary historian, the spectacle of a great
poet turning out trash while both perilous stuff and intense
emotion must have been stirring in his depths, is most interesting. [8]
I say 'must' because what appears in his notebooks of 1847 was
surely fermenting yeastily in '41 and '42.

Late in 1842, as a supplement to *The New World*, one of the
many newspapers for which Walt worked at printing sporadically
in this decade, he published 'Franklin Evans,' a novel intended
to illustrate the curse of alcohol. It was reprinted in *The Brooklyn
Eagle* by Walt himself in 1846, and is said to have sold twenty
thousand copies in supplement form, which I very much doubt.
He wrote it rapidly for cash down. Now Walt, as a youth, was a
Puritan without being sour about it. He never touched strong
liquor, so he said to Traubel, until he was thirty, and not much
then, hated tobacco, and apparently had little to do with young
women. The story that he attacked intemperance under the in-

fluence of gin cocktails is surely not true. He was a good choice as writer of a tract, so far as his Puritanism (unusual in a journalist) was concerned, but not for the reasons stated in *The New World:* 'This novel,' said the newspaper, 'will create a sensation, both for the ability with which it is written, as well as the interest of the subject, ... It is written by one of the best novelists of this country ... to aid the great work of reform.' So egregious a blurb would scarcely have been risked except on Walt's urging. In fact, I have no doubt that the blurbist was Walt himself.

The first chapters of 'Franklin Evans,' describing the journey down from Long Island to New York of the youthful teller of the tale, and his adventures in the great city before he takes to drink, are good conventional narrative. Whitman's gift was not for story-telling — he could never by any possibility have become 'one of the best novelists of this country' — but there are good scenes in this novel, fresh from Whitman's memory, of his apprentice days in New York, descriptions of the 'musical drinking-houses,' the streets, the shops, the typical characters encountered by a young fellow trying to get started in a great city. But when the tale goes to the South (of which Walt then knew nothing), 'melodramatic' is too weak a word to describe its incidents and characters, 'sentimental' too mild to define its morality, and 'tripe' too gentle a name for its eloquence.

The plain truth is that Whitman had no higher standards when he wrote for current fashion than such as are typically exhibited in the Annuals, those expensive gift books, which, far better than the Thoreaus, the Emersons, the Bryants, show what the popular taste of the day regarded as literature. The worst as well as the best literary writing in American history was done in the forties, and Whitman, in his copy-pad stage, followed the worst. He was a bad hack writer even according to the low standards of really popular writing of the time. But he was a good journalist, and journalism set him on a better track, and became an important part of the background of the 'Leaves of Grass.'

3

After selling Nina, his horse, Walt had gone to New York in the summer of 1839,[9] but was soon back and on *The Long Island Democrat*. It was in 1841 that he was printer in New York on *The New World*. In 1842 (writing on his own at the same time) he was associated somehow or another with a Democratic paper, *The Aurora*, with *The Sun*, and *The Tatler*. He describes himself as having been, when he was with *The Aurora*, a managing editor, working day by day beside Orpheus C. Kerr, a humorist who, as the 'scissors editor,' clipped the exchanges.[10] One must imagine a big fellow, serious though friendly, full-lipped, who looked much older than his age. William Cauldwell, an associate on *The Aurora*, described him as 'tall and graceful in appearance, neat in attire,' a cheerful, happy-looking countenance. 'He usually wore a frock coat and a high hat, carried a small cane, and the lapel of his coat was almost invariably ornamented with a boutonnière.' [11] Beard he must have had, for George said that he never had shaved. But the beard was probably trimmed and the hair black, long but not unruly, with probably a streak of white. The callow printer's assistant had, by the age of twenty-three, made himself at home in both New York and Brooklyn, one of 'the boys,' as he used afterward to call the newspaper and magazine crowd. He was boarding at various places — seven are named for 1842 and 1843! No wonder he wrote feelingly on the evils of boarding-houses in 'Franklin Evans.' In 1843, his job was on *The Statesman*, a New York semi-weekly, and he was contributing, now and later, to *The Columbian* and *The American Review* magazines as well as to *The Democratic Review*. In 1844, he was on *The Democrat*, a daily which sponsored Silas Wright, radical and expansionist Democrat who turned conservative later, for the governorship of New York. Then came his 'best sit' on *The Brooklyn Eagle*.

I do not agree that these constant shifts indicate a shiftless youth, without plans. The newspapers themselves shifted or died with changes of political opinion, and a promising young journalist then, as now, was likely to be distinguished more by the num-

ber of positions he could get than by what he held. Nor does the
one picture of Whitman we possess of these middle 1840's show
a vacillating dilettante. This early daguerreotype (see Plate IV),
now in the Whitman House in Camden, shows a frock coat,
careful dressing, short-trimmed beard, bare upper lip, tar-black
hair with one streak of white. His brother George said he turned
gray by thirty, so it is a good guess that this portrait is of 1846,
when he paid a visit, which he describes in an *Eagle* article, to
Plumbe's New York gallery of daguerreotypes and probably had
himself taken.[12] What must strike anyone is the seriousness of
this young man's face, the absence of that later bluff geniality
or the soulful pose of so many later pictures. And, indeed, by
1846 and at age twenty-seven — if that is the date — he was
mature as an editor; and as a poet, as will be seen, knew what he
must do, if he could do anything with poetry at all.

4

Here are the bare statistical bones of a typical career of the
kind of journalist we call a free lance, meaning that, while he does
not refuse a regular job, and may often hold a good one, his heart
is in the highlands of composition chasing the deer of his fancy.
Such a man is quite different from the closeted writer — a Longfellow, an Emerson, a Hawthorne — who may resort to teaching
or lecturing (which is just another kind of teaching) for income,
but whose work from the beginning represents himself and not
an institution like a newspaper or a magazine. Young Whitman
is more like the coffee-house scribblers of the previous century,
picking up what they could from the town, and retailing it hot
under cover of the editorial 'we,' or experimenting with popular
literature on the side.

It was therefore of very great importance for his career as a
writer, that, in February of 1846, Walt was made editor of *The
Brooklyn Eagle*, an influential and liberal newspaper in what he
regarded as his home town, and continued in charge until January of 1848. An editor, even an editor of a political newspaper,
was supposed to do some 'elegant' writing (of which Whitman

had done too much), but his chief concern was with a clientèle interested in local happenings, and political and social controversy. The born editor, said Whitman, writing from his desk at *The Eagle* in 1846, requires a union of rare qualities. He must love the public he serves. In general information he should be complete, particularly in that relating to his own country. He should have a fluent style; 'elaborate finish we do not think requisite in daily writing.' He has to press noble reforms, school the people, in opposition perhaps to their long established ways of thought, improve their politics, and be no 'mere monotonous writer after old fashions.' [13]

I submit that for a youth whose writing so far had been mawkish, ornate, and empty, this was just the medicine needed. It did nothing for his poetry, which would require a new language, but this daily writing for sound if somewhat overstated purposes did cure him of the pseudo-literary, as it has many a young journalist since. His first really honest writing was in daily editorial journalism.

Walt got his best 'sit' (situation) and most continuous job by succeeding William B. Marsh, an able editor of *The Eagle*, recently dead. This was not only a substantial promotion for a drifting printer and editorial writer of twenty-seven. It was success. He had, clearly, been picked as a coming man, and his conduct of his editorship, and the comments of his colleagues both in Brooklyn and in New York, indicate that he has become at least a minor figure in the journalistic world. Thanks to his writing, thanks, unquestionably, also to his political activities which were earnest and extensive, he gets an independent command, which might have led to the top of his profession. If, as seems probable, the picture described above was taken in the first year of his editorship, its stiff respectability, responsible jaw, formal clothing are easily explained in a man so photogenic and dramatic in his poses as Whitman. Small-town celebrity, I should call him at this stage.

He began in February of 1846.[14] Polk was President. The Mexican War was imminent. It was a good time to be an editor, for all kinds of winds were blowing, and one was to cost him his

job. Isaac Van Anden, the owner of *The Eagle*, was as strong a
party man as Whitman, but more conservative. As the war in
Mexico drew to its close in 1847, the ominous question of slavery,
suppressed, denied, compromised, began to show its hideous
implications. The young Whitman was no Abolitionist. He believed, like a good states-rights man, that slavery in the old South
was an affair to be settled — and which would be peacefully
settled — by the South itself. But this new part-continent, this
California and the vast Southwest added by the war — every
fibre in him believed it should be free soil. He became a so-called
Free-Soiler and wrote vehemently in *The Eagle* imploring his
party to see its manifest destiny, and its probable fate if it compromised on the New West. Van Anden seems to have been a
tolerant man, who had given his young editor entire independence. But the radical Democrats, Barnburners as they were
called, joined in forming a Free-Soil organization, and threatened
a split in the party. It was soon clear that the New West could
not be kept free without alienating the Democrats of the South.
Van Anden must have told Whitman that even if he refused to
attack, he could not continue to support, the Free-Soil Democrats in *The Eagle*. And so in January of 1848, refusing to compromise, Whitman was fired by the publisher 'in the course of
his business arrangements.' But Walt had enjoyed two years of
editing, at the head of the best paper in a city of over sixty
thousand people.

It was an agreeable job, in no sense easy, in fact highly responsible, yet not too exacting for profitable leisure.[15] We have
the reminiscences of Whitman's fifteen-year-old printer's devil,
Henry Sutton, recorded in 1920, to give us an intimate picture
of the young editor at work.[16] *The Eagle* was a four page paper.
When Walt took hold, he was still in a literary mood, and began
his innovations by inserting a couple of columns of literary material on the first page, hitherto given over to announcements.
Some of this was reprinted from current prose and poetry, sometimes the writing was his own. The second page was news and
editorial, followed by local news and the usual mélange of a
newspaper of that day, letters, comments, reviews. Walt must

have written a couple of columns a day, in addition to selecting and editing for the rest of the paper.[17]

Sutton liked him, and there are no memories of a lazy boss in his reminiscences. Walt was still boarding part of the time, though his father was living in Brooklyn, and, characteristically, trying in 1848 to sell his house. He came to the office early, worked hard all morning, and saw few visitors except 'politicians.' When his copy was ready, he went for a walk and came back in time to read proof. This done, he would take young Sutton for a swim at Gray's Bath at the foot of Fulton Street, staying in the water exactly twenty minutes, then have a shower at the pump, which the boy worked for him. So the Brooklyn day was finished, and he was off, usually across the ferry to New York, or for what he called a 'sun-down' walk. It sounds like a six- or seven-hour working day, which, as he certainly wrote, and must have read, much at home, made a full schedule. Van Anden gave him perfect freedom, and was evidently satisfied with his editor until politics separated them.

Here is a happy young man to all outward appearances, immersed in work which he liked, with plenty of opportunity to study the human animal both at first hand and in the news. It was his job, but also his delight. We know that he was physically vigorous, intensely healthy, and there is no evidence in his daily contacts and daily writing of any emotional or moral perturbation beyond the excitements of the times, which it was his duty as an editor to record. Much more, and far different, fermentation was at work beneath the surface, yet he functions so easily and so well as an editorial sermonizer, writes with such animation, is so tranquil, regular, and content with his external life, that it is difficult not to believe that in 1846 and 1847 he foresaw a life of editing, in which he might well come to lead opinion in the wider field of New York. Ten years later, when he was editing *The Brooklyn Times*, and had become, though few knew it, the most original poet of his day, he defended journalism as a career in words which certainly reflect his past if not his present: 'We are convinced that neither do the labors of journalism exceed, nor are its returns unworthy of comparison with, those of any other profession.' The income is satisfactory, the political opportunities great, and 'there is the consciousness of possessing power and influence, ... the silent veneration of the public who regard the terrible "We" as a semi-omniscient and omnipotent being, ... compliments, ... notes of thanks, ...' [18]

5

I am dwelling at some length upon the details of this first thoroughgoing experience as editor, because I think that Walt had even better reasons to be satisfied with what he regarded then as his profession than the personal gratifications stated above. And also that this experience was of far greater importance in making him the representative poet of the nineteenth century and democracy than has been hitherto supposed. At what Bernard De Voto calls the critical period of United States history, Whitman was at the listening post, the broadcasting station of a newspaper which, though small, was strategically central. These were years of war and vital decisions. They were the years when the leaders of the nation first began to suspect that a house divided against itself must fall, and that a state cannot exist half slave and half free. They were the years just preceding the European upheavals of 1848, when liberalism, for a while, seemed about to triumph throughout the Western world. In the later 1840's, the West was really won, the United States became a continental nation, the issues of slavery were seen to be unavoidable. It was one of the great expansionist periods among all recorded national histories, perhaps the greatest, certainly the most rapid. As De Voto writes in a passage later condensed on pages 8 to 10 of his 'The Year of Decision, 1846':

'It was a blind drive to free the nation's burgeoning industrialism to better functioning. But our elders ignored what their elders had known, that there also went into expansionism romance, Utopianism, and the dream that man might yet be free. And also the logic of geography, which any map makes clear to anyone today. You would experience a gnawing feeling of incompletion and even insecurity today, if you looked at a map of the United States in which Oregon, Washington, and Idaho were colored to represent joint occupation with a foreign nation and all the area south of them and eastward to Texas and the Arkansas River was marked foreign territory. Both the incompletion and the insecurity were a good deal more real to every American who looked at a map in '44. And finally, expansionism had acquired an emotion that was new — or at least a new combination. The Americans had always devoutly believed that the manifest superiority of their institutions, government, and mode of life would eventually spread, by inspiration and imitation, to less fortunate, less happy peoples. That devotion now took a new phase: it was perhaps the American destiny to spread out free and admirable institutions by action as well as by example, by occupying territory as well as by practising virtue. For the sum of these feelings, a Democratic editor found, in the summer of '45, one of the most dynamic phrases ever coined, Manifest Destiny.

'That phrase was both a revelation and a recognition. Quite certainly, it made soldiers and emigrants of many men who, without it, would have been neither, but its importance was that it expressed also the peculiar will, optimism, disregard, and even blindness that characterize the 1840's in America.' [19]

And there was not only the opening of vast sources of wealth, and the rush of population toward the unoccupied lands of the West, there was expansionism also in American literature, philosophy, and religion. The Mormons built their Utopia on its impetus. The Brook Farmers, who hated materialism, believed in it. Emerson's 'Essays' is an expansionist book; so, in its contrary and paradoxical way, is Thoreau's 'Walden.' 'Moby Dick' is as expansionist in its imagination as it is pessimistic in its conclusions. And emphatically, enthusiastically, the 'Leaves of Grass,' which has its roots in these years, is perhaps the type expansionist book of all literature.

Walt, a young expansionist mind in an expansionist country, had the good fortune to be perched (if I may change the figure) like a weathervane through these years. It was his business to note and record and guide for Brooklyn the impulses of the nation, and, in so far as he knew them, of the world. He was a weathervane at the great port of entry and departure, the bay of New York. Settled in a liberal if vague philosophy, in the midst of a great boom of liberalism, curious, with an imagination already intensely sensitive to his country, he was by necessity responsive to winds and counter winds. That is the danger but also the opportunity of an editor. The journalist and editorial writer, even more than the political leader or the intuitive man-of-letters of those days, had (to change the figure still again) his finger necessarily on the pulse of the public, and recorded, though he did not always interpret, the hot-flowing blood of the 1840's.

Such an editor was the young Whitman. It is impossible to understand the growth, the scope, and the bloodstream of the 'Leaves' without understanding how much editorial experience of the kind I have been describing lay behind it. Let me hasten to add that it is equally impossible to understand the book and its influence solely or chiefly by means of this journalistic experience.

CHAPTER VI

~~~~~

'Over the roofs of the world'

WALT, in his old age, when his too admiring friends tried to pump out from his memory reminiscences of his youth, said very little of his editorials, or his career as editor. Although he reprinted some of his early stories, which he must have found in the drifts of manuscript and memorabilia on his floor at Camden, he seems to have forgotten his voluminous editorial writing. Perhaps he lost his books of clippings, if he ever had any. But I think it more probable that the old man, who now identified himself as prophet, poet, and seer with the 'Leaves of Grass,' disclaiming any important existence outside of what was recorded in that volume, was willing to forget, if, indeed, he ever realized, the close connection between his editorial experience and the ideas and the objectives of his poems. With a sound instinct for publicity, he preferred to remember the struggling, unsuccessful, indomitable poet and let the successful editor remain in historical darkness. Hence the legend of the man of the people, toiling in obscurity toward the articulate and fame. And yet he made a revealing remark to Doctor Bucke which shows the truth. 'Remember the book arose,' he said, 'out of my life in Brooklyn and New York from 1838 to 1853, absorbing a million people, for fifteen years, with an intimacy, an eagerness, an abandon, probably never equalled.'[1] A million people! His rambling, his sun-down walks, his bus riding, his visits to prisons and theatres would never have given him such a consciousness of that million as his journalistic sense of the metropolitan communities upon whose pulse he kept his editorial finger.

Now that his admirers have exhumed his newspaper contributions and published them in several volumes, it is easy to follow the records of Walt the weathervane for nearly twenty years. Personally, I find his editorials good reading, except when too brashly patriotic, too smugly confident of the manifest destiny of the United States, too smugly flippant, or too full of platitudes. There is a fine conviction behind many of them of warring for a great cause which must prevail. He felt himself to be one of the young men described in a credo of the Democratic Party published in *The Democratic Review* of 1841. And he would certainly have agreed with the following sentence from that credo: 'For in truth our faith in the people — our confidence in the Providence which watches over the high destinies of mankind involved in the great political experiment of our system of institutions — our democratic optimism, so to speak — was a principle lying rather more than skin-deep.' [2] And there is a generous and sometimes daring humanitarianism in his writing which is evidently based on real feeling and real experience.

Most interesting of all to the modern reader, is the fervor of expansionism and progress which makes his plea for social betterment warm and vigorous, and trumpets from his editorials on war and politics and the future of the country. The continent was becoming a nation under his eyes, and here is that basis of fact which underlies the immense exuberance and expansive imagination of the national poems in the 'Leaves of Grass.' In the New World of America at that moment, everything good for body and soul seemed possible.

The Eagle editorials from which I intend to quote are evidently the results of precocious political knowledge, but of very young emotions and youthful thinking. Walt seemed mature intellectually at twenty-seven to twenty-nine, for he could write effectively of the right ideas for his time, his party, his paper, and himself. But this writing came from the upper levels of his mind. Below, as we know from his notebooks, was a confusing uprush of emotional thinking, and a hard and uncertain struggle to find a language to express it. As editor, Walt writes like a man of thirty-five; as poet in these years, he seems to be in the stage which powerful poets usually reach before twenty.

2

Whitman's editorials are only good vigorous journalism, in no sense literature, and are expressive of the editorial 'We,' not yet of the 'I' which was to dominate the 'Leaves.' To use modern terms, while he was a good news broadcaster, a commentator, and occasionally a columnist, his private imagination was still off the record. On the radio he would have done well, and would have enthusiastically welcomed this opportunity to speak with the voice (which he thought was so important) direct to the masses. He would have been particularly acceptable to the many listeners who like their news colored by temperament and interspersed with opinion, for his mind ran that way. This was the way he talked in later years, and this would have been his style as a broadcaster. Therefore, to arrange sentences from the editorials of his *Eagle* days in the form of a broadcast is a good way to represent Walt the editor letting his mind run for the benefit of his subscribers. Let him begin with the Democratic Party, which he still believed was going to win democracy for the country; then follow on through the news with ideas on the current Mexican War, on progress, reform, the arts, and his political enemies. It is 1846 and 1847, the turning point of the nineteenth century — for a poet-editor, 'A strange, unloosen'd, wondrous time,' for a youngster an opportunity both to yawp and be wise:

'To attack the turbulence and destructiveness of the Democratic spirit, is an old story.... Why, all that is good and grand in any political organization in the world, is the result of this turbulence and destructiveness.... The Democracy of this country never can be overthrown.... there is a mighty and restless energy throughout the length and breadth of this nation, for going onward to the very verge with our experiment of popular freedom.... Swing open the doors!... There is too much mankind and too little earth... *And then look at America.* Stretching between the Alleghany Mountains and the Pacific Ocean, are millions on millions of uncultivated acres of land.... That liberality toward "foreigners," and that generous hospitality for them, which *true American "public opinion" fixed upon at the beginning as one of the good elements of character here,* ... any party or public man, that defies that element, will ... surely fall into ruin.'

'Yes: Mexico must be thoroughly chastised! ... What has miserable, inefficient Mexico — with her superstition, her bur- lesque upon freedom, her actual tyranny by the few over the many — What has she to do with the great mission of peopling the New World with a noble race? Be it ours, to achieve that mission! Be it ours to roll down all the upstart leaven of old despotism, that comes our way! [Manifest Destiny. Let the eagle scream! We are the people! You will find it again in the 'Leaves of Grass' but in better English.] ... This war is the most bloodless one thus far, ... that ever was known on earth. ... Many classes in what is called a peaceful community have and do greater bitterness toward each other, than the Yankee army and the Mexicans — ... *Will not the future effect of even this war ex- tend the area of Peace Principles?* ... But hear *The Tribune* again — ... The black mouthed libeller. [Mr. Greeley, I suppose.] ... When will the war be ended? This talk about a peace party is all moonshine, until we are able to protect them from their own mili- tary tyrants. ... We must make our authority respectable — we must make our possession of the country safe to the people, and give them security in pursuit of their lawful occupations. ... If the work is well done, it must be quickly done. We must ... so manage that they stay beat. ... This cannot be done ... by barely keeping open our lines of communication, ... There is no middle course — either we must back out of it entirely, or we must drive it through with a vigorous hand. [As so often, quota- tions from Walt Whitman seem timely a hundred years later.] ... We have lofty views of the scope and destiny of our American Republic. It is for the interest of mankind that its power and territory should be extended — the farther the better. [Page Herr Hitler!] We claim those lands [Northwest Mexico] thus, by a law superior to parchments and dry diplomatic rules. ... We do not take them to be our inferiors in any respect, but to be our equals.' [Here Walt Whitman and Adolf Hitler part company.]

'You cannot legislate men into virtue. ... Why, we wouldn't

give a snap for the aid of the Legislature, in forwarding a purely moral revolution. It must work its way through individual minds. It must spread from its own beauty, and melt into the hearts of men — not be forced upon them at the point of the sword, or by the stave of the officer. [Thoreau was writing the same doctrine in New England.] . . . For our own part, one of the principal arguments against the gallows is, that while it stands, murderers are so often allowed to escape with impunity — because juries will not convict, where the penalty is death, unless the causes are very aggravated indeed. . . . Once open the eyes of men to the *fact* of the intimate connection between *poor pay* for women, and *crime* among women, and the greatest difficulty is overcome.'

'We believe the Brooklyn *Eagle* was the very first Democratic paper . . . expressing the conviction that it is the duty of its party to take an unalterable stand against the allowance of slavery in any new territory, under any circumstances, or in any way. . . . With the present slave States, of course, no human being anywhere out from themselves has the least shadow of a right to interfere. . . . The man who accustoms himself to *think* . . . will see the wide and radical difference between the unquestionable folly, and wicked wrong, of "abolitionist" interference with slavery in the Southern States — and this spirit of establishing slavery in fresh lands. . . . The influence of the slavery institution is to bring the dignity of labor down to the level of slavery, which God knows! is low enough.'

'All conservative influence is pestilential to our [the Democratic] party. It may succeed for a day or a year — but . . . the more liberal doctrines will gradually become paramount, and their advocates be honored and trusted. [Forecast of the careers of Woodrow Wilson and F. D. Roosevelt.] . . . Thinking, as we do, that hardly any evil which could be inflicted on the people of this hemisphere, and the cause of freedom all over the world, would be so great as the disunion of these States — their parting in bitterness and ill-blood — we believe it incumbent on every Democrat always to bear testimony in the same spirit and the same words, as one now in heaven [Jackson] — "the Union! it must and shall be preserved."'

'Most of the squibs of the *Advertiser* toward us, are simply impertinent; and we disdain even to crush such pitiful malevolence. [Walt Whitman had been charged with being a Whig in 1841.] ... As to our "grammar," [which the 'pack of English cockneys' running the *Advertiser* had attacked] it is of course perfectly correct [see above for one instance where it definitely wasn't], or we shouldn't presume to write for an intelligent community. ... We never sacrifice at the shrine of formal construction, however. [The Whig paper *Star* accuses him of partisanship] ... *Star*! go wash thy venerable eyes, that thou mayst see how the world has not been sleeping for these fifty years. Mere precedent is nothing, and will oftener warrant wrong than right. ... It is quite impossible to make a silk purse out of the Brooklyn *Advertiser*.'

'Now, Democrats of King's County! now, close up your ranks and prepare for the contest. ... King's County ... wants the vote fully out. [This was Walt Whitman's responsibility both as political worker and editor.] ... Well; the Whigs have triumphed in Brooklyn. ... But ... one can take these things with coolness and serenity enough, after all. It varies the monotony, for *our side* to be beaten; almost as much as it does for the Whigs to succeed — ... As for the *ins*, alas! they are always more or less to be pitied! Civil strife, rivalry for appointments, and other turmoil, spread among them all the waters of bitterness. Poor devils! ... We feel perfectly serene about the whole affair.'

'We think that importations should be kept to as low a point as possible, consistently with the freedom and best interests of commerce. But we can't have trade without imports. ... Cut us loose from the antiquated bondages of the tariff system — ... and we will show the world ... a spectacle of solid commercial grandeur. ... How nice a game they play in asking a high tariff "for the benefit of the workingman"! What lots of cents have gone out of poor folks' pockets, to swell the dollars in the possession of owners of great steam mills!'

'There may be some, doubtless, who may not be blamed — whom peculiar circumstances keep in the bands of the solitary; but the most of both sexes can find partners meet for them, if

they will. Turn, Fools, and get discretion. Buy cradles and double beds; make yourself a reality in life — and do the State some
service.'

'Beautiful Brooklyn, with its saucy-browed Heights jutting
out on the river.'

'We do not want a rich government.... We had far rather
have a rich average population.'

'Not one single independent dramatic critic seems to be among
many talented writers for the New York press. Or rather, we
should say, not one single upright critic is permitted to utter
candidly his opinion.... The Park, once in a great while, gives a
fine play, performed by meritorious actors.... It is (however)
but a third-rate imitation of the best London theatres.... One of
the curses ... is the *star* system.... Give us American plays ...
fitted to American opinions and institutions.... The drama of
this country *can* be the mouthpiece of freedom, refinement, liberal philanthropy, beautiful love for all our brethren, polished
manners and an elevated good taste. It can wield potent sway to
destroy any attempt at despotism.'

'Hardly anything which comes to us in the music and songs of
the Old World, is strictly good and fitting from our notions....
The music of feeling — heart music as distinguished from art
music — is well exemplified in ... several ... bands ... of American vocalists.... Because whatever touches the heart is better
than what is merely addressed to the ear.' [3]

And so young Whitman looks around and beyond his Brooklyn world. He is a democrat, a Jeffersonian, an idealist, a violent
patriot, a humanitarian, a reformer who believes that morals begin in the heart, an ardent defender of progress for the people, a
fighter for democracy who knows that democracy has to be fought
for. Also a somewhat heavy-handed humorist, an earnest but
quite untechnical economist, an expansionist everywhere, a lover
of life who feels himself to be a rambling incarnation of the best
of Brooklyn. He is already egoistic (the presence of *The Eagle* 'at
any public place — at *any* place is a *special favor*'), intensely loyal,
a firm believer in health, cleanliness, marriage, and the rights and
virtues of the workingman, and in whatever furthers the great

ideal of a New World being made in America. And he is always an individualist. In an editorial not quoted above, he even maintains that every man's disease demands its own drug, not what may have cured the same in someone else!

After reading these excerpts, you will know young Walt as Brooklyn knew him. For it may be guessed that, except for fits of abstraction and reserve, when no one then would have understood what was going on, these freely written editorials represent the genial, ardent, liberal way of the young editor in his human contacts. Whatever was preparing underneath that was perturbed, mystical, and heavily egoistic, did not show in the confident optimism of the successful reporter and lecturer of the town. And you will know Walt of the first 'Leaves of Grass' too, as far as his general social and political ideas are involved in his poetry, for he did not much change in this respect until the years just before the Civil War, and not radically then. When he begins to write poetry, the effect of this editorial experience at one of the world's listening posts will be evident in what he called the 'kosmic' quality of his themes. The 'Leaves' have the vigor, the spaciousness, the vanity, the social importance, and the continental massiveness of America in its great moment of expansion, as a keen young journalist saw and was part of it. Also the disorder and overemphasis. It was the 'sit' on *The Eagle*, more than his reading, I should say, which broke through the partitions of a provincial mind. Walt must be regarded as very definitely a product of American journalism — although, of course, that tells only a quarter of the story.

CHAPTER VII

'Walt Whitman, a kosmos, of Manhattan the son'

THERE is much more to be told of Whitman's life in the 1840's. He was too much of a man, both physically and emotionally, to tie all his energies to an editorial desk. It was the varied experiences of his youth, between sixteen and thirty, he once said, 'on which everything else rests.' [1] Absorbing Brooklyn for the benefit of his subscribers, when the office day was done there was New York waiting for him across the river.

The Brooklyn ferry took him to a New York with which he was extensively familiar. He was no apprentice now, or hanger-on at the skirts of magazine literature, but a representative man of his profession, with an entrée to all events of public importance, and a name known at least to the 'boys' of the journalistic, critical, political, and publishing trades. New York itself was a cosmos of expanding humanity. It was, as he said of himself in the lines which in *Song of Myself* follow the title line of this chapter:

Turbulent, fleshy, sensual, eating, drinking and breeding.

But there is not the slightest evidence that Walt himself deserved this collection of adjectives, unless applied to his imagination. A loosening, an expansion, and an escape from his country inhibitions was unquestionably happening to him in these editorial years. He did not have to wait for New Orleans to become a Bohemian and a 'caresser of life,' as appears clearly enough in his lighter editorials. When in Brooklyn, on *The Eagle*, he was a responsible citizen going to clambakes at Coney Island with the local officials, keeping an eye on the condition of the streets, visiting the schools, urging his subscribers to marry and buy double beds, preaching sound Democratic doctrine — a combination of Uncle Don, Walter Winchell, and Dorothy Thompson for the town. For such a dramatization, the frock coat and respectable air which his first daguerreotype exhibits were indispensable.[2] But the New York Walt was probably easier of dress and of manner. He was certainly not 'turbulent' or 'fleshy,' yet an independent, carrying himself with confidence, a hearty intellectual, a democratic man. And a roving reporter such as seldom comes out of newspaper offices. Read the packed lines of re-membered experience in *A Song for Occupations*, written probably in the early fifties, and realize that the tall young fellow with the rolling gait had used his senses and his absorptive mind on everything that New York could offer.

Walt's New York, in these forties and fifties was, prevailingly, what we should call below Twenty-Third Street, and most of it below Fourteenth Street. Much of its domestic regions still remain in the rows of decorous red-brick houses ('quadrangular' he calls them) on such side streets as Eleventh or Nineteenth or Charlton. It was a New York of villainous slums, now mostly cleared away, and of a waterfront still fringed with masts, instead of the dock terminals and warehouses that hide the rivers. Up and down the business streets the iron-columned buildings, symbolic of the new industrial age, and so much admired by Walt, were beginning to rise eight or ten stories. Trinity spire still dominated the toe of the island, and that region was still the heart of human as well as of financial activity. There, the leading hotel was the great Astor House, and the Battery was, as yet, the chief park of the city, where thirty thousand people would assemble to watch the fireworks on Independence Day. And slanting through the city from the ocean end to the open country, the Fifth Avenue of its day, was Broadway, then for miles, as now for a few blocks only, one of the great streets of the world. This was the street of shops, of parades, the see-and-be-seen avenue for distinguished visitors, such as the first Japanese envoys and the Prince of Wales. It was an artery of traffic, a symbol of metropolitanism. Not the Champs Élysées, or Unter den Linden, or the Strand have had more memorable praise than Whitman's for his Broadway:

> Give me faces and streets — give me these phantoms incessant and endless along the trottoirs!
> Give me interminable eyes — give me women — give me comrades and lovers by the thousand!...
> Give me such shows — give me the streets of Manhattan!
> Give me Broadway, with the soldiers marching — [3]

And Broadway, leading on and on to the northwestward, was, like the great Hudson waterway beside it, a symbol of the expanding nation. The New York it epitomized was in the lusty youth of what was to become the greatest commerce of the world. When Whitman came back in the 1840's, it was still enjoying the heroic age of its theatre, the decline of which into trivial comedy was mourned by *The Eagle.* Already New York, though Boston and Philadelphia were not ready to admit it, was becoming the mouthpiece, if not yet the centre, of American culture. It was to New York, not to Boston, that Thoreau came in these forties, hoping to establish himself as a magazine writer or editor.

Walt went to the art shows, spent long hours in the new Egyptian Museum, patronized the phrenologists, was soon to study the Old World, which he had known only by books, in a great exposition. Most of all he revelled in the theatre and the opera. His own reminiscences are more evocative than any fabricated descriptions.[4] There his memory bubbles and boils again, as it does in his poems:

'Living in Brooklyn or New York City from this time forward, my life, then, and still more the following years, was curiously identified with Fulton Ferry, already becoming the greatest of its sort in the world for general importance, volume, variety, rapidity, and picturesqueness. Almost daily, later, ('50 to '60,) I cross'd on the boats, often up in the pilot-houses where I could get a full sweep, absorbing shows, accompaniments, surroundings. What oceanic currents, eddies, underneath — the great tides of humanity also, with ever-shifting movements. Indeed, I have always had a passion for ferries; to me they afford inimitable,

streaming, never-failing, living poems. The river and bay scenery, all about New York island, any time of a fine day — the
hurrying, splashing sea-tides — the changing panorama of steamers, all sizes, often a string of big ones outward bound to distant
ports — the myriads of white-sail'd schooners, sloops, skiffs, and
the marvellously beautiful yachts — the majestic sound boats
as they rounded the Battery and came along towards 5, afternoon,
eastward bound — the prospect off towards Staten Island, or
down the Narrows, or the other way up the Hudson — what re-
freshment of spirit such sights and experiences gave me years
ago (and many a time since). My old pilot friends, the Balsirs,
Johnny Cole, Ira Smith, William White, and my young ferry
friend, Tom Gere — how well I remember them all.

'Besides Fulton Ferry, off and on for years, I knew and fre-
quented Broadway — that noted avenue of New York's crowded
and mixed humanity, and of so many notables. Here I saw, during those times, Andrew Jackson, Webster, Clay, Seward, Martin
Van Buren, filibuster Walker, Kossuth, Fitz-Greene Halleck,
Bryant, the Prince of Wales, Charles Dickens, the first Japanese
ambassadors, and lots of other celebrities of the time. Always
something novel or inspiriting; yet mostly to me the hurrying
and vast amplitude of those never-ending human currents. I
remember seeing James Fenimore Cooper in a court-room in
Chambers Street, back of the City Hall, where he was carrying
on a law case — (I think it was a charge of libel he had brought
against some one.) I also remember seeing Edgar A. Poe, and
having a short interview with him, (it must have been in 1845 or
'6,) in his office, second story of a corner building, (Duane or
Pearl Street.) He was editor and owner or part owner of *the
Broadway Journal*. The visit was about a piece of mine he had
publish'd. Poe was very cordial, in a quiet way, appear'd well
in person, dress, etc. I have a distinct and pleasing remembrance
of his looks, voice, manner and matter; very kindly and human,
but subdued, perhaps a little jaded. . . .

'One phase of those days must by no means go unrecorded —
namely, the Broadway omnibuses, with their drivers. The vehi-
cles still (I write this paragraph in 1881) give a portion of the

character of Broadway — the Fifth Avenue, Madison Avenue, and Twenty-Third street lines yet running. But the flush days of the old Broadway stages, characteristic and copious, are over. The Yellow-birds, the Red-birds, the original Broadway, the Fourth Avenue, the Knickerbocker, and a dozen others of twenty or thirty years ago, are all gone. And the men specially identified with them, and giving vitality and meaning to them — the drivers — a strange, natural quick-eyed and wondrous race — (not only Rabelais and Cervantes would have gloated upon them, but Homer and Shakspere would) — how well I remember them, and must here give a word about them. How many hours, fore-noons and afternoons — how many exhilarating night-times I have had — perhaps June or July, in cooler air — riding the whole length of Broadway, listening to some yarn, (and the most vivid yarns ever spun, and the rarest mimicry) — or per-haps I declaiming some stormy passage from Julius Caesar or Richard (you could roar as loudly as you chose in that heavy, dense, uninterrupted street-bass.) Yes, I knew all the drivers then, Broadway Jack, Dressmaker, Balky Bill, George Storms, Old Elephant, his brother Young Elephant, (who came after-ward,) Tippy, Pop Rice, Big Frank, Yellow Frank, Yellow Joe, Pete Callahan, Patsey Dee, and dozens more; for there were hundreds. They had immense qualities, largely animal — eating, drinking; women — a great personal pride, in their way — per-haps a few slouches here and there, but I should have trusted the general run of them, in their simple good-will and honor, under all circumstances. Not only for comradeship, and sometimes affection — great studies I found them also. (I suppose the critics will laugh heartily, but the influence of those Broadway omnibus jaunts and drivers and declamations and escapades undoubtedly enter'd into the gestation of *Leaves of Grass*.)'

At the old Park Theatre, just opposite the Astor House, and home of heroic drama, his 'young manhood's life' expanded in response to the great art of dramatic communication. Later came music, 'the deep passion of Alboni's contralto,' 'Bettini's pensive and incomparable tenor.' Booth and Forrest played at the Bowery Theatre, which was 'pack'd from ceiling to pit with its audience mainly of alert, well-dress'd, full-blooded young and middle-aged men, the best average of American-born mechanics — the emotional nature of the whole mass arous'd by the power and magnetism of as mighty mimes as ever trod the stage — ... tempests of hand-clapping ... from perhaps 2,000 full-sinew'd men.' [5]

Reading the text of the play when he was young, finding his seat, later, with the other critics and patrons, standing (like a good newspaper man) to scrutinize the audience, he followed with indescribable tensity the romance and the heroism (for this is what interested him) of the acting, delighting in the expressiveness of body and speech. The story was secondary, whether in play or opera,[6] and it is questionable whether he gave it much attention. In opera, voice and delivery inspired such a real passion of aspiration that dozens of poems in the 'Leaves' can be described as recitative with solos. He heard concerts, of course — a Beethoven septette once, which he interprets in a literary fashion [7] — but music as pure composition meant no more to him than to Emerson or Thoreau. It was the quality of single sounds, the tune, or the elocution of a Badiali, 'the finest in the world,' that enraptured him, and surely made him think hard of how he too could transmit great emotions to the masses. At the theatre, he shouted with the thousands when life and death were made articulate by the superb oratory of the tragedians. When the stage became merely comic and sentimental in the later 1840's, he lost interest.

All this attendance at theatre, concert hall, and opera was part of his editorial job, as were indeed his visits to prisons, hospitals, courts, and schools. But what distinguished Walt from the roving reporters of his day was a passion for people in the mass, the 'full-sinewed' workers, the crowds in the streets, the drovers, ferrymen, bartenders, prostitutes, every item of the moving pageant which was a great city. In his poems it will be noted that he has seen all these and hundreds of other types, rural as well as urban, and noted them as individuals, each described with his adjective or verbal accompaniment, but nearly always in relation to the streaming masses of which they are a part. Hour upon hour of Walt's leisure time in the forties, which, except when he was on *The Eagle*, was considerable, must have been spent in absorbing and stamping on his imagination these catalogues of American life. There was some deep need here for the concrete and the definite, proceeding from his subconscious imaginings, now becoming articulate:

The machinist rolls up his sleeves, the policeman travels his beat, the gate-keeper marks who pass,
The young fellow drives the express-wagon, (I love him, though I do not know him;) ...
The groups of newly-come immigrants cover the wharf or levee, ...
The connoisseur peers along the exhibition-gallery with half-shut eyes bent sideways,
As the deck-hands make fast the steamboat the plank is thrown for the shore-going passengers, ...
The conductor beats time for the band and all the performers follow him, ...
The regatta is spread on the bay, the race is begun, (how the white sails sparkle!)
The drover watching his drove sings out to them that would stray,
The pedler sweats with his pack on his back, (the purchaser higgling about the odd cent;)
The bride unrumples her white dress, the minute-hand of the clock moves slowly,
The opium-eater reclines with rigid head and just-open'd lips,
The prostitute draggles her shawl, her bonnet bobs on her tipsy and pimpled neck,
The crowd laugh at her blackguard oaths, the men jeer and wink to each other,
(Miserable! I do not laugh at your oaths nor jeer you).

2

It is commonly supposed that it is in these years, when we know so little of his personal life, or in the fifties, that Walt began those wide and intimate contacts with the common man and woman of every kind which seem to be the democratic basis of the 'Leaves.' I doubt it. He *saw* the en-masse with observant and sympathetic eye; but that his close associations were among them is supported by no real evidence. His friends in the forties and fifties, if mention by name means anything, were in the professional, bourgeois world of journalism. There he was already a character, although not until the fifties a Broadway figure. William Cullen Bryant, editor of *The Evening Post*, and another boy from the country, was his friend probably as early as this. They rambled together for miles in the Brooklyn countryside where Bryant joined him, talking about Europe, and doubtless, also about New York politics. And it was only the violent unrestraint of the 'Leaves' when it was published which caused them to drift apart. 'Powerful, uneducated people' were, of course, impressing him strongly now as later. It was, however, almost certainly of such a person as his mother, whose intuitive strength of mind meant so much to him, that he was thinking when he wrote those words, and not of the roughs and toughs. No records have come down to us from these years of close friendships with 'the people,' though many reminiscences of contacts and acquaintances exist. Walt himself, in a burst of candor, admitted later, as we shall see, that he had never really known the American common, average man until he was brought into greatest intimacy with him in the hospitals of the Civil War.

In fact, not only his reportorial observations but also the descriptive poems of the masses which go back to this vital formative period, are intensely personal of Walt, but curiously impersonal of the people. He was passionately encountering them, but for his own purposes of absorption as if (and this, of course, was the fact) to illustrate some inner philosophy beginning to seek expression. He saw them as any good reporter does, for news of life, not for themselves. Who is more impersonal than a reporter, unless it is a press photographer? Reporters are friendly with all the world, but friends with none. So was Walt in the forties, unless there was some unrecorded Pete Doyle to whom he gave a deeper affection.

His associates who begin to describe him a little later as he sat at Pfaff's restaurant under the sidewalks of Broadway (called Pfaff's privy), or make reference to him when he gets and loses a job, give little more than an impression of ample size, rolling gait, open friendliness, and geniality. The truth is that Whitman at this age was unquestionably a deeply self-absorbed man, intensely absorbing also the outside world for his own purposes, but making no close personal contacts with it, and probably no close emotional contacts of an imaginative kind. He was shaping his own figure for the dramatic representative man of a great poem (we know this, as will be shortly seen); he was registering every phenomenon of his beloved America, not so much in his memory as in his imagination. Whitman the editor and critic was real enough; but Whitman the genial friend of all the world was a front behind which lay a creative personality that had not yet exposed itself to public view. When it did, he began to attract to himself with irresistible fascination — *not* the masses upon whom he spent his leisure — *not* the roughs, one of whom he described as himself with complete inaccuracy in the first version of his great poem — but sensitive, rebellious men and women of his own white-collar world.

3

It is certain, however, that these were the years when he seriously began his self-education in books. Walt had been a reader all his life. In his early youth, he had found his bookshelves in the second-hand bookstores of Brooklyn and New York. He was familiar with them all, he told Horace Traubel, searched them through and through. And there was a small library at one of his apprentice jobs. Yet all told, and including the few books, such as Scott and Epictetus which he owned and kept all his life, Walt was never a bookish man. He was indiscriminate, beginning with a passion for romantic novels, and ending with what he called the disease of newspaper reading; read what he liked and could understand, absorbed what he needed, and passed on. Yet, of course, when he became an editor, responsible for book reviews, and with books in plenty under his hand, he made up as well as he could for lost time. With enough education to teach school, he must have known very well that he was deficient for the job of editor, and deficient for the cosmic poetic purpose he was beginning to generate, which was no less than to 'project the history of the future.'

Doctor Bucke, Whitman's most trusted biographer, published many manuscripts entrusted to him at the death of the poet.[8] Among them are records, which probably begin in the 1840's, of an experiment (you cannot call it a system) of self-education which would be pathetic if coming from a lesser man. Whitman was plunging through books of every description, but especially factual books, and setting down elaborate digests and commentaries, which are all distinguished by the lack of any frames of reference. When he tries to analyze Hegel's philosophy, or the periods of English literature, the result closely resembles the attempts of an ill-prepared student to get ready in a hurry for an examination in a survey course. Yet, like so many powerful minds, he gained as well as lost from this process of self-education. His mind took what it wanted and stayed original.

With his daily editorial job requiring a ballast of knowledge and ideas, and his vast poetical projects now forming, it is clear that he was using anything hit or miss to fill the vacuum in his mind. Fortunately, an editorial office was an excellent place for extra-curricular work. Poe had broadened his education by reading the English reviews. So did Whitman, and he found, also, among the new books sent in for review, a large percentage of reprints of standard works. The reviewing shelf, he said in *The Eagle*,[9] 'enables *editors* to keep up in some sort, with the foremost ones of the age.' Substitute 'catch up' for 'keep up' and you have a fair statement of another activity of Walt in the forties.

His brief reviews in *The Eagle* were, as he admits, 'a dash at the meaning of a book,' which did not preclude a more careful reading afterward, but in practice seldom did include it. Holloway says he quoted from a hundred books in these two years and reviewed a hundred more. And among these were many of high value in a course of self-education. Boswell, Bryant, Carlyle, Coleridge, Goethe, Hazlitt, Keats (he might have become 'distinguished'), Longfellow, Lamartine, Milton, Ruskin, George Sand all roused him to comment. What is interesting in the extensive list recorded is the surprising proportion of solid or otherwise valuable books by comparison with any list of popular titles that could be drawn from the American publishing of these years. Whitman is omitting most of the sentimental trash and tripe. He is clearly trying to educate his readers, and, more particularly, himself. It is doubtful if many American writers or editors (the Concord and Boston group excepted) were reading more widely and with as earnest a search for values.

Studying his voluminous notes, one sees that he was usually searching for facts, and especially facts about human nature. Here he differs sharply from such a reader as Emerson, who seeks ideas, beauty, thought. Whitman was collecting fuel for his own fires, and anything that would warm his generalizations went into his bin. Characteristically his habit, later, and quite surely now (since he never collected a library), was to tear out from books or magazines or newspapers what he wanted and throw the rest away. Imagine Emerson tearing leaves from a Goethe! Emerson and Thoreau and all scholarly writers read to know and savor the truth. But the truth (so he clearly thought) was already in Whitman. He wanted (as his notes show) helpful, evidential, illustrative facts.

4

It should be clear by now that young Walt kept himself happily busy in the days of his twenties — and felt it, and looked it, and thought of himself justly as a man who had arrived. As I have tried to show in the last chapter, he definitely had, though not at his true destination. His life was crowded full, fuller than this narrative has shown so far, since there was another by-product of his editorial job which must have taken much of his time and given him valuable insights into human history.

As a youngster in Long Island, Walt had gone in for politics. All through the forties he was active in politics, sometimes as writer, sometimes as speaker, often as a worker in the Democratic organization. It will be indispensable to remember that the man who became the most optimistic of democratic idealists was the American man-of-letters with the most extensive, first-hand knowledge of the machinery of practical politics. He knew specifically what kind of work, clean or dirty, kept government going, and a party in power. Although his own record shows a fight for principle, he did not stop with writing about principle. He helped get out the vote.

At the age of nineteen, he had electioneered in Jamaica. At the age of twenty-one, he was one of the speakers at a Democratic rally of from eight thousand to fifteen thousand people in New York, and had his speech reported in *The Evening Post*. He was for two years secretary of the Brooklyn Democratic organization, and later a member of Tammany Hall in New York, not then malodorous. Said the twenty-one-year-old orator, 'It is our creed — our doctrine not a man or set of men, that we seek to build up.' Nevertheless, he went to the later convention of the Free-Soil Democrats at Albany as a delegate, to help choose a leader. According to John Burroughs, who is reporting a conversation with Walt, he was sent down to Long Island to make addresses in the tumultuous conflicts between Whigs and Democrats in the 1840's.[10] Walt was a Van Buren supporter and in at least one Long Island district followed Daniel Webster in the campaign.[11] And, of course, his job as editor, in the days when patronage was more important than advertising profits, was in the area of practical politics. Rival papers accused *The Eagle* of a financial interest stronger than principle in the local victories of the party. Sutton said he saw no one in Whitman's office except politicians. And he lost his job because he would not sacrifice his opinions as to the extension of slavery in order to play safe practical politics. It is clear, I think, that by 1848 he was regarded as one of the intellectual leaders of the Free-Soil Democrats.[12] Yet it was local politics he knew best, and it was there he must have got his knowledge of how, in practice, democratic government is maintained.

Until the slavery issue made him an independent, Whitman was as much a professional Democrat as a professional journalist. But after the great splits of the Civil War period, he sublimated his political action in poetry and pamphlets. More of this later. It shall be noted here merely that even in his twenties Whitman knew how much grease was needed to make the democratic wheels go round, and when he wrote of democracy wrote of a system whose mechanics he perfectly well understood.

5

I think one troublesome and persistent question about Whitman can be answered from the experiences, the loyalties, and the achievements described in these chapters on the forties. Writers of depth and scope can be roughly classified as those who have essentially loved life and those who have essentially hated it. Shakespeare loved life, though by no means always. Swift hated life. Emerson loved life. Thoreau wavered, and compromised on nature. In our 1920's and 1930's of the twentieth century, we have had a powerful American school — the Lewises, the Hemingways, the Faulkners, the Steinbecks, the O'Neills, and an army of minor debunkers and satirists — who have been so much against the current tendencies of their times that they must be grouped with those who have hated the manifestations of life as they have seen them, and often life itself.[13] Many of these writers have been hurt in youth, and such a hurt may have come from circumstances with which the climate of the times has little or nothing to do. Nevertheless, and even so, such a man or woman becomes peculiarly vulnerable to irritants and opposition. If he has enough creative power to get beyond his own personal wounds, he ranks himself easily with the haters.

Now Whitman, the democratic idealist, had some reason to emerge as a hater of life. His youth shows no wounded soul, but by his thirties and the 1850's his idealism was so disturbed by the great splits preceding the War Between the States, and (as we shall see) his own personality was so perturbed and clouded by emotional disturbances, that veritable explosions followed in his life and writings. From being current with his times and his fellow men, he seemed to become counter. Those who read him only in anthologies, which choose usually his most exuberant and objective poems, do not know how steadily (like most great writers) he was in the opposition whenever he was most himself, or they are deceived by failing to note that his optimism is nearly always in the future tense. He hated war as such, exploitation, commercialism, the genteel, throughout a lifetime in which all these evils burst bounds in his beloved country. The Civil War was to be a frontal attack on his passionate faith in the Union. He was to see the ugly failure of Reconstruction. He would see the West, which was hope for the common man, exploited by the rich, and industrialism regimenting the independent workman, whose welfare was his dream. His brotherhood of American men and women was to sideslip into class divisions of monopolies and labor unions. There was to be plenty to sour his liberalism and make both his faith in democracy and his dream for America seem just another New World illusion.

It did not go that way with him. Any careful reader of Whitman knows that often he did hate life in some of its aspects, but instead of breaking down into a general hate, he lifted into a general love of mankind. There were reasons of temperament undoubtedly, but to them must be added these responsible and enthusiastic years when he was a 'son of Manhattan' happily wandering its streets, lay moralist and commentator for the town of Brooklyn, and friend to every manifestation of vital living.

As for Manhattan, which I use as he did symbolically for the en-masse of a city, there, among the crowds of mechanics, ferrymen, bus drivers, women of the streets and shops, most of them unconscious of convention and respectability, he seems first to have broken through the bourgeois life of office and print shop, and learned to admire and praise, even if he did not intimately know, democratic, unsophisticated human nature, whether in the city or on the farm. This is what he *means* by en-masse, and in these common people, sexual, turbulent, independent, eating, drinking, and breeding, he put his trust.

The drifter, who was soon to become the great rebel against convention, was for a while in his best 'sit,' a known and accepted figure in the extensive community of Brooklyn. He was also a young leader in a party to which millions of his countrymen belonged. Personally and professionally he had, what he was never to have again after the early 1850's, the sense of being in, not out, with and not always against, and this is an experience which seems to be needed at some time in life if a man is to keep his faith in human nature. Walt's radically expanding ideas of democracy soon were to take him far beyond the ideology of any existing party, and even if the Democrats had not split over slavery it is questionable whether he could have remained the good party man he was in the mid forties. But he had for a while the experience of what the sociologists, I suppose, would call a supporting structure, and never, even when most disillusioned, gave up the faith that once again there would be a party which he could inspire, perhaps lead, and to which he would be loyal.

The attempts to discuss the later Whitman as a potential Socialist, or visionary, or a solitary warring against the state, are off centre, because all his life he was a Democrat as he conceived the Democratic faith to be when he fought for it in the forties, even though he had extensively expanded it in his own imagination. His emphasis upon what might be called sexual democracy, and upon the place of women in society, and many other emphases, aroused so much opposition and alarm among those who read his books, that for years he seemed to be a party of one man with a handful of none too discriminate admirers. But listen to the old revolutionary talking to Traubel in his cluttered room in Camden, and you learn that his faith in the ultimate triumph of the people was just as strong as ever. And he still thinks in terms of party, going over painfully the past and the present to count those who should or could be regarded as 'ours.'

My point, of course, is that Whitman set out upon his self-explorations from a good and friendly harbor. He was a happy familiar of streets and market-places, and a spokesman for society, before he began to be egoist, rebel, and prophet. Whatever they said of him afterward, no one could have called him either morbid or neurotic in his twenties.

CHAPTER VIII

～～～～～

'The open road'

WHEN Whitman lost his job on *The Eagle*, he was adrift again, but only for a few weeks. On a night in February of this same 1848, a newspaper proprietor from New Orleans, named McClure, approached him in the lobby of the Broadway Theatre, and after fifteen minutes' conversation between the acts, and a drink, engaged him for the staff of *The Crescent*, a new daily paper about to be started by a Mr. Hayes and himself in New Orleans.¹ The meeting, of course, was not entirely accidental, nor did Mr. McClure pay two hundred dollars in advance without knowing very well just whom he was employing; but it was a surprise to Walt, and probably he would not have accepted with such alacrity if he had not just lost his best 'sit.' ²

New Orleans was enjoying a war boom. It had been the chief American base for the Mexican War; now the army was drifting back that way after victory, and the city was buzzing with enthusiasm and news. Politically, the Mexican conquest seemed to mean for the great city an extension of slavery through the great Southwest and a tremendous boom for the slave trade, which the Creoles controlled; commercially, it meant in any case, new markets for one of the greatest trading centres of the Union.

McClure was seeking an experienced newsman and contributor, and did not engage Walt as an editorial writer. Whitman's known Free-Soil principles would have made him a dangerous spokesman for a paper in the South in these critical days of conflict and compromise. There were several editors on *The Crescent*. Walt's job was to assemble and select the news (he was 'scissors editor'), which in those days came from exchange papers rather more often than direct. Of course, his familiarity with the Northern press made him valuable for this rewrite job, and presumably accounts for his appointment. Evidently he was asked, also, to do some feature writing, probably to describe New Orleans and its 'types' as he had already described Brooklyn in *The Eagle*. This is what he did in the occasional articles which can be ascribed to his pen.

He set off for the South in two days (February 11, 1848), taking his favorite brother, fifteen-year-old Jeff, with him. It was his first lap on the open road outside of New York and Long Island, away from the North and East, into the West which had so stirred his imagination, down to the South, which, so far, had meant to him only arrogance, brutality, pluck, and melodrama. It was a visit, not a migration, otherwise he would scarcely have taken Jeff.

They went by way of Baltimore, crossing the Alleghenies by coach at night, stopping at roadhouses where tough drovers lounged before vast fires of soft coal, dropping down the steep western escarpment of the range to Uniontown, and then on to the Ohio. Walt's true record of his first sight of the West is not to be found in his routine narrative published in *The Crescent*, but in flashes throughout the 'Leaves' — the lifted broad axe in the forests, the pioneers on the flatboats, the vast untenanted spaces inward and westward. Yet, while his venture from his tidewater homes gave color to his imagination, it cannot be said that it was this first sight of the continent which made him resolve to be the bard of expanding America. He carried that project West with him, and would have given a continental scope to the 'Leaves' if he had never crossed the mountains. In his notes for lectures and poems published by Doctor Bucke are lists of European cities, of famous men-of-letters abroad, and of 'the localities and persons of my own land.' 'Look in the census,' he suggests, 'if more material is needed.'[3] Had he never seen the Alleghenies, the Ohio, or the Mississippi, I feel sure he would have projected his poetic self there, as he had already projected his editorial self in many an eloquent tribute to the new men and the new lands. It was New Orleans itself that gave him something new for his imagination.

However, the interior of the continent became a reality as he

travelled west and southward. Yet it seems to have been a somewhat disappointing reality. The great rivers were muddy, unlike
the blue sounds and inlets of his Long Island coast, the land was
rich and the steamers were heaped with its products, but the
shores were barren of interest. And as for those great democrats,
the Westerners, whom he had described before he met them as
hardy and untutored of impulse, scorning mere precedent and
imitation, they seemed to be represented by a multitude of rough-
clad and rough-shod idlers around each landing place. He says
rather defensively that they were probably manlier than the
citizens of the East, yet a satirical-minded person might find an
ample field for his powers in describing their manners and appearance. Dickens had not been so far wrong after all! Nevertheless,
the Kentucky youths were tall and strapping, and he had forgotten mud and shiftlessness by the time he came to write *Pioneers!
O Pioneers!*

On this trip, Walt did not really see the South. He saw New
Orleans, which was a very different experience. Planters, slaves,
the cotton economy have little place in the sketches he wrote for
The Crescent and in his later reminiscences. Even the brooding
heat, the relaxation of the South, seem to have caught his imagination in some later experience, symbolized in his poems by
laughter and the magnolia. It is very probable that the 'magnet
south' for him was Washington rather than the New Orleans of
1848, or the Texas he said he visited. His biographers have too
often forgotten that Washington, especially in the years when he
lived there, was emphatically a Southern city, in mood, as well as
in climate and vegation.

But he was not disappointed in New Orleans. Into the life of
that extraordinary city, the Broadway lounger entered with delight. In the hours before eleven, when he was due at the office,
on his noonday strolls, and at night after ten or eleven, he was
free to wander and study a multitude of new human types — soldiers fresh from the wars, dandies of a breed different from New
York's, bravoes looking for a fight, rivermen from Kentucky —
most of all the quadroons and octoroons of mixed Negro, French,
and Spanish blood, beautiful, sexual creatures, born outside of

Puritanism, and natural caressers of life. It was perhaps symbolic that Walt, who had abstained from stimulants, now took his morning coffee from the vast kettle of a mammy in the French district, and many years later was still talking to Traubel of the charm of the dusky grisettes who sold love as well as flowers on the streets of New Orleans.

In the vast bars of the great hotels, he was an eager looker-on. He rose at dawn to see the life of the turbulent waterfront, and the markets beginning to stir. At the 'living picture' of the 'Circassian Slaves' he saw General Taylor in mufti, and joined in the cheering.[4] He visited, with a humanitarian eye, the police courts, went to a ball, had (or invented) an episode with a fascinating married lady, and heartily enjoyed one of the most picturesque and cosmopolitan cities of the world.

Yet Walt's one really new experience seems to have been his first encounter with a different culture in being. Men and women of many races he had seen and known in New York. New Orleans, however, still preserved a French civilization — tropical French. In the lovely courtyards of the houses of Spanish West Indian type, palm-shaded and decked with curious flowers, in the quaint European streets of the French quarter, where priests pattered and youngsters shouted in patois, he felt, though he did not adequately express it then, an extension of his kosmos to Europe and the Indies. At the cathedral and in the Latin balance and charm of the Place St. Louis, his sensitive eye encountered the esthetics of a civilization different from English New England or disorderly New York. And if the ritual of Catholicism in the cathedral did not impress his Quaker consciousness, the devotion and the democracy of the crowding worshippers did.

Whitman's descriptive writing in the sketches he wrote for *The Crescent* is flippant, and often sentimental, and sometimes very bad, partly, I think, because he was trying to be humorous in the fashion long since set by Irving, and Walt in his light, humorous vein is like a revivalist trying to tell a funny story. When he writes with any feeling, it is of the French-speaking quadroons and octoroons, or of the Creole women at the cathedral or on the streets. With French Creole society he seems to have had little or no intimate contact. It was then, and for a generation or two afterward, a city within a city, and apart. And yet these New Orleans writings show how sharply this roving reporter from the North was impressed with a Catholic Latin *mores*, and a tropical environment utterly new in his experience.

This was Whitman's first hearing also of another language used as an instrument of a native culture. With the dangerous acquisitiveness of the self-educated, he picked up phrases from the French he had heard on the streets, and used them in his writing, as he had used clichés, trite quotations, and Latin words in his editorials. But French, being a living language, caught his imagination. He never learned to read it. He never learned to read any language but his own. Yet from this time on he tries to enliven and enrich his vocabulary with tags of spoken French, often half understood, sometimes entirely ungrammatical. It was a bad habit which makes many a line from the 'Leaves' or from his Prefaces sound cheap to the cultivated ear. The purpose unquestionably was to enlarge the vocabulary of democratic America by such additions as he could make with expressive words from another culture. Unfortunately, there was too much bluff, and of all his naïve borrowings, only one has stuck, and that the word 'en-masse,' which was learned from George Sand, and not in New Orleans.

Whitman did his work, as far as we know, faithfully. Jeff's letters, which have been preserved, account for most of his time and leave not much margin for the 'jolly' bodily experiences which he assigned to his 'times South.' His lounging in barrooms and loafing on the streets and waterfront were evidently parts of his assignment. Whether he did his work well is another question. He seems to have thought so, and the pseudo-literary style of his feature writing probably did not offend contemporary New Orleans taste as it does ours. These Louisianans liked the bland and the sentimental, as the pictures and furnishings of contemporary houses show. When his proprietors began to be cold and distant and an advance of necessary cash was refused, he was surprised and hurt, the more so since, just before this, he had written his mother that his financial prospects were bright.[5] Holloway's guess that the two hundred dollars was advance in salary and not against expenses, with subsequent misunderstanding, is as good as any. But if his backers had been satisfied, that would have been cleared up. My guess would be that his Free-Soil opinions had been aired in the office and perhaps showed in the rewrites of news he sent to the copy room. Whatever happened, there were causes enough, without imagining irate husbands or deserted lovers on his trail, for his leaving so soon. Jeff was homesick, with a touch of dysentery. No mail came from the family. Walt was homesick too. So, after some formal objections, he resigned and they were off again to the North, and back in Brooklyn by June 15.

I make no mention of quadroon love affairs in this New Orleans interlude, or half-breed illegitimate children springing from it, or a sexual entanglement with an aristocratic married woman, because there is no evidence whatsoever that anything of the kind happened. Whitman's sexual 'perturbations' began, as we shall see, before he went to New Orleans. There was scarcely time to mature a serious and responsible love affair in the three months he was in the city, particularly with a young brother on his heels. Perhaps he was seduced by Miss Dusky Grisette, of whom he wrote. But Walt's difficult sexual make-up, as it shows itself later, and his own words, suggest a caresser of the voluptuous female in the imagination rather than in actuality. If we have to look for the origins of the six illegitimate children and one grandchild, of which he boasted to John Addington Symonds in 1890, it will not be in the New Orleans of 1848.

2

He came back — and this is the important item — still an aspiring political editor, and by September, 1848, was put in charge of *The Freeman*, a Free-Soil Democratic paper, launched by the wing of the party with which Whitman was in sympathy. It is a tenable guess that his trip to New Orleans was an interlude until some such opportunity should come to him. *The Freeman*, after one number, was burned out in a fire, but got under way again in two months. Something, however, was going wrong in

Whitman's editorial and political career. In September of 1849, he resigned with a bitter farewell to his enemies, and 'old Hunkers generally,' by which he meant conservative Democrats ready to sacrifice free soil in order to keep the party in power.

This — and I feel sure that Walt realized it — was the end of his career as political editor. Walt was not only a Free-Soiler like his friend Bryant, he was a 'Barnburner,' willing to sacrifice patronage and power to principles, and ready to split the party if necessary. And like many leading members of this faction, he later deserted the Democrats entirely and went over to the new Republican Party, where, however, he never functioned as a politician or editor. His journalistic career had many years to go; he was, as we shall see, to hold another editorship, though not a political one; but, from this crucial year of 1849, he becomes more and more distrustful of American politics, more and more resolved to speak for himself.

It is a tenable guess, again, that his trip West and his residence in New Orleans had made him more determined to keep slavery out of the new lands west of the Mississippi, though he was still in no sense an Abolitionist. He was certainly becoming more radical, too radical for *The Freeman*. He was also becoming more revolutionary in his social ideas, and that change was to reveal itself powerfully and soon.

The important thing to note for 1849 and 1850, after his return from the South, is that this stalwart Democrat had lost his party, and was ideologically adrift. Thousands of his countrymen were in the same predicament, but they were neither political editors nor poets. In 1850, he wrote a poem — not yet in his own new style, with which he was already experimenting, but so vigorous and sincere by comparison with his earlier 'literary' contributions as to mark a new stage in his intellectual history. It was called *The House of Friends* and was printed, significantly, in Horace Greeley's Abolitionist *New York Tribune*:

> Virginia, mother of greatness,
> Blush not for being also the mother of slaves.
> You might have borne deeper slaves —
> Doughfaces, Crawlers, Lice of Humanity —
> Terrific screamers of Freedom, ...

> Muck-worms, creeping flat to the ground,
> A dollar dearer to them than Christ's blessing;...
>
> Arise, young North!
> Our elder blood flows in the veins of cowards —
> The gray-haired sneak, the blanched poltroon.[6]

Through these lines breathes — one might almost say screams — the wrath of lovers of liberty who now, in the North, thanks to the Fugitive Slave Law, were forced to take part in the maintenance of slavery, and found their own states and own political parties controlled by compromising politicians bootlicking the vested interests of slavery. It was this year that aroused Emerson, that aroused Thoreau, it was the year when the great Daniel Webster's reputation disappeared in what was felt to be appeasement. Even Free-Soil Democratic leaders, reading this poem, must have thought that young Whitman, who had been so staunch, was becoming too radical, since he was urging the Democrats of the North to throw their party allegiances overboard.

It was true, and his growing radicalism was not confined to domestic politics. The great revolutionary movements in Europe of 1848 had failed, and were being suppressed by reactionaries. But liberty was unquenchable. In the same year, and also in *The Tribune*, he published *Resurgemus*, the first of his poems in the new style of the 'Leaves of Grass.'

> Suddenly, out of its stale and drowsy lair, the lair of slaves,
> Like lightning Europe le'pt forth,
> Sombre, superb and terrible,...
> God, 'twas delicious!
> That brief, tight, glorious grip
> Upon the throats of kings....
>
> ...Frightened rulers come back:....
> And the king struts grandly again....
> Meanwhile, corpses lie in new-made graves,
> Bloody corpses of young men;...
> Those corpses of young men;...
> They live in other young men, O, kings,...
> Liberty, let others despair of thee,
> But I will never despair of thee.[7]

This man is clearly bottling up too much steam for a party already split, and for an era of cowardly compromise which dodged the great issues. Like Thoreau again, he admired the ruthless determination of the South to fight for its interests, while the crawlers, the doughfaces, the weak and inefficient leaders of the North temporized and appeased. Now he had no party that he was willing to call his own. Though he did not desert journalism, political journalism as a career was deserting him. He writes a plea for waterworks in Brooklyn for *The Advertiser* in 1850, contributes to *The New York Evening Post* in 1851, attacks with reason, balance, and common sense Sunday closing in Brooklyn in 1854, and publishes other bits and oddments. But this was with his left hand. With his right he turned at last to what was to be the great job of his life. Sometime in these early fifties he put upon his table the motto, 'Make the Works.'

CHAPTER IX

'House-building, measuring, sawing the boards'

THESE early fifties are the end of the formative period of Whitman's life — the years when, as he said, he absorbed the soul and spirit and mind and behavior of the hundreds of thousands of Americans swarming in the cities of New York Bay, to which what he drew from the West and New Orleans was added. The years also, as he did not say, but which should now be obvious, when he absorbed the ideology of a great party, and also the events and ideas of the world as they came across the news desk of an editorial office, or had to be discussed in reviews of books.

And we are at the beginning of that decade which has so puzzled every thoughtful Whitman biographer, the decade when, from the pen of a political editor and literary dilettante, appeared the first radical, revolutionary, egotistic, powerful poems of the 'Leaves of Grass.'

There is actually no mystery in the matter except the eternal mystery of creative genius. But there is drama, surprise, and what seemed to be disaster.

The story comes to the surface in 1847 while Walt, still in broadcloth, and serious-browed, was editing *The Eagle*, and it can be written concretely from then on. But the critical years are after 1849, when Walt was turned adrift again as his party split under his feet.

The Whitman legend takes charge of Walt's biography in these years. Says that Walt dropped from the journalistic world. Says that he had mystical experiences. Says that he became a laborer among the proletariat, that he thought of himself as a journeyman carpenter and dressed like one, and from then on spoke with the authentic voice of the workers.

This is what Whitman in his later years was willing to have thought of him. This is the reason he called himself 'one of the roughs' in the first 'Leaves' of 1855, which he hoped was to bring him some money and more fame as the poet of the common man, and did neither. This is why he had a print made from the remarkable 1854 daguerreotype, which emphasizes the workman's clothes, and the flannel undershirt conspicuously showing. The legend is not altogether true, or rather it is one of those halftruths that conceal the truth.

But that something of the deepest importance had happened to the man is made evident by a simple comparison of the two daguerreotypes — one of probably 1846, the other of about 1854 (see Plates IV and I).[1] Walt was extraordinarily photogenic, before the camera he was always histrionic. He posed, precisely as an actor in costume poses so as to look like the part he is playing. This is obvious to anyone who will take the pains to leaf through the photographs in this book. If he is a weary beaten old man, he looks it. If he is a bearded angel visiting the sick in the hospitals, he looks it. If he is a powerful and venerable bard, speaking for a New World, and sure of his message, he looks it. If he is a respectable editor of a small-town newspaper, he emphatically looks that way. He can look Bohemian too, when he was Bohemian.[2] And the most posed, and also the most revealing, of all his photographs is this 1854 daguerreotype from which looks out the pensive, yet burning, soul of a poet who has dedicated himself to chants for all America, and put on a workman's garb so as to feel one of the en-masse which he proposes to celebrate. There is simply no use in deprecating this theatrical sense of identity in Whitman, for it is as much a part of the man as his instinctive passion for democracy.

Walt said that after he left his newspaper office and was at work on the 'Leaves,' he helped his father in the carpentering trade, and lived at home in Brooklyn. We know that he was also free-lancing, but he was without a regular job, and must have had to make additional money somehow, for he always paid his board at home, and money had to be saved if he was to print and publish a book on his own. Carpentering was not the obvious way out, but it was a natural one, especially since his father, who was failing by 1853, and was to die in 1855, must have needed help. And yet I doubt whether Walt did much carpentering, although he is known to have worked regularly at the trade for a week, or weeks at a time.[3] His friends said later that he handled carpenter's terms better than carpenter's tools. Though he earned wages with hammer, plane, and saw, I question whether he spent more hours than were necessary in actual manual labor. George said that he was considering lecturing at this time, which was true, and would lie abed late, write for a few hours, and perhaps go off for the rest of the day. 'We were all at work — all except Walt.' By which he meant, of course, regular work.[4] And we know that Walt was not only accumulating material for lectures in case he could not get his 'message' over any other way, but also working hard, first at the composition, then at the actual printing, of the 'Leaves,' in addition to what time he spent on journalistic writing.

A cryptic remark made to Traubel, that he might have got rich if he had stuck to building in Brooklyn, and some autobiographical notes published by Holloway,[5] make it possible to guess with reasonable probability as to what was happening externally in this curious part of Whitman's life.

To begin with, he seems to have dropped out of the journalistic world of New York, and the society of the 'boys' and the increasing Bohemianism of the town. Not entirely, one supposes, yet his references to experiences at Pfaff's, and on Broadway, and among the theatres and publishing houses, seem to date from the last half of the decade.

Freed from his job because of his growing radicalism, disgusted (as his poems show) with the cowardice and incompetence of the leaders of his party, he was driven in upon himself. The time had come to 'make the works.' Now, a truly creative writer bent on the immense effort of making his imagination articulate can do almost anything in his free hours — except daily, routine writing which has no relation to his main purpose. From such writing Whitman was set free when he lost his political editorship with no prospect of getting another. The problem was to make a living without giving up his main purpose, and without spending too much precious time. What happened may be revealed by these notes, dull in themselves: 'I built the place 106 Myrtle av. the winter of 1848–9, and moved in, the latter part of April '49.' [This would have been while he was editing *The Freeman*. The house was also used as a printing office and bookstore, which might indicate that Whitman was beginning to set up for himself.] 'I sold the Myrtle av. house in May '52, and built in Cumberland street, where we moved Sept. 1st, '52. Sold the two 3 story houses in Cumberland street, March 1853. . . . Built in Skillman st., and moved there May, 1854.' These dry details are revealing. He was certainly not carpentering in 1848–1849. From George's account, he could not have spent much time on a building job in the years just following. The series of items seems to be not so much the diary of a regular worker as the record of a speculative builder, building and then selling, precisely as Walter Whitman senior had been doing all his life. Walt may have brought some money back from New Orleans to help in the turnover; and he certainly put on jeans now and then, and worked for others or himself. The engraver of his portrait met him in a Brooklyn restaurant wearing his red workman's shirt.

No, he worked with his hands when he felt like it, or needed the wages, or was called to help by his father. But the extra cash with which he paid for the material costs of his first edition may have come from profits on the turnover of speculation. When, in the same year of 1855, his father died and the 'Leaves' (which had become his career) failed to bring him either fame or money, he dropped a business which could never have interested him — you could not interest Whitman in making more money than the minimum which he needed — and went back, not to politics, which were bitter in his mouth, but to journalism. And also to the revision and expansion of the 'Leaves,' which now had acquired a momentum that assured their continuance. Add, that the dress and the occupation of a worker with his hands was good publicity for the representative man, one of the people, 'one of the roughs,' whom he was dramatizing as Walt Whitman in the

'Leaves.' This is, at least, a probable outline of Whitman's external life in the first half of the 1850's.

What was the deep concern which absorbed Whitman's real energies for from three to five years while his front was of a carpenter or builder or idler, and which resulted in a book of such cryptic and intensely original poetry as to have startled its few readers? The shrewd and intuitive Emerson gave the clue when, in 1855, he greeted the, to him, utterly unknown Whitman, 'at the beginning of a great career, which yet must have had a long foreground somewhere for such a start.' He was right of course. There was a long foreground. Part of this foreground and a very important part was Whitman's political and especially editorial experiences to which the preceding chapters have been devoted. Of this the Whitman legend takes no account. But there was also a mysticism, a dynamic personality, an essential poetry, a technique in these first 'Leaves' which nothing in this narrative so far explains. The legend describes some mystical illumination of the consciousness, or sudden outrush of genius in the 1850's, to account for the unexpected birth of a savage masterpiece in the thirty-sixth year of Whitman's age. Great conceptions, novel methods, original poetry do not happen that way. They must have their foregrounds, and these shadowy foregrounds in Whitman's experience are to be found in an inner life which has not expressed itself in the activities so far recorded, and in a subconsciousness charged with the electricity of environment and itself a transforming instrument. Fortunately, we have records of these formative inner experiences, though to find them we must turn back. We must turn back to eight years before the 1855 volume, the startling originality of which aroused so much speculation, turn back to the black-coated, respectable editor of *The Brooklyn Eagle*, who had not yet been to New Orleans, nor broken with his party.

CHAPTER X

'Out of the cradle endlessly rocking'

OLD WHITMAN in his untidy upstairs room in Camden would rake over with his cane bundles of manuscripts, stuffed scrapbooks, and the letters, notes, and clippings of a lifetime, saying, 'Here is the foetus of the *Leaves of Grass.*' His executors and later editors have printed most of this material, including numerous drafts of poems, and of prefaces and other prose pieces, and voluminous notes on his reading or for use in possible lectures or poems. But the most interesting item among this prefatory material is a series of notebooks, of which the first four date before the first publication of the 'Leaves.' [1]

The earliest of these notebooks is dated 1847, and contains several of his home addresses in Brooklyn at the time when he was editing *The Eagle.* It concludes with a routine journal account of his arrival in New Orleans, written on the spot on March 18, 1848, followed by a brief statement of his editorial experiences and life in New Orleans set down on the way home, and an even briefer record of the last stage of his journey.

In all human probability, the intervening entries, which contain such surprising revelations, were made in Brooklyn in 1847 or early in 1848, for they are not such records, or such copies of earlier writing, as would be written down on a journey. We can therefore say with assurance that this poetic, apocalyptic prose, and this poetry differing in depth and strength as much as in form from anything Walt had published, and revealing a Whitman who so far has given no articulate sign in this biography, were recorded, if not composed, by the young man of twenty-eight or twenty-nine with the Lincoln features, the stern appearance, the conventional clothing, who was writing so vehemently but so conformably and respectably for his Brooklyn paper. Eight years later most of this poetry, somewhat revised and fitted into a larger pattern, will come out in the first 'Leaves.' And most of this prose will either be used in his first Preface, or be the basis of later poetry. Thus we are lucky enough to possess a rare record of a creative imagination at work in its first struggles to become articulate. Here is a poet emerging in the mind of a successful professional writer of competent journalism. The extraordinary fact is that in spite of crudeness and muddle, most of all that Whitman was to be, was to believe, and was to say is at least suggested by these jottings set down by a journalist who had never given the slightest indication of possessing anything which by the longest stretch could be called genius, nor caused anyone to suppose that he was abnormal or supernormal in any way whatsoever except in a gift for meditative indolence.

2

Imagine the surprise of young Sutton, the printer's devil in *The Eagle* office, if, returning from the afternoon swim with Walt, he had picked up from the desk of his genial, athletic boss, the friend of politicians, the stalwart Democrat, a little notebook, and read: 'If I walk with Jah in Heaven and he assume to be intrinsically greater than I it offends me, and I shall certainly withdraw from Heaven!'

Imagine the mystification of Whitman's Quaker-minded mother, to whom Walt's letters were always so simple, so tenderly affectionate, so youthful, if she could have read: 'I am not so anxious to give you the truth. But I am very anxious to have you understand that all truth and power are feeble to you except your own. — Can I beget a child for you?'

This egoism, this somewhat mystical preaching, whence did it come? What did it mean? For it is contemporaneous with the earnest platitudes of the young editor who was advising his subscribers to take more baths, buy double beds, and vote the Democratic ticket — who was a solid and respectable citizen of Brooklyn, not of Heaven!

There is an interesting clue in the notebook itself. 'I cannot understand the mystery,' he writes, 'but I am always conscious of myself as two — as my soul and I: and I reckon it is the same with all men and women.' And it is true that the inner life, the self reflecting his subconscious, the imaginative, intuitive self which he calls 'soul,' is definitely different from the 'I' he exhibits to the outer world, or the 'We' of his editorials. And it is also true that all men and women who are conscious of their mental processes are aware of such a division between their inner and outer selves. There is no real duality here, only a difference in attitude, a difference in reception, a difference in influence. But in Whitman, as these notebooks will show, this difference was extraordinary, both in its extent, and in his dramatization of it. 'Soul' for him becomes an identity, *the* poet, *the* prophet, *the* spokesman for all he has absorbed. 'I' and 'We' are the editor, the free-lance writer, the friend of many, the devoted son of his mother, the elephantine lounger rolling down Broadway. 'Soul' writes the poems, 'I' writes the letters, 'We' the editorials. And yet, of course, they are all a unity — the 'kosmos,' the American, the soul-and-body, Walt Whitman.

'Be simple and clear. — Be not occult.' So this notebook of 1847 begins. Some writers are always advising themselves and Whitman was one of them. The paragraphs that follow are in an oracular, poetic prose, very different from anything Whitman was publishing or had published. They are not occult — that word clearly refers to the poetry which follows and which I shall discuss later. But they are not simple, and they are none too clear. Here, evidently, is a mind struggling with ideas and emotions that have been rising from deep in his consciousness and which ordinary journalistic style is quite incapable of expressing without loss of imaginative content. I shall quote freely, for here *is* the foetus of the 'Leaves of Grass.'

'True noble expanded American Character is raised on a far more lasting and universal basis than that of any of the characters of the "gentlemen" of aristocratic life.... It is to accept nothing except what is equally free and elegible to any body else. [This is to become "By God. I will accept nothing which all cannot have their counterpart of on the same terms."] . . . Prudence is part of it, because prudence is the right arm of independence. . . .

'I never yet knew how it felt to think I stood in the presence of my superior. — If the presence of God were made visible immediately before me, I could not abase myself. . . . I will not be the cart, nor the load on the cart, nor the horses that draw the cart; but I will be the little hands that guide the cart. — . . .

'The soul or spirit transmits itself into all matter — . . . A man only is interested in anything when he identifies himself with it. . . . I guess the soul itself can never be anything but great and pure and immortal; but it makes itself visible only through matter — a perfect head, . . . a twisted skull. . . . Wickedness is most likely the absence of freedom and health in the soul. . . .

> Every soul has its own individual language, often unspoken, feebly
> Or lamely spoken; but a true fit for that man and perfectly haltingly

adapted for his use. — The truths I tell to you or to any other may not be plain to you, because I do not translate them fully from my idiom into yours. — If I could do so, and do it well, they would be as apparent to you as they are to me; for they are truths. — No two have exactly the same language, and the great translator and joiner of the whole is the poet. . . .

'The universal and fluid soul impounds within itself not only all good characters and heros but the distorted characters, murderers, thieves. . . . When I walked at night by the sea shore and looked up at the countless stars, I asked of my soul whether it would be filled and satisfied when it should become god enfolding all these . . . and the answer was, No. . . . When I see where the east is greater than the west, — . . . then I guess I shall see how spirit is greater than matter. . . .

'I will not be a great philosopher, and found any school. . . . But I will take each man and woman of you to the window . . . and my left arm shall hook you round the waist, and my right shall point you to the endless and beginningless road. . . . Not I — not God — can travel this road for you. . . .

'What is this then that balances itself upon my lips and wrestles as with the knuckles of God, for every bite, I put between them, and if my belly is victor, cannot even then be foiled . . .? — And what is it but my soul that hisses like an angry snake, Fool! Will you stuff your greed and starve me? . . .

'The ignorant man is demented with the madness of owning things . . . I will not descend among professors and capitalists — I will turn the ends of my trousers around my boots, and my cuffs back from my wrists [just what he did in a picture of 1855], and go with drivers and boatmen and men that catch fish or work in the field. . . . In other authors of the first class there have been celebraters of? (low life) and characters — holding it up as curious observers — but here is one who enters it with love. . . .

'My right hand is time, and my left hand is space — both are ample . . . — what I shall attain to I can never tell, for there is something that underlies me, of whom I am a part and instrument . . . . (The heart of man alone is the one unbalanced and restless thing in the world). . . . Greatness is the other word for development. . . .

'As to the feeling of a man for a woman and a woman for a man, and all the vigor and beauty and muscular yearning — it is well to know that neither the possession of these feelings nor . . . having them powerfully infused in poems, is any discredit . . . but rather a credit. . . . Most of what is called delicacy is filthy or sick and unworthy of a woman of live rosy body and a clean affectionate spirit.'

Here, of course, is a Whitman new to this biography — but new only because it has been impossible earlier to see what was happening in his inner life. There is no abnormal phenomenon of a double mind. Rather these paragraphs represent, as I have said, an inner consciousness trying to express itself, and succeeding, by lines brilliantly, by paragraphs not succeeding at all. 'The truths I tell to you . . . may not be plain, because I do not translate them fully from my idiom into yours.' He has not yet found his language. That is the job of the poet, the 'joiner of the whole,' which he is only beginning to become. But how different this language will be from the prose which in this same year the competent editor of *The Eagle* was writing, will be evident to anyone who compares these extracts with the excerpts of Walt's contemporary editorials in Chapter VI. Here, in this far more vital record, he stumbles, he is ungrammatical. These truths that he has been laboring with are not new to the world (he must have known that), but when he identifies himself with them — a dilated soul capable of anything in a New World where anything is possible — they become original. And they have the confidence of felt inspiration — the same confidence that one hears in the voice of the untutored Quaker speaking out of his concern, repeating in sentences that halt, but are usually rhythmic, what the inner voice has seemed to say to him. I do not mean, of course, that the doctrines in these passages are Quaker; only that Whitman had lived in his youth with men and women who took inspiration seriously, and regarded themselves as possible mouthpieces for eternal truth. Emerson, though he was critical of miscellaneous inspiration, made this his point of departure from orthodoxy. 'Powerful, uneducated' inspiration he might have called these emotional stammerings, paraphrasing Walt's later line.

The new quality in young Whitman, so dramatically discoverable in these notebooks, is not of ideas abstractly considered. The intense individualism of his religion was no invention of his own; his ideas of democracy are not new, though they are given vitality by his passion to draw them from the common ground and share them with the common man, who is to be loved, not just observed. His insistence that the soul must find its own way is a commonplace of mysticism. All this merely represents the first transmutations of a stock of thought and feeling into articulate poetry. The surprise is to discover that the young editor intends to become the poet needed by the New World.

This new Walt Whitman proposes to inspire because he is inspired. Greatness is growth, he says, and his soul has become great because in mystical, imaginative experiences it has grown until it identifies itself with the power of the universe. Yet he is not content to be a god enfolding nature. Matter and spirit are of equal importance, and he, the poet of earth, will speak for both and to both. He has the power, if he can find a way.

Double exclamation marks seem to be called for at this point. This self-assumed apostleship, this mantle of a prophet put on at the age of twenty-eight, seems a little strong. But to do so would be to fall into the error of Whitman's contemporaries, who could not stomach a man speaking like a god in one stanza, and, so they thought, like a beast in the next. It was not, as Whitman would have said, the 'I' which was speaking, and certainly not the editorial 'We' of *The Eagle*, but 'my soul,' by which he meant an identification of himself with the power for greatness which he felt intuitively to be entering his own spirit. The problem was to dramatize this soul, to let it speak in its own language as soon as he could devise it, to present a 'Walt Whitman' who was symbolic, yet in his knowledge of men and cities and scenes and emotions of the common man was also representative of the merely human Walt who had been absorbing the life of America so passionately for many years. And this, of course, was what he did in his first important poem, the *Song of Myself*.

3

But let us turn to the poetry in these pre-1855 notebooks. Whitman may very well have written the prose self-searchings, from which I have quoted, at a few sittings. But it is incredible that the somewhat less than two hundred lines of poetry, arranged as such, on the pages of the first notebook should have been composed at the time when he was writing them down. There are passages in this section of poetry less poetical than the prose which precedes it, and lines of the prose that are definitely poetry. Yet this part of the notebook is spaced at the beginning and clearly set aside to record the sum total so far of his attempt to create a new idiom of verse which would make his truths 'as apparent to you as they are to me.' We know how Whitman composed his poetry later, a line or two at a time on scraps of paper, worked over, made more rhythmical, shaped into his own style, though never polished for what he called literary effect. The same process must have gone on here preceding the copying down, for unskilful as is some of this verse, not 'right' as he said a poet's speech must be, it shows every sign of difficult labor not yet completed. The poetry, not the prose, is probably the oldest stratum represented in the notebook. And it is — much of it — occult.

Of course it is occult. The prefatory prose (like the famous Preface to the first edition which uses so much of it) states, not too coherently, his 'truths' and his purposes as a poet. But here, in this section of poetry, these truths and others come surging up in a series of symbols and pictures which require a highly articulate style if they are to be intelligible. The old poetic language would not say what he wanted to say, and the old metres would not carry it. This he says explicitly later, telling how hard he worked to get literary convention out of his poems before he was ready to publish. He has to be indirect, suggestive, symbolic (though he would not have used that word). He has to make his poem *be* something as well as *say* something. And the way to do this seemed to be to project himself as a simple, separate person, who nevertheless is representative and can identify himself with all of you or any man or woman. It must have been very difficult and confusing for a good journalist accustomed to say what he meant simply and clearly. Now it is what he substantially is, or what his soul is, that is demanding words, and that soul has dilated until it desires to speak for America. Here are samples of what he wrote down, or copied into this little notebook:

> I am the poet of the body
> And I am the poet of the soul
> I go with the slaves of the earth equally with the masters
> And I will stand between the masters and the slaves,
> Entering into both, so that both shall understand me alike.

This is simple and clear, not occult, yet note the free, flowing rhythms, bound together by repetition of I, And, I, And, a technique of verse not yet perfected, yet utterly different from the current poetry of the time. The poem continues:

> I am the poet of Strength and Hope....

> I am the poet of reality
> I say the earth is not an echo
> Nor man an apparition;...

> I am the poet of little things and of babes
> Of gnats in the air, and of beetles rolling balls of dung.

> Afar in the sky was a nest,
> And my soul flew thither and squat, and looked out

> And saw the journeywork of suns and systems of suns,
> And that a leaf of grass is not less than they . . .
> And the running blackberry would adorn the parlors of Heaven. . . .
>
> I am the poet of Equality.

And now the going gets difficult. Only symbols, and what a modern critic would call symbolism, will express his next idea, which is more emotion than thought, and which has expansions that must be felt before they can be understood, if, indeed, it is necessary to understand them at all —

> I dilate you with tremendous breath,
> I buoy you up,
> Every room of your house do I fill with armed men
> Lovers of me, bafflers of hell.
> Sleep! for I and they stand guard this night
> Not doubt, not fear, not Death shall lay finger upon you
> I have embraced you, and henceforth possess you all to myself, . . .
> God and I are now (?) here (?)
> Speak! What would you have (?) of us?

From the prose of the notebook I have already quoted a direct and pithy statement, 'The ignorant man is demented with the madness of owning things' — an inferior, though entirely independent, version of Thoreau's remark at about the same time, that most men live lives of quiet desperation. Thoreau wisely stopped with that admirable line. His genius was for prose. Whitman, however, is still feeling for his idiom. He is not content to be a philosopher, he must 'hook' as he says each reader round the waist, and translate his truth into the personal and the concrete:

> It were easy to be rich owning a dozen banks
> But to be rich
>
> It was easy to grant offices and favor being President
> But to grant largess and favor
>
> It were easy to be beautiful with a fine complexion and regular features
> But to be beautiful.

The suspended answer is to run in the mind of the reader. This is a creative imagination at work, feeling its way, experimenting, seeking a form, a style. Note again the succession of It, But, and the balance of each first and second line. Eight years before his book is to be charged with prosodic illiteracy, he has not only something passionate and burning (if still fluid and inchoate) to say, but is definitely and consciously working on a technique.

Yet what follows in the first notebook is not so easily defined, nor is it paralleled by any known experience in Whitman's life, nor can it be assigned to the ideological climate of his youth. So far we have an individualist, a democrat, and a mystic, sucking in from the climate of opinion which surrounds him, and subjecting his absorptiveness to a poetic metabolism. But new emotions are crowding for expression which he either cannot or will not explain, except in symbols so occult as to be what Jean Catel, his French critic, justly calls, in describing another and later passage, sur-realism, with all that means for the art of the twentieth century — a sur-realism untranslatable into direct statement without loss of its emotional truth. And this truth is not to ideas, but to something intensely intimate and personal to the senses of this young editor, who outwardly is so respectable with his frock coat and his frank statement that he knows little of sex and women:

> One touch of a tug of me has unhaltered all my senses but feeling
> That pleases the rest so, they have given up to it in submission. . . .
> They move caressingly up and down my body. . . .
> Each brings the best she has,
> For each is in love with touch. . . .
> Unloose me, touch, you are taking the breath from my throat!
> Unbar your gates you are too much for me
> Fierce Wrestler! do you keep your heaviest grip for the last?
> Will you sting me most even at parting?

I shall not try to unravel here the sexual imagery of these lines, or the curious identification of the senses with man or woman, each symbolic of the other. It is enough to learn from this notebook that either our knowledge of Whitman's love life up to this year has great gaps in it, or that there is dangerous material in his imagination which has found no outlet in human contact, and left no shred of evidence in what he has so far writ-

ten. Gates have been opened. Strange symbols have come float-
ing up from below. The question is not whether this is good
poetry, or good symbolism. It is a process we are following, the
attempt of a creative mind to find expression for the turbulent
passions as well as for the intuitive truths in the depths of his
personality. It is occult, it is crude and imperfect, it is also, regarded as a language, original and audacious. As with the rest of
the poems in the notebook, here is obviously an attempt, an almost painful attempt, to expose the inner man with complete
sincerity. That, of course, was Whitman's later definition of his
purpose in the 'Leaves,' to express in and out, up and down,
nineteenth-century man by a full revelation of himself.

4

I add one more passage, this time from the second notebook.
It appears again in the *Song of Myself*, heightened and rhythmi-
cally improved, but the first version is vivid and powerful:

The hunted slave who flags in the race at last, and leans up by the fence,
    blowing and covered with sweat,
And the twinges that sting like needles his breast and neck
The murderous buck-shot and the bullets,
All this I not only feel and see but am....
Damnation and despair are close upon me
I clutch the rail of the fence
My gore presently trickles thinned with the [plentiful sweat-salt] ooze of
    my skin as I fall on the reddened grass and stones
And the hunters haul up close with their unwilling horses,
Till taunt and oath swim away from my dim and dizzy ears.

This is an early example of Whitman's most skilful art, the art
of representative scenes, for which he has never been sufficiently
praised. But it is much more than that, for it gives a clue to the
new powers (and new difficulties) which make this Walt of the
notebooks seem such a different person from Walt on Broadway
or in *The Eagle* office.

First there is the boy whose career we have been following,
intensely absorptive (that much we know), a caresser of life, as
he describes himself. Then the youth in an expansive society,

expansive himself. Then the man with a warm and crowded imagination stirring, who discovers in himself an extraordinary power of *identification* with whatever moves him, whether thought, emotion, history, or people. 'A man,' he wrote in his notebook at this time, 'only is interested in anything when he identifies himself with it,' and then, getting Transcendental, 'he would be growing fragrantly in the air, like the locust blossoms — ... he would spring like a cat on his prey — he would splash like a whale. ...' Next the dilating ego begins to identify itself with everything human, and with mysterious forces behind humanity. This ego becomes creative, organizes, conceives a vast cloudy project to represent truth by itself.[2] Then Whitman realizes that, if he is to make himself articulate, these representative poems must have a new form, which means a new poetical idiom. And these experiments, especially his attempt to capture his deeper consciousness in symbols, release curious sexual identifications probably not any too clear to himself, and certainly occult.

He has never seen a wreck,[3] though there were terrible wrecks on the dangerous South Shore of Long Island while he was living near-by, but in *Song of Myself*, he identifies himself completely with the courageous devotion of the rescuers: 'I am the man, I suffered, I was there.' He has never seen a runaway slave captured, but he can identify himself with tortured humanity. He knows, at this time, not too much intimately about drovers and fishers and axemen and criminals and carpenters and vigorous farmers, though he has seen them all, talked with them, lived with them. Yet he feels capable of representing them, because he enters into their personalities, not as an observer merely, but with love. He makes so complete an identification between his soul and what he will write, that he will be able to say truly when the 'Leaves' have expanded into a real book, 'Who touches this touches a man.'

Thus this young editor had determined, as he says in his second notebook,[4] to 'elevate, enlarge, purify, deepen and make happy the attributes of the body and soul of a man,' and so prepare for an ideal democracy. It was a large order. For to the reader of this biography who knows the flow, the style, the imagery of later poems in the 'Leaves,' it must seem that Whitman has not yet found his idiom, that his technique is only just begun. He will not, indeed, be sure of himself in it for another ten years.

This fact probably accounts for the 'barrels' of lectures his family said Walt was accumulating while he lay in bed and wrote in the Brooklyn house in the early 1850's. Not barrels, but sheaves of notes for lectures do remain from this period.[5] Still more editor and evangelical than artist, this young Whitman whose career we have been following seems to have resolved that if his poetry failed, he would spread his 'truths' by word of mouth. The attempt, of course, was foredoomed to failure. Emerson (whose career he presumably wished to imitate), Emerson, clear and shrewd of mind, a famous man, with his air of aristocratic otherworldliness, and his theme of the perfectibility of the soul in a cool and rational world, could talk as he pleased, and be heard with pleasure, though seldom understood, except by passages. But Whitman, a confused and prophetic thinker, striking out powerful lines, but proceeding by circles in circles, also a sexual radical, and with the pedantry of the self-educated, would have bored or frightened his audiences if he had tried to pour out the doctrines of the 'Leaves' in lectures. It was poetry or nothing for him — the poetry of prose, and also sheer poetry, when he learned how to write it. This was the task he set for himself when he put on his desk the self-command 'Make the Works,' and sat there, as he said in his fifth notebook 'suffused as with the common people.... It is I who live in these, and in my poems, — O they are truly me!'

The struggle of a growing self to be born into consciousness and action has never been better illustrated than in Walt the editor giving birth to Walt the poet, who nevertheless is more truly a twin brother than a son. Nor is there anywhere a more interesting example of a sophisticated and professional writer putting aside his sophistication and dropping his acquired professionalism in order to learn how to become articulate for what he felt was a new society. But first (being Walt) he had to dramatize himself as a new and different man.

CHAPTER XI

'The American poem'

A<small>ND</small> so about 1850 probably, though it may have been a little later, Whitman settled down with the family in Brooklyn, and must have found his first opportunity since his preliminaries of 1847 to 'make the works' out of his notes in prose and verse. His mother, George, and Jeff, also Eddie and his father, till his death in 1855, were living on Cumberland Street, then Skillman Street, then Ryerson Street, and in '56 on Classon Avenue, from which Walt walked the two miles to the river with Thoreau. George and Jeff were what we should call engineers (Jeff, of course, just beginning). Walt, as has been said, had a finger in the building speculations which kept them changing homes, carpentered some, wrote, revised, noted, meditated, and was soon to be ready to print.

Free-lancing a little, he seems at this time to have contemplated being a printer and publisher himself. In his little office on Myrtle Street, he had printed and issued an advertising sheet. That shop had been given up in 1852, and probably it was then that he went in for building, and began to concentrate his writing and publishing energies on the hoped-for edition of the 'Leaves.' He seems to have run a small bookshop, too, on Myrtle Street. But by 1855 the twelve poems he proposed to publish were in shape, and he found two printer friends, Tom and James Rome, at Fulton and Cranberry Streets, Brooklyn, who let him use their press.

By now Whitman had dedicated himself to poetry, not to poetry as literature, but to a poetry which by definition was to give new ideals, a new esthetics, and a new philosophy of body and soul to the American democracy. Even if he had not stated this to have been his purpose, it would be possible to guess at what the man essentially meant by studying the remarkable daguerreotype already referred to and reproduced in Plate I of this book.

The costume of shirt sleeves and flannel undershirt without a tie are, as has been said, significant in themselves. That he had a daguerreotype taken in this workman's uniform is proof enough that he was dramatizing himself as one of the common people, the en-masse his poems were to celebrate. But more significant is the face. The pontifical look of the young editor of the earlier daguerreotype is gone. His hair is grayer. The white lock so impressively visible in the earlier picture is brushed under his hair and just shows. He is trying to be like, not unlike, the average man now. But there is nothing average in the face, which seems to me to be the most revealing portrait of Whitman. Later pictures, when he was far more accomplished as a man of letters than now, are all a bush of hair and beard. But this close-cropped chin, the full, sensuous, speaking lips, and most of all the dreamy penetrating eyes, say what Whitman seems to be saying himself as he poses:

I speak the pass-word primeval, I give the sign of democracy,
By God! I will accept nothing which all cannot have their counterpart of on
　　the same terms.

Through me many long dumb voices,
Voices of the interminable generation of prisoners and slaves,
Voices of the diseas'd and despairing and of thieves and dwarfs,
Voices of cycles of preparation and accretion,
And of the threads that connect the stars, and of wombs and of the father-
　　stuff,
And of the rights of them the others are down upon,
Of the deform'd, trivial, flat, foolish, despised,
Fog in the air, beetles rolling balls of dung.

Through me forbidden voices,
Voices of sexes and lusts, voices veil'd and I remove the veil,
Voices indecent by me clarified and transfigur'd.

In spite of the self-dramatization, the man in this picture is, I believe, more relaxed, more his inner self than in other photographs. The curious lengthening of the left eyelid, which in Whitman's more nervous (or more posed) pictures sometimes keeps that eyebrow almost at the horizontal while the right eyebrow arches high, is not so noticeable here. Nor, in spite of the workman's clothes is this a picture of 'one of the roughs,' but rather of the chanter of songs, loafing and inviting his soul, and permitting Nature to speak through his lips, 'for good or bad,' 'at every hazard,' 'without check, with original energy.'

2

It is unlikely that Whitman even considered a regular publisher for the book that now filled his mind. The format of the first edition of the 'Leaves' was to be as original as its contents — had to be, in order to give the right effect to the new long looping lines he had adopted as part of his idiom for a democratic, all-inclusive poetry. The large sheets were unlike those of contemporary books. It was best, since he could set type, that he should set up enough of his verses for a lay-out, saving labor charges also.

Except for the cover, a purchaser, looking at the 'Leaves,' might think that it was an attempt to revive the quarto of Shakespearean times. Only the cover (of such as were later bound in leather) was conventional, for, in spite of the golden roots winding down from the letters of the title, as if to indicate the origin of these 'Leaves' in the fertile earth itself, the effect was definitely Victorian, and not unlike a previous book by the popular female author, Fanny Fern. No author's name appeared on the title page, though Walt declared himself the writer in the course of the poem. No publisher's name either. But the book was put on sale on July 4, 1855, at Swayne's bookshop in Brooklyn and (more importantly) at Fowler and Wells, the phrenological emporium and home of *Life Illustrated* (to which Walt later contributed) in New York. A small advertisement ran for a month in *The Tribune*, and Fowler and Wells, through *Life Illustrated*, kept plugging the book, without success. Swayne had enough of it after four days. The edition was about a thousand copies.

One S. Hollyer made for him a steel plate (since reproduced

*The 'New House,' Walt Whitman's birthplace
at West Hills, near Huntington, Long Island*

From a drawing by Joseph Pennell

PLATE II

Walter Whitman   George Washington Whitman

From daguerreotypes of the 1850's

Louisa Van Velsor Whitman

From a later portrait

PLATE III

Walt Whitman in the 1840's or earliest 1850's

Probably taken while he was editor
of THE BROOKLYN EAGLE
From a daguerreotype now in the
Walt Whitman House at Camden, New Jersey

PLATE IV

From HARPER'S WEEKLY, used by permission of
Harper & Brothers and John A. Kouwenhoven,
editor of ADVENTURES OF AMERICA, 1857–1900

Broadway in New York in the latter 1850's

PLATE V

Walt Whitman, probably in the late 1850's

Dated in his hand as of 1849,
but much more probably of the late 1850's

PLATE VI

Walt Whitman in 1860

From a photograph by W. Kurtz

PLATE VII

Walt Whitman in 1860

From a photograph by W. Kurtz

PLATE VIII

Walt Whitman about 1864

From a photograph by Alexander Gardner

PLATE IX

Washington in 1866

By Frederick Dielman

From HARPER'S WEEKLY, used by permission of Harper & Brothers and John A. Kouwenhoven, editor of ADVENTURES OF AMERICA, 1857–1900

PLATE X

Walt Whitman about 1865

*Possibly by J. Gurney & Son, who photographed him
in the same striped shirt about 1865*

PLATE XI

Walt Whitman in 1872

From a photograph by Pearsall, Brooklyn

PLATE XII

WALT WHITMAN, INCITING THE BIRD OF FREEDOM TO SOAR

Walt Whitman inciting the Bird of Freedom to soar

By Max Beerbohm, from THE POET'S CORNER, 1904

PLATE XIII

'Conversation Piece'

A painting by Herbert Gilchrist of Whitman, Mrs. Gilchrist, and her daughter Grace at tea at the Gilchrist home in Philadelphia. Painted between 1882 and 1884, but representing a scene of the late 1870's. Whitman, however, would have looked younger at this time. Now in the possession of Mrs. Frank J. Sprague

PLATE XIV

From the E. R. Pennell collection

Whitman's House in Mickle Street, Camden, New Jersey

From an etching by Joseph Pennell
Now in the possession of Mrs. Frank J. Sprague

PLATE XV

Walt Whitman at seventy-two

From a photograph by Thomas Eakins
who also painted his portrait

PLATE XVI

again and again) based on the daguerreotype of 1854. There is a broad hat now, hands negligently thrust, workman's trousers, but the face has lost its penetrating beauty. Meeting him in a Fulton Street restaurant where Walt was supping in red flannel shirt, minus coat, his broad-brimmed hat at a rakish angle, the artist made a few alterations to please the poet, perhaps the carpenter's flap pocket in the trousers.[1] This plate, and (presumably) the design for the cover, were contributed. But all the rest of the make-up of the book was from Whitman's own hand.

A strange book it was, perhaps the strangest to be published in English since Blake's mystical poems. Emerson called it 'The American Poem.' It is easy to imagine a drifter in Fowler and Wells picking up the green volume and leafing it through. He would note the curious apocalyptic and symbolic prose of the long Preface, and even more its strange punctuation by dots and dashes, and abundant parentheses and italicization. Turning to the first poem, he would have been struck by the sublime egoism of —

> I celebrate myself,
> And what I assume you shall assume,
> For every atom belonging to me as good belongs to you.

It is much more probable, however, that his attention was caught by the strange style of the lines. It was not poetry as he knew poetry, since there was neither rhyme nor metre; not prose either, for see how the lines were printed on the broad page as if each was a verse. Conditioned by Poe, Tennyson, Bryant, Longfellow, this possible purchaser and reader would have probably considered the book only a strange experiment in writing; and in truth the poem of Walt Whitman, an American, as it was to be called the next year, was still experimental in its rhythms, still feeling toward a form. So (we can say with reasonable certainty) he dropped the book, which was unfortunate if he was a collector, since this edition is now very valuable — thought it probably the production of some eccentric — there were plenty about in the 1850's — Brook Farmers, Shakers, Abolitionists. This is a fair sample of the sales history of Whitman's first attempt to reach the public with his 'truths.'

He confessed to Horace Traubel in the 1880's that he did not know of one copy sold.[2] That can scarcely have been true, and his memory always tended toward exaggeration. However, he had been liberal with gift and review copies, as, being the sole owner as well as maker of the book, he was free to do. It was, as he said later, his *carte de visite* [3] to posterity, and most probably what he hoped for was not so much cash as fame, fame of the kind that would enable him (as he wrote to Emerson in 1856) to sell thousands of later copies of his poems. It would be absurd to suppose that Walt expected an easy popular reception for the twelve poems of these first 'Leaves.' He was not descending from an ivory tower into an unknown commercial world. On the contrary, he knew from long experience what the book- and magazine-buying public wanted. Had he not tried again and again to give it to them! If he did not know how to write what was widely salable, he certainly knew how *not* to write if he wished a quick commercial success. 'Be simple and clear — not occult' had been his prescription (not filled) as long ago as 1847. That he hoped to shock his critics and his readers with a sensation and so point toward success, is much more probable. Unfortunately, he puzzled more than he shocked. The shock was to be stronger from later editions.

Nevertheless, though from the sales angle the first 'Leaves' was one of the great flops of literary history, this is by no means true of its critical reception. In spite of Thoreau's protest against the 'reprobates' among the reviewers who attacked him, the book, as will be seen, was not unfortunate in its reception by the professionals, who got their copies free. It was thoroughly and rather widely discussed, and with a realization by no means confined to Emerson that here was something new and powerful in American writing. If the most frequent reaction was anger and even scorn, that was, considering the subject, success of a kind. The 'Leaves' registered far better than Poe's first production, and at least as well as Thoreau's 'A Week on the Concord and Merrimack Rivers.'

As for this first experimental book itself, a book which was narrow, uneven, defensively aggressive by comparison with the greatly expanded 'Leaves' which was to follow, it should be said that the few Americans who read it were not judging the Whitman with whom we are familiar, but only an eaglet with ruffled feathers. One should remember also Walt's saying, 'Who touches this book touches a man.' While it will be necessary to diverge into criticism in order to explain what Walt was doing, and what he accomplished, most of the discussion of this and later editions of the 'Leaves' is as strictly biographical as the narrative of his adventures on the streets of New York. 'I... live in these, and in my poems, — O they are truly me!'[4]

3

At least a third of this slender volume was prose, consisting of a Preface which, like Wordsworth's Preface to the 'Lyrical Ballads,' is one of the important documents of modern literature, and, like Emerson's *American Scholar*, one of the fundamental statements of American criticism. We have already peeped at the ideas and ill-assembled materials of this Preface in the notebook of 1847. Later much of its rhythmic prose was given more rhythm and taken over into a poem, *By Blue Ontario's Shore*, and, unfortunately, the Preface does not appear as a whole in its original form in many modern editions. But in 1855 it seemed vitally important to Whitman.

For Whitman was still distrustful, and rightly, of his poetry. He knew that it was 'occult,' felt that its purpose might be no clearer than its symbols, was sure that he was writing in a new way, and was enough of an editor to wish to tell his readers why he did so before they should run aground on obscurity or refuse to carry on with a style that would seem to them neither poetry nor prose. Later, when he grew more audacious, more skilful, and more confident, he dropped prefaces, and trusted to the poems, since (even by 1856) there had been enough written about him to inspire curiosity among those likely to buy. But in the first edition he tried to explain why what he had done was worth doing. His 'Leaves' were not to be regarded as polite literature. They were intended to dilate the imagination with a faith, a doctrine, a religion embodied in a personality. That, at least, must be understood by the reader.

It is a long Preface. For the purposes of biographical discussion I shall excerpt and sometimes paraphrase as if Whitman himself were telling the story, keeping as many as possible, in so little space, of his magnificent epigrammatic phrases:

America does not repel the past, but sees that a new era has come in which past forms, politics, and religions are not sufficient. Compared with the expanding history of the common man on this continent, the small theatre of the antique seems tame and orderly — the Americans themselves are a greater poem. Here in their history is action untied from strings, necessarily blind to particulars and details, magnificently moving in masses. The genius of America is in its common people through all our mighty amplitude.

America is the race of races. Faith, which is the antiseptic of the soul, pervades the common people of America and preserves them — they never give up believing and expecting and trusting. Thus the American poet must be transcendent and new, indirect and not direct or descriptive or epic. His theme must have vista for the American future.

Whatever is past is past. The American poet must expose superior models for life. Illiterate persons, the en-masse, are as good as he; but it is he who can indicate the path between reality and their souls.

The form of poetry is dependent upon its nature. All beauty comes from beautiful blood and a beautiful brain. Love the earth and sun and animals, despise riches, hate tyrants, argue not concerning God, have patience toward the people, go freely with powerful uneducated persons, re-examine all you have been told, and your very flesh shall be a great poem and find its own expression.

There is a precision and balance about the proper expression of beauty. One part does not need to be thrust above another. The art of art is simplicity. To speak in literature with the perfect rectitude and insouciance of the movements of animals is the flawless triumph. The great poet is the free channel of himself.

He swears to his art, I will not be meddlesome, I will not have in my writing any elegance to hang in the way. The clearest expression is that which finds no sphere worthy of itself, and makes one. The greatest poet does not only dazzle his rays over characters and scenes and passions — he finally ascends and finishes all — he glows for a moment on the extremest verge.

The American bard shall delineate no class of persons, nor one or two out of the strata of interests, nor love most, nor truth most, nor the body most. For the eternal tendencies of all toward happiness make the only point of sane philosophy. The direct trial of him who could be the greatest poet is today. If he does not flood himself with the immediate age as with vast oceanic tides — if he be not himself the age transfigured, let him wait his development.

Whom the great poet takes he takes with firm sure grasp into live regions previously unattain'd. Every man in America shall be his own priest and be responded to from the remainder of the earth. No great literature can long elude the jealous and passionate instinct of American standards. An individual is as superb as a nation when he has the qualities which make a superb nation. The soul of the largest and wealthiest and proudest nation may well go halfway to meet that of its poets.

These words — which can truly be described as simple, sensuous, passionate, and hence themselves poetry — are at the heart of this Preface. I suppose they could be defined as one part epicureanism, one part emotional democracy, and one part the romance of an expanding America. But romance should not have too much emphasis. There is nothing in Whitman's dream of an American standard to which the world would prove to be responsive which was not perfectly realizable if the idealists had their way. Some of it has already been realized, and in part because of the vitality of this dream. And democracy, while spoken of in political terms elsewhere in this Preface, is here a new and indirect democracy, a call for a poet who can find a tongue for the released consciousness of the common people, their beauty, their vitality, their trust. Also, the epicureanism has been extended beyond the antique philosophy of a tendency toward happiness in both soul and body, to a recognition that in the new world powerful uneducated people have as much to teach as the philosophers. The poet's task is to reveal to them their souls.

It was this Preface, I feel sure, that impressed Emerson and led him to write so quickly his warm-hearted letter. He remembered, of course, his own earlier and passionate appeal in *The American Scholar* for a self-confident, self-directing America. The reviewers of this first edition also, except when they were too horrified by the frank language of the poems that followed to remember anything else, read and discussed the poetic sermon with interest and appreciation. But they failed (and perhaps Emerson failed also) to carry on Whitman's explanations into their reading of the poems. Nearly all of them missed his most significant statement, that the poet *himself* must be the age transfigured, and when they encountered a Walt Whitman who seemed to have indulged in everything from rowdyism and sensuality to mystical identifications with the controlling spirit of the universe, they were confused and amazed.

4

The first poem they read was what afterward was to be called *Song of Myself*. Like Emerson's first and famous essay, *Nature*, it was a fertile concentrate of everything the author at the time possessed, and of most of what he was, at any time, to possess. It is the heart of Whitman, though not yet Whitman at his best. This chant illustrates, and was intended to illustrate, what Whitman meant by poetry, and its text was in its first line already quoted:

I celebrate myself, and sing myself.[5]

What Whitman meant by poetry was something alive and to be lived. It was as alive as its writer because it represented him in a song. It was not a statement or a description or a doctrine, though it might carry all of these. It was indirect, not direct like saying this or that is true. It was a living thing in action; not an idea or an emotion, but the result of an idea or emotion. You understood it and absorbed it as you understood and absorbed a person who powerfully impressed you — not so much through what he said as what he was. Hence the poem had to be in a language exactly expressing the poet. He could not use any rhythm, any form, any diction that was not his and no one else's. Some writers were skilful enough to make the old verse forms express everything they had to say. But Whitman had to make his own, partly because that was the only way he could express himself accurately, partly because of the nature of what he had to express.

Furthermore, if the poem was to be important, then the man it expressed had to be representative of his age and its experiences, as well as of his narrow self. He would have to be able to identify himself with aspects of humanity in his time. If he could, then the strength, scope, beauty, truth, and even the form of the poem would be dependent upon how deeply, widely, and truly he could make himself stand for humanity. Ornament, polish, allusion would be only curtains hung in front of the real excellence. If democratic America was the subject, or inspiration, of his poem — and, with Whitman, it usually was — then the poem must be as good as America, could only be as good as was America in a real and an ideal sense. Could only be as good as Whitman, because if he were to speak for representative man, fully and freely, the poem would have to be about himself; for his excuse for writing at all was that he believed himself to be symbolic of America.

And if these 'Leaves of Grass,' which connected earth and sky and were offered as the celebration and revelation of Walt Whitman, an American — if they were to be real poems, and if America was something new in the world, and the common man as he expanded in America something new for literature, why then the poems had to be new themselves, had to be experiments, catalogues, repetitions, symbols, descriptions of the flow of consciousness of this representative Walt Whitman until the whole became a man, not just a book, and the man was felt to be a microcosm of you and me and all people, good and bad, poor and rich, strong and feeble, here in America, and perhaps in the world also. This required a new eloquence, a new approach, a new objective. Walt Whitman would not get it right the first time. He would never get it right completely, though he would spend the rest of his life at the job.

With this in mind, the flaunting egoism of the first poem in the little book is intelligible and may be allowed to justify or fail to justify itself. With this in view, the series of moods, pictures, catalogues, sensations, prophetic orations, intimate confessions, bold claims to spiritual power in this strange medley which called itself a song, are to be regarded as an attempt to dramatize a 'simple separate person' as a symbol of humanity. Unfortunately none of this was obvious to his startled (or contemptuous) critics. They might at least have understood what kind of one-man revolutions they were encountering if they could have read some of Whitman's later and simpler descriptions of what he had been trying to do:

'Leaves of Grass... is ... the song of a great composite *democratic individual*, male or female. And ... the thread-voice ... of an aggregated ... vast, composite, electric *democratic nationality*.' [6]

'I saw' that to 'express my own distinctive era,' there 'must be an identical body and soul, a personality — which personality, after many considerations and ponderings, I deliberately settled should be myself — indeed could not be any other.' [7]

'*Leaves of Grass* ... has mainly been ... an attempt from first to last, to put *a Person*, a human being (myself, in the latter half of the nineteenth century, in America) freely, fully and truly on record. I could not find any similar personal record in current literature that satisfied me.' [8]

And all this was to be so written as to let Nature, by which he seems to mean human nature, speak unchecked, 'with all its original energy.'

5

This is what Whitman meant by the function of poetry. What he meant by a poem, and what he was trying to do in the *Song of Myself* and the other eleven poems of this first edition, was much more eccentric to the modes of any earlier century and puzzled, even when it did not shock, his first readers. Of the twelve poems in this edition, most were as confusing (not to say offensive) to the contemporary critic as the music of Wagner when first played to hearers conditioned by Mozart or Haydn. And since the readers of this edition were most of them professionals, sensitive to form, it may be said that it was probably not the realistic sexuality of *I Sing the Body Electric* or the egoism of the *Song of Myself*, but what seemed anarchy in every poem that offended them most. Here was no story like *Evangeline*, no single emotional pattern like Poe's, no moral like Emerson's, no device of the usual sort to secure unity and coherence. Each poem was like a pianist improvising, or a savage chanting his needs and deeds. Was this poetry, which has to communicate or be only words? They thought not. Like their predecessors in another art who had said that Wagner and Beethoven were not music, they said that Whitman's 'Leaves,' whatever else it might be, was not poetry.

A poem for Whitman was, in truth, not a poem as Tennyson, Longfellow, or Browning conceived a poem to be. It was a chant — like the chant of a medicine man. The savage witch doctor heats up his consciousness with mumbo-jumbo until he feels himself sucking in the power of the gods and can represent them; then his chant becomes his expanded self and can kill or cure. In much the same way, a poem for Whitman was a series of spells evoking all the senses of man, and his relations with Nature and human experience, until the reader identifies himself with the chanter and becomes a poet himself, and the purpose of the poem is achieved. There is an analogy with the mystery of transubstantiation in the Mass. But Whitman was dealing neither with 'creeds nor schools' nor with the primitive gods either, but with common men and women in a democracy, the rising class in history, no longer primitive, not susceptible to the literary incantations of the past, because so little of earlier literature touched the expanding freedom of their lives in a free continent. A poem by him was meant to evoke what *they* felt, and *their* original energy, by opening his own nature to its depths and speaking for them, if not to them.[9] And he was right — this had not been tried before.

It was not easy. Try yourself, if you have a rich nature, not without strong experience, not devoid of imaginative sympathy. Believe, as is presumably true, that what floats up from the depths of your consciousness is your own, yet also symbolic of the flow of life and thought everywhere. Believe (as Whitman did) that all whisperings from your inner life are important, especially those which conventions have taught you to disregard. Then note what energy of interest is released, provided you let nature go unchecked. There seems no end to what can be said, even of a 'simple, separate person.' You will feel as Whitman did, *'Walt, you contain enough, why don't you let it out then?'* [10] Later, try to make a complete exposure of yourself, coherent, unified, audacious. Blurring, confusion, shame, or babbling is likely to be the result.

Whitman by 1855 had got past shame and had learned to be confident of his intuitions. He was not afraid to seem incoherent, the unity was in himself; and he had too much personality to babble. Furthermore, he had learned a language for such a revelation. His first real poem — the *Song of Myself* — is confusing only if you do not see that it is a creation in words of a personality, not of an idea, and that it is incoherent only as a picture gallery of the works of one artist is incoherent by comparison with a treatise on logic. And it has a unity which amateur attempts at complete self-expression lack, because, as the medicine man's chant is always in reference to the gods, so Whitman's song is in reference everywhere to his idea of completely developed man — soul *and* body — as the unit of a new democracy. If it is sometimes definitely not poetry, not even prose poetry, that is because Whitman had not mastered his style, or because his imagination is profusely experimental, like nineteenth-century democracy. But certainly this all-out celebration of a man who contained multitudes was the right way to make an expansive society of energetic individuals articulate; for this society was represented by a stream-of-consciousness, moving-picture life of words. The method, even in its crude and egoistic state, fitted America, and was the most interesting attempt in literature anywhere to present the masses of the new age. Naturally, its novelty made offense inevitable to all but the most discerning critics. Whether

Whitman himself was representative enough to fit his own formula, is another question. He will prove to be much less typical than he thought.

6

With magnificent courage (and considerable effrontery) the printer-poet in 1855 assembled and published at last his experimental fragments, and with the opening poem began to celebrate his symbolic self.

What he wrote was not so much a description of this self as an invocation of the life of his senses and of his spirit which he called his soul. This is the continuity of the poem, which passes from idea to emotion, from emotion to experience, from experience to memory, from memory to promise and prophecy. The logic is not sequent but centripetal. I mean that this man is preaching no sermon, but rather putting record after record on his victrola, each one a self-revelation, and each related to the next only by association of ideas or sensations. All good poets rely on evocation, but this poem is given its unity and coherence by evocations. It centres in, it is unified by, the personality of the writer and the reactions of the reader:

I loafe and invite my soul,
I lean and loafe at my ease observing a spear of summer grass.

My tongue, every atom of my blood, form'd from this soil, this air,
Born here of parents born here from parents the same, and their parents the
    same,
I, now thirty-seven years old in perfect health begin,
Hoping to cease not till death....

I have heard what the talkers were talking, the talk of the beginning and the
    end,
But I do not talk of the beginning or the end.

There was never any more inception than there is now,
Nor any more youth or age than there is now,
And will never be any more perfection than there is now,
Nor any more heaven or hell than there is now....

The big doors of the country barn stand open and ready,
The dried grass of the harvest-time loads the slow-drawn wagon,
The clear light plays on the brown gray and green intertinged,
The armfuls are pack'd to the sagging mow.

I am there, I help, I came stretch'd atop of the load,
I felt its soft jolts, one leg reclined on the other,
I jump from the cross-beams and seize the clover and timothy,
And roll head over heels and tangle my hair full of wisps.

Alone far in the wilds and mountains I hunt,
Wandering amazed at my own lightness and glee,
In the late afternoon choosing a safe spot to pass the night,
Kindling a fire and broiling the fresh-kill'd game,
Falling asleep on the gather'd leaves with my dog and gun by my side.

The Yankee clipper is under her sky-sails, she cuts the sparkle and scud,
My eyes settle the land, I bend at her prow or shout joyously from the
    deck. . . .

In me the caresser of life wherever moving, backward as well as forward
    sluing,
To niches aside and junior bending, not a person or object missing,
Absorbing all to myself and for this song. . . .

I am of old and young, of the foolish as much as the wise,
Regardless of others, ever regardful of others,
Maternal as well as paternal, a child as well as a man,
Stuff'd with the stuff that is coarse and stuff'd with the stuff that is fine,
One of the Nation of many nations, the smallest the same and the largest
    the same,
A Southerner soon as a Northerner, a planter nonchalant and hospitable
    down by the Oconee I live,
A Yankee bound my own way ready for trade, my joints the limberest joints
    on earth and the sternest joints on earth,
A Kentuckian walking the vale of the Elkhorn in my deerskin leggings, a
    Louisianian or Georgian,
A boatman over lakes or bays or along coasts, a Hoosier, Badger, Buck-eye;
At home on Kanadian snow-shoes or up in the bush, or with fishermen off
    Newfoundland,
At home in the fleet of ice-boats, sailing with the rest and tacking,
At home on the hills of Vermont or in the woods of Maine, or the Texan
    ranch,
Comrade of Californians, comrade of free North-Westerners, (loving their
    big proportions,)

Comrade of raftsmen and coalmen, comrade of all who shake hands and wel-
    come to drink and meat,
A learner with the simplest, a teacher of the thoughtfullest,
A novice beginning yet experient of myriads of seasons,
Of every hue and caste am I, of every rank and religion,
A farmer, mechanic, artist, gentleman, sailor, quaker,
Prisoner, fancy-man, rowdy, lawyer, physician, priest...

I am the poet of the Body and I am the poet of the Soul,
The pleasures of heaven are with me and the pains of hell are with me,
The first I graft and increase upon myself, the latter I translate into a new
    tongue.

I am the poet of the woman the same as the man,
And I say it is as great to be a woman as to be a man,
And I say there is nothing greater than the mother of men.

I chant the chant of dilation or pride,
We have had ducking and deprecating about enough,
I show that size is only development.

Have you outstript the rest? are you the President?
It is a trifle, they will more than arrive there every one, and still pass on.

I am he that walks with the tender and growing night,
I call to the earth and sea half-held by the night.

Press close bare-bosom'd night — press close magnetic nourishing night!
Night of south winds — night of the large few stars!
Still nodding night — mad naked summer night.

Smile O voluptuous cool-breath'd earth!
Earth of the slumbering and liquid trees!
Earth of departed sunset — earth of the mountains misty-topt!
Earth of the vitreous pour of the full moon just tinged with blue!
Earth of shine and dark mottling the tide of the river!
Earth of the limpid gray of clouds brighter and clearer for my sake!
Far-swooping elbow'd earth — rich apple-blossom'd earth!
Smile, for your lover comes.

Prodigal, you have given me love — therefore I to you give love!
O unspeakable passionate love.

I am the mash'd fireman with breast-bone broken,
Tumbling walls buried me in their débris,

Heat and smoke I inspired, I heard the yelling shouts of my comrades,
I heard the distant click of their picks and shovels,
They have clear'd the beams away, they tenderly lift me forth.

I lie in the night air in my red shirt, the pervading hush is for my sake,
Painless after all I lie exhausted but not so unhappy,
White and beautiful are the faces around me, the heads are bared of their
    fire-caps,
The kneeling crowd fades with the light of the torches....

The spotted hawk swoops by and accuses me, he complains of my gab and
    my loitering.

I too am not a bit tamed, I too am untranslatable,
I sound my barbaric yawp over the roofs of the world.

The last scud of the day holds back for me,
It flings my likeness after the rest and true as any on the shadow'd wilds,
It coaxes me to the vapor and the dusk.

I depart as air, I shake my white locks at the runaway sun,
I effuse my flesh in eddies, and drift it in lacy jags.

I bequeath myself to the dirt to grow from the grass I love,
If you want me again look for me under your boot-soles.

You will hardly know who I am or what I mean,
But I shall be good health to you nevertheless,
And filter and fibre your blood.

Failing to fetch me at first keep encouraged,
Missing me one place search another,
I stop somewhere waiting for you.

Is it surprising that readers of Bryant, of Irving, of Cooper, of
Tennyson, of Longfellow did not see what Whitman was trying
to do, did not understand how he was doing it, wondered if it was
worth doing? For this poem, in spite of its magnificent passages,
is a *mélange* of confession, evangelical preaching, identities, memories, symbols, organized as a dramatized Walt Whitman, and
written like a mystical chant. It seemed to the most sympathetic
like a magnificent if somewhat humorless attempt to expand an

ego to the dimensions of some pirate's great gun, then cram the muzzle with every oddment from the decks of America, and blast the whole at the nineteenth century.

Few heard the blast, and none were hurt this time but a few delicate-minded critics who never had supposed that sexual intercourse would be a subject of poetry in their century! But Walt loads again, or, to drop the figure, keeps on with his little books made up of scraps of paper, preparing for a vast composite poem of which these twelve chants are only the beginning, a poem which is to be as expansive as America. *Song of Myself* is a blueprint for a much greater whole — which will never be quite achieved. It is the birth-song of the symbolic Walt Whitman, who is decidedly not yet the kosmos he keeps calling himself. But here in this 1855 volume is the purpose of his poetry, and the pattern for his poems.

CHAPTER XII

'We have positively arrived'

W ALT, as I have already suggested, had not been in the writing game for nearly twenty years without knowing what the public would take easily, and what they would not take at all. Furthermore, he must have been well aware that the soul-and-body doctrine of the 'Leaves' could have been most easily put over to a susceptible populace (as many cults of this decade of strange religions were being put over) by sentimental writing, oratorical eloquence, or by sheer sensationalism. He was too serious to attempt the first, too unskilled and too little known for the second, too much of a real poet and prophet for the third.

The en-masse are conservative in their literary tastes. They like accepted forms and familiar metres. Even *Hiawatha* seemed a strange performance to Mrs. Whitman. And the public like easy references. To shoot at them a series of preachments and pictures, where the only coherence was to be found in the stream of consciousness of an extraordinarily self-confident individual, was like giving them the disintegrated symbols of a killer whale arranged in a pattern by a Pacific-Indian artist, and expecting them to see and like the animal. The Cubists and the sur-realists were to try an equivalent experiment half a century later, and with equal unsuccess.

Nor do the en-masse, particularly the workers and the white-collar class, like sensual descriptions virtuously put. And still less obscure symbols of phallic experiences. Symbolism was familiar in the Bible, but belonged to religion and not to sexual intercourse! Even deacons told dirty stories (as many memoirs record) in the years when Whitman was writing. But praises of the sexual

organs written with the moral elevation of hymns would have
shocked the most foul-mouthed pioneer. The very beautiful
description of sexual intercourse in *I Sing the Body Electric*, also in
this first edition, and to be quoted later, if understood at all
would have seemed only indecency to the public of 1855, and did
so seem to many 'genteel' critics who did not regard themselves
as belonging to the en-masse at all.

Nor could the public, Protestant or Catholic, have been expected to encounter without, to put it mildly, extreme discomfort
the shocking spiritual egoism of these poems. For Whitman had
gone his Quaker friends one better. They, in their inner life, felt
indirect communion with God, and spoke as from God. But he
identified himself with God, who for him was manifest entirely in
man. It is too much to say that he thought he was God, but he
was of God, and felt no inferiority: 'In the faces of men and
women I see God, and in my own face in the glass.'

Walking the old hills of Judea with the beautiful gentle God by my side,
Speeding through space, speeding through heaven and the stars, . . .
Storming, enjoying, planning, loving, cautioning,
Backing and filling, appearing and disappearing,
I tread day and night such roads.[1]

Who is this fellow anyway — Christ, the holy Ghost — or an
escape from the asylum?

But, of course, he was not publishing for the en-masse, or even
for the reading public, but for the critics, teachers, preachers, editors who made public opinion and could get him a hearing. And
there he expected, not praise I should say, or acceptance, but at
least a recognition that his was a new voice, and a powerful one,
whether they liked it or not. 'I expected hell: I got it,' he said
to Horace Traubel in the 1880's.[2] The 'hell' actually did not come
in full fierceness until later, when he had affronted prudishness on
a wider circle. He said to Traubel on another occasion, speaking
of Howells and Aldrich, 'I have met them and like them (Howells
especially is genial and ample — rather inclined to be big — full
size) — but they are *thin* — no weight: such men are in certain
ways important — they run a few temporary errands but they are
not out for immortal service.'[3] What he hoped for was an agree-

ment that he was out for immortal (even if very unpopular) service. He did not get that, perhaps did not deserve it on the basis of these first 'Leaves.' Yet, so far as recognition of his vigor and originality was concerned, these first poems did surprisingly well, better, I should say, than the first offering of any other revolutionary poet in modern history, better than his own later books. When the count was all in for both the 1855 and 1856 editions, Whitman was justified in saying, though the sales were almost zero, 'We have positively arrived.'

2

One of the first reactions to the 'Leaves' was such a letter as many a young author has dreamed of receiving about his first would-be masterpiece. It is impossible to overrate the importance to Whitman of Emerson's letter, addressed to Mr. Walter Whitman only two and a half weeks after the publication of the 1855 book. Emerson was at the height of his reputation, he was the acknowledged custodian of the idealism of America, and its premier man-of-letters. But that was not all. His religious and moral individualism had been one of the chief influences upon Whitman's thinking. 'I simmered, simmered,' he said later, 'Emerson brought me to a boil.' And no subsequent statements that he did not read him till after he wrote the 'Leaves' (Whitman's memory was bad, his later vanity great) could subtract from that admission, whose substantial truth must be evident to any reader of the two men's works. Even more important, Emerson stood for high-standarded, ethically obsessed New England; and he was as emphatically *the* good man of America as he was the defender of its spiritual expansiveness. For him to give the radical, revolutionary 'Leaves,' with its emphasis upon the infinite importance of sexuality, a blanket approval was as if, being published in England, the Archbishop of Canterbury had blessed it. Here is the famous letter:

Concord, Mass., 21st July, 1855

Dear Sir, — I am not blind to the worth of the wonderful gift of *Leaves of Grass*. I find it the most extraordinary piece of wit and wisdom that America has yet contributed. I am very happy in reading it, as great power makes us happy. It meets the demand I am always making of what seems the sterile and stingy Nature, as if too much handiwork, or too much lymph in the temperament were making our Western wits fat and mean. I give you joy of your free and brave thought. I have great joy in it. I find incomparable things said incomparably well, as they must be. I find the courage of treatment that so delights us and which large perception only can inspire.

I greet you at the beginning of a great career, which yet must have had a long foreground somewhere, for such a start. I rubbed my eyes a little to see if this sunbeam were no illusion; but the solid sense of the book is a sober certainty. It has the best merits, namely, of fortifying and encouraging.

I did not know, until I last night saw the book advertised in a newspaper, that I could trust the name as real and available for a post-office.

I wish to see my benefactor, and have felt much like striking my tasks and visiting New York to pay you my respects.

R. W. EMERSON

Is it surprising that Whitman carried this letter in his pocket and displayed it to all his friends, or that, having shown it to Charles A. Dana, then managing editor of *The Tribune*,[4] he allowed it to be printed? It is surprising, however, but understandable that he had the bad taste to print it again himself, this time in the second edition of 1856, with a fulsome and (so far as sales of his book were concerned) mendacious letter of reply, and the quotation, 'I greet you at the Beginning of a Great Career — R. W. Emerson,' on the cover.

Emerson was shocked, but he stuck to his guns. He was disappointed in Whitman's later poetry, as he was disappointed in Thoreau's poetical progress. Neither followed the specifications he had laid down in his own mind. But he never doubted Whitman's essential Americanism, or his importance. What signs of distaste and irritation he showed to later questioners were natural enough. Four reviewers out of five for the next ten years were to

wonder in print how the godly Emerson came to condone indecency. This annoyed him naturally, and the women in his family
still more.

Whitman himself was not dismayed by the hell he got, and
printed some of it with the praise in an appendix to his second
edition. In order to show how his own nineteenth century received his first work, I shall do the same.

Fanny Fern was sister of N. P. Willis, the most popular jour-
nalist-columnist-poet of his day, and herself one of the most successful of sentimental novelists. Whitman had money difficulties
with her husband, James Parton, and she was reported to have
been 'sweet' on him, though he certainly had not been sweet on
her — so the frank praise of his first woman reviewer is interesting. She wrote in *The New York Ledger* of May 10, 1856, reprinted in *Life Illustrated*, May 17, 1856:

'Well baptized; fresh, hardy, and grown for the masses. Not
more welcome is their natural type to the winter-bound, bed-
ridden, and spring-emancipated invalid. "Leaves of Grass" thou
art unspeakably delicious, after the forced, stiff, Parnassian ex-
otics for which our admiration has been vainly challenged. . . .
Walt Whitman, the world needed a "Native American" of thor-
ough out-and-out breed — enamoured of *women*, not *ladies*, —
men, not *gentlemen*; something besides a mere Catholic-hating
Know Nothing.[5] It needed a man who dared speak out his strong,
honest thoughts in the face of pusillanimous, toadying, republican aristocracy.'

William Howitt, the English Quaker poet, in *The London Dis-
patch*, reprinted in *Life Illustrated*, April 19, 1856:

'It is of a *genus* so peculiar as to embarrass us, and has an air at
once so novel, so audacious, and so strange, as to verge upon absurdity, and yet it would be an injustice to pronounce it so, as the
work is saved from this extreme by a certain mastery over diction
not very easy of definition.'

From *The London Leader*, reprinted in *Life Illustrated*, July 19,
1856:

'Walt is one of the most amazing, one of the most startling, one of the most perplexing creatures of the modern American mind; but he is no fool, though abundantly eccentric.... The poem is written in wild, irregular, unrhymed, almost unmetrical "lengths" ... by no means seductive, to English ears.... It seems to resolve itself into an all-attracting egotism — an external presence of the individual soul of Walt Whitman in all things, yet in such wise that this one soul shall be presented as a type of all human souls whatsoever.... Much ... seems to us purely fantastic and preposterous, ... disgusting without purpose, and singular without result. There are so many evidences of a noble soul in Whitman's pages, that we regret these aberrations.'

The London Critic, April 1, 1857:
'Walt Whitman is as unacquainted with art as a hog is with mathematics.'

R. W. Griswold, (Poe's detractor) in *The New York Criterion*, November 10, 1855:
'Thus, then, we leave this gathering of muck to the laws which, certainly, if they fulfil their intent, must have power to suppress such obscenity.... It is entirely destitute of wit.... We do not believe there is a newspaper so vile that would print confirmatory extracts.... We have found it impossible to convey any, even the most faint idea of its style and contents, and of our disgust and detestation of them ... but ... some one should ... undertake a most ... disagreeable ... duty.... Monsters have gone on in impunity, because the exposure of their vileness was attended with too great indelicacy.'

Edward Everett Hale, author of 'The Man Without a Country,' in *The North American Review*, January, 1856:
'Walter Whitman, an American — one of the roughs, — no sentimentalist, — no stander above men and women, or apart from them, — no more modest than immodest, — ... Everything about the external arrangement of this book is odd and out of the way ... it is well worth going twice to the bookstore to buy it ... one reads and enjoys the freshness, simplicity, and reality of what he reads, just as the tired man, lying on the hill-side in summer, enjoys the leaves of grass around him....'

Putnam's Monthly, September, 1855. Written by *Charles Eliot Norton* at the age of twenty-eight: [6]

'Lawless ... poems ... in a sort of excited prose ... a compound of the New England transcendentalist and a New York rowdy. A foreman (of intelligence) might have written this gross yet elevated, this superficial yet profound, this preposterous yet somehow fascinating book.'

National Intelligencer, Washington, D.C., February–March, 1856:

'Walter Whitman is a pantheist. Without, perhaps, ever having read Spinoza, he is a Spinozist. Without, perhaps, much deep insight into Plato the divine, he is a Platonist 'in the rough' ... The world as he finds it ... is good enough for Walter Whitman who is himself a "kosmos." ... Mr. Whitman thinks ... he would like to turn and live awhile with the animals. ... Everyone to his liking, as remarked the venerable dame in the proverb when she kissed her cow. ... No one, we may say, however, in all candor, can read this singular prose-poem without being struck by the writer's wonderful power of description and of word-painting. It is only ... his transcendental sinuosities of thought ... which ... become narrower and narrower and at last dwindle to a squirrel path and run up a tree.'

3

The charge of lack of art from these reviewers was to be expected, and was justified by many a defective passage in the first volume. The charge of indecency certainly was to be expected. What is surprising in these and other reviews, is the number of critics who glimpsed that Walt was experimenting in a new and not unpromising form, and the number (among them Fanny Fern, and Mrs. Gilchrist, not quoted here) who praised his frankness and refused to be shocked. Praise of the rough Americanism of his democracy was to be expected also, especially among the English liberals. Yet the omissions seem curious. The writer of *The London Leader* review very well understood Walt's conception of a representative man. Yet the others, almost without exception, did not see that the ego of the poems was a dramatized symbol, and took it literally to be Whitman himself — which means that the 'immortal service,' the spiritual quality, the daring scope of the poems went over their heads altogether. No contemporary American, so far as I am aware, really understood the significance of the spiritual and bodily expansiveness of these poems for an expanding democracy, though Emerson glimpsed it, and Thoreau felt it in the man himself. To no one did it occur that the expansiveness of the common man in an expansive democracy would inevitably bring somehow into the spotlight all the aspects of hidden human nature, and all the catalogues of experience, which seem to have been regarded by his critics as merely eccentricities of his poems. It is probable that it would have taken as great a man as Whitman at that moment of time to see the prophecy of new releases for human energy in his blatant poems, and a new art in his walloping verse.

But Whitman was right in calling attention to those reviews, though wrong in printing so many of them in his second edition — he was usually unfortunate in the methods of his publicity. The balance of what they said did not swing against his book. There was nothing of the lukewarm (that fatal quality) in them. The vituperation (as any publisher would say) was good sales talk. There was basis enough for an advertising campaign, but no money, and no publisher. Readers simply would not buy, either the first or the second edition. The book was a good subject to write about — but it was not good to read.

Some time before most of these and many other reviews had appeared, the most interesting criticism of all had been published. It was printed in *The Brooklyn Times* of September 29, 1855, and was written by the man who best understood the purposes of the poems and was not unaware of their faults and probable reaction of the public. The author was Walt himself:

'Very devilish to some, and very divine to some, will appear the poet of these new poems ... an attempt, as they are of a naïve, masculine, affectionate, contemplative, sensual, imperious person to cast into literature not only his own grit and arrogance, but his own flesh and form, undraped, regardless of models, regardless of modesty or law; and ignorant or silently scornful, as at first it appears, of all except his own presence and experience, and all outside of the fiercely loved land of his birth. . . . Politeness this man has none, and regulations he has none. . . . The effects he produces in his poems are no effects of artists or the arts, but effects of the original eye or arm, or the actual atmosphere, of tree, or bird. . . . His . . . purpose to stamp a new type of character, namely his own, and indelibly fix it . . . for the present and future of American letters and American young men. . . . [He is] a person singularly beloved . . . by young men and the illiterate . . . not an extraordinary person . . . but has the easy fascination of what is homely and accustomed . . . the begetter of a new offspring out of literature . . . preferring always to speak for himself rather than have others speak for him.'

And so he does, and very modestly for a Whitman who from now on proposes to fight the world until it accepts his poems. He writes as one who knows he will be misunderstood, and so, breaking an editorial law (as of course he was well aware), writes his own defence and explanation. What he felt was needed, as this and other self-reviews show, was a word to the readers that behind his egotism was sincerity, that the duty of speaking for a new democracy of the common people had been laid upon a man who was at least honest and courageous, not afraid to be gross where democracy was gross, passionate where hearty men and women were passionate, and egoistic where only a dilated ego could contain the composite and confused attributes of the en-masse.

I cannot blame him for plugging his own book. He knew so much better than those whose experience had been only literary what the press in which he had been brought up would missay, misunderstand, understate, and exaggerate about him. He was well aware that the common people of whom he wrote would never come to testify for him. Having inside opportunities to speak for himself, he took them. So did Falstaff on a famous occasion, so did Elijah until the Lord rebuked him, so does any modern author seeking success, although he or his publisher usually employs a publicity man to do the job.[7]

4

By midsummer of 1855, it must have been clear that Whitman's hope that his book would give him a revolving fund on which he could live and publish again was an illusion. What he had hoped to do is evident from what he said he was going to do, in his decidedly disingenuous letter to Emerson accompanying his second edition:

'Here are thirty-two Poems, which I send you, dear Friend and Master.... The first edition ... was twelve poems — I printed a thousand copies, and they readily sold; these thirty-two Poems I stereotype, to print several thousand copies of.... I keep on till I make a hundred, and then several hundred — perhaps a thousand.... A few years, and the average annual call for my Poems is ten or twenty thousand copies — more, quite likely. Why should I hurry or compromise?'

This was sheer bluff as far as the 1855 edition was concerned, meant to cover its complete failure until his second edition should have a chance for financial success. If Emerson had come to New York, he would not have found Whitman counting his profits. Instead, he was restoring his courage on the beaches of his beloved Paumanok, rambling, loafing, swimming, until he could come back to Brooklyn confident and ready for his second round in the battle for fame. His resolution to go ahead did not come from the reviews I have quoted. Nothing less than to have been called the John the Baptist of the new democracy would have really satisfied him! No author of any originality is ever satisfied even with the most appreciative reviews unless they crack the ceiling of praise. Whitman's confidence came from within, and carried him through the hard work of preparing the new and extended edition which was to be ready, according to *Life Illustrated*, on September 1 of 1856. Relieved of the lengthy Preface, enriched by twenty new poems, and backed by Emerson's letter, it was a good bid for success.

Alas, the results were the same. Although it contained such memorable poems as *Salut au Monde*, *Song of the Broad-Axe*, *Crossing Brooklyn Ferry*, and *Song of the Open Road*, poems which have since carried Whitman's reputation across the world, a few copies only seem to have been sold, and Fowler and Wells soon withdrew as distributors because of the unfavorable criticism of Walt's freedom of speech. The super-Walt, the colossal egotist of the spirit, the sovereign of the flesh as Alcott called him, who had hoped from now on to make poetry his support as well as his profession, had to go back to journalism, because no one would buy his books. Some celebrity had come to him. He had arrived as a man to be talked about, if not to be read. When he wrote for the August 16, 1856, number of *Life Illustrated* an anonymous description of street life and street character in New York, he was justified in describing himself as known to be a poet: 'Tall, large, rough-looking man, in a journeyman carpenter's uniform. Coarse, sanguine complexion; strong, bristly, grizzled beard; singular eyes, of a semi-transparent, indistinct light blue, and with that sleepy look that comes when the lid rests half way down over the pupil; careless, lounging gait. Walt Whitman, the sturdy, self-conscious microcosmic, prose-poetical-author of that incongruous hash of mud and gold — *Leaves of Grass.*'

But by 1857 he had returned to editing again and the clothes, if not the mind, of an editor.

CHAPTER XIII

~~~~~

'I sit and look out'

A ND SO Walt came back from the cosmos of spiritual expansion, the roll call of a continent, the incarnation of expanding America in a dramatized Walt Whitman, to his familiar rôle of free-lancer and writer of editorials. He had little choice, except to continue as carpenter and builder, and that, if I am right in my hypothesis, was no longer attractive after his father's death in 1855. For he clearly would have had to take on the speculative building trade alone, or give full time to the carpenter's trade. The first, as he told Traubel, he had enough of, the second was incompatible with his ambitions, now fully aroused, and would have been impossible for a man of Whitman's large aspirations anyway. A carpenter worked ten hours in these days, unless he was just lending a hand in a family job.

In 1855 and 1856, while the reviews were coming in, and he was still setting up in type his self-reviews and the new poems of the 1856 edition, he began a series of articles for *Life Illustrated*. *Life Illustrated* was a weekly of wide distribution throughout the country, and with a circulation of perhaps seventy-five thousand. It was published by Fowler and Wells, his phrenological friends who had taken on his first edition of the 'Leaves.' For them, he wrote on 'wicked architecture,' which was an attack on high rents, tenements, and boarding houses, also on the opera at the new 14th Street Theatre written for the uninitiated, on Christmas at church, on Doctor Henry Abbott's Egyptian Museum, this last with much erudition supplied by the owner, on the English language, and on night life in New York. He was, in most of these contributions, the reporter of a populous city, as he had once been of New Orleans. But there is far more solidity, far less flippancy in these later descriptions.

By 1857 he had become editor of *The Brooklyn Times*, an ambitious newspaper, independent and proud of it in politics, and much concerned with local topics and local welfare.[1] In sharp contrast to his editorship of *The Eagle*, he did not — did not have to apparently — concern himself much with politics. The editorials which Professor Holloway has reprinted are extraordinarily broad in their scope. They are literary, descriptive, humanitarian, reforming, on women's health and morals, on civic subjects, on international affairs, and many of them can only be described as excellent of their kind. They are daring too in their social ideas, touching upon such delicate subjects as the sexual problems of the unmarried, upon prostitution, upon abortion, upon slavery. Traditionally, he lost his job sometime in 1859 because he ran afoul of the churches. It seems most probable, for his social radicalism was beginning to come to the surface, even in sober editorial writing.[2] The powers that were in the churches (and Brooklyn has been called the city of churches) may have found his topics suggestive of greater frankness to come, especially since he was now known as the author of a book which had been called indecent.

By June 26 of 1859, he is writing in his notebook, 'It is now time to *stir* first for *money* enough *to live and provide for M*—— *To Stir* — first write stories and get out of this slough.'[3] He had evidently lost his job, and did not expect another. But why 'stories,' when he must have been already ashamed of those he had written? Doubtless because even bad stories were easy to sell. As for M——, some think she was a mistress. The reference was certainly not to his sister Mary, who was getting on well enough as far as we know, but why not to his Mother, whom he did help to support until her death? Walt was capable of any abbreviation in his notes.

All this has to do only with Whitman's trade of journalism in this decade. His vital interests lay deeper, and must have engaged far more of his creative energies and his anxious thought. He kept afloat in the newspaper and magazine world, but his true concern was with the state of the nation and with poetry.

For *The Times*, he wrote a handful of political editorials dealing with those 'dead rabbits,' the office-seekers and pro-slavery leaders of the Democratic Party, and with Douglas, the 'Little Giant,' whose moderate policies pleased him better than the fanaticism of the Abolitionists. It was Douglas who would preserve the Union by letting popular sovereignty in each state determine the issue of slavery. Yet Whitman's real feelings, which were intense and destructive of his interest for the time being in all parties and in all politics, only peep out now and then from these editorials.

His party had been 'diverging, splitting, forking off' [4] until there was no firm ground for feet like his. Yet that was only half of the story. If he had wished to seek another party to work for, he could have found one in the new Republican organization, and, indeed, he had voted for Frémont in 1856. One could be a Republican without becoming an Abolitionist. Whitman did not believe that slavery was the one crying sin of the universe,[5] but neither did Lincoln. Unhappily for Walt, his faith in the 'good old cause' had been so great, and his loyalty to the Democrats who represented it so strong, that to break with his party was to break with faith in all parties. His first reaction to political disillusion was into violent distaste for the whole business of party politics. Like many another idealist who has been disappointed in the machinery by which life in society is carried on, he wanted to smash all machines.

An extraordinary pamphlet, published for the first time by Mr. Clifton Furness in 1928, is evidence.[6] I doubt Mr. Furness's belief that *The Eighteenth Presidency* was written to aid the cause of the Republicans and Frémont. It had been, apparently, begun earlier in the fifties and completed in 1856, when Frémont was to run against the spineless Buchanan nominated by the Democrats, and Fillmore, candidate of the Whigs and Know-Nothings. But this diatribe — for no milder word can describe this pamphlet — did not stop with attacks on Fillmore and Buchanan, nor was it written to aid Frémont. It is an outburst against all parties and particularly against the method of choosing presidential candidates.

Whitman is fed up with practical politics. The time has come for men to count, not parties. Party machines are run by office-seekers and creatures of the President. It sounds like an attack on the French Third Republic of 1939, or, shall we say, any American presidential convention seen through a red haze of rage. Will six millions of honest American workmen submit to this? 'Are not political parties about played out? I say they are, all round.' 'I would be much pleased to see some heroic, shrewd, full-informed, healthy bodied, middle-aged, beard-faced American blacksmith or boatman [or rail-splitter?] come down from the West across the Alleghanies, and walk into the Presidency. I would certainly vote for that sort of man.' [7]

This pamphlet is magnificent propaganda, but it is not politics as Whitman had played politics in the past. For what does he propose — that some rich person (none offered) shall circulate and reprint 'this Voice of Mine and deluge the States with it: No man knows what will happen next, but all know that some such things are to happen as mark the greatest moral convulsions of the earth. Who shall play the hand for America in these tremendous games?' [8]

Well, it was the full-informed, middle-aged, and shrewd Abraham Lincoln who came (smooth-shaven then) down from the West across the Alleghanies. Yet, even though Whitman voted for him, it was not until 1863 that he recognized the heroic in the Republican politician. Nor would Lincoln ever have been elected, if the prescription to abolish all parties had been followed by the millions of prospective readers of this really superb outburst. Walt is still a prophet, more of a prophet than ever, but he has lost faith, for a while, in the democratic system, though not in democracy. His political-editorial days are over (he was never a kept editor), his interest in getting out the vote has been swallowed up by his interest in giving ideals to his country. In other words (and as so often with Milton when he was Latin Secretary), it is a poet who writes.

One needs only to read *The Eighteenth Presidency* to see that Whitman would never again have a career as the editor of a newspaper supporting a party — any party. One has only to read the first 'Leaves' to see that his career as a commentator on doings of the day and a writer of magazine stories would end as soon as he was able to support himself otherwise.

Actually, his work upon poetry must have been his most intense life and hardest work between 1850 and 1860. 'By July 28, 1857, he was confessing to his friend Hector Tyndale that he had a hundred poems ready.' [9] There were many more when the third edition was ready to print in 1860. And this poetry contained material of such a startling nature, and individual poems of such outstanding excellence, that one wonders how he had time to do anything else. These new poems, however, and the new Whitman that surges up in them, represent, as did his first twelve, a Walt quite unknown to the Bohemians of Broadway, his family, and his friends and acquaintances, who now become not only numerous, but accessible in the records they have left. For them, Whitman was still the lounger and friend of all the world, who wrote as late as the 1860's, 'Give me the streets of Manhattan!... The life of the theatre, bar-room, huge hotel, for me.'

CHAPTER XIV

'Camerado, I give you my hand'

WE MUST think of Whitman in the latter fifties and early sixties as having multitudinous acquaintances and many real friends among both men and women, in New York as well as in Brooklyn. I believe that he had no real intimates — or, if he did, the record is only in his poems, and these are not a record of shared inner life but of love, which is a somewhat different thing. I doubt whether he ever had intimates who broke through the extraordinary reticence with which he veiled his inner life in letters and in conversation, even while he was exposing it, as no man of his century had exposed it, in his poems.

And even more cogently, we must think of Whitman in 'perfect health,' with an immense gusto for living, enjoying, absorbing, seeking for every kind of contact with life.[1] The great port and city and centre of American entertainment and heart of American enterprise gave him unexampled opportunities. Creating in such an environment was for him the end-product of intense living. The catalogue and picture poems written in this decade are electric with vivid reactions, like flying sparks from a dynamo, the results of an immense, indiscriminate, utterly satisfying interest in life. I am thinking especially of *Song of Myself, Salut au Monde, Song of the Open Road, Crossing Brooklyn Ferry, Song of the Broad-Axe, A Song for Occupations, The Sleepers, To Think of Time.*

New York, then as now, was a place like London, of many societies, sometimes intersecting, and all set in the composite multitude of a great city. Walt moved freely among them. He took parts at the amateur theatre up Broadway — 'full of fun and enjoyment'[2] — haunted theatres and the opera, and listened to the reformers and the Abolitionists speak at the 'Tabernacle' to audiences of three or four thousand. There were riots at the meetings, but 'the Anti-Slavery and Quaker and Temperance, and Missionary speakers were tough, tough, and always maintained their ground.' Emerson he heard, too. That he was a companion to many of the unsophisticated and embittered of this multitude, stage-drivers, criminals, bartenders, street-walkers, mechanics, is evident from his own statements and from the realistic descriptions in his poems. That he was well known on Broadway by many who had never heard of and never would read his poetry, is certain also.

He took his new front of Bohemian-journalist as seriously as his recent mask of carpenter-poet, and clearly hoped that interest in the man as a dramatic character, who looked the part of a celebrity, might lead to interest in his books. Here is a vivid self-written description of himself,[3] not I think hitherto reprinted, and perhaps never printed, but written certainly with self-advertisement in mind. It belongs to 1860:

'A fine warmish afternoon — and Broadway in the full flow of its Gulf-stream of fashion . . . Omnibuses! — There they go incessantly — the Broadway line, Yellow Bird, Twenty-Third Street, . . . Everything appertaining to them is a study. — One man appears to think so at any rate — Do you mind him, as the driver of that handsome Fifth Avenue pulls up casting at the lounger a friendly and inquiring glance, as much as to say, come take a ride, Walt Whitman? For none other than Walt is it who in response turns off from the pave, and seizes the handle, swings himself up with spring and elastic motion, and lights on the offhandside of the stage, with his hip held by the rod as quietly as a hawk swoops to its nest.

'That man is the subject for the whole of this week's Plaza Sketch — that pet and pride of the Broadway stage-drivers.

'As onward speeds the stage, mark his nonchalant air, seated aslant and quite at home. — Our million-hued, ever-changing panorama of Broadway moves steadily down; he, going up, sees it all, as in a kind of half dream. — Mark the salutes of four out of each five of the drivers, downward bound; — salutes which he silently returns in the same manner — the raised arm, and the upright hand. —'

To which I must add the equally naïve account of the interest he aroused on the streets of Boston when he was at work in that classic city on his 1860 edition. It is in a letter to Abby Price, of whom more later:

'I go on the Common — walk considerable in Washington street.... I create an immense sensation in Washington street. Everybody here is so like everybody else — and I am Walt Whitman. — Yankee curiosity and cuteness[4] — for once is thoroughly stumped, confounded, petrified, made desperate.'

We know what he looked like and how he dressed in these years after 1856 from several descriptions, of which the most detailed was written by a young German poet, Frederick Huene, a revolutionist of 1848, who was a printer on *The Brooklyn Times* when Whitman was editor.[5] This description dates from 1858:

'He was a tall, well-built man, wore high boots over his pants, a jacket of heavy dark blue cloth, always left open to show a woolen undershirt, and a red handkerchief loosely tied around his brawny neck. Outside the office he wore a broad-brimmed hat. He often came upstairs and walked up and down on the part of the floor where the job office was located, without speaking a word. Sometimes he was very conversible, and as he once saw a little book of poetry of mine which I had printed in the Grand Street *Times* office, he presented me with one of his books, *Leaves of Grass*. He wished I should translate it into German.'

This agrees with the doubtfully dated picture of Whitman in Plate VI, except for the tie, which may have been assumed for outdoor wear, and the boots, of which the same may be true, if indeed they are not below the margin of the photograph. There is a close resemblance between this picture and Charles Hines's painting of 1859 which was reproduced as a frontispiece for the 1860 edition. Here is a somewhat conventionalized Whitman with beard and hair much as in the photograph, tighter tie, a slightly more formal coat, but much the same man, of the same age, and the same dramatization of a Bohemian man-of-letters. Curiously enough, the painting shows his hair and beard as dark brown, only slightly grizzled. Why? I do not know, for he was certainly quite gray by 1850. Perhaps he asked the painter to make him look young.[6]

2

I have used the word 'Bohemian' with a reference more specific than to manners and morals. There was a very definite and so-called Bohemian group in New York of the mid and latter fifties, which had its own organ in *The Saturday Press*, a leader in its editor Henry Clapp, and enemies among the ultra-respectable and orthodox in both New York and the outlying literary capital of Boston. Some brilliant men and women joined in the rather extensive coterie that assembled to eat and drink ale, beer, or champagne, in 'Pfaff's Privy.' Fitz-James O'Brien, the young Irish celebrity who wrote two famous short stories, still often reprinted, before he lost his life in the war: *The Diamond Lens* and *What Was It?*, met with them. Ada Clare was another habitué, the author and beauty who died tragically from the bite of a mad dog, and whose name was often on Walt's lips. It seems improbable that he knew her well, or romantically. Thomas Bailey Aldrich, Stedman, Fitz-Greene Halleck, 'Willy' Winter the dramatic critic, Clapp himself with his sparkling, cynical wit, and many now forgotten were among the frequenters. This miscellaneous assortment of writers, musicians, painters, editors, for whom Pfaff's was a favorite rendezvous, had little resemblance to the more authentic Bohemians of Paris. It was only a society of journalists and artists who, thanks to their profession, were likely to be on the streets at all hours, and were marked by this singularity, if for no other, in a city where men and women spent most of their free time at home.

The especial coterie at Pfaff's seems to have gathered with and around the editor and contributors of *The Saturday Press* — *The New Yorker* of its day, which was brief. Founded in October, 1858, it was suspended in December of the critical year of 1860, and when it was revived after the war it had lost its Bohemian tone.[7] *The Saturday Press* was Whitman's friend and champion, and it was natural that he should often join the group where Clapp met his authors and arranged for contributions. Clapp paid only by promises, yet (so said William Dean Howells) for a while *The Saturday Press* gave prestige to a new author second only to what *The Atlantic* could do for him. It was 'clever,' said Howells who wrote for it, attacking 'all literary shams but its own,' 'and full of the wit that tries its teeth upon everything.' [8] The unconventionality and iconoclasm must have pleased Walt, but the wit was not his métier. By his own testimony he sat much at Pfaff's, but talked little.

It was in 1860 that the young William Dean Howells, having established himself, after many heart shakings, in the old centre of American culture at Boston, decided to follow up his numerous (and unpaid for) contributions, to New York, the new metropolis of literary journalism. Howells did not like Bohemia at all. Boston was to be his spiritual home and he did not return to New York until twenty years after the smart Bohemian set had died of its own smartness and the Civil War. In 1860, he was taken to Pfaff's and 'the long board spread for the Bohemians in a cavernous space under the pavement,' listened to whirling words, ate pancakes, but being a good youth from the Middle West neither drank nor smoked. He was somewhat disappointed at the 'orgy' he had been told he would find there. A few head-aches seemed to be the only indication. But Whitman was there, and this proved to be 'the chief fact in my experience.' As usual, Walt sat in the background.

Howells had read the first 'Leaves,' and felt that it was the materials of poetry, not poetry itself. Whitman's prose seemed to him, to be preferable. He had thought of Whitman as the apostle of the rough and the uncouth, whose barbaric yawp was shocking, and whose printing of Emerson's private letter was evidently not the act of a gentleman. But the man he met was 'the gentlest person,' with an address of singular quiet, delivered in a voice of winning and endearing friendliness.

'I remember how he leaned back in his chair, and reached out his great hand to me, as if he were going to give it to me for good and all. He had a fine head, with a cloud of Jovian hair upon it, and a branching beard and mustache, and gentle eyes that looked most kindly into mine, and seemed to wish the liking I instantly gave him, though we hardly passed a word, and our acquaintance was summed up in that glance and the grasp of his mighty fist upon my hand. I doubt if he had any notion who or what I was beyond the fact that I was a young poet of some sort, but he may possibly have remembered seeing my name printed after some very Heinesque verses in the *Press.*' [9]

This seems to be the Walt who looks out of Kurtz's photograph of 1860, in Plate VII of this book, though the man Howells met was not posing as a bard and revolutionary, as he does so very significantly in the photograph. Nor did Howells guess that the kindly gentleness of this unexpected Whitman concealed a passionate intensity which would have surprised (and probably bored) these somewhat second-rate Bohemians.

Only the year before, Walt had set down in his notebook what seems to be a reference to Pfaff's and the literary bargaining that went on there, which would not have pleased *The Saturday Press* coterie:

But that shadow, my likeness, that goes to and fro seeking a livelihood, chattering, chaffering,
I often find myself standing and looking at it where it flits — That likeness of me, but never substantially me.[10]

And still more pertinently in a notebook of 1862: [11]

The vault at Pfaff's where the drinkers and laughers meet to eat and drink and carouse,
While on the walk immediately overhead, pass the myriad feet of Broadway ...

Laugh on Laughers!
Drink on Drinkers!
Bandy the jest! Toss the theme from one to another!
Beam up — Brighten up, bright eyes of beautiful young men!
Eat what you, having ordered, are pleased to see placed before you — after the work of the day, now, with appetite, eat,
Drink wine — drink beer — raise your voice,
Behold! Your friend as he arrives — Welcome him, when, from the upper step, he looks down upon you with a cheerful look

Overhead rolls Broadway, the myriad rushing Broadway (?)
The lamps are lit — the shops blaze — the fabrics vividly (?) are seen through
     the plate-glass window
The strong lights from above pour down upon them and are shed outside
The thick crowds, well-dressed — the continual crowds as if they would never
     end
The curious appearance of the faces — the glimpse first caught of the eyes
     and expressions as they flit along,
O You phantoms! oft I pause, yearning to arrest some one of you!
(Oft I doubt your reality whether you are real — I suspect all is but a
     pageant.)

3

'With a cheerful look.' Whatever was going on in the depths
of his mind, the cheerfulness of Whitman's usual appearance
in these days was genuine, not posed. This aspect of the man it
is necessary to stress particularly because, if studied only through
the poetry he had been writing, he seems to be a set of tensions,
suppressions, and exuberances, all coiled about genius. In his
daily contacts with friends and family he was just the sweet-
natured man that Howells describes. 'I never think of Walt
without thinking of his cheerful face,' his unhappy sister, Hannah,
wrote to the old mother in a letter of about 1860.[12] (It was
Hannah alone of all the family that liked the 'Leaves.' She found
them 'fascinating.') If Walt had not been such a man it would
have been impossible for him to write the truly remarkable letters to his mother describing hospital scenes which will be
quoted in a later chapter. Prophet and poet, apostle of sexual
honesty, passionate defender of democracy, orator in the cause
of freedom, he was also just the lovable friend of all simple
genuine people which these descriptions suggest.

The Prices, for example, mother and two daughters, friends of
the Whitman family as well as himself, kept a superior boarding-
house in Brooklyn, a guest-house, we should call it, and Whitman
in the late fifties was often with them. Helen Price has left an
account of Walt as she knew him, which deserves reprinting
from Doctor Bucke's biography:

'My acquaintance with Walt Whitman began in 1856, or about

a year after he published the first edition of "Leaves of Grass." I was at that time living with my parents in Brooklyn, and although hardly more than a child in years, the impression made upon my girlish imagination by his large, grand presence, his loose, free dress, and his musical voice will never be effaced. From that date until the death of his mother, in 1873, he was often a visitor at our house, as I at his, his mother being only less dear to me than my own.

'So many remembrances of him in those by gone years come crowding to my mind that to choose what will be most characteristic, and most likely to interest those who know him only from his books, is a task to which I fear I shall prove unequal. On the other hand, *anything* I might write of him, his conversation especially, when deprived of the magnetism of his presence and voice, and of the circumstances and occasions which called forth the words, will, I am painfully aware, seem poor and tame. . . .

'No one could possibly have more aversion to being lionized than Mr. Whitman. I could not say how many times, after getting his consent to meet certain admirers at our house, he has vexed and annoyed us by staying away. At one time an evening was appointed to meet General T., of Philadelphia, and a number of others. We waited with some misgivings for his appearance, but he came at last. Soon as the introductions were over, he sidled off to a corner of the room where there was a group of young children, with whom he talked and laughed and played, evidently to their mutual satisfaction. Our company, who had come from a distance to see Mr. Whitman, and did not expect another opportunity, were quite annoyed, and my mother was finally commissioned to get him out of his corner. When she told her errand, he looked up with the utmost merriment, and said, "O, yes — I'll do it — where do you want me to sit? On the piano?" He went forward very good-naturedly, however, but I knew that his happy time for that evening was over.

'A friend of ours, a very brilliant and intellectual lady, had often expressed a great desire to see him — but as she lived out of town it was difficult to arrange a meeting. One day she came to our house full of animation and triumph. "I have seen Walt

Whitman at last," she said. "I was sitting in the cabin of the Brooklyn ferry-boat when he came in. I knew it was he; it couldn't be any one else; and as he walked through the boat with such an elephantine roll and swing, I could hardly keep from getting right up and rolling after him." The next time he called we related this to him; he laughed heartily, and frequently afterward alluded to his "elephantine roll."

'Mr. Whitman was not a smooth, glib, or even a very fluent talker. His ideas seemed always to be called forth or suggested by what was said before, and he would frequently hesitate for just the right term to express his meaning. He never gave the impression that his words were cut and dried in his mind, or at his tongue's end, to be used on occasion; but you listened to what seemed to be freshly thought, which gave to all he said an indescribable charm. His language was forcible, rich and vivid to the last degree, and even when most serious and earnest, his talk was always enlivened by frequent gleams of humor. (I believe it has been assumed by the critics that he has no humor. There could not be a greater mistake.) I have said that in conversation he was not fluent, yet when a little excited in talking on any subject very near his heart, his words would come forth rapidly, and in strains of amazing eloquence. At such times I have wished our little circle was enlarged a hundred-fold, that others might have the privilege of hearing him.

'As a listener (all who have met him will agree with me) I think that he was and is unsurpassed. He was ever more anxious to hear your thought than to express his own. Often when asked to give his opinion on any subject, his first words would be, "Tell me what you have to say about it." His method of considering, pondering, what Emerson calls "entertaining," your thought was singularly agreeable and flattering, and evidently an outgrowth of his natural manner, and as if unconscious of paying you any special compliment. He seemed to call forth the best there was in those he met. He never appeared to me a conceited or egotistical man, though I have frequently heard him say himself that he was so. On the contrary, he was always unassuming and modest in asserting himself, and seemed to feel, or at least made others feel, that their opinions were more valuable than his own. I have heard him express serious doubt as to what would be the final judgment of posterity on his poems, or "pieces" as he sometimes called them.

'I have, however, seen in his character something that, for want of a better word, I would call vanity. I think it arose from his superabundant vitality and strength. All through those years he gloried in his health, his magnificent physical proportions, his buoyant and overflowing life (this was in the first ten years of my acquaintance with him), and whatever so-called oddity there was in his dress and looks arose, I think, from this peculiar consciousness or pride. We all thought that his costume suited him, and liked every part of it except his hat. He wore a soft French beaver, with rather a wide brim and a towering crown, which was always pushed up high. My sister would sometimes take it slyly just before he was ready to go, flatten the crown, and fix it more in accordance with the shape worn by others. All in vain; invariably on taking it up his fist would be thrust inside, and it would speedily assume its original dimensions.

'One day, in 1858 I think, he came to see us, and after talking awhile on various matters, he announced, a little diffidently I thought, that he had written a new piece. In answer to our inquiries, he said it was about a mocking bird, and was founded on a real incident. My mother suggested that he bring it over and read to us, which he promised to do. In some doubt, in spite of this assurance, we were, therefore, agreeably surprised when a few days after he appeared with the manuscript of "Out of the Cradle Endlessly Rocking" in his pocket. At first he wanted one of us to read it. Mr. A. took it and read it through with great appreciation and feeling. He then asked my mother to read it, which she did. And finally, at our special request, he read it himself. That evening comes before me now as one of the most enjoyable of my life. At each reading fresh beauties revealed themselves to me. I could not say whose reading I preferred; he liked my mother's, and Mr. A. liked his. After the three readings were over, he asked each one of us what we would suggest in any way, and I can remember how taken aback and nonplussed I was when he turned and asked me also.

'He once (I forget what we were talking about — friendship, I think) said there was a wonderful depth of meaning ("at second or third removes," as he called it) in the old tales of mythology. In that of Cupid and Psyche, for instance; it meant to him that the ardent expression in words of affection often tended to destroy affection. It was like the golden fruit which turned to ashes upon being grasped, or even touched. As an illustration, he mentioned the case of a young man he was in the habit of meeting every morning where he went to work. He said there had grown up between them a delightful silent friendship and sympathy. But one morning when he went as usual to the office, the young man came forward, shook him violently by the hand, and expressed in heated language the affection he felt for him. Mr. Whitman said that all the subtle charm of their unspoken friendship was from that time gone. . . .

'One evening in 1866, while he was stopping with us in New York, the tea bell had been rung ten minutes or more when he came down from his room, and we all gathered around the table. I remarked him as he entered the room; there seemed to be a peculiar brightness and elation about him, an almost irrepressible joyousness, which shone from his face and seemed to pervade his whole body. It was the more noticeable as his ordinary mood was one of quiet, yet cheerful serenity. I knew he had been working at a new edition of his book, and I hoped if he had an opportunity he would say something to let us into the secret of his mysterious joy. Unfortunately most of those at the table were occupied with some subject of conversation; at every pause I waited eagerly for him to speak; but no, some one else would begin again, until I grew almost wild with impatience and vexation. He appeared to listen, and would even laugh at some of the remarks that were made, yet he did not utter a single word during the meal; and his face still wore that singular brightness and delight, as though he had partaken of some divine elixir. His expression was so remarkable that I might have doubted my own observation, had it not been noticed by another as well as myself.

'I never heard him allude directly but once to what has been so severely condemned in his books. It happened in this way. He had come on from Washington and was stopping with us at the time (it was in 1866), preparing the new edition of "Leaves of Grass" just spoken of. My mother and I were busy sewing in the sitting-room when he came back from a two hours' absence and threw himself on the lounge. He said he had been offered very favorable terms by a publisher down town (we were living in the upper part of New York at that time) if he would consent to leave out a few lines from two of his pieces. "But I dare not do it," he said; "I dare not leave out or alter what is so genuine, so indispensable, so lofty, so pure." Those were his exact words. The intense, I might almost say religious, earnestness with which they were uttered made an impression upon me that I shall never forget.'

See also the simple affection of Walt's correspondence with Mrs. Abby Price in Brooklyn, after he has left New York for Washington in 1863:

Washington, October 11, 1863

Dear Friend: your letters were both received, and were indeed welcome ... You must write me just as often as you conveniently can. — Tell me all about your folks, especially the girls ... Tell me about Mrs. U. and the dear little rogues ... You wrote about Emma, her thinking she might and ought to come as nurse for the soldiers. Dear girl, I know it would be a blessed thing for the men to have her loving spirit and hand. But, my darling, it is a dreadful thing — you don't know these wounds, sickness, etc., ... sometimes the wounds full of crawling corruption.... Abby, I think often about you and the pleasant days, the visits I used to pay you, and how good it was always to be made so welcome. Oh, I wish I could come in this afternoon and have a good tea with you, and have three or four hours of mutual comfort, and rest and talk, and be all of us together again. : ... [13]

These simple, heartfelt letters reveal a Whitman more like a lonely boy away from home than the great democrat Thoreau had visited a few years earlier, or the blusterer celebrating his ego we must inevitably associate with the early poems of the 'Leaves of Grass.' And it is a true Whitman, no 'shadow,' but Whitman as he was with those he was fond of, when he was neither defensive nor creative. There was also a Whitman obsessed with passion in love of whom we know very little outside of his poetry. But the loving, affectionate, kindly Whitman, liking people who liked him, not for his poems, but for himself, can easily be forgotten in a biography, where aspects of eternity, abnormalities, exaggerations, and the dramatic generally tempt a biographer to make his book a series of posed portraits like Whitman's own photographs.

There was, for example, a reason for his frequent presence at Pfaff's which was not even remotely commercial. He liked, as he said, to observe, and had to keep up his own stock with writers, and with editors like Henry Clapp. But his pleasure there (as well as elsewhere in the city) seems to have been in the company of quite undistinguished young men of whom he was fond, and who, very clearly, regarded him not as a potential celebrity, but as a friend.[14] I quote these letters from Washington here, because the reference is to an earlier New York:

Washington, March 19, 1863
Dear Nat and Fred Gray:
... Now you write to me good long letters, my own boys. You, Bloom, give me your address particular, dear friend. . . . Also write me about Charles Chauncey. Tell me about everybody. For, dearest gossips, as the heart [sic] panteth, etc., so my soul after any and all sorts of items about you all. My darling, dearest boys, if I could be with you this hour, long enough to take only just three mild hot rums, before cool weather closes.

Washington, August 7, 1863
Dear Hugo,[15] ... Write oftener — you express your thoughts perfectly — do you not know how much more agreeable to me is the conversation or writing that does not take hard paved tracks,

the usual and stereotyped, but has little peculiarities and even kinks of its own, making its genuineness — its vitality? Dear friend, your letters are precious to me — none I have ever received from anyone are more so.... And Charles Russell — how I should like to see him — how like to have one of our old times again — Ah Fred, and you dear Hugo, and you repentant one with the dark shining whiskers — must there not be an hour, an evening in the future when we four returning concentrating New Yorkward or elsewhere, shall meet, allowing no interloper, and have our drinks and things, and resume the chain and consolidate and achieve a night better and mellower than ever, — we four?

Washington, October 8, 1863

Dear Hugo, ... Dear comrade, you must be assured that my heart is much with you in New York, & with my other dear friends, your associates.... I want to see you, to be within hand's reach of you, and hear your voices, even if only for one evening for only three hours — I want to hear Perk's fiddle ... — for so it happened for our dear times, when we first got acquainted, (we recked not of them as they passed,) were so good, so hearty, those friendship times, our talk, our knitting together, it may be a whim, but I think nothing could be better or quieter & more happy of the kind — & is there any better kind in life's experiences? —

And this was the tone of Whitman's affectionate letters to his family, and especially his mother, who was the emotional centre of his life. He is colloquial with these friends, he is often downright ungrammatical with her, as if responding affectionately, as he probably did in conversation, to her homely talk.

CHAPTER XV

'Are you the new person drawn toward me?'

EXCEPT for Bryant, Whitman had never met on terms of equality, respect, and friendliness any man of his own calibre, had never associated with minds capable of understanding the width and depth of his imagination. Now the 'Leaves,' his *carte de visite* to posterity, began to bring to his door the first of a lengthy succession of visitors who sought him out for what he had written rather than for friendly contacts. As early as 1856, this began.

Emerson had lent his copy of the first edition to Henry Thoreau, or bought another for him. Thoreau, who had published his *carte de visite* for the future, 'Walden,' only two years before, possessed a mental nose as long as his physical one for radical thinking. He had been engaged in the autumn of 1856 to survey Marcus Springer's proposed colony of serious thinkers in New Jersey, near Perth Amboy. On the way, at the urging of Alcott who had also read the 'Leaves,' he met that peripatetic philosopher in New York, and went to see what manner of man this Walt Whitman might be. Both knew of Emerson's mighty greeting to the book, and they evidently regarded themselves as surveyors of the new genius, if genius he was. For Emerson had committed himself deeply to the reputation of 'the American poem,' as he called it, written by a man who was quite evidently in temperament vastly different from himself.[1]

In 1855, he had described Whitman in a letter to J. E. Cabot as 'hurt by hard life & too animal experience,' which was a bad guess.[2] And two years later he was to write to his dear friend, Caroline Sturgis Tappan, of 'Our wild Whitman, with real inspiration but choked by titanic abdomen,' an excellent criticism of the more turgid and symbol-choked passages of the *Song of Myself*, provided one understands, as Caroline probably did, all that Emerson meant by 'abdomen.' It was difficult for a Brahmin to be specific in writing of Whitman to a New England lady!

Clearly the man as well as the book should be seen by his Concord defenders. As Emerson's letter to Walt has been said to be the most important letter in American literary history, so the meetings between Thoreau and Whitman are among the most interesting in our biographical record. Here were two men determined to be ranked as major in nineteenth-century literature, but as yet, in spite of their maturity, regarded, if regarded at all by the knowing, as obscure eccentrics. Here were two rebels against the materialism of their expansive epoch and two byproducts of its spiritual expansiveness. Here were two preachers of the same doctrine: make a living when you have to, but first of all and last of all, really live. And two intuitive philosophers who called for simplicity, and a life of the mind and the spirit and the healthy, hearty body, in an age and a country that was making a cult of comfort, luxury, wealth, and the power of wealth. Two men who wrote from inner necessity, and to lift and chasten, not to please or drug their neighbors. Two personalities, two individualists *à outrance*, two deep and intense lovers of their native soil, though one loved, Transcendentally, a continent, and the other just the fields and streams of Concord. Also two men who would have assuredly walked upright even in God's presence, because they had dedicated themselves to the religion of love. Call them two representative, though not typical, men of the American 1840's and 1850's, or call them two unique specimens of *genus homo*. Both statements are true.

But the differences were even more significant, and Henry and Walt felt them as instinctively as two dogs of different households. Henry was a spiritual democrat, which is not very different from an intellectual aristocrat. He would be governed by no dictator, but no en-masse either. One earned one's right to liberty, and he thought that even his Concord farmers were not deserving of their freedom any more. All things were accomplished by one man, he felt. The individual can be what he wills, but he must will it. As for Walt, it was the masses, our common humanity, who really achieved — their welfare was the objective, their leaders must be chosen from among themselves. He himself was interested in becoming articulate only when he represented them — the good, the indifferent, and the evil. Evil was a deficiency of good, to be hated perhaps but not scorned. So Thoreau thought also, but Whitman was prepared to love all genuine men and women, which Henry definitely was not.

Yet they differed far more as to means than as to ends. I suspect that Walt in thinking of their conversation must have been reminded of his favorite book of youth, the 'A Few Days in Athens' of the reformer Frances Wright.[3] There, Epicurus, noble of visage as Walt wished to be and was, meets the equally noble Zeno, teacher of Stoicism. Epicurus follows pleasure wherever pleasure nobly can be found. Zeno refuses the pleasures of the senses because they are so often uncontrolled. Whitman felt and said that the austere Thoreau, who did not like sweaty politics and clearly was neither an esthete nor a lover of women, was prejudiced, which was precisely what Epicurus said of Zeno. Thoreau, as I have said elsewhere, believed that there was too much pleasure per pound of uplift in Whitman's passion. Only the pure could afford to be passionate. The fault was not with Whitman's honesty, which he approved, but with the low ideals of love as currently practised.[4]

And, indeed, and finally, Henry was a congenital Puritan and Walt, whatever his puritanisms may have been before his blood began to run, was definitely not. Henry was New England, a perfectionist in morals as well as in the intellect. Walt was a half-Quaker who consulted his flesh as much as his inner light. And Henry was a countryman, Walt a Cockney. Perhaps that made them feel ill at ease together more than anything else. Can you imagine Walt at Walden Pond? Yes, with some hot rum and women visitors, and someone to do the gardening. Yes, after he was paralyzed. Can you imagine Henry reading one of God's lessons in the eyes of a New Orleans quadroon? The answer is in the negative.

In Brooklyn, in November of 1856, the two Concordians called on Whitman. He was out the first time, but Mrs. Whitman, whom Henry evidently took to, was baking cakes and let Thoreau get some in the kitchen, which indicates an unbending from Thoreau's usual stiffness with strangers and is a tribute to Mrs. Whitman. The next day, taking a Mrs. Tyndall with them, a 'solid walrus of a woman,' so Alcott described her, they went again, and found Whitman in his attic study, probably in his striped calico jacket, red flannel undershirt, and overalls, as Alcott had seen him in October.[5] He had told Alcott that he had never been sick, nor taken medicine, nor sinned, and so was quite innocent of repentance, which would have pleased Thoreau, who did not believe in repentance.

As for Henry and Walt, at first 'each seemed planted fast in reserves [Alcott speaking], surveying the other curiously, — like two beasts, each wondering what the other would do, whether to snap or run; and it came to no more than cold compliments between them.'[6] I doubt whether they snapped. It was not Whitman's way, and Thoreau was clearly interested to a high pitch. Walt was always a little distrustful of Bostonians and if Thoreau surveyed curiously 'the savage sovereign of the flesh,' as Alcott called Whitman, it was no more than his usual manner with the woodchucks he was so fond of. It took two letters to his friend H. G. Blake to discharge his strong impressions from this interview:

'He is apparently the greatest democrat the world has seen. Kings and aristocracy go by the board at once, as they have long deserved to. A remarkably strong though coarse nature, of a sweet disposition, and much prized by his friends. Though peculiar and rough in his exterior, his skin (all over [?]) red, he is essentially a gentleman. I am still somewhat in a quandary about him, — feel that he is essentially strange to me, at any rate; but I am surprised by the sight of him. He is very broad, but, as I have said, not fine. He said that I misapprehended him. I am not quite sure that I do. He told us that he loved to ride up and down Broadway all day on an omnibus, sitting beside the driver, listening to the roar of the carts, and sometimes gesticulating and declaiming Homer at the top of his voice. He has long been an editor and writer for the newspapers, — was editor of the *New Orleans Crescent* once; but now has no employment but to read and write in the forenoon, and walk in the afternoon, like all the rest of the scribbling gentry.'

'That Walt Whitman, of whom I wrote to you, is the most interesting fact to me at present. I have just read his second edition (which he gave me), and it has done me more good than any reading for a long time. Perhaps I remember best the poem of Walt Whitman, an American, and the Sun-Down Poem.[7] There are two or three pieces in the book which are disagreeable, to say the least; simply sensual. He does not celebrate love at all. It is as if the beasts spoke. I think that men have not been ashamed of themselves without reason. No doubt there have always been dens where such deeds were unblushingly recited, and it is no merit to compete with their inhabitants. But even on this side he has spoken more truth than any American or modern that I know. I have found his poem exhilarating, encouraging. As for its sensuality, — and it may turn out to be less sensual than it appears, — I do not so much wish that those parts were not written, as that men and women were so pure that they could read them without harm, that is, without understanding them. One woman told me that no woman could read it, — as if a man could read what a woman could not. Of course Walt Whitman can communicate to us no experience, and if we are shocked, whose experience is it that we are reminded of?

'On the whole, it sounds to me very brave and American, after whatever deductions. I do not believe that all the sermons, so called, that have been preached in this land put together are equal to it for preaching.

'We ought to rejoice greatly in him. He occasionally suggests something a little more than human. You can't confound him with the other inhabitants of Brooklyn or New York. How they must shudder when they read him! He is awfully good.

'To be sure I sometimes feel a little imposed on. By his heartiness and broad generalities he puts me into a liberal frame of mind prepared to see wonders, — as it were, sets me upon a hill or in the midst of a plain, — stirs me well up, and then —throws in a thousand of brick. Though rude, and sometimes ineffectual, it is a great primitive poem, — an alarum or trumpet-note ringing through the American camp. Wonderfully like the Orientals, too, considering that when I asked him if he had read them, he answered, "No: tell me about them."

'I did not get far in conversation with him, — two more being present, — and among the few things which I chanced to say, I remember that one was, in answer to him as representing America, that I did not think much of America or of politics, and so on, which may have been somewhat of a damper to him.

'Since I have seen him, I find that I am not disturbed by any brag or egoism in his book. He may turn out the least of a braggart of all, having a better right to be confident.

'He is a great fellow.' [8]

2

Mrs. Gilchrist later reminded Whitman that even Nature has her reticences, which is a better criticism than Thoreau's of Whitman's sexual frankness. It is certain that if the beasts spoke, they would say nothing resembling the *Songs of Adam* or *Calamus*, and it was the intellectual and spiritual delight in sensuousness which offended the genteel age. Beasts would use four-letter words where Walt used symbols, which is another difference. However, Thoreau's estimate of values in the 'Leaves' is superior to any criticism written at the time of first publication. He got what so many missed, that this was one of the greatest sermons preached in the nineteenth century.

Walt, as might be expected, had only one criticism of Thoreau, once he saw that he was not Bostonian but a plain fellow who would eat cakes in the kitchen and went to the heart of the matter about life. He said to Traubel of this meeting:

' "Thoreau had his own odd ways. Once he got to the house while I was out — went straight to the kitchen where my dear mother was baking some cakes — took the cakes hot from the oven. He was always doing things of the plain sort — without fuss. I liked all that about him. But Thoreau's great fault was disdain — disdain for men (for Tom, Dick, and Harry): inability to appreciate the average life — even the exceptional life: it seemed to me a want of imagination. He couldn't put his life into any other life — realize why one man was so and another man was not so: was impatient with other people on the street and so forth. We had a hot discussion about it — it was a bitter difference: it was rather a surprise to me to meet in Thoreau such a very aggravated case of superciliousness. It was egotistic — not taking that word in its worst sense." Corning broke out: "He was simply selfish, that's the long and short of it." W. replied: "That may be the short of it but it's not the long. Selfish? No — not selfish in the way you mean, though selfish, sure enough, in a higher interpretation of that term. We could not agree at all in our estimate of men — of the men we meet here, there, everywhere — the concrete man. Thoreau had an abstraction about man — a right abstraction: there we agreed. We had our quarrel only on this ground. Yet he was a man you would have to like — an interesting man, simple, conclusive."' [9]

And later, to Mrs. Gilchrist, Walt said that he was offended for 'my Brooklyn' when Henry, walking with him on what was evidently another occasion, perhaps in May of 1858,[10] asked what he saw in the people, in 'all this cheating political corruption.' This is Henry sneering at the town and its dregs and dragglements, as he did at New York in his letters and his journals, not, I should say, Thoreau sneering at democracy. Politics and democracy meant different things to him, and he had never, like Whitman, had to bring them together. But Thoreau did shrink from the full implications of democracy. That is what Emerson must have meant when he said to Walt, 'Henry...shrinks from some formidable things in you — in your book, in your personality — over which I rejoice.' [11]

Yet, talking later with his friend Harned,[12] Whitman hesitated whether to put Emerson or Thoreau first in eminence. 'Thoreau was a surprising fellow...one of the native forces...not so precious, tender, a personality as Emerson: but he was a force —

he looms up bigger and bigger.... One thing about Thoreau keeps him very near to me...his lawlessness — his dissent — his going his own absolute road let hell blaze all it chooses.' And Whitman remembered gratefully Henry's surprise when he questioned 'reprobates' as too severe a term for the critics of the 'Leaves.' 'Do you regard that as a severe word? reprobates? what they really deserve is something...more caustic.'[13] This was hardly a cold compliment. New England and Long Island, Concord and New York. They could not melt, the extraordinary thing is that they recognized that God spoke in both languages and had been understood.

3

Would that the cosmic Emerson (more truly cosmic in a scholar's sense than Walt) had left pen portraits equivalent to these. He had many sessions with Whitman, the first of which was probably at the Astor House in New York in January of 1857.[14] For he saw, better than Thoreau, the scope of the man, how representative he was of the expansive and uncontrolled vigor of the United States. This is what he meant when he said to Moncure Conway, 'Americans abroad may now come home: unto us a man is born.'[15] It was what he meant by calling the first 'Leaves' 'the American poem.' But Walt, as John Burroughs said, was too physical for Emerson. He had too much abdomen, as Emerson euphemistically put it. The Sage of Concord did not like Whitman's calling for beer in a tin mug at Emerson's hotel (wasn't it perhaps pewter, and wasn't that the right way to drink beer anywhere in New York?). He did not like some fireman friends into whose company Whitman introduced him. He was disappointed in some of his later poems. 'I expect — him — to make — the songs of the Nation — but he seems — to be contented to — make the inventories,'[16] so he said later, a touch of the kind of wit of which Walt was incapable, but superficial except as esthetic criticism. He remarked that he would have made the *buts* stronger in his famous letter if he had known it was to be published. Though Whitman asserted that Emerson wrote him many letters after the first, none have been found, which probably indicates that they were only notes. He probably did not wish to risk another blanket statement, which might again be used for publicity.[17] Yet it is certain that Emerson was not repelled by the frankness of Whitman's poems — he was only disturbed. He wanted the 'Leaves' to be read, and he knew that the franker passages would make trouble, and limit acceptance, as they did. So did Walt, at least after 1855, but he felt that sexuality was vital to his scheme, and, leaving questions of taste aside, he was right.

And Whitman, who called Emerson master until he got his roots in the ground,[18] was unquestionably right in saying that Emerson never went back on his first endorsement, though wrong in asserting in later life that the 1855 book owed nothing to his influence. 'The atmosphere between us was always sweet. . . . He belonged to us,' not just to the 'literary classes.' They met more than twenty times, best when strolling up and down the Boston Common.

If there was a blind spot in Emerson, it was for Whitman's superb technique in his later poems. Apparently he shared Whitman's own opinion that *the* American bard would come later — took it literally as Whitman did not, for he failed to include anything of Whitman's in his anthology of American poetry. As a man, as a promise, as a representative, he never ceased to believe in him, but, fastidious to a fault, when his friends accused him of too high praise for Whitman's virility, he may have often made a 'whinnying sound' as he did to Edward Carpenter,[19] and been content to say at the worst, that Whitman had promise, '*burt* he is a wayward fanciful man.' He would unquestionably have preferred a Whitman house-broken to Concord, precisely as he would have preferred a Thoreau who stuck to Transcendental natural history. Yet Whitman was right, he never went back on his prophecy of greatness, though he felt, as he felt with Lincoln at first, that it was too rough for his perfectionist taste. Whitman said that Emerson loved him always for 'something I brought him from the rush of the big cities and the mass of men,' [20] and that was the truth. He loved him, I think, rather too much to set down a characterization in which he would have had to be rather unpleasant about abdomens and egoisms and sexualities, which were difficult for a Concord man to describe without falsifying greatness. It is doubtful whether he felt, as Thoreau did, that this surprisingly gentle representative of the American roughs was really a gentleman, but he was too much of a gentleman himself to say so, too much of a scholar to think this deficiency detracted from greatness, too much of an experienced man-of-letters not to feel that it might defer the recognition and perfection of greatness — as it did.

4

I shall quote one more intellectual's impression of the Whitman of this period. It belongs to the early sixties, but would have surely been the same in the fifties, and it suggests in Whitman those elements of scope, freedom, and wide-sweeping airs in a kindly nature which his family and his New York and Brooklyn cronies missed because they were too close to their friend.

John Burroughs, the naturalist, had been powerfully impressed by the 'Leaves.' As a young clerk in Washington, he met Whitman, and soon became a close friend and companion of his walks. Perhaps he also would not have felt the continental breadth of the man if he had not read his book, but at least the impact upon him of the personality was as strong as had been his reading. I quote from 'Whitman A Study' which was a revision of Burroughs' early 'Notes on Walt Whitman, as Poet and Person,' the first book on Whitman:

'When I came to meet the poet himself, which was in the fall of 1863, I felt less concern about his [egoism and his attitude toward evil] ... ; he was so sound and sweet and gentle and attractive as a man, and withal so wise and tolerant, that I soon came to feel the same confidence in the book that I at once placed in its author. ... I saw that the work and the man were one, and that the former must be good as the latter was good. There was something in the manner in which both the book and its author carried themselves under the sun, and in the way they confronted America and the present time, that convinced beyond the power of logic or criticism. . . .

'One would see him afar off, in the crowd but not of it, — a large, slow-moving figure, clad in gray, with broad-brimmed hat and gray beard — or, quite as frequently, on the front platform of the street horse-cars with the driver. . . . There were times during this period when . . . the physical man was too pronounced on first glance. . . . One needed to see the superbly domed head and classic brow crowning the rank physical man. . . .

'Whitman was of large mould in every way, and of bold, far-reaching schemes, and is very sure to fare better at the hands of large men than of small. The first and last impression which his personal presence always made upon one was of a nature wonderfully gentle, tender, and benignant. . . . I was impressed by the fine grain and clean, fresh quality of the man. . . . He always had the look of a man who had just taken a bath.'

Burroughs, as much an enemy of the genteel age as Whitman himself, was a little timid. Like many nature lovers, he was hesitant in the face of carnal nature when it showed itself to be as instinctive in a man or woman as in a stag or a woodchuck. Whitman loved him, but doubted sometimes whether he was 'one of us,' a true believer that the flesh and the spirit are intertwined in an equal importance. But he misjudged Burroughs' devotion, which knew no criticism except when Walt began to write about birds and nature generally, where, indeed, even Thoreau had failed to satisfy the naturalist's professional competency. Burroughs' description is a real picture of a real man, only slightly posed, a man who in his appearance and his personality was clearly not the aggressive egoist of his book. Nevertheless, as Burroughs said, and as will easily be made manifest, the two were one, the difference was between the expression of personality in love and kindliness and its expression in art.

5

Slightly posed. There is another aspect of Whitman which belongs in this chapter, and which must have been familiar to all his friends, as it was to Burroughs, though it was not displayed for their benefit. Unhappily, it is too familiar to those who knew only a little about Whitman. They see in his numerous pictures always a pose, an attitude, as of one who knows that he is photogenic and has thought of a new posture of expression to present to the camera. Whitman's own frequent remarks to his admirers about the defect of this bust, or that photograph, would seem faintly absurd if they were not so acute in criticism, and so revealing of a purpose beyond vanity. For even as he felt that as representative man, he should be clean, healthy, handsome, full-blooded, and virile, so he wished his pictures to represent his idea of the editor, the journalist, the Bohemian, or of the seer, the prophet, the bard, or whatever he felt that he was at the time.

The vanity — for there was some vanity — was philosophical. He was a simple, separate person, but, according to his faith, he was large, ample, able to identify himself with anyone. A great man should look great. He must stand out in the street like a crag in the woods. He must be felt on first view to be someone; on second view, to be Walt Whitman. If Lincoln, as reported on fair authority, noting Walt on the sidewalks, said 'Well, *he* looks a *man*,' why, that was as it should be. He must be a *man*, or he would never carry out his 'Leaves of Grass.' And if distinctive clothing helped, let it be adopted. He was angry when in Morse's bust the brim of his hat was made too narrow. Not even the Prices could induce him to bash down the crown. As he wrote to Mrs. Price in the letter already quoted: 'Everybody here is so like everybody else — and I am Walt Whitman.'

Whitman's attitudinizings were not really poses, they were parts, like the tragedian's parts he followed with such enthusiasm in youth. He was playing up to his duty and his destiny of being the bard of democracy. If he needed a prompter's cue, he might have got it from Fanny Wright's description of Epicurus in his favorite book, already mentioned, 'A Few Days in Athens.'

'The features were not cast for the statuary; they were noble but not regular. Wisdom beamed mildly from the eye, and candour was on the broad forehead: the mouth reposed in a soft, almost imperceptible smile, that did not curl the lips or disturb the cheeks, and was seen only in the serene and holy benignity that shone over the whole physiognomy. . . . The hair indeed seemed prematurely touched by time for it was of a pure silver, thrown back from the forehead, and fringing the throat behind with short curls. . . . "We want but the will said Epicurus to be as great as Zeno. . . . Without confidence Homer had never written his Iliad — No, nor would Zeno now be worshipped in his portico."'

And even so, writing an anonymous blurb, does Whitman describe himself. Though he sometimes 'appears gross, repellent, and dangerous' —

'His complete and permanent character — and that is the only just method of comprehending him — is nevertheless healthy, free, manly, attractive, and of a purity and strength almost beyond example. The basis of his principal poetry is the intuitional and emotional actuated by what the phrenologists term self-esteem and adhesiveness. Like all revolutionists and founders, he himself will have to create the growth by which he is to be fully understood and accepted. This will be a slow and long work, but sure.'[21] Add, from another self-portrait already quoted: 'Coarse, sanguine complexion; strong, bristly, grizzled beard; singular eyes, of a semi-transparent, indistinct blue, and with that sleepy look that comes when the lid rests half way down over the pupil; careless, lounging gait.'

He was clearly trying, sometimes at least, in these photographs, to appear an Epicurus of his own times, since, like Epicurus, he believed virtue could be learned through pleasure, and that life was to be lived, not shrunk from. As Epicurus, in Fanny's story, looked like a god to the startled Theon, so Walt Whitman should look like a man to the petrified Yankees.[22] 'How can you stand it?' Emerson was to ask Whitman later, speaking of his hospital experiences, surprised at the gaiety of tone, the flirting with life, which is evident in some of his letters. The answer is, that not only a passionate pity for suffering, but also the ferment of the 'Leaves,' and a deep, sometimes agonizing concern for the fate of the Union, were perturbing his inner life through all these years. He had to keep confidence in himself and in his book, and perhaps this attitudinizing, like his genial gaiety, helped him as much as it helped his publicity.

CHAPTER XVI

〰〰〰

'The people sprawl with yearning, aimless hands'

WE OF this generation, who have seen two wars, and the loud-voiced divisions which inevitably, in a democracy, precede a conflict, can better understand the fifties and sixties of the American nineteenth century than did our immediate predecessors. Looking backward to such a turbulent period, it is easy for the inexperienced to assume that all were supporters of this or that extreme and partisan view, and that all were excited together. But the decade of the 1850's, like the decade of the 1930's, shows fewer clear blacks and whites than series of blending and rapidly changing grays. And interest in the approaching crisis ran, in the earlier decade as in the later, all the way from a determination to make war down to no concern whatsoever.

Politically, Whitman belonged with the grays to the very outbreak of the war, but in no sense with the unconcerned. I have explained in an earlier chapter why and how he threw over politics as a profession — yet it would be a grave error to deduce from the long series of poems of passion in the 1860 edition of the 'Leaves' that he was too obsessed with unresolved sexuality to think and feel politically, as he had so strongly in the past. It is probably true that he suffered more from the progress of the Union toward disruption than from all of his personal problems combined. Certainly his most violent outbursts (too violent to be poetical) in these years deal with what he thought was the decadence of democracy, not with the opposition to his book or the pangs of passion unsatisfied. Sexuality for him was indispensable to love, and there were deep perturbations of sexual passion troubling him in the latter 1850's. But love, for Walt, had for its ultimate objective the binding together of men and women in an ideal democracy. And this was a decade of rising hate.

Democracy was on trial, both the democratic processes of our government, and essential democracy itself. With both, Whitman was deeply concerned, but most of all with essential democracy. I shall explain just what he meant by that in a later chapter.

As a young editor, Whitman had been a fanatical believer in the future of the Republic, provided the ideas of Jefferson and Jackson could be made to prevail. His first great disillusion, as has been recorded, was with parties. His second was with presidents. In the 1850's, not only did his party disintegrate beneath his feet, but in three 'presidentiads,' as he called them — Fillmore's, Pierce's, Buchanan's — he saw cowardice and compromise bring his beloved country to the brink of disunion, with the great brotherhood of the American democracy, whose strength and love and new virility he had chanted, silent, helpless, or inflamed with prejudice and hate. When it was all over and war and destruction had settled what democratic statesmanship could not, he wrote sadly that the villainy and shallowness of rulers (back'd by the machinery of great parties) are just as eligible to these States as to any foreign despotism, kingdom, or empire — there is not a bit of difference. 'Once before the war,' he continued, 'I was filled with doubt and gloom.' A foreigner had said to him, 'putting in form, indeed, my own observations,' that America was honeycombed with infidelism, even as to its own program. The brazen hell-faces of secession and slavery were gazing defiantly from every window. Thieves and scalawags were arranging the nominations to office. The North was as full of bad stuff as the South. Millions of honest democrats were the 'helpless supple-jacks' of comparatively few politicians. Parties shamelessly usurped the government for their own party purposes.[1]

He went further in his reaction from confidence. In a remarkable document, most of it written, apparently, in the late sixties or early seventies, but not published until 1882, and called then 'Origins of Attempted Secession,'[2] he put the blame for the Civil War upon the incapacity of the rulers of both sections. There was as much ultimate responsibility for the war, and about as much sympathy for the vested interests of slavery, in the North as in the South. Secession was not more favored by the slave-owners than by those who traded with them. The great surprise for the politicians was that, in the North, the people were resolved to fight for the Union, while so many of their supposed leaders were quite willing to let the South go its way. It was clear that there had been a breakdown in representative government; appeasers had got hold of this government, and, failing to stop the extremists, or to represent the real will of the people, North or South, had made war inevitable. This is how Whitman felt, and he believed that the root of the trouble was not so much in the South as in New York, Pennsylvania, Ohio, where politicians were most in control. 'I say secession, below the surface, originated and was brought to maturity in the free states.' And those presidents to whom the defence of the Union was entrusted, who symbolized that Union, how had they been chosen, why were they such weaklings that only an emergence of a strong man at the last possible moment and the terrible resort to Civil War had saved from disruption the great American experiment?

I have already printed on page 131 of this book his earlier answer to that question, but now he repeats his invectives against that still malodorous evil of national politics, the presidential convention, and adds a new range of epithets as he realized how near the country had come to destruction, and might again. It is a classic among American diatribes, and should be better known especially among those who think of Walt as a blend of sweetness, light, and sensuality:[3]

'Let me give a schedule, or list, of one of these representative conventions for a long time before, and inclusive of, that which nominated Buchanan. (Remember they had to be the fountains and tissues of the American body politic, forming, as it were, the whole blood, legislation, office-holding, &c.) One of these conventions, from 1840 to '60, exhibited a spectacle such as could never be seen except in our own age and in these States. The members who composed it were, seven eighths of them, the meanest kind of bawling and blowing office-holders, office-seekers, pimps, malignants, conspirators, murderers, fancy men, custom-house clerks, contractors, kept-editors, spaniels well-train'd to carry and fetch, jobbers, infidels, disunionists, terror-ists, mail-riflers, slave-catchers, pushers of slavery, creatures of the would-be Presidents, spies, bribers, compromisers, lobbyers, sponges, ruin'd sports, expell'd gamblers, policy-backers, monte-dealers, duellists, carriers of concealed weapons, deaf men, pimpled men, scarr'd inside with vile disease, gaudy outside with gold chains made from the people's money and harlots' money twisted together; crawling, serpentine men, the lousy combings and born freedom-sellers of the earth. And whence came they? From back-yards and bar-rooms; from out of the custom-houses, marshals' offices, post-offices, and gambling-hells; from the Presi-dent's house, the jail, the station-house; from unnamed by-places, where devilish disunion was hatch'd at midnight; from political hearses and from the coffins inside, and from the shrouds inside of the coffins; from the tumors and abscesses of the land; from the skeletons and skulls in the vaults of the federal alms-houses; and from the running sores of the great cities. Such, I say, form'd, or absolutely controll'd the forming of, the entire personnel, the atmosphere, nutriment and chyle, of our munic-ipal, State, and national politics — substantially permeating, handling, deciding, and wielding everything — legislation, nomi-nations, elections, "public sentiment," &c. — while the great masses of the people, farmers, mechanics, and traders, were helpless in their gripe. These conditions were mostly prevalent in the North and West, and especially in New York and Phila-delphia cities; and the Southern leaders (bad enough, but of a far higher order) struck hands and affiliated with, and used them. Is it strange that a thunder-storm follow'd such morbid and stifling cloud-strata?'

Impossible to believe, after reading this, that Walt Whitman in the 1850's, is to be regarded merely as a victim of suppressed and warped sexuality, or as an ignorant optimist trumpeting an easy triumph for democracy.

2

Many decisions of belief and policy were troubling him — as they were troubling Lincoln at the same period. He thought that Lincoln had the advantage in the war of words in the famous Illinois debates, but was pleased when Douglas won the election. A congenital Democrat in spite of his attacks upon the 'dead-rabbit' conservatives and wire-pullers for slavery in the party, he was still not enough of a Republican to take no satisfaction in an Independent Democrat's victory against the opposition of a cowardly administration. Also, as I have said, Douglas's policy, which was essentially to 'let the popular will defeat slavery, first in the new states where it was not yet an institution, and afterward by the logic of a changing world, in the Slave States themselves,' was close to Whitman's own. Whitman never believed with Seward and Lincoln in the 'irrepressible conflict,' and the 'house divided against itself,' although he was one with the war administration in pressing on to complete victory. He was simply incapable of feeling that sectionalism could be a primary issue in his great democracy. The enmasse were neither slave-holders in the South nor capitalists in the North. They did not make the war. Ergo, it could have been prevented.

But, like Lincoln, he distrusted reformers and extremists. His hatred grew for the slave trade, which in the fifties showed signs of revival under the stimulus of immense profits in the new cotton lands along the Mississippi. He did not approve of John Brown's attempt to begin revolt in the South, though he admired the courage of the old man.

I would sing how an old man, tall, with white hair, mounted the scaffold in
     Virginia,
(I was at hand, silent I stood with teeth shut close, I watch'd.)

But he appeared at the trial of F. B. Sanborn in Boston, who had been charged with conniving in John Brown's raid, ready, with others, to resist by force any infringement of the liberties of the individual. Yet as the Calhounites seemed to him arrogant, so his practical politician's mind grouped the Abolitionists with useless, if not dangerous, meddlers. They were idealists, but they looked to him, when he attended their convention in 1857, like a 'line of bald-headed Quaker-looking gentlemen, mostly wearing white neckcloths, generally surmounted by benevolent faces.' [4]

How far his moderation was influenced by his somewhat romantic affection for the South, it is hard to say. Certainly this was genuine enough to make him temperamentally opposed to any sectional policy based on hate. There is a naïve and charming naturalism in all of Whitman's comments on his country. He expected, and he seems usually to have got, the same response from the kind of people he liked, South and West, that he encountered in their fellow souls on Long Island. In spite of its interesting divergences, he felt as much at home on Canal Street in New Orleans as upon Broadway. Psychologically he was right. But not politically. The moral split and the economic split between North and South was greater than he had supposed, and faith in the Union was less, except, perhaps, in the West. Thoreau's first reaction to secession was to let the slave states go, and then to proceed to the moral purifying of New England. Whitman, like Lincoln, felt that the Union was the issue transcending all. He simply could not and would not believe that the common people of 'these States,' South as well as North, would not support it as he did, if only they could be heard.

Probably it was Walt's romantic affection for the South more than his faith in the West which made him keep his balance when so many Northern intellectuals were willing to sacrifice everything in order to be rid of slavery. Only Alcott among them all seems to have shared his admiration of the Southerners and the South, as persons and as a region. I am inclined to think that this enthusiasm was more romantic than realistic, bred undoubtedly in his vivid New Orleans experience, fed in the years after the war by his long life in Washington, yet always warmed by his passion for diversity in the unity of his country. There may of course have been, as his later biographers think, other journeys, other residences in the South before 1860 — perhaps lovers, perhaps a mother of his alleged children. We do not know, and there is no real evidence. The key poem for this discussion is *O Magnet South*, which he published in 1860 on the eve of armed conflict:

O MAGNET-SOUTH! O glistening perfumed South! my South!
O quick mettle, rich blood, impulse and love! good and evil! O all dear to
    me!

But this poem is a dramatization of a man whose 'birth-things' were in Virginia ('O to be a Virginian where I grew up.') and who wants to go back there, or to the Carolinas or to Tennessee. If it is Whitman speaking, then he had never been in the Carolinas. Otherwise, he would not have written

> I coast up the Carolinas,
> I see where the live-oak is growing, . . . the lemon and orange.

The orange, even in the eighteenth century when it was warmer, was a rarity on that coast, the lemon never grew there. It is Whitman's romantic affection, not Whitman's experience, which enters the poem. But whatever the cause, this romanticism must have influenced his politics. And of course he believed that under democracy there should be no sectionalism at all, except in rivalry to produce the finest men and women and the richest, most natural life.

3

There is surely enough in this chapter to prove that Whitman's passionate appeals to the common man to rise and make a new and better world are not based exclusively upon romantic optimism. He believed, with reason, that he was living in a crisis for democracy, when all his hopes for the future of the people in a New World were on the verge of frustration. Human nature itself was disappointing him. There is a bitter poem, written in, or just before, 1856, and published in that year, in which he speaks with far more directness than is usual with him when writing verse. It is not always good poetry, and probably that is why he removed it from later editions of the 'Leaves.' But it is revealing:

Respondez

Let men and women be mock'd with bodies and mock'd with Souls!
Let the love that waits in them, wait! let it die, or pass stillborn to other
    spheres!
Let the sympathy that waits in every man, wait! or let it also pass, a dwarf,
    to other spheres!
Let contradictions prevail! let one thing contradict another! and let one line
    of my poems contradict another! —
Let the people sprawl with yearning, aimless hands!...
Stifled, O days! O lands! in every public and private corruption!
Smothered in thievery, impotence, shamelessness, mountain-high;
Brazen effrontery, scheming, rolling like ocean's waves around and upon
    you, O my days! my lands!...
Let the Asiatic, the African, the European, the American, and the Aus-
    tralian, go armed against the murderous stealthiness of each other!
    let them sleep armed! let none believe in good will!

Then, with a burst of ironic, despairing egotism:

Let him who is without my poems be assassinated! [5]

And there is a sad and mellower poem, called *I Sit and Look Out*, published in 1860 and written then or a little earlier, in which his melancholy doubts of human nature under stress and temptation are imperishably recorded:

I sit and look out upon all the sorrows of the world, and upon all oppression
    and shame,
I hear secret convulsive sobs from young men at anguish with themselves,
    remorseful after deeds done,
I see in low life the mother misused by her children, dying, neglected, gaunt,
    desperate,
I see the wife misused by her husband, I see the treacherous seducer of young
    women,
I mark the ranklings of jealousy and unrequited love attempted to be hid, I
    see these sights on the earth,

I see the workings of battle, pestilence, tyranny, I see martyrs and prisoners,
I observe a famine at sea, I observe the sailors casting lots who shall be kill'd
    to preserve the lives of the rest,
I observe the slights and degradations cast by arrogant persons upon labor-
    ers, the poor, and upon negroes, and the like;
All these — all the meanness and agony without end I sitting look out upon,
See, hear, and am silent.[6]

We should realize and remember that the great poems of love and democracy which Whitman was also writing from the latter fifties onward were drawn (in a kind of Hegelian synthesis of opposites) from a confidence which transcended, but also and certainly included, the experience of complete disillusion.

CHAPTER XVII

'It is a man, flushed and full-blooded — it is I'

B ut let us get back to the main line. I say main line because whatever Walt's secret adventures, whatever his emotional perturbations, whatever his patriotic distresses and personal disappointments, all, everything fed into the poems which he was now steadily writing. 'These are indeed me.' In spite of the relative failure of his first two editions, he had hardened his resolve to make the 'Leaves' his life-work. Certainly the edition of 1860, his third, is a planned book — in order and emphasis better planned than any subsequent edition, though, of course, not so rich; very much better as a book of poetry than the famous first of 1855, as well as far more inclusive.

To an Unknown Correspondent
Brooklyn, July 20, 1857
... Fowler & Wells are bad persons for me. — They retard my book very much. — It is worse than ever. — I wish now to bring out a third edition — I have now *a hundred* poems ready (the last edition had thirty-two.) — and shall endeavor to make an arrangement with some publisher here.... In the forthcoming Vol. I shall have ... no other matter but poems — (no letters to or from Emerson — no Notices or anything of that sort.) — It is, I know Well enough, that *that* must be the *true Leaves of Grass* — and I think it has an aspect of completeness, and makes its case clearer.' [1]

He found a publisher, not in Brooklyn or New York, but in Boston — the young firm of Thayer and Eldridge. Charles W. Eldridge, who became Whitman's lifelong friend, and his close associate in the Washington years, was a young man of progressive tastes, who probably found out the 'Leaves' for himself, though it is conceivable that Emerson may have spoken a helping word. The edition was successful, although it met with the same contradictory criticisms as the first two, and, thanks to its contents, a more violent reaction from the prudish. According to Burroughs, several thousand copies were 'taken up,' but I doubt whether these figures are trustworthy.[2] Then the outbreak of the war extinguished the Southern credits of the firm, and they went bankrupt. A hypocritical and predatory publisher, Richard Worthington, called 'Holy Dick,' bought the plates, and for many years troubled Whitman with piratical issues.[3]

It may be doubted whether Whitman collected much of the royalty due him, for he gives no evidence of cash in hand in 1861, and was dependent for livelihood when he got to Washington upon free-lancing for the press. Nevertheless, his Boston experiences, while he was seeing his poems through the press, were memorable. Through Eldridge he met William O'Connor, later to be his fiery champion, also J. T. Trowbridge (author of *Darius Green and his Flying Machine*), who also befriended him in Washington. He was invading Boston, temple of American culture, at last, and in person. As a happy introduction, Lowell, in January of 1860, accepted his *Bardic Symbols*, later called *As I Ebb'd with the Ocean of Life*, and published it in *The Atlantic Monthly* for April. This was an omen of rising reputation. Lowell had not liked the 'Leaves of Grass.'

To Mrs Abby H. Price, Brooklyn.
    March 29, 1860
... I have been here in Boston, today is a fortnight, and, ... my book is well under way.... It is to be very finely printed, good paper, and new, rather large-sized type. [It was selling for five dollars a copy after the bankruptcy, according to Traubel.] ... I am more pleased with Boston than I anticipated. It is full of life, and criss-cross streets. I am very glad I came, if only to rub out of me the deficient notions I had of New England character.

2

And so he read proof, went to listen in a waterfront chapel to that apostle to the sailors and the poor, Father Taylor (whom Thoreau also admired), and walked up and down the streets of the old city. But if he flaunted for the benefit of the public his flowing beard and broad hat set slantwise, those who met him privately found a much simpler and kinder man than they expected. In 1860, said J. T. Trowbridge in his memoirs,[4] he was 'a simple, well-mannered man.'

And it was here, in this three months stay in Boston, that he talked through with Emerson the question of sexuality in his poems:

October 10–13, 1881

I spend a good deal of time on the Common, these delicious days and nights — every mid-day from 11.30 to about 1 — and almost every sunset another hour. I know all the big trees, especially the old elms along Tremont and Beacon streets, and have come to a sociable-silent understanding with most of them, in the sunlit air (yet crispy-cool enough), as I saunter along the wide unpaved walks. Up and down this breadth by Beacon street, between these same old elms, I walk'd for two hours, of a bright sharp February mid-day twenty-one years ago, with Emerson, then in his prime, keen, physically and morally magnetic, arm'd at every point, and when he chose, wielding the emotional just as well as the intellectual. During those two hours he was the talker and I the listener. It was an argument — statement, reconnoitring, review, attack, and pressing home (like an army corps in order, artillery, cavalry, infantry), of all that could be said against that part (and a main part) in the construction of my poems, 'Children of Adam.' More precious than gold to me that dissertation — it afforded me, ever after, this strange and paradoxical lesson: each point of E.'s statement was unanswerable, no judge's charge ever more complete or convincing, I could never hear the points better put — and then I felt down in my soul the clear and unmistakable conviction to disobey all, and pursue my own way. 'What have you to say then to such things?' said E., pausing in conclusion. 'Only that while I can't answer them at all, I feel more settled than ever to adhere to my own theory, and exemplify it,' was my candid response. Whereupon we went and had a good dinner at the American House. And thenceforward I never waver'd or was touch'd with qualms (as I confess I had been two or three times before.) [5]

Again and again he discussed with Traubel this advice of Emerson's. It seems to have been directed at the *Children of Adam* rather than the more ambiguous *Calamus* poems, which is another indication that Whitman's conclusion not to heed it was right. For it was not the inherent sexuality to which Emerson seems to have objected, so much as the frankness of expression. Whitman later removed some unnecessarily gross words, but he could not meet Emerson's objections without omitting whole poems. And the poems to be omitted, though frank according to the standards of that day, might be precisely the most essential to the 'rondure' of the 'Leaves': such poems as *A Woman Waits for Me* and *To a Common Prostitute*, which all could understand. When the test came years later and his book was threatened with suppression, some objectionable lines and these poems were exactly what the prosecutors finally asked should be dropped. Whitman was definitely obstinate in insisting upon his tiresome and tasteless references to, for example, 'seminal wet.' But he felt instinctively that to yield at all would not be enough unless he yielded all along the line. He was right; but so, unfortunately, was Emerson in saying that these violations of the genteel refinements of the day would be red herrings throwing his readers off the scent of greatness, and restricting his sales.

These walks and talks with Emerson, initiated by the older poet, made this visit memorable, but left Whitman more firmly convinced than ever that in his nature he represented a vigor and warmth of humanity that neither Transcendentalism nor the exalted Puritanism of Concord could satisfy or express.

'Emerson,' he said years later, in *Collect*,[6] 'is best as critic or diagnoser. Not passion or imagination or warp or weakness, or any pronounced cause or speciality, dominates him. Cold and bloodless intellectuality dominates him. (I know the fires, emotions, love, egotisms, glow deep, perennial, as in all New Englanders — but the façade, hides them well — they give no sign.) ... His final influence is to make his students cease to worship anything. ... Suppose these books becoming absorb'd ... what a well-wash'd and grammatical, but bloodless and helpless, race we should turn out! ... Of *power* he seems to have a gentleman's admiration —' This is not a fair indictment, though it is accurate as far as it goes. Nor is it generous. Not once in their many talks did Emerson complain of the sneers and innuendoes directed at him for sponsoring a foul-mouthed Brooklyn rough.

Burroughs was wrong in saying that Walt was Emerson in the concrete. Rather, he was Emerson's complement in the representation of America. Taking the master's conception of a viable spirit in all things, he extended it into familiar human nature, where Emerson could not reach for lack of knowledge; and indeed, this familiar humanity never could become Emersonian because what was possible for the saint was impossible, and undesirable, for the mass. As they walked and talked together, Whitman must have felt, as he felt with Thoreau, that too much love of intellectual perfection was not consistent with a love for democracy — and the latter seemed to him more important. But he was never impatient with Emerson as he definitely was with Thoreau. There was no arrogance in Emerson. Thoreau was a Milton of his day, obstinate, lofty, and narrow in his humanity (Walt did not like Milton); Emerson was a Saint Francis, eternally true, eternally insufficient for humanity as it was. And always after a discussion backward and forward under the elms, or in a room in New York, the two went for a good dinner at Emerson's expense, understanding each other without agreeing. From Emerson, Whitman, and perhaps Mark Twain, it would be possible to reconstruct a typical American, but from no one of them alone, least of all from Emerson.

3

Walt was aware that with real publishers at last, and he himself with a background of usable publicity, a great opportunity had come. His hundred new poems had increased to a hundred and twenty-four; he had rewritten and improved much in the old poems; it was definitely worth while to drop everything else and settle down in Boston for these months. The two young Yankee publishers, unlike Emerson, raised no question apparently as to text. They sent him to the stereotypers, where, being a printer himself, he could see that a good job was done.

It sounds as if he had arrived with a complete manuscript ready for printing, probably much of it already in type, so that he could spend his time in correcting and perfecting the lines as they came from the press. If so, the most important work had been done beforehand. This was the rearrangement of the 'Leaves' into a book with a beginning, a middle, and an end, whose structure would represent the edifice of the imagination which he was building. He felt that he had succeeded in this organizing of his material, otherwise he would not have said in the course of the poems:

> Lift me close to your face till I whisper,
> What you are holding is in reality no book, nor part of a book,
> It is a man, flushed and full-blooded — it is I.[7]

If the book was a man, it was certainly a broader and more complex Whitman than has been discussed so far in these pages. New areas of his inner life and its absorptions from experience have become articulate. The 'Leaves' in this edition for the first time takes on the aspect of a wheel, a composite unity revolving around a central theme. The figure is Whitman's own, for he was to say later, when the war had taught him so much about democracy, that his 'Drum-Taps,' which recorded that experience, had become the hub of the 'Leaves.' In 1860, the central theme is love — between the sexes in *Children of Adam*, and the love of male comrades in *Calamus*. It was the centrality of a love which was sexual as well as spiritual, that Walt could not successfully explain to Emerson, and so kept silent. Freud would have readily understood, and would have approved of his thesis.

The hoop of the wheel is Whitman's faith in himself as able to dramatize representative man. The spokes are the aspects of dramatic life he speaks for. Once such a poetic purpose was clear to the maker of the 'Leaves,' some organization became inevitable. And, indeed, he had only to expand the simple method, half lyric, half prophetic and didactic, of the *Song of Myself* to produce a book representing a personality which itself represented 'multitudes.'

He began the new edition with a new poem *Proto-Leaf*, afterward called *Starting from Paumanok;* this is Walt's own intellectual biography. It is a blueprint of his purposes, and from now on will always be kept as an introduction to the 'Leaves.'

> Free, fresh, savage,
> Fluent, luxuriant, self-content, fond of persons and places,
> Fond of fish-shape Paumanok, where I was born,
> Fond of the sea — [8]

so the poem began in its 1860 version, and each word of the first line is indicative. He is free now 'to make the works' of a great composite poem reflecting his country through his own personality; he is fresh in his approach to the common people and their democracy; he is savage (the one note of pose) in his willingness to speak 'nature, without check, with original energy.' He is a national figure, aware of the continent, identified with all its activities, who, singing in America, strikes up for a New World. For this New World he has digested the past, and now will make a program of chants for the future of America, chants in which all time converges upon his own place and day. He will make a song of the equality of the states, a song of the masses threatening the rulers with whom they are dissatisfied, songs of heroes, companionship, comradeship, and love, songs of evil and good as the realities of a democracy, songs of 'the greatness of Love and Democracy, and the greatness of Religion.'

> I will effuse egotism and show it underlying all, and I will be the bard of personality,
> And I will show of male and female that either is but the equal of the other,

And sexual organs and acts! do you concentrate in me, for I am determin'd
    to tell you with courageous clear voice to prove you illustrious,
And I will show that there is no imperfection in the present, and can be none
    in the future, . . .
And I will show that nothing can happen more beautiful than death. . . .

I will not make poems with reference to parts,
But I will make poems, songs, thoughts, with reference to ensemble, . . .
And I will not make a poem nor the least part of a poem but has reference to
    the soul. . . .
Behold, the body includes and is the meaning, the main concern and in-
    cludes and is the soul.

  His voice will announce:

    A new race dominating previous ones and grander far, with new contests,
    New politics, new literatures and religions, new inventions and arts.

You will see in these poems not only the forest, fields, animals
tame and wild, but steamers, locomotives, printing-presses, cities
and commerce. So 'haste on with me.'

Starting from Paumanok is more of a program than a poem,
just as Whitman's verses, as Emerson said, are often more inventories than imaginative projections of America. Nevertheless, merely as a program, it shows the courage and breadth of
his resolve. A mystic who believes in the spiritual unity of the
universe, proposes to show that his own tumultuous country is
as miraculous as Scripture, that there is no activity of man or
machine that does not involve the soul, and that the greatest
miracle of all is possible, which is a perfected democracy.
'Bearded, sun-burnt, gray-neck'd, forbidding,' he has arrived,
to be wrestled with for the solid prizes of the universe. Learn
to love humanity through him. No less than a plan for idealizing
the New World is what he proposes to accomplish with his
'Leaves,' and from now on it is impossible to take Whitman's
purpose at less than his own estimate. Can he do it?

The question cannot be answered now. There are too many
fine poems unwritten. Yet there was enough scope, variety, and
power in this edition to convince an enlightened and unprejudiced
critic that a poet of major importance had appeared and was
ripe for judgment. Walt now clearly knows what he wants to do.

Out of the Cradle Endlessly Rocking,[9] his superb new chant of remembered love, was in this book, a poem showing a complete mastery of the technique he had so painfully developed. In this poem his style, which I shall discuss in a later chapter, has reached maturity.

Here is the *Song of the Open Road,* reprinted from the 1856 edition, and containing lines which have been quoted since in every civilized country. Why did not its magnificent phrasing catch immediate attention? I hope to give an answer in a later chapter.

> Afoot and light-hearted I take to the open road,
> Healthy, free, the world before me,
> The long brown path before me leading wherever I choose.
>
> Henceforth I ask not good-fortune, I myself am good-fortune,
> Henceforth I whimper no more, postpone no more, need nothing,
> Done with indoor complaints, libraries, querulous criticisms,
> Strong and content I travel the open road.

The open road, the long brown path, has been romantically chosen as a slogan by thousands of nature lovers, and, naturally, Walt did walk it, composing this poem slowly as he went. But symbolically, of course, the road is the world, or, from the soul's point of view, the universe, and the basic idea is spiritual evolution open to those who will follow a leader who loves them. This is a poem on values in living, and its thesis is very close to Thoreau, that other individualist philosopher, who saw that in the expansionist New World spiritual values were being neglected for what was falsely called success. Whitman is the inner voice proclaiming that life is good if loosed from limits and imaginary lines, because the individual holds more goodness than he thinks — particularly good if lived in the open air where great personal deeds have room, and all are done with love. Hence let those who follow him seek the great Companions — swift and majestic men, the greatest women, the trusters of human nature, journeyers who go through youth to an old age 'flowing free with the delicious near-by freedom of death.' He pleads with his friends to come out from convention, and their secret silent loathing and despair, come out to the struggle for a life so vital that always some greater struggle will lie ahead.

This is an intensely American poem, a call to the strenuous life, like Theodore Roosevelt's, but more spiritual, with deeper values. It is a chant of freedom, more subtly and more philosophically put than the rhetoric tinged with materialism of the American President. Impossible, one might say, to have written it anywhere but in a New World where anyone was free to get up and out and seek the great Companions, and thus an authentic song for expansionist America. But, of course, not about contemporary expansionist America, since, like Emerson's essays, and more so, it is a summons to a possible future, in no sense realized. And this poem is compact, unified, not arrogant, yet confident, its message, like a great speech, foreseeing its end at the beginning, its style exactly adequate. Here is the mature Whitman.

Thoreau's favorite, and a favorite of many since, *Crossing Brooklyn Ferry*, was also reprinted here from the neglected second edition. It is a symbolic description of familiar sights and sounds of city and water, 'appearances' which the senses register — seabirds, tall masts of Manhattan, beautiful hills of Brooklyn, voices of young men, gorgeous clouds of sunset, fires of foundry chimneys:

You have waited, you always wait, you dumb, beautiful ministers,
We receive you with free sense at last, and are insatiate henceforward,
Not you any more shall be able to foil us, or withhold yourselves from us,
We use you, and do not cast you aside — we plant you permanently within
    us,
We fathom you not — we love you — there is perfection in you also,
You furnish your parts toward eternity,
Great or small, you furnish your parts toward the soul.

One of the most mystical of his poems, with perhaps his fullest use of symbols in terms of what we call now sur-realism, also appeared in this 1860 edition, and for the first time. This is the *Bardic Symbols* which Lowell published, certainly without understanding it, now called *As I Ebb'd with the Ocean of Life*. Here Whitman passionately regrets the 'blab' of his 'arrogant self' as it had appeared in his earlier poems; says that it leaves 'the real me' unreached and untouched. So he writes a poem made entirely out of symbols of the ebbing and flowing sea which he knew so well, and the shores on which are flotsam and jetsam, 'tufts of straw, fragments, buoy'd hither from many moods, one contradicting another.' Putting lines together from the correlative poems, *As I Ebb'd with the Ocean of Life* and *Out of the Cradle Endlessly Rocking*, one gets the heart of the appeal of the former poem:

> I perceive I have not really understood any thing, not a single object and
> that no man ever can.

So he wrote in *As I Ebb'd* and completed the theme in *Out of the Cradle:*

> O give me the clew! (it lurks in the night here somewhere;)
> O if I am to have so much, let me have more! [10]

But there is no answer. He can only symbolize what comes up from the 'fathomless workings fermented and thrown, ... capricious, brought hither we know not whence, spread out before you.' This poem, as it is the fashion to say now, does not try to explain life — it *is* life unexplained.

And the volume ends with *So Long*, a phrase said to have been the carpenter's farewell at the end of work, but more probably in colloquial usage generally as now. And this, in contrast to *I Ebb'd with the Ocean of Life*, is a clear and direct statement of intentions:

> To conclude, I announce what comes after me....
> When America does what was promis'd,
> When through these States walk a hundred millions of superb persons, ...
> Then to me and mine our due fruition.
> I have press'd through in my own right, ...
> I have offer'd my style to everyone, I have journey'd with confident step;
> While my pleasure is yet at the full I whisper *So Long!* ...
>
> I announce natural persons to arise,
> I announce justice triumphant,
> I announce uncompromising liberty and equality, ...
> I announce the Union more and more compact, indissoluble, ...
> I announce a life that shall be copious, vehement, spiritual, bold.

It was not 'so long' yet; indeed there is so much more to come that it is wrong at this point to try to see the 'Leaves' as a whole. Yet Whitman's so-called chaos had definitely become a kosmos. He knew he had arrived.

4

I have spoken of the really great poems in this edition. I have not yet mentioned what, biographically, was its most significant feature. Here in this book which was to represent in all his aspects, at last, a full-blooded man of the nineteenth century, the sexuality which was so strong in Whitman was given full release and expression. The new organization of the 'Leaves' made it possible to separate and concentrate these poems of passionate sexual love. They are to be found in two divisions, one called *Enfans d'Adam* in his borrowed French, later changed to *Children of Adam*, the other *Calamus*, the name of the wild flag, with its stiff phallic leaves and phallic-shaped root. In *Children of Adam* he gathered his poems of passion for women; in *Calamus* were placed his chants of 'adhesiveness,' the love of men for men. Scattered through the 'Leaves,' these poems, most of which are short, would not have been so emphasized. Gathered together, they naturally seemed, and were, a defiant *Apologia* for that sexuality which he said was the blood, if not the heart, of the 'Leaves of Grass.' He wrote no more really sexual poems after this. *Children of Adam* and *Calamus* were his challenges to Victorian ethics and the genteel age.

What this meant for Whitman, what the poems mean, I shall discuss in the next two chapters. No understanding of Walt Whitman is possible without the most careful consideration of these revolutionary and revealing poems. Upon them have been based the libels still directed against him. As a result of their publication, his way to a just fame was made immensely more difficult. These difficulties, which Emerson had so truly forecast, were evident in the reception of a volume which should have been recognized as Whitman's first mature and rounded book.

Before the new edition had been published, the smearing had

begun. Charles Gayler, a playwright and journalist, described as a 'picturesque ruffian,' had been Whitman's predecessor on *The Brooklyn Times*. We do not know what cause he had to hate Whitman, nor what poems he had read, but he had a poisoned pen. In 1860, while Walt's Boston edition was preparing, he was editor of a comic daily *Momus*, in which he published, and presumably wrote, these scurrilous lines: [11]

> Walt Whitman well names his obscene productions,
> Where he riots in filth, on indecency feasts,
> For 'tis plainly the simplest of simple deductions,
> That such 'Leaves of Grass' can but satisfy beasts.
> Humanity shrinks from such pestilent reekings
> As rise, rotten and foul, from each word, line and page,
> Of the foulness within him the nastiest leakings,
> Which stamp him the dirtiest beast of the age.

But far more dangerous were some of the reviews in serious, not to say godly, papers which followed upon the publication of the book in May of 1860. *The Springfield Republican* headed its comment 'Smut in Them.' Clearly the hounds were to be set upon the hare of indecency, as, indeed, a review of the 1856 edition in *The Christian Examiner* had warned.[12] This time, Whitman was not unprepared. He had put together a little pamphlet for Thayer and Eldridge which was to be issued in the same season as the book, and serve both for promotion and defence. 'Leaves of Grass Imprints' they called it. In sixty-four pages of small type, he reprinted mingled praise and abuse from earlier reviews. Critics of this new volume were to be told that, while some condemned him, there had been many who believed that a new poet of power had appeared. They would see that the vigor of his democracy had been recognized, that, even if rough and tough, he was a live dog and not a dead poodle. But even in these early reviews, three-quarters of the attack was upon his indecency. Against charges of egoism and irreligion, this edition, with its strong and superb poems might be a final answer to readers with a sense for literature and sincerity. But neither pamphlet nor book could acquit him of indecency. By the literary standards of 1860, he was indecent. To deny it, would be only a waste of energy and time.

5

And so, in June of 1860, Walt came back from Boston to Brooklyn again to live with his family, watch the progress of his book, ride up and down Broadway, intending, apparently, to free-lance for a livelihood. In June of 1861, he began a series of twenty-five reminiscent and historical articles on Brooklyn, called 'Brooklyniana,' publishing them in *The Brooklyn Weekly Standard*. Except for the liveliness of his own memories, they are hack work. In 1862, he was writing articles for *The New York Leader*. Thus he brought in some income, while he worked upon a new series of poems, and saw his hopes for a publisher's success with the 1860 'Leaves' wrecked by the onset of war.

It is questionable whether literary failure this time seemed important. The new poems he was writing, which were to become 'Drum-Taps,' are new in every sense, powerful in patriotism, not sexual, not egoistic, with the kind of objectivity which subjective men attain only in crises of such scope that their own fortunes are involved in a great emergency. The national crisis had come. On the 13th of April, 1861, Whitman, strolling down Broadway after the opera, heard in the distance the loud cries of newsboys announcing the attack on Fort Sumter. The Civil War had begun.

'I bought an extra and cross'd to the Metropolitan hotel (Niblo's) where the great lamps were still brightly blazing, and, with a crowd of others, who gather'd impromptu, read the news, which was evidently authentic. For the benefit of some who had no papers, one of us read the telegram aloud, while all listened silently and attentively. No remark was made by any of the crowd, which had increas'd to thirty or forty, but all stood a minute or two, I remember, before they dispers'd. I can almost see them there now, under the lamps at midnight again.' [13]

In July of 1861, Bull Run shocked him, as it did all Northerners, into a realization that what had seemed an armed quarrel was to be a great war:

'All this sort of feeling was destin'd to be arrested and revers'd by a terrible shock — the battle of first Bull Run. . . . In Washington, among the great persons and their entourage, a mixture of awful consternation, uncertainty, rage, shame, helplessness, and stupefying disappointment. The worst is not only imminent, but already here. In a few hours — perhaps before the next meal — the secesh generals, with their victorious hordes, will be upon us. The dream of humanity, the vaunted Union we thought so strong, so impregnable — lo! it seems already smash'd like a china plate. One bitter, bitter hour — perhaps proud America will never again know such an hour. She must pack and fly — no time to spare. Those white palaces — the dome crown'd capitol there on the hill, so stately over the trees — shall they be left — or destroy'd first? For it is certain that the talk among certain of the magnates and officers and clerks and officials everywhere, for twenty-four hours in and around Washington after Bull Run, was loud and undisguised for yielding out and out, and substituting the Southern rule, and Lincoln promptly abdicating and departing.' [14]

On December 16 of 1862, he left for Washington and the front. It is the end of his life as a Broadway Bohemian, and journalist of Brooklyn and New York.

CHAPTER XVIII

'Children of Adam'

I HAVE stressed the emphasis upon sexuality in the third edition of 1860–1861 because this volume marks the moment in Whitman's career when his eroticism, his abnormality, if any, his supernormality, if that is the word, must be faced and discussed. In the critical years of 1861 and 1862, a passion of patriotism was gradually driving other obsessions from his poetry. After he gets to Washington, new experiences vitalize his relations with the common people, and shift the emphasis in his 'Leaves' from self-expression to a religion of democracy. These experiences were transforming in their power because, sexually and psychologically, Walt Whitman had been neither a 'dirty beast' nor 'the sovereign of the flesh,' but a complex erotic type, neither mysterious nor pathological, but requiring the most careful analysis and explanation. For this we must go back to *Children of Adam* and to *Calamus*.

Yet it is not possible — and I shall quote his own words in defence of this statement — to discuss the sexuality of Whitman's poetry without reference to his actual experiences in life behind the poetic sublimation. There is no question here of the private, irrelevant aspects of a great man's career. It is neither dirt nor a skeleton in the closet that we are seeking. This man's greatness is in some respects a function of his excessive sexuality. Whole sections of the 'Leaves' are either sheer rhetorical fantasy or the articulation and sublimation of experience. Of that experience we know actually very little, but enough to make the essential connection between Walt the 'I' and Walt Whitman the poetic personality of the 'Leaves.'

He does not help the biographer in his own published reminiscences. There seems to be no instance in literary history where an author has tried so consistently, from middle age to death, to identify his life with his book. When he is pushed into a corner, asked to explain himself, challenged as to his meaning for his times, urged to add to his personal history, he falls back, sooner or later, always upon the 'Leaves.' The book is both his testimony and himself. He does not understand all of it, does not praise all of it, regards it as unfinished — but the 'Leaves' *are* Walt Whitman, and Walt Whitman apart from the 'Leaves' is of little importance. So far as I am aware, he makes only two exceptions to this complete identification. Walt the hospital visitor, who comforted and strengthened so many disabled soldiers — this Walt (who definitely did not function as a poet) he never tires of describing. And there was another Walt of whom he did not boast but who was always an 'essential me,' the Walt who was the center of his family's welfare, and the affectionate friend of so many unliterary men and women. It is to be noted that in both these aspects of his personal life apart from his book, the dominating factor is love.

Yet Walt the 'I' records in his private notebooks perturbations of unsatisfied passion, and writes in his letters to young soldiers of a love which is more than friendship. That this 'I,' this living personality, is unimportant, critically and biographically, is, of course, nonsense. The Whitman that edited, free-lanced, went to Fowler and Wells to have his bumps read by the fashionable pseudo-science of phrenology,[1] haunted Broadway, worried over the Union, and loved and was loved, is, naturally, a source for the poetic personality that appears in the 'Leaves.' It is less important, but no biographer can follow Whitman's lead and omit from his life whatever does not seem appropriate in the background of a prophet and bard of democracy. Unfortunately, much has to be omitted because we simply have no facts, and in all probability never will have.

The *Song of Myself*, which was the heart of Whitman's first 'Leaves' and, indeed, of all of the poems of the first two editions, failed adequately to present this poetic personality. Or, to put it differently, and in Whitman's words, the typical democratic man of the nineteenth century whom he intended to portray fully through the imaginative personality called Walt Whitman in the poem, had got only part of himself into the first editions of the 'Leaves.' I think this accounts for the brash self-assertiveness of the earliest poems, as of a man still not fully articulate or even mature, who makes up by overemphasis what he lacks in wholeness of representation. The lack of wholeness may also be responsible for the dispersed sexual imagery in these early poems, obscure, difficult, never getting itself into the open except in the *I Sing the Body Electric.*

There were strange passions, full-blooded and perturbing in the man which had not yet got themselves fully expressed in the still incomplete revelation of his poetry. Whitman thought that these passions were typical of the representative, democratic man he was trying to put into literature for the first time. There he was partly wrong. They were more typical of Walt's peculiar nature than of the average American, no matter how full-blooded. But he was right in believing that he must make them articulate, must sublimate them into imagination, if he was to get all of himself, as a poet must, into poetry.

2

One of Whitman's great services was to restore sexuality to literature, but it is equally true that he himself was afflicted by his sexuality. There was, to quote Kipling, too much ego in his cosmos. There will always be too much ego in him to be as completely representative of humanity as he wished, but in the 1840's and 1850's, he seems to have been bubbling and steaming with highly personal passions which, until they boiled off into the 'Leaves,' and took their rightful place as part of his poetic personality, kept him in a state of diffused eroticism which distracted both his readers and himself. When the *Children of Adam* and the *Calamus* poems got themselves written and published, the discharge of eroticism, of what he called perturbation, into his poetry ceased almost entirely. That this is true, the unchronological arrangement of the 'Leaves,' as they are printed today, conceals; but it is easy to prove by looking at the dates of the constituent poems.[2] Democracy and the democratic, death and spiritual love, are never going to get an unclouded articulation from this poet until he blows off the sexual steam of his own private passion. The Oriental mystic knows that nothing clarifies the spiritual vision like a stern refusal to indulge in any sensuality. Walt was not that kind of mystic. He felt that he had to lift the sexual into place by the fullest and most courageous expression, or fail to present his en-masse of the nineteenth century in all its essential aspects. And first he had to lift his private sexuality from a problem to a triumph of the soul. This is the real explanation of the important position given by Whitman to the *Calamus* and the *Children of Adam* poems in the 1860 edition.

I shall take the love of woman, heterosexual love, in his poems first, as presenting the least difficulties. The questions to be asked are these: Was Whitman undersexed; were his explosions (this seems to be the fitting word) into poems of intense passion, or into passages of vivid sensuality, to be explained by a suppression of the normal outlets of sexual desire by inhibitions of various kinds? Was he an abnormal man physically who got his sexual satisfactions only in phantasy?

Well, he never married, and yet through all his writings he attacked free love, and defended matrimony as the ideal state for men and women, deploring constantly (in both prose and verse) prostitution and adultery. When he was asked in old age why he had never taken a wife, he gave his favorite answer to close questioners on subjects where he wished to be uncommunicative, 'That cat has a very long tail.'

Yet part of the tale is obvious. He never had income enough at any time to marry and raise a family without shifting his energy toward productions more salable than the 'Leaves.' He never, until after his mother's death, escaped from at least a part responsibility for a family with two defectives, and an aging mother whose welfare was his dearest concern. Also there was Andrew who died of tuberculosis, leaving his unpleasant wife and dependent children. We know that one fixed ambition of Whitman's, which he never realized, was to set up a home for his mother and Eddie, where she would be in no danger of becoming a servant in the house.³ I do not believe that this was the only reason he never married, but it was a good one as far as it went. If he had a mother fixation, as any psychiatrist I think would say, here was another cause for his long bachelor's life into which the question of possible sexual energy did not enter.

But the critics and interpreters of Whitman who believe that his failure to marry was the result of a physiological deficiency or a homosexual tendency (which I shall discuss in the next chapter) go further. They think that he may have been incapable of sexual intercourse, and that physical love for him was always a phantasy.

Whitman's own theory of poetry, so often stated, would be made ridiculous by such an assumption. 'There is no trick or cunning,' he says, 'no art or recipe by which you can have in your writing that which you do not possess in yourself — that which is not in you can [not] appear in your writing. No rival of life — no sham for generation — no painting friendship or love by one who is neither friend nor lover.' ⁴ We know he was capable of friendship. Was he a lover, and, if so, what kind of lover?

Friendship — in its broadest sense, including rare affection of extraordinary scope — need not be argued. Whitman could be friends with anyone who was genuine, not a snob, not a prig, not a pedant, not a mere money-maker. He could be and he was. And this held for women as well as for men. Nelly O'Connor, of whom more later, was very close to him. Mrs. Gilchrist, a powerful woman and an intellectual, who came from England to marry him, went back his dear friend. The faculty for friendship he powerfully possessed, and there is plenty of testimony that even until old age he had an extraordinary personal magnetism which made a man, particularly a young man, his friend at first encounter, and which attracted women. Once in Washington, says Burroughs, a woman on a horsecar gave him shyly as she passed, a rose.

'Now, Henry made no account of love at all,' wrote Ellery Channing of his dead friend, Thoreau, who was as intense an individualist as Whitman. 'He had notions about friendship.' ⁵

The remark was a half-truth only, but it is easy to see what Channing meant. These Transcendentalists, to whom Whitman owed so much inspiration, were constantly trying to lift love above sex. But Walt was constantly striving to lift sexuality into love. Love, for Thoreau, was an emotionally intense friendship. Friendship, for Walt, was simply a diffused and unperturbing love.

In one sense Walt always loved — it was his natural reaction toward any man or woman spiritually kin to him. But what experience did he have of love that, unlike friendship, perturbs and grips the whole being, and whose natural expression is sexual intercourse?

It is usually unwise to take passages of poetry out of their context. Nevertheless, and admitting the risks, I ask the reader to ponder upon the excerpts which follow, most of them from *Children of Adam*, and ask whether this man has or has not known passionate, sensual, sexual love:

(Hark close and still what I now whisper to you,
I love you, O you entirely possess me,
O that you and I escape from the rest and go utterly off, free and lawless,
Two hawks in the air, two fishes swimming in the sea not more lawless than
   we;) . . .
From the master, the pilot I yield the vessel to,
The general commanding me, commanding all, from him permission taking,
From time the programme hastening, (I have loiter'd too long as it is,)
From sex, from the warp and from the woof, . . .
From plenty of persons near and yet the right person not near, . . .
From the close pressure that makes me or any, man drunk, fainting with
   excess, . . .
From the cling of the trembling arm, . . .
From side by side the pliant coverlet off-throwing, . . .
From the hour of shining stars and dropping dews.

I sing the body electric, . . .
This is the female form,
A divine nimbus exhales from it from head to foot,
It attracts with fierce undeniable attraction, . . .
Mad filaments, ungovernable shoots play out of it, the response likewise un-
   governable,
Hair, bosom, hips, bend of legs, negligent falling of hands all diffused, mine
   too diffused,

Ebb stung by the flow and flow stung by the ebb, love-flesh swelling and
    deliciously aching,
Limitless limpid jets of love hot and enormous, quivering jelly of love, white-
    blow and delirious juice, . . .

So much for passion and sensuality. Now add this, perhaps the
most beautiful and imaginative description of sexual intercourse
in all literature in English:

Bridegroom night of love working surely and softly into the prostrate dawn,
Undulating into the willing and yielding day,
Lost in the cleave of the clasping and sweet-flesh'd day.

3

As for the experience which you must possess if you are to have
it in your writing, of that, for Whitman, we know surprisingly
little. And yet it is highly important to form an opinion, since no
final estimate of the 'Leaves of Grass' can be made without set-
tling the question of the truth or phantasy of Whitman's love.
For unless it had been real to him, he falsifies his own theory of
poetry.

Walt's relations with women outside his own family are highly
unspecific in the record. Of direct testimony that he had known
actually, and not merely in the imagination, the sexual ecstasy of
passionate embrace with a woman he loved or lusted for, there is
none — unless his own statement to Symonds that his life in the
past had been 'jolly' in the bodily sense be taken as evidence. It
cannot, I think, be proved legally that Whitman was not virgin
through life, but the law allows many absurdities! There are
many stories, such as Nelly O'Connor's of a married woman with
whom he was in love,[6] the quadroon tales of New Orleans, or the
letters of his Washington friend Will Wallace, a hospital steward
which sound like an invitation from one libertine to another
offering new experiences.[7] John Burroughs hints that his life was
not blameless, when tried by the standards of a Northern intellectual. Most significant, and most inconclusive of all, is the great
secret which on so many occasions Whitman proposed to tell to
Traubel, but never did tell. Traubel assumed from the context of

the conversations that this was to be the account of a secret love life and perhaps of the illegitimate children of which he wrote to Symonds on August 19, 1890:

...Though unmarried I have had six children — two are dead — one living Southern grandchild, fine boy, writes to me occasionally — circumstances (connected with their fortune and benefit) have separated me from intimate relations. [8]

This, presumably, was the grandchild who, so Walt told Traubel, had visited him in Camden.

And, as if the cat with the very long tail had to be shown again to somebody in this year which he knew was near his end, he wrote to his executor, Doctor Bucke, on May 23, 1891, of his tomb now nearly finished:

I have two deceased children (young man & woman — illegitimate of course) that I much desired to bury here with me — but have ab't abandoned the plan on account of angry litigation and fuss generally, and disinterment from down South. [9]

The credibility of his boast of six illegitimate children would be greater if it had not been made to Symonds, who had shaken him seriously by suggesting that the *Calamus* poems were definitely in defence of homosexuality. Yet if any part of this tale is true, it would seem to be the other account of two dead young children. Six children by one woman, or by several women, seems incredible without the knowledge of someone who, sooner or later, would have blabbed. For Walt was not, after early youth, a person whom one could see and forget. Many, it would seem, would have known or guessed and afterward remembered.

Indeed, it will be difficult for the most fictionizing biographer to provide Whitman with time and money to beget six children in a faraway place or places, except in an extravagance of libertinism which nothing in the record suggests. In Washington, which not only seemed Southern to Walt, but in the mid-century was definitely a Southern city, it might have been possible — the two children of the letter to Doctor Bucke, let us say, might have been possible. There he was living for a decade alone and away from his family and his wide circle of friends and associates in New York — and from 1865 to his paralysis in 1873 was financially better off than in any other part of his life. Two children born then might well have been spoken of, in 1890, and after their death, as young people. And the reference to angry litigation could very well have meant that the mother had married after the liaison, or had never acknowledged her offspring to be other than her husband's.

Personally I do not believe a word of either of these stories, though quite willing to admit that I may be wrong. Both letters were written when Walt was smarting from the charge of homosexuality. Nor do I believe that an unchecked, utterly unconventional man like Whitman, who wrote with affection even of prostitutes and criminals, would have drifted slowly into death, leaving living or dead children with no sign or message or bequeathal. It seems to be certain that the close friends of his old age knew of no such sign.[10]

4

Yet his love affairs were certainly not all in his phantasy. The 'M—' of the notebook of 1859 may have been only his mother; however, there is a tintype pasted in this notebook which deserves mention here, though it is not evidence. The face is of a young and self-conscious woman, rather carelessly dressed, sensuous mouth and eyes, heavy ringlets, revealing on one side of her face what seems to be an eardrop, graceful hands and wrists of which she seems to be proud. Her clothes are heavy but not unfashionable — a plaid waist under a coat with flowing sleeves, tied at the breast by a corded collar, with a pleated, heavy skirt — apparently a brunette. I record my opinion — for what it may be worth — that this obviously unintellectual, probably 'unrefined,' evidently sensuous, and presumably passionate girl from the undifferentiated people is the kind of woman, and probably the only kind of woman, with whom the complex Whitman could have had rewarding physical experiences — whether for a night or a year.

But evidence that Walt had pursued love of a most real and physical kind is to be found in the later notebook dated 1868, when all passion of this kind had long been spent in his poetry, though the personal perturbations remained:

Cheating, childish abandonment of myself, fancying what does not really exist in another, but is all the time in myself alone — utterly deluded & cheated by *myself* & my own weakness — REMEMBER WHERE I AM MOST WEAK, & most lacking. Yet always preserve a kind spirit & demeanour to 16. But PURSUE HER NO MORE. . . .

June 17 —
It is IMPERATIVE, that I obviate & remove myself (& my orbit) *at all hazards* [away from] this *in-
 cessant* [*enormous*] & enormous PERTURBATION. . . .

June 15– 1870
TO GIVE UP ABSOLUTELY & *for good, from this present hour,* [all] this FEVERISH FLUCTUATING, *useless undignified pursuit of 164 — too long* (*much too long*) persevered in, — so humiliating — *It must come at last* & had better come now — (*It cannot possibly be a success*) LET THERE BE FROM THIS HOUR NO FALTERING [or] NO GETTING — *at all henceforth,* (NOT ONCE, *under any circumstances*) — *avoid seeing her, or meeting her, or any talk or explanations — or* ANY MEETING WHATEVER, FROM THIS HOUR FORTH, FOR LIFE. . . .

Depress the adhesive nature

It is in excess — making life a torment

All this diseased feverish, disproportionate adhesiveness.

One feels apologetic for quoting these intense, morbidly self-critical lines, meant only for the private eye. I do so only because they show a kind of passion not consistent with anything called friendship. Also because a woman is clearly involved.[11] The important item in the confession is *pursuit,* feverish, undignified pursuit, this time condemned to unsuccess. It is impossible to believe that the man who wrote these lines had not desired with all his being the reality of passion, and not been always unsuccessful.

A little superficial but perhaps useful common sense applied to all this problem would seem to lead toward rather obvious conclusions. The suppressed sexual imagery of the earliest notebooks and the poems of the early fifties, and the outspoken amativeness of the *Children of Adam* section of the 1860 edition, had a basis in real experience. If he was still perturbed and feverish in pursuit of a real woman in 1870, it is nonsense to suppose that he is inventing his sexual ecstasies ten years earlier, or that he had never known love except in vain chase never consummated, or in his fancy. I do not believe that Walt was ever a libertine, but that he was virgin after New Orleans and probably after the mid forties seems most improbable. Whatever may be said of the *Calamus* items, the poems of the *Children of Adam* are the sublimation of the passion of real love. That the passion was not all sublimated is clear enough from the Journal quotations above. But he had got it out of his imagination, segregated it psychologically where it was no longer infusing itself through his poetic personality, and was clearly trying to purify his 'I' as well as his soul. The love poetry of Whitman is sometimes unpleasantly carnal, sometimes magnificently imaginative. But it is not mere phantasy. 'There is no trick or cunning, no art or recipe by which you can have in your writing that which you do not possess in yourself.'

CHAPTER XIX

'Here the frailest leaves of me'

WHITMAN was no phantom lover, and yet he was no simple, amative heterosexual either. Probably in his life, certainly in his poetry, there is no sharp boundary between phantasy and reality. And if he loved women, he also loved men, and sometimes, more than either, himself.

As for his love of men, who were usually, and probably always, young men or youths, there is abundant evidence of its extraordinary power, tenderness, and continuity from early maturity to old age. He testifies himself, with confirmation from the family, that in youth he had little interest in girls. Pete Doyle, who knew him so well in Washington, had never heard of 'Walt's being bothered up with a woman.' [1] But from the time he went swimming with young Sutton of *The Eagle*, we know of a long series of recorded intimacies with young men. He writes to them with palpitating affection:

To Pete Doyle

Brooklyn, August 7 [1870] Dear Boy Pete... It is a beautiful quiet Sunday forenoon.... I have just taken out your last letter and read it over again — I went out on a kind of little excursion by myself last night — all alone — It was very pleasant, cool enough and the moon shining — I think of you too Pete, and a great deal of the time.... Your welcome letter of the 8th has come this morning, dear loving son, and has pleased me, as always.... [August 12] My darling son, I will send you $5 every Saturday, should you be idle — as I can easily spare that, and you can depend on it.... Many, many loving kisses to you, dear son. [2]

To Elijah Fox

Brooklyn, Nov. 21, '63. Dear Son and comrade ... I know I am a great fool about such things but I tell you the truth dear son. I do not think one night has passed in New York or Brooklyn when I have been at the theatre or opera or afterward to some supper party or carousal made by the young fellows for me, but what amid the play or the singing I would perhaps think of you, ... I would see your face before me in thought as I have seen it so often there in Ward G, and my amusement or drink would be all turned to nothing, and I would realize how happy it would be if I could leave all the fun and noise and the crowd and be with you.... I hope you are quite well and with your dear wife.... I must indeed bid you good night my dear loving comrade, and the blessing of God on you by night and day my darling boy.[3]

These tender letters are, of course, essentially the outpourings of a thwarted paternalism in a man childless, either in actuality or by circumstance. Yet 'I know I am a great fool about such things.' This 'adhesiveness,' as he called it, this almost feminine love for men, must often have led him into that same feverish perturbation which he deplores with *16*, and such perturbation is evident in the *Calamus* [4] poems. It will be remembered that in the notebook passage quoted above and written in the same year as this letter to Pete Doyle, he urges himself to 'Depress the adhesive nature.... It is in excess — making life a torment ... diseased, feverish, disproportionate.' Adhesiveness, as he defines the phrenological term elsewhere for his own purposes, is 'intense and loving comradeship, the personal attachment of man to man — which, hard to define ... seems to promise ... the most substantial hope and safety of these States, ... the counterbalance and offset of our materialistic and vulgar American democracy.' But apparently this adhesive love, 'at least rivalling the amative love hitherto possessing imaginative literature,' could get out of hand, be disproportionate, seem like a diseased emotion.[5]

Many feel that it did get out of hand in his poetry. They think that such a passage as the following from the *Song of Myself* is merely homosexual:

I mind how once we lay such a transparent summer morning,
How you settled your head athwart my hips and gently turn'd over upon
    me,
And parted the shirt from my bosom-bone, and plunged your tongue to my
    bare-stript heart,
And reach'd till you felt my beard, and reach'd till you held my feet.

But this is addressed to 'my soul,' and ends with the noble lines:

Swiftly arose and spread around me the peace and knowledge that pass all
    the argument of the earth,
And I know that the hand of God is the promise of my own,
And I know that the spirit of God is the brother of my own.

One gets closer to the truth in the *Calamus* poems:

Here the frailest leaves of me and yet my strongest lasting,
Here I shade and hide my thoughts, I myself do not expose them
And yet they expose me more than all my other poems.

For an athlete is enamour'd of me, and I of him,
But toward him there is something fierce and terrible in me eligible to burst
    forth,
I dare not tell it in words, not even in these songs.

Or again:

And that night while all was still I heard the waters roll slowly continually
    up the shores,
I heard the hissing rustle of the liquid and sands as directed to me whispering
    to congratulate me,
For the one I love most lay sleeping by me under the same cover in the cool
    night,
In the stillness in the Autumn moonbeams his face was inclined toward me,
And his arm lay lightly around my breast — and that night I was happy.

2

There are two alternative conclusions which can be drawn from these *Calamus* poems, the first of which I reject, as I think all close students of Whitman's life must. This is, that Walt Whitman, the 'I,' was actively homosexual, and that his poems are not merely a sublimation of what he calls manly love, but a blind and an excuse. There has, so far, been educed not one scrap of evi-

dence of actual homosexuality in Whitman's life. And it must be
remembered, that after the publication of the first 'Leaves,' and
especially after the 1860 edition with its *Calamus* section, Whitman must have been marked by suspicion from those (and there
would be many) ready to suspect. He was, as I have said with
reference to his affairs with women, a conspicuous man. It would
seem probable that if he yielded to the 'fierce and terrible' in him,
ready to burst forth, somewhere, somehow, in that unpsycholog-
ical age, he would have been branded for future if not immediate
discovery.

One is driven to a second conclusion, which is not only in accord
with the known facts of Whitman's life, but consonant with the
man's curious blend of Puritan idealism and passionate sensuousness. Into that rich and moving love for men which made him an
angel of compassion in the hospitals, blending with it, and changing it sometimes into passionate longing, was infused an erotic
sexualism, to be distinguished from love of women only by its
objects. That this eroticism was sometimes, as he says, disproportionate, a disease of adhesiveness, which destroyed his serenity
and made idealizing difficult, he does not deny. But that this
might mean a physiological and psychological difference from the
normal man never seems to have occurred to him, until, in old age,
John Addington Symonds, an unhappy homosexual himself, made
clear by his praise of Whitman's courage that he believed him
to be, like himself, an unrepresentative man. The old poet was
horrified:

August 19, 1890

... About the questions on *Calamus* etc., they quite daze me.
Leaves of Grass is only rightly to be construed by and within its
own atmosphere and essential character — all its pages and pieces
so coming strictly under. That the *Calamus* part has ever allowed
the possibility of such construction as mentioned is terrible. I am
fain to hope that the pages themselves are not to be even mentioned for such gratuitous and quite at the time undreamed and
unwished possibility of morbid inference — which are disavowed
by me and seem damnable.[6]

I believe this letter to be entirely sincere. But what so upset the old man has been frequently misunderstood. He is not denying, of course, that passion, which implies sexuality, had inspired him in his love for men. This is implied, often stated, in his poems. It is one of the 'paths untrodden' into which he proposes in the first of the *Calamus* poems to lead his readers. Men must love their fellow men with the passion with which they love women, or there can be no comradeship strong enough to hold together an ideal democracy:

> Come, I will make the continent indissoluble...
> By the love of comrades,
> By the manly love of comrades.

He resented the charge that the power to lift such love above sex barriers was pathological, for he believed that good poetry could come only from what he called 'beautiful,' meaning healthy, 'blood.' Yet this power is certainly abnormal, though supernormal is I think the better term, and not representative of his democratic man, though he believed that ideally it should become so. Subconsciously at least he was aware of a dilemma. The sex-infused love of man for man had bad associations, was usually manifested by unhealthy human types. This, I should say, was one reason for his tiresome insistence throughout his poems upon his own perfect manliness and perfect health, his constant repetitions of 'robust,' 'vigorous,' 'rough,' his description of himself as 'rude, unbending, lusty.' These adjectives show a malaise. We are close here to an emotional and psychological weakness in Whitman. He was very definitely not the normal animal in both body and mind he described. But we are close to one of the secrets of his poetic strength also.

Science as well as common sense can be used to sum up this discussion. Whitman was a psychological type now clearly recognized, though not adequately named. Psychologically (and perhaps in the obscure dominance of the hormones physiologically), he was intermediate in sex. By which one means that exalted, yet passionate, physical love for a man was as possible for him as was the same kind of love for a woman — and in Whitman's case easier. Such men are very common, especially among strong cre-

ative intellects, whose imaginative sympathies penetrate beyond
sexual differences. They are very seldom homosexuals in the vulgar sense of the word. In Whitman's case, the eroticism diffused
itself in sexual imagery, and was sublimated into a fatherly love
of innumerable 'sons,' and into magnificent poems of the comradeship of true democracy. Let him speak for himself:

> Come, I will take you down underneath this impassive exterior, I will tell
>   you what to say of me,
> Publish my name and hang up my picture as that of the tenderest lover, . . .
> Who was not proud of his songs, but of the measureless ocean of love within
>   him, and freely pour'd it forth.

3

And yet this theory of a love overflowing sex boundaries still
oversimplifies the curious sexual nature of Walt Whitman. Nor is
it sufficient to say with some biographers that in his sex life he
was a delayed adolescent who, like a child, made few sexual dif-
ferentiations. There is some truth here, of course, but neither an
intermediate nor an adolescent sexuality explains the intense personal fervor with which Whitman dwelt upon and returned to the
physiology of love.

Numerous and revealing passages in the 'Leaves' suggest another source of sexual passion and sexual fluidity much more relevant to the 'measureless ocean of love' which obsessed Whitman
in so many of his poems. He was in love with himself, in love
with his own body, erotically in love with it on some occasions,
as when he says in the *Song of Myself*,

> I will go to the bank by the wood and become undisguised and naked,
> I am mad for it to be in contact with me.

Sublimated, spiritualized as this passion becomes in other lines
less faintly absurd, it is nevertheless usually erotic in its
imagery.

This auto-eroticism in diffused form penetrates, invigorates,
and sometimes debilitates many of the 'Leaves.' It is the physi-

ological expression of his egoism — narcisstic, I should say, but not onanistic, if these words can be used with a precise differentiation. Here is another and a positive reason for his obsession with healthy bodies, athletic women, hearty vigorous workmen, beautiful swimmers, rosy-bodied wives, virile husbands, all projections of his own body, so healthy in his youth. It is this obsession which makes so many of Walt's poems of the mid-century seem prophecies of our own athletic age of semi-nudity and the cult of exercise. Which make his poems prophetic also of the vigorous, self-dependent women who have succeeded the wasp-waisted, migrained, and dyspeptic girls and wives of the mid-century, when to faint was fashionable and to be an invalid was the profession of too many wives after the loss of their first bloom. From this springs, as much as from self-defence, Walt's boasting of his beautiful blood, his virility, his freedom from every ill. He was magnificently healthy when most of his best poems were written, but you would never guess from his later ones that after his early forties he was constantly sick, and finished life with a horrifying combination of internal breakdowns and diseases. It was love of his own body, sometimes rather unpleasant, sometimes flaunting, and sometimes magnificent, that made him so value his physical health.[7]

Divine am I inside and out, and I make holy whatever I touch or am touch'd
    from,
The scent of these arm-pits aroma finer than prayer, ...
If I worship one thing more than another it shall be the spread of my own
    body, or any part of it, ...
I dote on myself, there is that lot of me and all so luscious, ...

I find no sweeter fat than sticks to my own bones.[8]

The not too tasteful reference to armpits is no more unhealthy or decadent than modern advertisements about B. O. I prefer Whitman's coarseness to theirs. But this love of his own body very naturally tended to concentrate itself upon the genital regions, sometimes defiantly, sometimes because there the nervous sensibilities are most intense. And this, of course, shocked the prudish. We ourselves are not shocked by the seminal imagery, which runs so pervasively through the early 'Leaves' that only those most patient with symbols have discovered a half of it. We are more amused than shocked by the orgiastic vanity of his imagination:

> On women fit for conceptions I start bigger and nimbler babies,
> (This day I am jetting the stuff of far more arrogant republics.)

or

> The supernatural of no account, myself waiting my time to be one of the supremes,
> The day getting ready for me when I shall do as much good as the best, and be as prodigious;
> By my life-lumps! becoming already a creator,
> Putting myself here and now to the ambush'd womb of the shadows.

This is as amusing as the boasting of a humorless child, but, for those who wish to understand the poet and his poetry, it is very significant.

Whitman was perhaps more auto-sexual than anything else. The dilation of his ego until he felt himself creative and all-embracing was given confidence by this immense passion for his own physiology (or vice-versa; I would leave that to a psychiatrist to decide). Psychologically, he could feel like the *dea creatrix* of the ancients, or all-fertile Jove. Love sprang from him. He could breed love in others. There is no mistaking his certainty of this. What in other men might have been only a neurosis, with him became creative, was lifted into religion and expressed in poetry. Since his sexuality was not primarily objective, it lay deeper than sexual differentiation, precisely as the sexual organs show forms and functions which have come from an earlier biological level where sex was undifferentiated. With Walt, auto-eroticism was apparently not physical. It was psychological. He could feel like a woman. He could feel like a man. He could love a woman — though one suspects that it was difficult for him to love women physically, unless they were simple and primitive types. He could love a man with a kind of father-mother love, mingled, as such love often is, with obscure sexuality. Because all reference was back to his own body, he seemed to himself to be a microcosm of humanity. There are, I think, no truly objective love poems in the 'Leaves of Grass.'

This is perhaps the final explanation of the extraordinary boldness and cosmic breadth of Whitman's sexualism which he makes to pervade men, women, children, animals, nature, and is, truly, as he says, as much soul as body. This is the secret of his capacity for undifferentiated passion which knows no bounds to its sympathy and understanding, and is able thus to project itself into poems which celebrate love as a world solvent, and the cement of the perfect democracy.

The scientist will say, of course, and rightly, that he was a neurotic. But then all great men and women, in the eyes of science, are neurotic! It was a fallacy of Whitman's to insist, as he so frequently did, that great poetry can come only from a perfectly sound, evenly developed, completely healthy man in both body and mind. Of what great artist is this true? In Whitman's case, enough of this supernormality, based on an abnormality, crept into his work to make his attempt to write a textbook of personality good for *all* men and women a failure. The average man is repelled by emotional excess, especially if it is of an unusual kind. But his neurosis, if it is that, helped, of course, more than it hampered his efforts in poetry.

This auto-sexuality, which made him feel like a creative god, is probably a chief cause of the opposition amounting to repulsion his sexual poetry set up in the mid-nineteenth century. The reactions of his critics were often ignorant and unfair, and still more often indicative of a sexual neurosis on their part of a different kind. Walt is hardly ever morbid, and not diseased, not dirty, not irreligious; but the instinct of the public is hard to deceive. There was something a little unnatural in these poems of unchecked nature. There was a tension in his religious egoism, a strain in his sexuality. His finest work came when, as he said, his need for violent self-expression had passed.

And, to conclude this chapter, there is nothing really abnormal in Whitman except his excess. Every fully developed human being has the potentiality of everything that Walt strove with. There are apparently no absolutely pure sexual types. Whitman was large; he contained, as he said, multitudes. It was his excess that enabled him to make the most powerful as well as the most erratic passions articulate:

> Fast-Anchor'd eternal O love! O woman I love!
> O bride! O wife! more resistless than I can tell, the thought of you!
> Then separate, as disembodied or another born,
> Ethereal, the last athletic reality, my consolation,
> I ascend, I float in the regions of your love O man,
> O sharer of my roving life.[9]

CHAPTER XX

'Long too long America, . . . you learn'd from joys

and prosperity only'

IT WAS probably in 1861 or 1862 that Whitman wrote the magnificent marching song afterward published in 'Drum-Taps':

Forty years had I in my city seen soldiers parading,
Forty years as a pageant, till unawares the lady of this teeming and turbulent city,
Sleepless amid her ships, her houses, her incalculable wealth,
With her million children around her, suddenly,
At dead of night, at news from the south,
Incens'd struck with clinch'd hand the pavement.

Of course, it was not Manhattan but Whitman himself who, at dead of night, at news from the South, clinch'd his hands in uncontrollable anger. The attack on Fort Sumter in April, and the disaster of Bull Run in July of the same terrible year of 1861, were shocks which he felt in common with all Americans whose hopes were linked with the indissoluble union of these states. Bull Run, with its crass confidence, its demoralization, its rout, was like a terrible fulfilment of his warnings against the complacent rottenness of Northern politics and the decline of leadership in the United States. His immediate reaction was a burning patriotism and rage, not so much against the South ('The South,' he wrote years later, 'was technically right and humanly wrong'[1]) as against the appeasers and the disunionists of the North.

There was nothing in these emotions that Walt did not share with hundreds of thousands. In 1861 and 1862, and indeed throughout the war, Walt, for a revolutionary, conforms in his political opinions with extraordinary exactitude to the average opinions of the Unionist North. Not an Abolitionist until Abolition became politically necessary,[2] at first distrustful of Lincoln but later whole-heartedly supporting him, he was as representative a man of the faction that won the war as you could have found anywhere. In his war politics, he seems to have followed, instead of trying to lead. The rambunctious ego of the *Song of Myself* now desires to serve, passionately believes in victory, is contemptuous of trivial hardships, and forgets for the duration all personal ambition, except to continue to publish his poems, which now are poems of war.

If it were not for his letters and his poetry, we should not know that in 1861 and 1862 Whitman was even this much moved by the crisis of the nation. He protested violently in Pfaff's one night at a toast to the Southern arms offered by George Arnold of *The Saturday Press*, which had printed his *Out of the Cradle Endlessly Rocking* and championed the 'Leaves.' A quarrel followed which must have nearly come to a fight, since Arnold grabbed him by his long hair. Yet, like many a middle-aged American of such war years as 1917 or 1941, he chiefly went about his business, which, after the Boston edition was published, was free-lancing again, and the writing of the 'Brooklyniana' for *The Brooklyn Standard*. He took time off for visits in Greenport and rambles and sails around Long Island, and, seemingly, he contemplated no active part in the war. But this was not true. As the Wound-Dresser in Whitman's poem of that name says of himself when making his routine rounds among the wounded, 'Yet deep in my breast a fire, a burning flame.'

2

Those who know Walt realize that it could not have been otherwise. Why, then, did he not enlist and fight with the boys in blue? I ask this question only because it has been, and still is, raised by opponents of Whitman, out of sympathy with him for other reasons, and with little understanding of the man, the circumstances, or the times. Whitman was forty-two when the war began, about twenty years older than the average age of the Northern ranks, and, of course, without military training or predilection. It would have been a magnificent gesture, and also a nine days' wonder, if he had carried his already gray beard into the lines of the Brooklyn boys who joined Lincoln's first seventy-five thousand, or any later thousand.

It was, in the opinion of both North and South at first, to be a short war. But as the conflict broadened, Walt began to be sick with worry over the possible dependency of his family. George, ten years younger, had gone off and was to emerge as Colonel Whitman. The worthless Andrew (so Walt says in a letter) became a soldier, too, but probably not for long.[3] Jeff, who when George had gone was the only real money-maker, had a wife, a child, and another soon to come. Later his salary was cut to fifty dollars a month, and he was threatened by the draft, for which, it should be said here, Walt also registered.[4] Whitman had always paid his board and 'helped out' at home. From Washington he sent back money regularly from the scanty sums earned by free-lancing, which, while he was still in hospital service, were his means of support. There was his mother, the mentally deficient Eddie, and also Jesse, the insane brother, who was now living with the family in Portland Street. It was a picture of threatened dependency and Whitman's letters are full of foreboding. One does not wonder that when there was danger of Jeff's being taken too, he unhesitatingly promised to raise three hundred dollars somewhere to purchase a substitute lest the unfortunate household and the beloved old woman become destitute. The idea of a levy en-masse was not familiar in war, which was still regarded (North and South) in 1861–1865 as a job for fighters and professionals. Only those eligible in a strict military sense, and the young and unattached, seem to have been criticized in 1863 for sending a substitute instead of themselves to the front.

But disregarding this fact of dependency, no acquaintance of Whitman would have wished him to go into actual fighting, provided he could serve otherwise. Carnage and violence were deeply repugnant to his nature — one may say impossible to him except in the extreme of self-defence. He did not lack courage, since he faced smallpox and other contagious diseases in the hospitals, against advice and without hesitation, and risked and lost his health there. Nor had he any inflexible principle against war as an instrument. His Quaker conditioning had made him distrust war as such. War as an instrument he had learned to believe in morally, as he had believed in it for less creditable reasons at the time of the Mexican invasion. His spiritual fathers in the Society of Friends would not have frowned upon this attitude. Yet even without this background of dislike for bloodshed and violence, the sensitive fibre and still more the passionate love for mankind of Whitman were enough to make his 'call' (he uses this word in its Quaker sense with reference to the demands of war) a call to a different kind of service. He was capable of killing, but not of preparing to kill some unknown, simple, separate person.

I have devoted this much space to an unnecessary defense only because so many critics of Whitman have attacked his war record, as if he had been a slacker, a coward, or a bluff. This is nonsense and belongs to a now outmoded debunking. One might as well attack Henry Ward Beecher for propagandizing in England instead of carrying a knapsack. If he had done nothing but write 'Drum-Taps' and 'Democratic Vistas,' one would say that Whitman's services to his country ranked far above the contributions of the vast majority of men of his age. But since he did not fight, did not give up his usual occupations for war service until the end of 1862, it has been difficult for many of his critics to understand why, in so many later writings and conversations, he insists that the 'Leaves,' finally, are to revolve like a wheel on its hub around the Four Years War.

The answer is that, while Whitman the citizen throbbed with rage and pride and patriotism like his fellow Unionists, Whitman the poet drew deep and lasting emotions from his own personal experiences and the lessons of the conflict. This big-hearted fellow believed that he never really knew the American democracy, never joined hands with it, until after his war experiences. His war biography is a story of a rebirth of idealism, and the sublimation of one of the most powerful egoisms in literary history. It is the story of how Walt became actually the bard of democracy, with his remarkable 'Democratic Vistas' as a commentary in prose.

3

For a sensitive man like Whitman, the desperate years of the Republic were, as has been said above, not 1861–1865 but, say, 1850–1860. In the war years there was frightful danger, but also an immense release. (What sensitive knowledgeable man of our times would not say the same of 1933 to 1939 in comparison with the years after 1941.) With actual war (and Emerson and Thoreau both record this) came not only the physical satisfactions of violence returned for violence, but a spiritual reaction equally strong, though less consciously realized except by idealists and intellectuals, against political decadence. The traitorous presidentiads of weak Northerners were over. If the Republic was to go down now, it would go down fighting, not sitting.

All of this distress with the fatness of content, this hardening of purpose, this idea of release in test and trial and action, Whitman put in a brief poem of a nation that must be aroused before it is too late. It is called *Long, too Long America*, and is as pertinent to later years of crisis as to 1861 or 1862, when it was probably composed:

Long, too long America,
Traveling roads all even and peaceful you learn'd from joys and prosperity
    only,
But now, ah now, to learn from crises of anguish, advancing, grappling with
    direst fate and recoiling not,
And now to conceive and show to the world what your children en-masse
    really are. . . . ⁵

And it is certainly true that Whitman's first intentions in the war years was to serve his country as he believed a poet should, with the pen, if not the gun and sword:

Arous'd and angry, I'd thought to beat the alarum, and urge relentless war,

he wrote in *The Wound-Dresser*. But, alas, he still had no real public, and no one would publish his poems. The next two lines tell the story:

But soon my fingers fail'd me, my face droop'd and I resign'd myself,
To sit by the wounded and soothe them, or silently watch the dead.

There are other poems of this critical period which show how deep was his personal response to the rising storm even while he seemed to be going about his business as usual. One is the *Song of the Banner at Daybreak* written about 1860,[6] an inferior poem but revealing, for the reader sees that Whitman was aware that commercialism was willing to let the Union break up rather than risk profits and prosperity.

A child questions its father what the call of the banner and its pennant flying in the wind can mean, why it talks to him, why it is alive and must be listened to. And the father says (I paraphrase freely): This talk of patriotism, this stirring of the adrenal glands, this moonshine idealism for what the flag of the Union stands for, is dangerous nonsense. Look, child, at the solid-walled houses and good pavements in the city we have built, and don't risk death for an idea; look at these dazzling things in the houses and see the money-shops opening, and the goods and chattels we have worked so hard for, and stop yearning for the heights where this flag is 'cutting the air, touch'd by the sun, measuring the sky.' A poet has been listening in. 'I do not decry,' he says, 'the precious results of peace,' but I see that they will not stand fast an hour unless there is an idea, an ideal, out of reach and worthy to be 'furiously fought for' by men 'risking bloody death.' Otherwise there is no hope for the democracy. Houses and machines of themselves are nothing, the talk of thrift is chatter. America has grown dangerously materialistic, and must face crises of anguish, or the Republic is lost.

This is not chauvinism, though the language runs in that direction. It is Whitman in recovery from a profound depression. The sensual satisfactions and distributed wealth of America which he had been celebrating in his long inventories as the rich promise of the New World had become its disease. The fat has gone rancid in degenerate politics, vested interests have been unwilling to change the *status quo* lest money be lost. Only determined, sacrificial action for the sake of an idea can provide an antidote for gross materialism. War for its own sake is to be hated (and Whitman was to hate it still more before he was through);[7] yet with a spiritual resolve to risk danger and destruction, a man could look up.

Thus Whitman's deeper broodings on the Civil War in its

opening stages, when as yet he had done nothing relevant except to write unread poems, was not upon rights and wrongs of North and South, but upon the will to struggle North *and* South for something more essential than 'countless profit,' 'earn'd wages' (houses of peace) — 'if need be you shall again have every one of these houses to destroy them.' In short, like the best of the pioneers he had just celebrated in *Pioneers! O Pioneers!*, he felt the necessity of pushing on where the elder races (and his own democracy) had halted, toward a future worth living in.

Twenty years ago, when economic man was still functioning in the textbooks, and the economic interpretation of history had reduced the War Between the States to a struggle between two kinds of capitalism, these explosive outbursts of Whitman's might have seemed rhetorical and ridiculous. Later students of the Civil War feel differently. They have seen in their own time economic man and economic interpretations bombed into cellars by a war where ideologies have been more significant than potential profits. They admit the vested interests in our great civil struggle, are aware (as was Whitman) of the vast private profits, yet do not try to explain a four-year conflict of the plain people in arms without taking into account emotional involvements in faith and in ideals, good or bad. As for Whitman, to quote again from 'Drum-Taps':

> ... I am fully satisfied, I am glutted,
> I have witness'd the true lightning, I have witness'd my cities electric,
> I have lived to behold man burst forth.

As he watched New York arm, as he saw the Brooklyn soldiers leave for the front, with ropes naïvely tied to their guns to bring back 'Secesh' prisoners, his heart beat high. You can hear its rhythms in these poems of 'Drum-Taps,' said to have been written to provoke enlistment, which, nevertheless, have more of pride and happy energy than propaganda — *First O Songs for a Prelude, Eighteen Sixty-One, Beat! Beat! Drums!, Rise O Days from Your Fathomless Deeps.* He had been living in a corrupted society. Action, armed action, seemed like light breaking through a dirty sky. Nor was the war an end in itself. The end was a

nobler society. So he felt in violent reaction to his despairs and
his depressions of the 1850's:

Beautiful that war and all its deeds of carnage must in time be utterly lost,
That the hands of the sisters Death and Night incessantly, softly wash again,
    and ever again, this soil'd world.

4

But of what avail is either insight or passionate and effective
expression, if no one reads you? These 'Drum-Taps' might become, and have become, a contribution to the spiritual and
artistic history of his country. But in 1860, 1861, and 1862 they
were irrelevant to the actual war in process, because they were
unheard. If Whitman wanted active and immediate service, he
still had to look for a job.

He found one, without a conscious plan so far as we know, and
by accident, yet it was work which he had already begun and for
which he was well prepared.[8] When he had settled down in
Washington to the profession of soothing the wounded and
watching the dead, he was able to say that the mission for which
he had volunteered 'deeply holds me.' [9]

For many years he had visited prisons and wherever misery
was to be found. In 1860, to be specific, he was regularly calling
at the old New York Hospital on Broadway, to comfort and
amuse his stage-driver friends, sick or disabled there.[10] By 1861
and 1862, he had begun to spend hours with the returned
wounded, probably at first Brooklyn boys he had known. He
speaks of going to one hospital at least twenty times.[11] Such an
addition to his daily round was, of course, only casual, a continuance of old practices. But in December of 1862, after the
disastrous battle of Fredericksburg, the name of his brother
George appeared in the casualty lists. It was always Walt who
took responsibility for the family in time of emergency, even
though he was the least reliable in daily affairs. Taking a carpet-
bag and fifty dollars with him, and losing the money when his
pocket was picked while changing trains in Philadelphia, he arrived in Washington 'without a dime,' and, after vexatious de-

lays, got to the near-by front, and found George not seriously wounded. Naturally he stayed on for a while to be with his brother, and then to look up wounded Brooklyn boys in the camp hospitals and afterward in Washington. In a few weeks he had, or rather created, his job for the war. Let him tell his own story in his simple and deeply moving letters, chiefly to his mother. But note in reading that, although 'Drum-Taps' are seething in his head, this Walt who is now in action is not the bard and prophet, but rather the affectionate friend of all the world, un-literary, unassuming, whom I have tried to describe in an earlier chapter. A Walt uncomplicated, and sometimes ungrammatical in his communications; a Walt who is again in the absorbing stage, but absorbing now from a novel and intense experience; a Walt whose ego, for the time being, has dropped toward his subcon-scious, while his whole being is centred upon transferring the riches of love, pity, and cheer in his personality to boys and men whose natures had been opened by suffering or the approach of death. No wrestling with 'You, Reader,' or 'Camerado' now, but such simple means as a letter written, a gift, a kiss, and especially the precept of Jesus of Galilee, Love your neighbor (and your enemy) as yourself.

CHAPTER XXI

'To sit by the wounded and soothe them, or

silently watch the dead'

Dear, Dear Mother — Friday the 19th inst. I succeeded in reaching the camp of the 51st New York, and found George alive

To his mother, Dec. 29, 1862

and well.... When I found dear brother George,... O you may imagine how trifling all my little cares and difficulties seemed — they vanished into nothing. And now that I have lived for eight or nine days amid such scenes as the camps furnish, and had a practical part in it all, and realize the way that hundreds of thousands of good men are now living, and have had to live for a year or more, not only without any of the comforts, but with death and sickness and hard marching and hard fighting (and no success at that) for their continual experience — really nothing we call trouble seems worth talking about. One of the first things that met my eyes in camp was a heap of feet, arms, legs, etc., under a tree in front of a hospital, the Lacy house.... I will stay here for the present, at any rate long enough to see if I can get any employment at anything, and shall write what luck I have.[1]

I can be satisfied and happy henceforward if I can get one meal

To his sister, Jan. 2, 1863

a day, and know that mother and all are in good health, and especially be with you again and have some little steady paying occupation in N.Y. or Brooklyn.

Yesterday I went out to the Campbell hospital to see a couple of Brooklyn boys, of the 51st. They knew I was in Washington,

To his sister, Jan. 3, 1863

and sent me a note, to come and see them. O my dear sister, how your heart would ache to go through the rows of wounded young men, as I did — and stopt to speak a comforting word to them. There were about 100 in one long room, just a long shed neatly white washed inside. One young man was very much prostrated, and groaning with pain. I stopt and tried to comfort him. He was very sick. I found he had not had any medical attention since he was brought there; among so many he had been overlooked; so I sent for the doctor, and he made an examination of him. The doctor behaved very well — seemed anxious to do right — said that the young man would recover; he had been brought pretty low with diarrhoea, and now had bronchitis, but not so serious as to be dangerous. I talked to him some time — he seemed to have entirely given up, and lost heart — he had not a cent of money — not a friend or acquaintance. I wrote a letter from him to his sister — his name is John A. Holmes, Campello, Plymouth county, Mass. I gave him a little change I had — he said he would like to buy a drink of milk when the woman came through with milk. Trifling as this was, he was overcome and began to cry.

The work of the army hospital visitor is indeed a trade, an art, requiring both experience and natural gifts, and the greatest judgment. A large number of the visitors to the hospitals do no good at all, while many do harm. The surgeons have great trouble from them. Some visitors go from curiosity — as to a show of animals. Others give the men improper things. Then there are always some poor fellows, in the crises of sickness or wounds, that imperatively need perfect quiet — not to be talked to by strangers. Few realize that it is not the mere giving of gifts that does good; it is the proper adaptation. Nothing is of any avail among the soldiers except conscientious personal investigation of cases, each for itself; with sharp, critical faculties, but in the fullest spirit of human sympathy and boundless love. The men feel such love more than anything else. I have met very few persons who realize the importance of humoring the yearnings for love and friendship of these American young men, prostrated by sickness and wounds.

From 'Hospital Visits,' *August, September, October, 1863*

To many of the wounded and sick, especially the youngsters,

there is something in personal love, caresses, and the magnetic

From 'Hospital Visits,' March and April, 1864
flood of sympathy and friendship, that does, in its way, more good than all the medicine in the world. I have spoken of my regular gifts of delicacies, money, tobacco, special articles of food, knick-knacks, etc., etc. But I steadily found more and more that I could help, and turn the balance in favor of cure, by the means here alluded to, in a curiously large proportion of cases. The American soldier is full of affection and the yearning for affection. And it comes wonderfully grateful to him to have this yearning gratified when he is laid up with painful wounds or illness, far away from home, among strangers. Many will think this merely sentimentalism, but I know it is the most solid of facts. I believe that even the moving around among the men, or through the ward, of a hearty, healthy, clean, strong, generous-souled person, man or woman, full of humanity and love, sending out invisible, constant currents thereof, does immense good to the sick and wounded.

As I write this, in May, 1863, the wounded have begun to arrive from Hooker's command, from bloody Chancellorsville. I

From 'Hospital Visits,' May, 1863
was down among the first arrivals. The men in charge of them told me the bad cases were yet to come. If that is so, I pity them, for these are bad enough.

This afternoon, July 22, 1863, I spent a long time with a young man I have been with considerable, named Oscar F. Wilber,

From 'Hospital Visits,' July, 1863
Company G, One Hundred Fifty-fourth New York, low with chronic diarrhoea and a bad wound also. He asked me to read him a chapter in the New Testament. I complied and asked him what I should read. He said, 'Make your own choice.' I opened at the close of one of the first books of the Evangelists, and read the chapters describing the latter hours of Christ and the scenes at the crucifixion. The poor wasted young man asked me to read the following chapter also, how Christ rose again. I read very slowly, for Oscar was feeble. It pleased him very much, yet the tears were in his eyes.

He asked me if I enjoyed religion. I said, 'Perhaps not, my dear, in the way you mean, and yet maybe it is the same thing.' He said, 'It is my chief reliance.' He talked of death, and said he did not fear it. I said, 'Why, Oscar, don't you think you will get well?' He said, 'I may, but it is not probable.' He spoke calmly of his condition. The wound was very bad; it discharged much. Then the diarrhoea had prostrated him, and I felt that he was even then the same as dying. He behaved very manly and affectionate. The kiss I gave him as I was about leaving, he returned fourfold. He gave me his mother's address, Mrs. Sally D. Wilber, Alleghany post-office, Cattaraugus County, N. Y. I had several such interviews with him. He died a few days after the one just described.

The soldiers are nearly all young men, and far more Americans than is generally supposed — I should say nine tenths are native *From* 'Hospital born. Among the arrivals from Chancellors-Visits,' *May, 1863* ville I find a large proportion of Ohio, Indiana, and Illinois men. As usual there are all sorts of wounds. Some of the men are fearfully burnt from the explosion of artillery caissons. One ward has a long row of officers, some with ugly hurts. Yesterday was perhaps worse than usual: amputations are going on; the attendants are dressing wounds. As you pass by you must be on your guard where you look. I saw, the other day, a gentleman, a visitor, stop and turn a moment to look at an awful wound they were probing, etc.; he turned pale, and in a moment more he had fainted away and fallen on the floor. I buy in the hot weather, boxes of oranges from time to time, and distribute them among the men; also preserved peaches and other fruits; also lemons and sugar for lemonade. Tobacco is also much in demand. Large numbers of the men come up, as usual, without a cent of money. Through the assistance of friends in Brooklyn and Boston, I am again able to help many of those that fall in my way. It is only a small sum in each case, but it is much to them. As before, I go around daily and talk with the men, to cheer them up.

I spent several hours in the Capitol the other day . . . the style is without grandeur, and without simplicity. These days, the *To Jeff, Feb. 13, 1863* state our country is in, and especially filled as I am from top to toe of late with scenes and thoughts of the hospitals, (America seems to me now, though only in her youth, but brought already here, feeble, bandaged, and bloody in hospital) — these days I say, Jeff, all the poppy-show goddesses, and all the pretty blue and gold in which the interior Capitol is got up, seem to me out of place beyond anything I could tell.

I believe I weigh about 200, and as to my face, (so scarlet,) and my beard and neck, they are terrible to behold. I fancy the *To his mother, April 15, 1863* reason I am able to do some good in the hospitals among the poor languishing and wounded boys, is, that I am so large and well — indeed like a great wild buffalo, with much hair. Many of the soldiers are from the West, and far North, and they take to a man that has not the bleached shiny and shaved cut of the cities and the East.

I generally go to the hospitals from 12 to 4 — and then again from 6 to 9; some days I only go in the middle of the day or eve- *To his mother, May 19, 1863* ning, not both — and then when I feel somewhat opprest, I skip over a day, or make perhaps a light call only, as I have several cautions from the doctors, who tell me that one must beware of continuing too steady and long in the air and influences of the hospitals. I find the caution a wise one.

As to the Sanitary commissions and the like, I am sick of them all, and would not accept any of their berths. You ought to see *To his mother, June 22, 1863* the way the men, as they lay helpless in bed, turn away their faces from the sight of those agents, chaplains, etc. (hirelings, as Elias Hicks would call them — they seem to me always a set of foxes and wolves). They get well paid, and are always incompetent and disagreeable; as I told you before, the only good fellows I have met are the Christian commissioners — they go everywhere and receive no pay.

Well, mother, I suppose you folks think we are in a somewhat dubious position here in Washington, with Lee in strong force *To his mother,* almost between us and you Northerners. *June 30, 1863* Well, it does look ticklish; if the Rebs cut the connection then there will be fun. The Reb cavalry come quite near us, dash in and steal wagon trains, etc.; it would be funny if they should come some night to the President's country house (Soldiers' home), where he goes out to sleep every night; it is in the same direction as their saucy raid last Sunday. Mr. Lincoln passes here (14th st.) every evening on his way out. I noticed him last evening about half-past 6 — he was in his barouche, two horses, guarded by about thirty cavalry. The barouche comes first under a slow trot, driven by one man in the box, no servant or footman beside; the cavalry all follow closely after with a lieutenant at their head. I had a good view of the President last evening. He looks more careworn even than usual, his face with deep cut lines, seams, and his *complexion gray* through very dark skin — a curious looking man, very sad. I said to a lady who was looking with me, 'Who can see that man without losing all wish to be sharp upon him personally?' The lady assented, although she is almost vindictive on the course of the administration (thinks it wants nerve, etc. — the usual complaint). The equipage is rather shabby, horses indeed almost what my friends the Broadway drivers would call *old plugs*. The President dresses in plain black clothes, cylinder hat — he was alone yesterday.

Mother, one's heart grows sick of war, after all, when you see what it really is; every once in a while I feel so horrified and dis- *To his mother,* gusted — it seems to me like a great slaugh- *Sept. 8, 1863* terhouse and the men mutually butchering each other — then I feel how impossible it appears, again, to retire from this contest, until we have carried our points (it is cruel to be so tossed from pillar to post in one's judgment).... One of the things here always on the go is long trains of army wagons....

They have great camps here in every direction...and small hospitals. I go to them (as no one else goes; ladies would not venture). I sometimes have the luck to give some of the drivers a great deal of comfort and help. Indeed, mother, there are camps here of everything — I went once or twice to the contraband camp, to the hospital, etc., but I could not bring myself to go again — when I meet black men or boys among my own hospitals, I use them kindly, give them something, etc. — I believe I told you that I do the same to the wounded Rebels, too — but as there is a limit to one's sinews and endurance and sympathies, etc., I have got in the way, after going lightly, as it were, all through the wards of a hospital, and trying to give a word of cheer, if nothing else, to every one, then confining my special attentions to the few where the investment seems to tell best, and who want it most. Mother, I have real pride in telling you that I have the consciousness of saving quite a number of lives by saving them from giving up — and being a good deal with them; the men say it is so, and the doctors say it is so — and I will candidly confess I can see it is true, though I say it of myself. I know you will like to hear it, mother, so I tell you.

I have cut my hair and beard — since the event Rosecrans,
To his mother,   Charleston, etc., etc., have among my ac-
Oct. 6, 1863   quaintances been hardly mentioned, being
insignificant themes in comparison.

Well, dear mother, how the time passes away — to think it will soon be a year I have been away! It has passed away very
To his mother,   swiftly, somehow, to me. O what things I
Oct. 27, 1863   have witnessed during that time — I shall
never forget them. And the war is not settled yet, and one does not see anything at all certain about the settlement yet; but I have finally got for good, I think, into the feeling that our triumph is assured, whether it be sooner or whether it be later, or whatever roundabout way we are led there, and I find I don't change that conviction from any reverses we meet, or any delays or Government blunders. There are blunders enough,

heaven knows, but I am thankful things have gone on as well for us as they have — thankful the ship rides safe and sound at all. Then I have finally made up my mind that Mr. Lincoln has done as good as a human man could do. I still think him a pretty big President. I realize here in Washington that it has been a big thing to have just kept the United States from being thrown down and having its throat cut; and now I have no doubt it will throw down Secession and cut its throat — and I have not had any doubt since Gettysburg. Well, dear, dear mother, I will draw to a close. Andrew and Jeff and all, I send you my love. Goodbye, dear mother and dear Matty and all hands.

Mother, I wonder if George thinks as I do about the best way to enjoy a visit home, after all. When I come home again, I *To his mother,* shall not go off gallivanting with my com-*Jan. 29, 1864* panions half as much nor a quarter as much as I used to, but shall spend the time quietly home with you while I do stay; it is a great humbug spreeing around, and a few choice friends for a man, the real right kind in a quiet way, are enough.

There is quite a number of sick young men I have taken in hand, from the late arrivals, that I am sorry to leave. Sick and *To his mother,* down-hearted and lonesome, they think so *Feb. 5, 1864* much of a friend, and I get so attached to them too — but I want to go down in camp once more very much; and I think I shall be back in a week. I shall spend most of my time among the sick and wounded in the camp hospitals. If I had means I should stop with them, poor boys, or go among them periodically, dispensing what I had, as long as the war lasts, down among the worst of it (although what are collected here in hospital seem to me about as severe and needy cases as any, after all).

I could not keep the tears out of my eyes. Many of the poor young men had to be moved on stretchers, with blankets over *To his mother,* them, which soon soaked as wet as water in *March 29, 1864* the rain. Most were sick cases, but some badly wounded. I came up to the nearest hospital and helped.

Mother, it was a dreadful night (last Friday night) — pretty dark, the wind gusty, and the rain fell in torrents. One poor boy — this is a sample case out of the 600 — he seemed to be quite young, he was quite small (I looked at his body afterwards), he groaned some as the stretcher bearers were carrying him along, and again as they carried him through the hospital gate. They set down the stretcher and examined him, and the poor boy was dead. They took him into the ward, and the doctor came immediately, but it was all of no use. The worst of it is, too, that he is entirely unknown — there was nothing on his clothes, or any one with him to identify him, and he is altogether unknown. Mother, it is enough to rack one's heart — such things. Very likely his folks will never know in the world what has become of him. Poor, poor child, for he appeared as though he could be but 18. I feel lately as though I must have some intermission. I feel well and hearty enough, and was never better, but my feelings are kept in a painful condition a great part of the time. Things get worse and worse, as to the amount and sufferings of the sick, and as I have said before, those who have to do with them are getting more and more callous and indifferent. Mother, when I see the common soldiers, what they go through, and how everybody seems to try to pick upon them, and what humbug there is over them every how, even the dying soldier's money stolen from his body by some scoundrel attendant, or from [the] sick one, even from under his head, which is a common thing, and then the agony I see every day, I get almost frightened at the world. Mother, I will try to write more cheerfully next time — but I see so much. Well, good-bye for present, dear mother.

Of the many I have seen die, or known of, the past year, I have not seen or heard of *one* who met death with any terror. Yester-

To his mother,   day afternoon I spent a good part of the after-
May 23, 1864   noon with a young man of 17, named Charles
Cutter, of Lawrence City, Mass., 1st Mass. heavy artillery, battery M. He was brought in to one of the hospitals mortally wounded in abdomen. Well, I thought to myself as I sat looking at him, it ought to be a relief to his folks after all, if they could

see how little he suffered. He lay very placid in a half lethargy with his eyes closed. It was very warm, and I sat a long while fanning him and wiping the sweat. At length he opened his eyes wide and clear and looked inquiringly around. I said, 'What is it, my dear? do you want anything?' He said quietly, with a good natured smile. 'O nothing; I was only looking around to see who was with me.' His mind was somewhat wandering, yet he lay so peaceful, in his dying condition. He seemed to be a real New England country boy, so good natured, with a pleasant homely way, and quite a fine looking boy. Without any doubt he died in course of night.

2

And thus Whitman's great rolling figure, his flowing beard till he cut it, became familiar in Washington hospitals and on Washington streets. His broad, light-colored hat, blue flannel coat, shirts (by his mother) with frilled Marseilles collars, and flowing tie must have made his appearance in a hospital ward a stage entrance. He knew it, and enjoyed it, but this time with no pose, or desire to court publicity. That he was obviously a personage, whom the guards sometimes saluted, made, however, his position easier. He was entirely on his own, had to win his way with officials, doctors, and nurses, in order to have recourse to his boys. He did so, disliking the officials, praising the doctors and nurses.

There were some fifty hospitals, good and bad, mostly bad, in Washington at the height of the war, and in them were (according to Whitman) twice as many sick as there were wounded. As there were three times as many casualties from sickness as from wounds in the Union armies, his estimate was probably right. Readers of Mrs. Leech's 'Reveille in Washington' will remember her documented account of the distressing conditions under which the rescue of casualties was conducted in the Civil War. The army department charged with the care of the wounded had been completely petrified since the Mexican War, and never caught up with this new conflict, but was always preparing for a battle after it was fought. They will remember that, in the first

years, the return of the wounded was entrusted to the teamsters
who carted up supplies and ammunition to the front. As a result, thousands of men lay unattended, sometimes for days, in
the field, thousands of both sick and wounded were dumped into
rough army-camp hospitals, where they stayed until their condition grew desperate. Then they were hauled, like the corpses
many of them became, to the steamboat landing at Aquia Creek
on the Potomac, and dropped on the wharves at Washington.
Naturally, there was a frightful aggravation of disease, especially
dysentery and pneumonia, and a horrible neglect of wounds.

In Washington, the hospitals were temporary sheds, grouped in
units, long, one-story edifices, each containing sixty cots, more in
an emergency. They were quite well organized in groups about an
administrative office, more or less heated, and much better than
the first destination of sick and dying men, which was the Patent
Office among glass cases of strange utensils and machines. Some
of these hospitals held a thousand men at a time, one, sixteen
hundred. It would seem probable that some thirty thousand were
usually under treatment in Washington. Thus Walt's field was
vast, but his energy was immense, and, at first, his health magnificent.

With the organization of the Union-wide Sanitary Commission
to supplement the tape-bound services, and the work of the Christian Commissioners,[2] conditions in the field improved. Yet in
characteristically American fashion, morality was mixed with
charity in a sometimes unfortunate blend. These worthy organi-
zations seemed to have determined to cure souls in their own way,
while the body was helpless. Only Whitman (so he said) gave
tobacco to the poor fellows when they craved it. As for the
Sanitary Commission, one annual report issued at the end of the
war, stated that it had distributed 787,276 pages of tracts, and
only thirteen reams of paper for writing letters!

Walt's approach was entirely different, as his letters show, and
it was an approach to suffering consciously calculated to soothe
the mind, lift the heart a little, and comfort the body. He stepped
in when doctors and nurses stepped out. These boys, as most of
them seem to have been, were not only suffering, they were lost,

unhappy, frightened, homesick. Walt gave them hope from his great reservoirs, and when there was no hope, love. Much went out of him to them, as he sat by their beds, or recited *Marco Bozarris* (never his own poetry) to the whole ward. As he had written years before:

> Behold, I do not give lectures or a little charity,
> When I give I give myself.[3]

With what we know now of psychology and psychiatry, and the relations between mental and physical health, it is not necessary to argue the value of Whitman's services. Twenty-eight per cent of all the American casualties in the first World War are now estimated to have been men who were psychologically unfit for the strain of combat service. Whether true or not of Whitman's soldiers, these youths were suffering from shock as well as from wounds or diseases. The will to recover was at least as important as the crude surgery and cruder medicine of the time. Whitman gave them that will.

Nor did the power that he exerted come merely from a strong personality and a kind heart. In these intimate contacts with young men from all over, New Englanders, Westerners, and Southerners also, for whom he showed special affection, the ease with which Whitman's love flowed toward the young of his own sex (a love dangerous only if too much particularized) resulted in tender relationships where he literally gave to his boys what a mother or a wife, but no nurse, friend, or doctor, could have given. They needed, as he said, and desired 'petting.' Many of them he came to love passionately, but entirely without that perturbation which, with him, was always a sign of unbalance and excess. He kissed them and they returned his kissing. The kiss of man and man was, of course, far commoner in the nineteenth century than in the twentieth, but Walt recognized that his kisses were more than comforting affection, which is shown by his care to explain that they were not sentimental. The Calamus in his nature was now an entire good. It gave to his love the intensity which is a tonic in distress.

That the hospital staffs appreciated his services is abundantly testified, and it would be easy to quote a sheaf of thanks from his soldiers. With his cane in his room in Camden, he would often poke at an old letter from some boy or another, home safe and well again, and be deeply moved when it was read. To anyone even superficially acquainted with human needs in time of trial, the letters quoted above are evidence enough that he was the right man in the right place.[4]

It is not necessary to assume that his old-age references to bivouacking with the troops and carrying a flag of truce to the enemy are either literally true, or tall stories intended to exaggerate his experiences. They were close enough to the truth he heard at firsthand from soldiers just back from what was usually, in the early years, defeat. Imagination and reality often intertwined in Walt's mind, especially when he was old. It is enough to say that his 'Drum-Taps' contains poems of this hospital period more truly descriptive than any other prose and poetry in that time, of the sights and emotions of the front.

In this war period, he supported himself by hack writing for the Washington newspapers, and his excellent hospital letters to *The New York Times* and *Tribune* and *Brooklyn Eagle*. (Raymond of *The Times* sent him fifty dollars once as a bonus for excellence.)[5] Out of these returns he lived, sent some money home, and added to the sums he raised by correspondence for dainties, paper, and knick-knacks for his soldiers. But his chief energy was mortgaged to the hospitals.[6] Whether an accidental wound on his hand in August, 1863, with blood-poisoning resulting, or (as he thought) malarial fever, broke him down, is not certain. More probably it was simply the strain of such continued emotional effort. In previous months his head had begun to trouble him. He thinks it a recurrence of a supposed sunstroke suffered years before. 'For two or three days I was down sick, for the first time in my life (as I have never before been sick).'[7] In October of that year he is still boasting of his health. In May of 1864 he is complaining again about his head, of its 'fullness.' In June, he was not feeling 'first rate' and was homesick — 'something new for me.' By June 7 he has had 'spells of deathly faintness.' The doctors warn him that he is 'going in too strong.'

The 'spells' continue. Soon he has to give up and go home to Brooklyn, writing Eldridge in October that still he does not feel as 'unconscionably hearty as before my sickness.' By 1869 the 'spells,' recurring, leave him temporarily little use of his limbs. Always his head troubles him. Finally came partial but irrevocable paralysis in 1873. He may have been weakened by some hospital disease, but it sounds like long-continued overstrain upon a system not able to take it — a full-blooded man with weakening arterial walls, who brings on a premature stroke by 'going in too strong' with all his emotions and all his physical energies, giving out every ounce of himself until his magnificent body yields, first to occasional leakage, and then to an actual break. The destroying flame (to change the figure) was lit in these war years; after 1873 he was burnt out. He was clearly right when he said (though he would not press an attempt to pension him) that he had lost his health in the Civil War as truly as did many a soldier he cared for.

3

The first impact of the war upon Whitman was (as I have said in different words) to tear a film from his eyes. He saw the cause of his depression in the bad years. He must have seen (though he does not admit) the weaknesses in his prophecy for New World democracy. He understood that the wave of expansion in his country had swept over the idea and the ideal and been diverted into a gross materialism. (The economist would say that it had never been diverted, but rather that time in its widening sweep had shown a weakness that it had always possessed, and perhaps this is the truth.) A great shock, a crisis, was necessary if what had been almost lost was to be retained. This realization roused Whitman's nature to accept carnage, conflict between brethren, destruction of his proud cities, death for his common people, deprivation for his rosy-fleshed women. So, aroused and angry, he welcomed the war.

But the second impulse from the war went deeper, for it ran with, not against, the current of his hopes. These years in the hospitals shifted his democratic faith from ideal to reality, from an often Utopian hope to a less rhetorical confidence in the worth of the individual. This we now know to be the essence of democracy, which can never be preserved by institutions alone.

It was in the hospitals that Whitman, for the first time, knew and loved for themselves, and not for any theory or temperamental wish of his own, young American men by hundreds and thousands, really representative of the whole of his country. The en-masse before this had been a symbol of his own prophetic ego, an extension of what he regarded as his representative self. Now, as in a controlled experiment, he sat with the youth of America at moments when all that they had was called to the test. 'I never knew what American young men were,' he wrote, 'till I have been in the hospitals.' [8] And they proved to be all that he had hoped for them.

This was not sentimentalism, nor even the bias of pity. Whitman describes, without varnish, the brutality, rascality, hoggishness he encountered in Washington. He hears, and is indignant at, atrocity stories. He is quite unconcerned with the past experiences of these soldiers, which he knew were trivial, and sometimes worse. But in a crisis, all these young fellows had been willing to risk their lives; after personal disaster they reacted like good men; they were lovable (most of them) and loved him. Nor did he choose the best for his attentions. He particularly charges the hospital visitor not to be influenced in his choice of duty by good looks, manners, or charm.[9] The divine average seemed to prove itself when called upon. Whatever was to be said of the leaders, he found the en-masse sound.

As a result, the amorphous Jefferson-Jackson ideology of his Democratic politics noticeably crystallizes after the experiences of war. He becomes less interested in himself as a religion incarnate, less rhetorical about democracy, more certain of his confidence that democracy has firm ground in human nature. Without being conscious of the philosophical implications, he is confirmed in that faith in the people which was implicit in the founding of the Republic, and in the long tradition of Catholic humanism. And this is the reason why the later editions of the 'Leaves' are made to revolve around the Four Years War. 'The meaning of America is democracy,' he writes in an unused preface of 1864.[10] The book as a whole shifts its final emphasis from democratic Walt to democracy.

And so at the end of the great war, emerging from a symbolic battlefield tent for good, 'loosing, untying the tent-ropes,' he enlists again for his own campaign, the cause of democracy now as broad as human nature itself:

Adieu O soldier,
You of the rude campaigning (which we shared,)
The rapid march, the life of the camp,
The hot contention of opposing fronts, the long manoeuvre,
Red battles with their slaughter, the stimulus, the strong terrific game,
Spell of all brave and manly hearts, the trains of time through you and like
     of you all fill'd,
With war and war's expression.

Adieu dear comrade,
Your mission is fulfill'd — but I, more warlike,
Myself and this contentious soul of mine,
Still on our own campaigning bound,
Through untried roads with ambushes opponents lined,
Through many a sharp defeat and many a crisis, often baffled,
Here marching, ever marching on, a war fight out — aye here,
To fiercer, weightier battles give expression.[11]

CHAPTER XXII

'O powerful western fallen star!'

WHITMAN was fortunate in his friends in Washington. Charles Eldridge was there, his Boston publisher, now an assistant in Major Hapgood's paymaster's office, and through this friendship, he was given a desk in the corner, and many of the letters quoted above were written there. Hapgood gave him also a little copying to do, which helped his slender finances. He found also William Douglas O'Connor, the fiery Irishman whom he had met in Boston. O'Connor, a novelist when Walt knew him before, was now in the Signal Bureau, and, what was more relevant, married to a woman who became one of Walt's dearest friends. A partisan, a pamphleteer, with an erratic but extensive education, O'Connor made the cause of Whitman and the 'Leaves' his own cause. At the moment he was of inestimable help by giving Whitman a home where he could relax after the tensions of hospital life. Walt got a room for a few dollars a month just below the O'Connors' apartment, breakfasted and dined with them when they were housekeeping, bought his stout meal for two bits when they were not, and made his own breakfast and tea. Sundays he spent usually with them and their many friends. John Burroughs, the naturalist, a country boy from Delaware County, New York, began his intimacy with Whitman at this time. He was now a treasury clerk who had not yet begun to capitalize his devotion to nature. Burroughs became the chief companion of Walt's long rambles through the adjacent country, and, incidentally, sharpened the ear and eye of a poet none too accurate in his observations of nature. But the powerful impression of personality in these early Washington days came from the man he saw almost daily, but with whom he never exchanged a word — Abraham Lincoln.

Yet his chief concern outside the hospitals was not the friendly life he was now leading, nor the great and the near great about him in Washington, but his poetry.

Whitman believed that the true story of the Civil War would never get into the books.[1] And he was right for his own times, since no war has had its complete history written until the shattering realism of the books that followed the first world conflict of 1914–1918. The readers of the 1860's did not want realism. Whitman's hospital journals (later published in *Specimen Days*) were offered, vainly, for publication in 1863; which is not surprising in that critical year when those responsible for public opinion were certainly not eager to advertise suffering and death and so discourage enlistment.[2] But the difficulty he encountered in getting 'Drum-Taps' into print is more surprising, for this is one of the most satisfying of all collections of war poems — stirring, noble, intensely pictorial, and intended to idealize what could be idealized in war.

He knew that it was a good book, yet in January of 1865 it was still in manuscript, and he was hoping to stereotype it himself and then find a publisher. Boston had refused it, so also must have New York, for eventually he had to bring it out himself. Why? Perhaps because, as toward the close and just after the close of the first World War, war books would not sell. Yet there is another, and even more probable, reason. After 1860–1861, when a beginning at least had been made of a real publication for the 'Leaves,' Walt had acquired a widening reputation but, except among the discerning, it was a reputation for being dirty in language, blasphemous, and often unintelligible.

His book did appear early in 1865, in pamphlet form, dated New York, 1865, but was recalled from sale, and reissued at the end of the year, with a sequel bound in, *When Lilacs Last in the Door Yard Bloom'd and Other Pieces*, dated Washington 1865–1866. For in April, Lincoln had been shot.

The best appreciation of the original 'Drum-Taps' is to be

found in a letter by Whitman himself to O'Connor of January 6, 1865, before the birth of the book in print:

'It is in my opinion superior to *Leaves of Grass* — certainly more perfect as a work of art, being adjusted in all its proportions, & its passion having the indispensable merit that though to the ordinary reader let loose with wildest abandon, the true artist can see it is yet under control. But I am perhaps mainly satisfied with *Drum-Taps* because it delivers ... the ... large conflicting fluctuations of despair & hope, the shiftings, masses, & the whirl & deafening din, (yet over all, as by invisible hand, a definite purport & idea) — with the unprecedented anguish of wounded & suffering, the beautiful young men, in wholesale death & agony, everything sometimes as if blood color, & dripping blood. The book is therefore unprecedently sad ...'— but it also has the blast of the trumpet, & the drum pounds and whirrs in it, & then an undertone of sweetest comradeship & human love. ... *Drum-Taps* has none of the perturbations of the *Leaves of Grass*. ... I have ... succeeded ... in removing all superfluity from it, verbal superfluity I mean, I delight to make a poem where I feel clear that not a word but is indispensable part thereof & of my meaning.' [3]

What a blurb writer Whitman would have made for his publisher, if he had only found one that could or would stick by him! No wonder that with his talent for conveying the soul of a book, he often wrote his own reviews! In this account of his manuscript, little is left to be added by another, unless in reference to the vivid pictorial quality of the poems. There is an excellence of depiction in 'Drum-Taps,' like the graphic illustrations which a great American school of art was to develop in the next generation. We have no such pictures of Civil War scenes elsewhere, except in Stephen Crane's little masterpiece, and the almost forgotten John William DeForest's 'The Conversion of Miss Ravenel from Secession to Loyalty.' [4] But Whitman is more concentrated and intense:

A sight in camp in the daybreak gray and dim,
As from my tent I emerge so early sleepless,
As slow I walk in the cool fresh air the path near by the hospital tent,

Three forms I see on stretchers lying, brought out there untended lying,
Over each the blanket spread, ample brownish woolen blanket,
Gray and heavy blanket, folding, covering all.

Curious I halt and silent stand,
Then with light fingers I from the face of the nearest the first just lift the
        blanket;
Who are you elderly man so gaunt and grim, with well-gray'd hair, and flesh
        all sunken about the eyes?
Who are you my dear comrade?

Then to the second I step — and who are you my child and darling?
Who are you sweet boy with cheeks yet blooming?

Then to the third — a face nor child nor old, very calm, as of beautiful yel-
        low-white ivory;
Young man I think I know you — I think this face is the face of the Christ
        himself,
Dead and divine and brother of all, and here again he lies.[5]

Still more like a fine illustration is *A March in the Ranks*:

A march in the ranks hard-prest, and the road unknown,
A route through a heavy wood with muffled steps in the darkness,
Our army foil'd with loss severe, and the sullen remnant retreating,
Till after midnight glimmer upon us the lights of a dim-lighted building,
We come to an open space in the woods, and halt by the dim-lighted building,
'Tis a large old church at the crossing roads, now an impromptu hospital,
Entering but for a minute I see a sight beyond all the pictures and poems
        ever made,
Shadows of deepest, deepest black, just lit by moving candles and lamps,
And by one great pitchy torch stationary with wild red flame and clouds of
        smoke,
By these, crowds, groups of forms vaguely I see on the floor, some in the pews
        laid down,
At my feet more distinctly a soldier, a mere lad, in danger of bleeding to
        death, (he is shot in the abdomen,)
I stanch the blood temporarily, (the youngster's face is white as a lily,)
Then before I depart I sweep my eyes o'er the scene fain to absorb it all,
Faces, varieties, postures beyond description, most in obscurity, some of
        them dead,
Surgeons operating, attendants holding lights, the smell of ether, the odor
        of blood,
The crowd, O the crowd of the bloody forms, the yard outside also fill'd,

Some on the bare ground, some on planks or stretchers, some in the death-
　　　spasm sweating,
An occasional scream or cry, the doctor's shouted orders or calls,
The glisten of the little steel instruments catching the glint of the torches,
These I resume as I chant, I see again the forms, I smell the odor,
Then hear outside the orders given, *Fall in, my men, fall in*;
But first I bend to the dying lad, his eyes open, a half-smile gives he me,
Then the eyes close, calmly close, and I speed forth to the darkness,
Resuming, marching, ever in darkness marching, on in the ranks,
The unknown road still marching.[6]

It is evident that in the letter quoted above Walt has not yet
thought of 'Drum-Taps' as the hub of the 'Leaves,' because he
has not yet seen its relevancy to the centre of his life's work —
the expression of democracy. He thinks of it (and naturally) as
a war book, a separate achievement, his first sustained attempt
at something more than the 'sharp-cut self-assertion,' which, in
the same letter, he states as the intention of his earlier 'Leaves.'
But soon he will know that he is building one composite poem in
the 'Leaves,' and set 'Drum-Taps' at the centre.

Eccentricity in style and vocabulary has almost disappeared
in 'Drum-Taps.' Some of the poems like the Lincoln ballad,
O Captain! My Captain! in the supplement, are regular both in
rhyme and in metre. It is clear that he could have written skil-
fully, now at least, in any metre he chose. But the instant he becomes regular he begins to sound imitative or insipid. Neither
metre nor regular rhyming lends itself to his style. To this I shall
make more detailed reference in a later chapter.

2

When the news came of Lincoln's murder, Whitman was at
home in Brooklyn with his family. He describes how they sat
all day, scarcely talking or eating. When he got back to Washington, there was Pete Doyle, who had been in the balcony of
Ford's Theatre, heard the shot, seen Booth leap for the stage,
and could put the whole drama in Whitman's imagination. A
powerful premonition had already been working in his mind.
Some tragedy, he felt, was overhanging a man he had come to

love.[7] The poems he now writes, with Lincoln as a theme, though finished (for Walt) so quickly, came from such depths of controlled emotion and were so interwoven with his own thoughts of love and death that they have not even a touch of the occasional. There are four of them, *When Lilacs Last in the Door Yard Bloom'd, O Captain! My Captain!, Hush'd be the Camps To-Day*, and *This Dust Was Once the Man*. They have become *the* poems of Lincoln, which raises a question of significant biographical interest. For with the exception of the last, which is only a quatrain, they are not poems of leadership, or poems of departed greatness, like Tennyson's ode on the death of the Duke of Wellington, nor even poems of democracy except by indirection. They are poems of love and death.

And as if in response to this fact, when Whitman came to arrange his 'Leaves' in their final order, putting 'Drum-Taps' as the hub of the wheel, he took the Lincoln poems out of 'Drum-Taps,' and made of them a separate section. One would have supposed that these tributes to the greatest democrat belonged in what Whitman regarded as the democratic heart of the book.

Perhaps they did belong there, and perhaps if Whitman could have lived on into another generation, and seen the history of the United States from our historical perspective, Lincoln would have become the symbol of democratic unity in a final 'Leaves.' Perhaps, but I doubt it. For the 'Leaves' is not a book of heroes, it is a book of the people, and its unity is not in individual achievement but in faith in the future of the common man, and in the principle of love. Actually, Whitman does not write of Lincoln as a hero in Carlyle's sense of the word. He writes of him as a common man with elements of greatness, but most of all as a man to be loved who has been lost to his generation. The hero-worship of Lincoln, now the accepted mode, was not Whitman's feeling about his President. When he went to Washington in 1862, he was still doubtful (like most Northerners) of the effectiveness of his leadership, and when he came to praise him, he praised him defensively. Like anyone at any time who lives in Washington when a strong man is President, he was too close to the necessary compromises and evasions of politics to be uncritical of his chief. By 1863, he has not so much changed his mind as given his respect, his loyalty, and his love entirely to a man whom he regards as one of the people struggling under a burden almost too great:

August 12, 1863

... Mr. Lincoln on the saddle generally rides a good-sized, easy-going gray horse, is dress'd in plain black, somewhat rusty and dusty, wears a black stiff hat, and looks about as ordinary in attire, &c, as the commonest man.... The sabres and ac-coutrements clank, and the entirely unornamental *cortège* as it trots toward Lafayette Square arouses no sensation, only some curious stranger stops and gazes. I see very plainly ABRAHAM LINCOLN's dark brown face, with the deep-cut lines, the eyes, always to me with a deep latent sadness in the expression. We have got so that we exchange bows, and very cordial ones.... They pass'd me once very close, and I saw the President in the face fully, as they were moving slowly, and his look, though ab-stracted, happen'd to be directed steadily in my eye. He bow'd and smiled, but far beneath his smile I noticed well the expression alluded to. None of the artists or pictures has caught the deep, though subtle and indirect expression of this man's face. There is something else there ... The current portraits are all failures — most of them caricatures. [8]

A curious relationship, as one sees, had formed between the men. It had already gone deep in Whitman, and Lincoln was presumably not unaware of some magnetism between them. A. Van Rensselaer, in a letter frequently quoted, reports that Lincoln remarked upon seeing him, 'Well, *he* looks like a *man.*' This may or may not be true to literal fact,[9] but it is emotionally true to the circumstances. They had surely never talked, for Whitman would certainly have recorded what would have been for him so momentous an occasion. They may, of course, have shaken hands at the President's last levee, where we know Walt was present. He says himself in two diary notes: 'October 31, 1863. Called at the President's house, on John Hay — saw Mr.

Lincoln standing, talking with a gentleman, apparently a dear friend. . . . His face & manner have an expression & are inexpressibly sweet — one hand on his friend's shoulder, the other holds his hand. I love the President personally.' [10] In later years, in those addresses on the anniversary of Lincoln's death which became a feature of his life, there is no distrust left of Lincoln's leadership, or doubts as to his quality of a hero. He has become in Whitman's memory an outstanding illustration of the line which Walt had written in 1856, 'Produce great Persons, the rest follows.' [11] But it was not this Carlylian sentiment which moved him in 1865, and it is not the theme of his poems.

I dwell upon this rather curious fact because it is so characteristic of the true and often misunderstood Whitman. Here was his wished-for leader who was to come up from the plain people. Here was precisely the kind of man whose absence he deplored in our military services, the leaders of which, as he wrote, had been trained in lessons of the past, or under foreign influence, could not adapt themselves to democratic conditions, and were responsible for three-fourths of our losses.[12] And it was Lincoln, he said, who 'kept the United States from being thrown down and having its throat cut.' Yet the group of poems inspired by the President's murder omits the laurels, except for the fine lines of the epitaph:

> This dust was once the man,
> Gentle, plain, just and resolute, under whose cautious hand . . .
> Was saved the Union of these States.

And even here it is service for the people by one of the people that is emphasized, rather than greatness.

The truth is that in his famous group of poems, Whitman mourns the loss of a beloved friend of the people, and even more of a friend deeply loved by himself — not the death of a great democrat, not the martyrdom of a hero. The fine elegy *When Lilacs Last in the Door Yard Bloom'd*, now in every anthology, is not a patriotic outburst, but the finest and most sublimated of those *Calamus* poems which celebrate the love of comrades. And if it is urged that this comrade, Lincoln, Whitman knew only by exchange of glances, the answer is that, for Whitman, this was enough. Walt's world, in spite of his far-flung talk of kosmoses, was a world of individuals, of persons. Intensely magnetic, as all his friends testify, Whitman was extremely sensitive to magnetism in others. He was seeking always for those he could love, and democracy, he believed, was to be bound together by a fraternity of affection stronger than politics. And he made his loves and his friendships alike, by a look or a touch on the arm or knee, as with Pete Doyle on his streetcar:

Passing stranger! you do not know how longingly I look upon you,
You must be he I was seeking, ...
I am not to speak to you, I am to think of you when I sit alone or wake at
  night alone,
I am to wait, I do not doubt I am to meet you again,
I am to see to it that I do not lose you.[13]

Lincoln, for Whitman, was at first such a stranger, a stranger of whom he knew much, but soon came to feel more. When the ship was 'anchor'd safe and sound, its voyage closed and done,' the murder of the great captain was for him, personally, the loss of a symbolic man of the people, one of the 'great companions,' 'the swift and majestic men,' the 'trusters of men and women,' whom he loved.

Therefore, in the Lilac elegy, which was written in the spring or summer after Lincoln's death, he describes the great President as a beloved stranger, and the greatness of our loss in his death as proportionate not so much to the eminence of the man as to the breadth of his capacity for love. Whitman himself, when he wrote this poem, had been ill and failing for the first time in his life. Death for him had also moved closer. The symbols of the sinking star for Lincoln, of the lilacs for his own youth, of the hermit thrush [14] chanting love in the cedars, unite to make a poem in the great classic tradition to which *Lycidas* belongs, but infinitely more personal, as befits the modern, subjective mind:

When lilacs last in the dooryard bloom'd,
And the great star early droop'd in the western sky in the night,
I mourn'd, and yet shall mourn with ever-returning spring. ...

O powerful western fallen star! ...
Over the breast of the spring, the land, amid cities, ...
Night and day journeys a coffin. ...

In the large unconscious scenery of my land with its lakes and forests, ...
Falling upon them all and among them all, enveloping me with the rest,
Appear'd the cloud, appear'd the long black trail,
And I knew death, its thought, and the sacred knowledge of death....

From the deep secluded recesses,
From the fragrant cedars and the ghostly pines so still,
Came the carol of the bird....

Come lovely and soothing death, ...
Dark mother always gliding near with soft feet, ...
Approach strong deliveress, ...
I float this carol with joy, with joy to thee O Death.

Thus with the sense of Lincoln's death at one side of him, and the thought of his own death 'close-walking the other side of me,' he mourns 'the sweetest, wisest soul of all my days and lands.' For Lincoln, the soiled world has been washed by night and death. And his loss is not so much a tragedy as a reminder that after struggle comes 'the delicious near-by freedom of death.'

It is clear that Whitman felt most strongly of Lincoln that he had too much love for the human kind. For such (in a soil'd world) only death can bring release, and, in mourning for them only their spiritual kin can say the final word, which is neither of power, nor of skill, nor of achievement, but of love. And who shall say that the triumph of Lincoln's memory over detraction and debunking has not been a triumph of that love which was the secret of the sadness in his face, and the essence of Whitman's poem!

CHAPTER XXIII

'I was looking a long while for Intentions'

WHEN Whitman settled down in Washington in 1863, he put off for the duration any real worry about his own career. More than once he writes his mother how trivial the cares and hardships of a civilian seem in the midst of so much tension and so much misery. It was, however, necessary to eat and sleep, and as soon as he decided to stay on, he got and used letters from Emerson to Charles Sumner and also from a Mr. Lane (who seems to have been Jeff's backer in the Brooklyn Water Department) in the attempt to get some kind of government job. Preston King, Senator from New York, once he had made sure that Walt's appearance as of a Southern planter did not indicate disloyalty, gave him recommendations for the State of New York to Chase and General Meigs of the Quartermaster Department. Nothing came of all this, and soon Walt had found his own way of getting a meagre support, and until his first breakdown in health, pulled wires, not for himself, but to get more money for his soldiers.

By 1864 and 1865 when the war was dragging to its end, he had become a figure in Washington, with services deserving recognition, and a circle of friends, some of whom were influential. Going home to Brooklyn in June of 1864, weary, sick, and on the verge of a breakdown, he expected to return quickly, but stayed to recuperate, as he so well knew how to do, in 'quiet lanes' of the country, sailing, and walking or bathing on the still lonely beach of Coney Island, or watching the political processions in New York. George was captured in September, imprisoned at Danville, but exchanged after many worrying months. By the end of the autumn, Whitman felt able to return to Washington.

It was the beginning of a new phase in his life. This time he proposed to establish himself in Washington, and could command influence to get himself a job. J. Hubley Ashton, Assistant Attorney-General in 1865, was a particular friend of the O'Connors, especially of Nelly O'Connor. Walt did not know which of them was the fonder of this generous and appealing woman, who, they thought, was treated by her Irish husband with too little consideration. Through Ashton and Judge W. T. Otto, Assistant Secretary of the Department of the Interior, who was Ashton's friend, and a reader of 'Drum-Taps,'[1] Whitman was given on January 24 of 1865 a twelve-hundred-dollar clerkship in the Office of Indian Affairs. It is interesting to note that his request for this appointment, which he was 'most desirous to get,' was based on his 'attentions to the soldiers, and my poems.'[2] Like the other appointments which he held later in Washington, his job was *honoris causa*, and while he discharged the duties assigned to him competently and satisfactorily, he had never to bother too strictly about office hours, and, indeed, used his Washington offices as warm and comfortable places to read and write when his work was done. In the history of the ingratitude of republics, Uncle Sam's record as far as Walt is concerned is good! And the financial stability came just in the years when Walt was consolidating his work, strengthening and extending his reputation, and needed security and freedom from the hazards of journalistic free-lancing.

There has been unnecessary speculation as to why the revolutionary and Bohemian Walt was so content with respectability in these latter 1860's. He draws his salary of from $1200 to $1600 a year (wealth for him), sends his mother money to buy her comforts, is liked by most (not all) of his fellow clerks, who never thought of him as a poet. He spends hours of talk with intellectuals like Edmund Stedman, who became the banker-poet, Ashton, O'Connor, Count Gurowski, the refugee, breakfasts (always late) with John Burroughs, and rolls his long stride through the woods and hills and streets with Burroughs and Pete Doyle. He has become a man-of-the-day whom, by 1872, while he was still in Washington, *The Fifth Avenue Journal* would be

caricaturing in his broad hat, bushy beard, and genial smile.[3]
If it were not for his decidedly unconventional friendship with
Pete Doyle and other probable but less publicized relationships,
one would say that Walt, the loafer through life, caressing all its
manifestations, had stabilized and conformed at last.

This is not so untrue as it is misleading. Something much
simpler, healthier, and more characteristic had happened to
Whitman. His restless egoism had burnt out of him. He no
longer felt that need of self-assertion which pushes the sensitive
mind into regions where it can make itself felt. There can be no
doubting the sincerity of his letters to his soldier friends in which
he says many times that his New York life has lost its savor.
He keeps his metropolitan friends, but more than ever he is the
onlooker he describes in his poem about Pfaff's. New York is
still a city of imagination, but his hospital experiences, where he
satisfied his deep need for action, have subtly transformed him
from an observer to a functional member of democratic society.
It is no longer the 'I' that pushes upon expression, but the 'We,
the people.' His significant poems and prose in these years deal
with democracy.

It was not only the need of continuing his work in the hospitals
that took Walt back to Washington after his illness, nor the
chance of financial stability, nor his new circle of friends among
men and women who were neither journalists nor uneducated.
His letters home, his writings, such as 'Democratic Vistas,'
which he was soon to be at work upon, his poems valedictory to
the war, such as *Adieu to a Soldier*, already quoted, all indicate
that Whitman's best spiritual climate was no longer a metropolis
of commerce and gaiety, but the new representative city (as he
had found it) of the democracy, where he was surrounded by
symbols of the 'Mother-of-all,' the Union, and in daily contact
with the business, the dangers, the problems of a nation recover-
ing from terrible wounds, and in a life-and-death struggle to determine its future. Walt the conciliator and idealist with deep
emotions constantly expressed, watched the conflicts of the
Republican radicals determined to dominate, the profiteers
bound to keep on and extend exploitation, the broken South, the

discouraged moralists who had thought that to win the war and free the slaves was to win all. It must have been a concern with him to stay at the heart of the battle. From this time on, New York and its pageants, the excitements of material expansion, the body's strong pull toward the ebullience and energy of the New World crowds, abate in his imagination. The last note of the old times is in *Give Me the Splendid Silent Sun*, published in 1865, but written before he left New York or on one of his visits back there, when he tasted still eagerly 'the life of the theatre, bar-room, large hotel,'

> Manhattan crowds, with their turbulent musical chorus!
> Manhattan faces and eyes forever for me.

But nothing like this after the war and his return to Washington. Now it is really, and not just rhetorically, the common people, their government, their personal development that fill his imagination. In 1889, he was still talking about it:

'Finally he got going with great feeling and vehemence: "I want the people: most of all the people: the crowd, the mass, the whole body of the people: men, women, children: I want them to have what belongs to them: not a part of it, not most of it, but all of it: I want anything done that will give the people their proper opportunities — their full life: anything, anything: whether by one means or another, I want the people to be given their due."' [4]

How? Just how, Walt did not know, which has displeased many of his critics who wish him to have been a socialist, communist, or what you will. He was a poet, not a statesman. But he did know what too many reformers have forgotten, that without such vision as he tried to give, ways and means are not enough.

2

His progress toward organizing and developing his poems was interrupted by a sensational incident which did more to extend his reputation than all his own rather feeble attempts at publicity.

The Secretary of the Interior, James Harlan, was an honest, obstinate, bigoted man, who had been put into the Cabinet by

Lincoln under pressure from the Methodists. He represented, as Mr. Mencken would say, the Bible Belt. Walt began well in the Indian Department of Mr. Harlan's establishment. In May, he was promoted from a first- to a second-class clerkship. His hours of nine to four were easy, and 'I don't come at 9, and only stay till 4 when I want, as at present, to finish a letter for the mail.'[5] His work was the copying of reports and bids, and apparently Judge Otto had told him not to waste his time in warming a chair. Harlan, himself, when the break came, had no complaint against his services. But since Whitman's afternoon and evening hours were spent largely in the hospitals, time was needed for the other and indispensable work upon which he was engaged — the preparation of a new edition of the 'Leaves.' In his desk, he kept a copy bound in blue paper, which must have been the Boston edition of 1860. This volume, so the testimony ran, was elaborately marked in pencil for revision. Unquestionably Walt kept it next his hand, so that in any interval he could work upon his text. Ironically, one of the distinctions of the edition of 1867, for which this volume was to serve as printer's copy, is the disappearance of certain 'rough terms and many references to sexuality.'[6] It was therefore rough terms and sexual passages which would be particularly marked for possible elision in the 1860 copy. And, of course, it is at marked passages that a reader first looks.

Someone who knew of Walt's reputation as a daring poet must have maliciously told Mr. Harlan that the Devil was at work in his own office. 'Examining' around the office building after hours in June of 1865, Harlan opened Walt's desk, and touching no other of the private papers there, picked up the 'Leaves,' found it 'odd,' and took it to his office to look over. He read in the book, probably in some of these marked passages, matter so outrageous that he determined to discharge the author. Mr. Ashton, from whose protesting interview (preserved in Walt's own handwriting) these statements are drawn, reminded Harlan of Whitman's laborious activities for the soldiers, insisted on his 'manly, pure, and patriotic life,' said that his appointment had been sought so that he might be able to spend his leisure hours in the service of

the maimed and the sick, and that he was now continuing quietly
and faithfully at that work. Mr. Harlan replied that his opinion
as to Whitman's personal character had been changed by this
information, but that the author of such a book should not be in
his Department. If the President should reinstate him, he would
resign. It is the old (and still new) story of a godly America even
more offended by a word than a deed, and unwilling to admit
that the part has significance only in relation to the whole.[7]

Walt was fired, but the results were fortunate. Harlan was not
popular, Lincoln had refused to have him as Vice-President on
his ticket, Whitman had become a figure of mercy in Washington,
and sentiment was with him. Furthermore, substantially no one
but Harlan outside the friendly Whitman circle had read the
'Leaves.' If his fellow clerks had seen anything of his, it would
have been the recently printed and perfectly respectable 'Drum-
Taps,' for whose printing in Brooklyn he had been given leave
only two months before the explosion. No objection was made
to his transfer to the office of the Attorney-General. There, as
he worked into the job, he prepared letters, answers to letters,
and opinions on law from rough drafts, to be sent to the President
and heads of Departments. He was, in short, a private secretary.
This work was by no means merely clerical. As he said, he had to
do 'only with big men.' [8] And his letters indicate that he did, on
the side, a little lobbying for his friends.[9] Here he stayed very
comfortably until January of 1872, when he was lent to the
Solicitor of the Treasury, a branch of the Department of Justice,
his appointment as a third-class clerk there being confirmed on
March 10, 1873. By this time and in his official capacity, he had
become a part, and a useful part, of the governmental machine.
'I guess they'll miss me,' he had written to his mother of his
transfer, '(as the old ladies say), a good deal more than they
'spected.' [10]

The only sensational result of Walt's encounter with the Bible
Belt was a notice served upon the official and literary world that
Whitman was now a national figure who could not be insulted
without insulting art. O'Connor, fiery radical that he was, uncompromising as to the rights of the slave, uncompromising later

in the Bacon-Shakespeare controversy, exploded as Whitman never could have done for himself.

In 1866, O'Connor published a pamphlet, 'The Good Gray Poet,' which his connections enabled him to distribute widely in the right directions. Unfortunately, like all of Whitman's followers, he struck too high, comparing him, with vast show of erudition, to the greatest in history, including Christ. Yet the vehemence with which he ransacked great literature to show the folly of condemning a poet's whole intention because his words offended the priggish, and the brilliance of his invective, made a strong effect. His pamphlet set the pundits of the genteel age talking, and persuaded the fair-minded that Whitman had been ill-used. They felt that a poet had been wronged, but also that this did not prove that he was a genius. As a long-time service, this powerful pamphlet was of great value to Whitman. After its publication, even those who detested him took him seriously, and the public, who were not interested in the controversy, got a name to call him which was an antidote to slander. This name, 'The Good Gray Poet' was not O'Connor's invention. It was suggested by Whitman himself.[11]

No name, of course, could have served as a better caption for his photographs. Whitman firmly believed that the voice, the gestures, the whole appearance of man should and could and, in a fully developed man, did reveal the personality, the power, the soul itself behind appearances. As he himself was highly expressive in countenance, as he had, and must have known he had, the ability to dramatize his moods, it was natural that he should like to be photographed. Photographers seem always to have been eager to photograph him, so he usually had an abundant supply of portraits on hand. In the early years in Washington he had copies sent to him in considerable quantity from home, apparently for distribution. The finest, perhaps the most beautiful (though not the most characteristic), of all the Whitman pictures was taken in the Washington years.[12] (See Plate XI.) The ripple of silvery hair down his chest, the quiet but powerful posture, the firm face, seem to belong to a man who had found release from inner troubles. Equally firm, but very different in effect, is the photograph by Gardner in 1864 (see Plate IX), taken after he had trimmed his hair and beard in October of 1863, and thus made a sensation among his friends. In this photograph he looks like General Grant, the current hero. Yet contrast these with the melancholy Whitman of Brady's picture of 1862,[13] or with the weary draggled Whitman in profile taken by Kurtz, probably in 1860 (see Plate VIII), or the eagle-faced Whitman defying the world, also by Kurtz in the same year (see Plate VII), and one begins to realize that even if these dates are not all accurate, the man changed not so much from year to year, as from hour to hour. His mood and his expression depend upon where the emphasis falls in his mobile soul, and this, within limits, held true for his writing also. He could write *Passage to India*, that poem of great serenity, in late 1868, and sink back into sexual perturbation, as his notebook shows, in the following year.

3

We have reached, however, the most satisfying period of Walt's life, and can be assured that, in spite of his failing health, it was the most satisfactory to him also. He has the immense gratification of being *en rapport* (as he would have said) with the plain man of the democracy, who would never read the poems he wrote about him. It has been his good fortune to have been intimate and affectionate with precisely those among his fellow citizens whom he would have chosen for steady companionship — the young, the unsophisticated young, the best product of a new and self-reliant country. He was in daily association with educated men like-minded with him in their freedom from the materialism of the Reconstruction period, and, like him, working, in office and out of office, on the business of democratic government. He was definitely out of the literary and journalistic atmosphere of New York, which, as we look back at it in perspective, with its Bayard Taylors, its Stoddards, its Curtises, its humorists and Orientalists, was brittle and artificial in comparison with the vast background of America and the still vibrating tremors of the war. As a journalist, he had been at home in New York, but he no longer had to be a journalist; as a celebrator of American expansiveness, he had been happily placed in New York and Brooklyn, but he never had belonged to any literary school there. That was the trouble with the Bayard Taylors and the rest — they wrote about literature, not about life in their country, not even about New York. He was free also from the sterile society of his family. He loved them all as much as ever, and especially his mother, but that family circle, where his work was quite unintelligible, was not a place in which the creative talent could feel at home. He had to go to Coney Island or on a bus top in the roar of Broadway, to shout even his Shakespeare or Homer.

As for the family, George was home again, able to take the place of Jeff, who had gone to a good job in St. Louis, and Walt could shift some of the responsibility of actual roof and food for his mother and Ed to his capable shoulders. Old Mrs. Whitman was failing, and a little querulous.[14] George and his new wife were too saving for her taste, which was reverting perhaps to the spacious ease of Dutch Long Island. And there was the constant worry over the neurotic 'Han' in Burlington, with her equally neurotic painter husband, who took his revenge for an unsatisfactory wife by extravagant insults to the family.[15] Walt was still the heart of the circle and his mother's dependence, but he was free. It all comes out in a talk he had with Traubel about the O'Connors to whom he felt nearer than to any others:

'A man's family is the people who love him — the people who comprehend him. You know how for the most part I have always been isolated from my people — in certain senses have been a stranger in their midst: just as we know Tolstoy has been. Who of my family has gone along with me? Who? Do you know? Not one of them... They have always missed my intentions. Take my darling dear mother:... she had great faith in me — felt sure I would accomplish wonderful things: but "Leaves of Grass"? Who could ever consider "Leaves of Grass" a wonderful thing: who? She would shake her head. God bless her! She never did. She thought I was a wonderful thing, but the "Leaves"? oh my, hardly the "Leaves"!... George is my brother; it may be said that I love him — he loving me, too, in a certain sort of a way....

I would say, God bless George my brother: but as to George my interpreter, I would ask God to do something else with him. . . . Nelly and William . . . were my unvarying partisans, my unshakable lovers — my espousers.' [16]

These ten or twelve years, if we include the early sixties when he was writing 'Drum-Taps,' were his last, but also his most mature, period of creation. He wrote *Chanting the Square Deific*, which he regarded (as did his friends) as one of his greatest poems — wrongly, I think. He wrote in 1868 and 1869, *Passage to India*, which included, so he said, more of himself than any other, and is surely a great poem. He wrote that most touching poem, *The City Dead-House*, he wrote *Proud Music of the Storm, In Cabin'd Ships at Sea, Whispers of Heavenly Death, Years of the Modern*, and, in prose, 'Democratic Vistas.' It was also the period of his widening reputation, and (most important for him) his sudden capture of a hearing in England, where William Rossetti published him, Swinburne praised him, Tennyson recognized his calibre and asked him to visit, and scholars like Edward Dowden, bred in the 'proud libraries,' from which Whitman was barred in America, discoursed at length on his merits.

4

It will be remembered that he wrote to O'Connor that 'Drum-Taps' had no perturbation. By this he may have meant only that his old self-assertiveness did not make these poems run like an engine without a balancing wheel. But he may also have meant, and more specifically, that the perturbations (as he used the word before) of sex no longer throbbed in this book — and, indeed, with slight exceptions they do not. So far as women are concerned, there is a possibility, though no direct evidence, that somewhere, somehow in these years he found sexual satisfaction, which with Whitman could scarcely have been in casual affairs. Of these there may have been many, also. He says that while he was in Washington, he received 'love letters galore.' He had, as Pete Doyle said, 'a good way with women.'

But that other, and more dangerous perturbation, which he

called adhesiveness, his love of young men — sometimes paternal, sometimes sexual though only in the images it engenders — that weakness, which was also his strength, had its full release. The soldiers he loved in the hospitals, addressed as 'son,' and to whom he was both father and mother at their bedsides, were to be numbered by scores. He lists them in catalogues of names in his letters written back from Brooklyn. And it was in these years that he began one relationship long continued, which may serve for all, and is fortunately open to our eyes because his letters have been kept and published.

Pete Doyle was an Irish boy in his twenties who had been a Confederate soldier, was captured, and paroled. He drifted into a job as conductor of a streetcar, and there Walt met him one night with instant recognition of some instinctive bond between them. Doyle, a simple, uneducated fellow, not very bright, never very successful, had an affectionate nature, trusting and dependent, and, like so many of his kind, no ambition except to keep going. Just one of the plain people with some inexplicable magnetism which answered a need in Walt's heart — 'a big rounded every day workingman,' Walt called him, 'full to the brim of the real substance of God.' [17] Here is Pete's story of their meeting: [18]

'You ask where I first met him? It is a curious story. We felt to each other at once. I was a conductor. The night was very stormy, — he had been over to see Burroughs before he came down to take the car, — the storm was awful. Walt had his blanket — it was thrown round his shoulders — he seemed like an old sea-captain. He was the only passenger, it was a lonely night, so I thought I would go in and talk with him. Something in me made me do it and something in him drew me that way. He used to say there was something in me had the same effect on him. Anyway, I went into the car. We were familiar at once — I put my hand on his knee — we understood. He did not get out at the end of the trip — in fact went all the way back with me. I think the year of this was 1866. From that time on we were the biggest sort of friends. I stayed in Washington until 1872, when I went on the Pennsylvania Railroad. Walt was then in the

Attorney-General's office. I would frequently go out to the Treasury to see Walt; Hubley Ashton was commonly there — he would be leaning familiarly on the desk where Walt would be writing. They were fast friends — talked a good deal together. Walt rode with me often — often at noon, always at night. He rode round with me on the last trip — sometimes rode for several trips. Everybody knew him. He had a way of taking the measure of the driver's hands — had calf-skin gloves made for them every winter in Georgetown — these gloves were his personal presents to the men. He saluted the men on the other cars as we passed — threw up his hand. They cried to him, "Hullo, Walt!" and he would reply, "Ah, there!" or something like. He was welcome always as the flowers in May.... It was our practice to go to a hotel on Washington Avenue after I was done with my car. I remember the place well — there on the corner. Like as not I would go to sleep — lay my head on my hands on the table. Walt would stay there, wait, watch, keep me undisturbed — would wake me up when the hour of closing came.'

The companionship between these two was very close until Whitman left Washington, and was never broken except by circumstance of removal, although Pete, a shy and humble fellow, kept away in later years from Camden because Walt's familiars there made him ill at ease. Whitman felt for him the palpitating affection, and the responsibility of a father:

[1869]

... Dear Pete, you must forgive me for being so cold the last day and evening. I was unspeakably shocked and repelled from you by that talk and proposition of yours — you know what — there by the fountain. [Pete, discouraged because he could not cure a badly erupted face, had said life was not worth going on with.] It seemed indeed to me (for I will talk out plain to you, dearest comrade) that the one I loved, and who had always been so manly and sensible, was gone, and a fool and intentional suicide stood in his place.... Dear Pete, dear son, my darling boy, my young and loving brother, don't let the devil put such thoughts in your mind again ... what would it be afterward to the mother?

What to *me*? ... [1870]. Pete there was something in that hour from 10 to 11 o'clock (parting though it was) that has left me pleasure and comfort for good — I never dreamed that you made so much of having me with you, nor that you could feel so downcast at losing me. I foolishly thought that it was all on the other side. ... [19]

So natural, so richly emotional a relationship as this was a happy release for the suppressions and the neuroticisms which forced their way into Whitman's earlier poems. Loving, uneducated persons, to alter Whitman's term, are no less desirable friends and companions because the appeal they make is not intellectual. Rather the more so with a man like Whitman, whose faith in democracy was confirmed by the simple people whose affection he craved and got.

And may it not be that the disturbing passage quoted in an earlier chapter from the notebook of 1869 was the last explosion of Whitman's sexual maladjustment? It was not love he foreswore there, not sexual relationships, but feverish, vain, unprofitable, egotistic pursuit.

Whatever happened in these years behind the veil of Whitman's private life, we may be sure that his known experiences were such as to extend his love of a 'simple, separate person' into a passion, no longer rhetorical, for humanity. Whitman was one of the great lovers of literary history, and that is why every biographer tries to discover secret recipients of his passion. They have failed, but his love for mankind is written in every poem of the 'Leaves' that shifts above egoism, and even in egoism his soul shares with the human race the inestimable privilege of living.

5

As far back as 1860 Walt Whitman had seen his goal and stated it in a poem, called *I Was Looking a Long While*:

I was looking a long while for Intentions,
For a clew to the history of the past for myself, and for these chants — and
    now I have found it,
It is not in those paged fables in the libraries, (them I neither accept nor
    reject,)

It is no more in the legends than in all else,
It is in the present — it is this earth today,
It is in Democracy — (the purport and aim of all the past,)
It is the life of one man or one woman today — the average man of today,
It is in languages, social customs, literatures, arts,
It is in the broad show of artificial things, ships, machinery, politics, creeds,
    modern improvements, and the interchange of nations,
All for the modern — all for the average man of today.[29]

I doubt whether this intention would have become fully realized if it had not been for Whitman's hospital experiences; I doubt whether it would have become so increasingly clear to him if he had not lived in Washington where the armies were returning, and become one of the people who helped to run the vast machine of government, a clerk among clerks, a dynamic cell in the central organism of a democracy.

This is not fanciful. There is a fine passage in a letter to his mother of 1866, describing the great Review which formally ended the war:

Washington, May 25, '65
Dear Mother, Well, the Review is over, & it was very grand — it was too much & too impressive, to be described — but you will see a good deal about it in the papers. If you can imagine a great wide avenue like Flatbush avenue, quite flat, & stretching as far as you can see with a great white building half as big as Fort Greene on a hill at the commencement of the avenue, and then through this avenue marching solid ranks of soldiers, 20 or 25 abreast, just marching steady all day long for two days without intermission, one regiment after another, real war-worn soldiers, that have been marching & fighting for years — sometimes for an hour nothing but cavalry, just solid ranks, on good horses, with sabres glistening & carbines hanging by their saddles, & their clothes showing hard service, but they mostly all good-looking hardy young men — then great masses of guns, batteries of cannon, four or six abreast, each drawn by six horses, with the gunners seated on the ammunition wagons — & these perhaps a long while in passing, nothing but batteries, — (it seemed as if all the cannon in the world were here) — then great battalions of blacks,

with axes & shovels & pick axes, (real Southern darkies, black as tar) — then again hour after hour the old infantry regiments, the men all sunburnt — nearly every one with some old tatter all in shreds, (that *had been* a costly and beautiful *flag*) — the great drum corps of sixty or eighty drummers massed at the heads of the brigades, playing away — now & then a fine brass band, — but oftener nothing but the drums & whistling fifes, — but they sounded very lively — (perhaps a band of sixty drums & fifteen or twenty fifes playing 'Lanningan's ball') — the different corps banners, the generals with their staffs &c — the Western Army, led by Gen. Sherman, (old Bill, the soldiers all call him) — well, dear mother, that is a brief sketch, give you some idea of the great panorama of the Armies that have been passing through here the last two days.

— I saw the President [Johnson] several times, stood close by him, & took a good look at him — & like his expression much — he is very plain & substantial — it seemed wonderful that just that plain, middling-sized ordinary man, dressed in black, without the least badge or ornament, should be the master of all these myriads of soldiers, the best that ever trod the earth, with forty or fifty Major-Generals, around him or riding by with their broad yellow-satin belts around their waists, — and of all the artillery & cavalry, to say nothing of all the Forts & ships &c. &c. — I saw Gen. Grant too several times — He is the noblest Roman of them all — none of the pictures do justice to him — about sundown I saw him again riding on a large fine horse, with his hat off in answer to the hurrahs — he rode by where I stood, & I saw him well, as he rode by on a slow canter, with nothing but a single orderly after him — He looks like a good man — (& I believe there is much in looks) — I saw Gen. Meade, Gen. Thomas, Secretary Stanton, & lots of other celebrated government officers & generals — but the *rank* and *file* was the greatest sight of all.[21]

Later he put it in poetry:

Pass, pass, ye proud brigades, with your tramping sinewy legs,
With your shoulders young and strong, with your knapsacks and your
    muskets; . . .

A pause — the armies wait,
A million flush'd embattled conquerors wait, . . .
They melt, they disappear. . . .
Other the arms the fields henceforth for you, or South or North,
With saner wars, sweet wars, life-giving wars.

And it was, as he believed, his boys who had done it. In spite of the generals, and the contractors, responding to such leadership as they got, the people had saved the Union.

Even in the corruption and pressure politics of Reconstruction, his faith kept burning. At his friend Harned's one day in 1888 they laughed at him when he said that while he was in Washington the prevailing atmosphere was of honesty. The old man was stubborn. 'I do not refer to the swell officials — . . . I refer to the average clerks, the obscure crowd, who after all run the government: they are on the square. I have not known hundreds — I have known thousands — of them. I went to Washington as everybody goes there prepared to see everything done with some furtive intention, but I was disappointed — pleasantly disappointed. I found the clerks mainly earnest, mainly honest, anxious to do the right thing — very hard working, very attentive. . . . Washington is corrupt — has its own peculiar mixture of evil with its own peculiar mixture of good — but the evil is mostly with the upper crust — the people who have reputations — who are better than other people.' [22]

Whatever else happened to Whitman in Washington, it was in the capital during the war and after the war — perhaps particularly after the war — that Walt sharpened his ideas of democracy, made a philosophy of them, worked them into the 'Leaves' without taking out earlier and more rhetorical conceptions, continued in the various editions and 'annexes' he worked on to make the evolution of his own faith in and understanding of democracy the rough Intention of the whole book. On the basis of the writing he did there we can decide whether his work is only a remembered faith and dream of a nineteenth-century democracy, or has unexpected energy still in it for Americans today.

CHAPTER XXIV

'Sail forth — steer for the deep waters only'

THE essential chapter in any life of Whitman must put to the test his idea of democracy. 'America *is* democracy,' he had written. A biographer must say, using the same overtones of meaning, Whitman *is* democracy — or only a chanter of songs, sometimes mellifluous, sometimes raucous, of himself and his loves. In Washington in the late sixties and early seventies, with the war and its 'million dead' still vivid in the streets of the capital, comes the right moment of time in Walt's life to estimate and assess the truth or falsity, good or bad prophecy, of his theories. By this decade Walt knew all that he needed for his faith and his doubts. After the mid-seventies he was a looker-on who neither changed his mind nor his expectations as the pageant of national development unrolled through the latter nineteenth century.

I believe myself that it is not the politicians, not the statesmen, not the historians who best speak for New World Democracy, but Walt Whitman. If you wish to know what heroism meant to the early Greeks, you must ask Homer. If you wish to know what moral unity meant to the Middle Ages, you must ask Dante. If you wish to know what aristocracy meant to the English Renaissance, you must ask Shakespeare. And if you wish to understand what was the, perhaps unconscious, ideal of democracy in the formative years of the nineteenth century, the question should be addressed to Whitman and his poems.

In everything that referred specifically to the development of his own country, Whitman was a strong nationalist. If he had died in, say 1854, he would have been remembered, if remembered at all, as a shrewd and outspoken political journalist, patriotic and partisan, and as a practical politician very useful in vote-getting and propaganda for the Democratic Party. There was little that anyone could have told him as to how government in the United States was made to work, why and how it failed when it did fail, and how it succeeded when it did succeed. He was as local and as national in most of his editorial writing as Horace Greeley.

But if his left hand was nationalist, his right hand and his imagination were both internationalist.[1] When he came at last to write from his own inner life, and in his own way, he was not content to speak only for the United States, nor was he much concerned (in his poetry at least) with the political organization of the northern Republic. He believed firmly that the system of government as such of the United States, a system inspired by the Declaration of Independence, based on the Constitution, worked out by representation in a balance of executive, judicial, and legislative powers, was good in principle and would endure. That is, it was good for us, and would endure with us. But this system, so he believed, was not the essence of democracy. It was only the machinery of *a* democracy — the United States in the nineteenth century. The essence of democracy was an ideal — and it should be noted that it was an ideal which he believed was most likely to succeed in the New World of both North and South America. When he says 'America,' he frequently means the New World, not just the United States. The terms are often used interchangeably:

I heard that you ask'd for something to prove this puzzle the New World
And to define America, her athletic Democracy,
Therefore I send you my poems.

2

I shall endeavor to interpret Whitman's noble and, I believe, valid theory of democracy, not by generalities, but by reference to his own words — and especially to a little-read book in prose, 'Democratic Vistas'[2] (1871). I do not choose this book arbitrarily, but because it was written against a background of intensest realism. A civil war of unprecedented magnitude had just been concluded, the unity of the country was assured, but democracy itself (though few but Whitman guessed it) was on trial as never before or after until our times. We had broken up the plantation system of the South; we had liberated the Negro without trying to fit him into any orderly evolution of self-government; we were opening up the richest continent in the known world, and allowing it to be exploited by a plutocracy. Corruption, strong-arm politics, the oppression of minorities were to be seen everywhere. Democratic idealism seemed to be dead, and democratic government seemed to be growing weaker as the country grew richer.

Whitman lived in no ivory tower. He was a clerk in Washington, and Washington was the centre of democratic degradation. Great power had been centred there in wartime, and now that power was being used by corrupt private interests. He was bitterly aware of what was going on. He saw, and I am quoting, 'the flippancy, and vulgarity, low cunning, ... youth puny, impudent ... half-brain'd nominees ... ignorant ballots ... elected failures and blatherers,' and he feared a breakdown. 'Democracy,' he said, 'grows rankly up the thickest noxious deadliest plants and fruits of all — brings worse and worse invaders.' Feudal reaction from the old Europe was no longer likely; and the dollar-chasers, who were using government for their own aggrandizements, were not the chief danger. The New World was strong enough to resist the one, and absorb the other — as indeed happened. What he dreaded was the invaders, the exploiters of democracy whether at home or from abroad, the shadowy figures of a Mussolini or a Hitler, still over the horizon, men who would recognize the vast new powers which the masses were acquiring, and would corrupt the people and use them for their own felonious purposes, and for the destruction of democracy.

In 1868, Whitman was 'fitting up my new piece for the *Galaxy* ... addressed to the literary classes' at his desk in the Attorney-General's office. *The Galaxy*, a New York magazine of quality, had paid him one hundred dollars each for two articles on democracy, and 'personalism,' his own word for the sacredness of the personality within the individual. It was to refuse the third, which then was to be worked in with the others to make 'Democratic Vistas,' published in 1871. Emerson and Alcott liked these essays. Where he wrote was irrelevant, but it was not irrelevant that as he wrote he was approaching fifty. He looked old with his gray-white hair and beard, but not aged; yet he began to feel old as a man will at fifty, when his life begins to come into perspective. The articles and the book into which they were made were probably the result of talk as much as of reflection. Many of the themes have appeared before, and the whole conception of New World opportunities for the common man is a repetition of his lifelong belief that the Americas could and would have a new history. But the backward and forward arguing of this vigorous book, and particularly the sentences, sometimes tiresomely full of parentheses and turnings aside — as of a man's head swinging when he answers this or that objection, or offers explanations — seem to come fresh from discussions at O'Connor's among a roomful. It may have been at one of these sessions that Whitman opposed the granting of an immediate franchise to the Negroes, thus offending O'Connor, a fanatical Abolitionist, and leading to a break of many years between these dear friends.

'Until the individual or community show due signs,' he wrote in the 'Vistas,' 'or be so minor and fractional as not to endanger the State, the condition of authoritative tutelage may continue, and self-government must abide its time' — which sounds like a peace program of the United Nations in the 1940's, sobering down the democratic Utopianism of a Woodrow Wilson.

Whitman wished to be judged as a prophet and a seer, and let us so judge him. He did not believe that the institutions of the Republic, or of any republic, were going by themselves to perpetuate democratic government:

'I would alarm and caution ... against the prevailing delusion that the establishment of free political institutions ... with general good order, physical plenty, industry, etc., ... do, of themselves, determine, and yield to any experiment of democracy, the fruitage of success.'

Nor did he believe that our particular institutions would have to be imitated by other countries of the New World in order to make a democracy fulfill what he believed to be its manifest destiny. Whitman did not draw his faith in democracy from the usual sources at all. 'I do not put it either on the ground that the People, the masses, even the best of them, are, in their latent or exhibited qualities, essentially sensible and good — nor on the ground of their rights; but that good or bad, rights or no rights, the democratic formula is the only safe and preservative one for coming times.' We endow the masses with suffrage for their sake, no doubt, but still more for the sake of the community. That is the direction in which the New World should move, not toward this or that imitation of foreign governments, but toward the development of every individual by any means. Ambitious men of the kind that make tyrants or fascists (the word is, naturally, ours) are 'always straining for elevations and exclusiveness.' The masterly ambition of a democracy is to see greatness and health in being part of the mass. Strength comes from a strong people. 'Nothing will do so well as common ground.'

So thinking, Whitman could not, and did not, feel that the dangers of a democracy come from controversy and the constant clash of opinion. He has a wise word for these dissensions, which arise from free speech, and which have been so much sneered at by the totalitarian states. They are like 'that perennial health-action of the air we call the weather — an infinite number of currents and forces, and contributions, and temperatures, and cross-purposes, whose ceaseless play of counterpart upon counterpart brings constant restoration and vitality.' This sentence shows not only foresight of the later conclusions of science as to the geographical sources of energy, but is a profound observation upon the trial-and-error basis of democracy itself. What a democracy loses in efficiency of plan, it makes up in right direction, endurance, and vitality.

Thinking this way, he believed, of course, that the real danger to democracy was a failure to produce in the masses men and women worth preserving, worth governing, able to defend themselves, able to govern themselves. It was a lack of faith in democracy which permitted the growth of rich cities rather than fine cities, concentrated wealth rather than made for general self-development, produced complacency rather than vigor, led to a dull pursuit of security instead of vitality and initiative.

The early biographers of Walt Whitman, and perhaps most of us who first read Whitman twenty or thirty years ago, misunderstood the emphasis in his definition of democracy and failed to heed his warnings. At the beginning of the century, it seemed, at least in the United States, that democracy had won its major battles, and was safe. By the time of Theodore Roosevelt, predatory plutocracy, which had used our institutions for its own ends, was clearly beginning a retreat. The greedy millions who had exploited a continent were coming to see that it was not enough to make a living out of a country. It had to be worth living in. We were on the way to social reform, but took democracy for granted. All that was necessary for us and for the New World generally, on our isolated continents, seemed to be to keep on reforming until we had made almost perfect states.

It was not to work out that way, as, first, the great depression of 1929, and then the second world war, showed with terrifying clarity. Democracy was not yet safe, not yet even successful. 'I say,' wrote Whitman in 1871, 'that our New World democracy, however great a success in uplifting the masses out of their slough ... is, so far, an almost complete failure in its social aspects and in really grand religious, moral, literary, and esthetic results.' We had achieved size, comfort, luxury, as had the democracies abroad, but monopoly, undirected industrialism, and the moral confusions of the nineteenth century had deadened idealism and substituted security for self-development as the goal of the individuals who make up the people. For democracy can corrupt, and had corrupted, the masses. Corruption, degeneracy, pettiness, both physical and spiritual, were as plainly visible to Whitman in the United States of 1871 as to us in, say, the France of 1940. In both there was a failure to function by the democratic masses, a failure to produce democratic leadership. The United States pulled through that crisis, perhaps because we were too busy getting rich when getting rich was easy to develop what Whitman calls 'invaders.' But they came elsewhere in the hard times of the 1930's, found a weary, devitalized democracy abroad, and picked off nations that seemed to be strong, one by one, like rotting apples from a tree.

Is Whitman's prophecy of a great democratic future good? We hope so. Was he a good prophet in his recital of the dangers to democracy lying just ahead? His prophecy was bitterly good, because bitterly true. A relatively small group of self-seeking politicians and militarists saw that the prosperous democracies had lost some of their vitality. The 'savage virtues,' which Whitman insisted were essential for a revolutionary and for an evolutionary democracy, had given way to complacency and security. The individual no longer felt responsible for his government, nor the government for more than the security of the individual. The sense of brotherhood among the common people had lessened. These democracies abroad were torn by ideologies, and even the most liberal were more concerned with distributing wealth than with making first-rate men. So, the invaders from autocratic states, having first corrupted their own people, turned with sneer, suggestion, and violence to the nearest democracies. Then they threatened the New World.

Yes, it was true prophecy. When Woodrow Wilson tried to make the world safe for democracy, these weaknesses were not so well understood, nor was Whitman as a poet of democracy rightly interpreted by those who read him. Now, both what he was defending and what he was fearing are much easier to believe in. The world, as he knew then, and as we see now, is safe enough for the right kind of democracy; for the right kind of democracy encourages freedom, expansion, self-expression, and also ideals of service and vitality among the individuals who create it. But the world will always be unsafe for a complacent, an appeasing, an unrealized, or a dead democracy, whatever our prosperity, or the apparent success of our political and economic institutions.

Whitman's final definition of democracy, as we find it in the 'Vistas,' contains, as a great concept should, the blood, sweat, and tears of personal experience. As I have said before, it was only after his years among the sick and wounded in the Civil War hospitals of Washington that he really learned to know the common people of his country and especially its youth. 'I know not whether I shall be understood, but I realize that is finally from what I learn'd personally mixing in such scenes, that I am penning these pages.' There they were by thousands, worn, ill, dying; and for thousands, literally, he became an intimate friend. From that time on, whenever he wrote of nationality and democracy, he thought of these young men from all over the states, a concrete, living democracy of the plain people, which he respected and loved. Therefore he enriched his idea of political democracy by fraternity, friendship, affection, love. And it was precisely, as I have said before, his bivalent auto-sexualism, with all it cost him of misunderstanding and frustration, that made him more sensitive than any other of his times to the emotional riches latent in his fellow kind, and usable for democracy.

Love, indeed, was the only antiseptic for the hate, the superiority, the condescension, the narrow selfishness which were congenital in human nature. A fraternal love, or at least affection, must be the cement of democracy. And this, of course, harmonizes with Whitman's ideas of self-development. The individual for whom democracy is conducted must know how to love and be loved, or the house of the state is built upon sterile sands. What literature claims for the heroes and the great lovers, Whitman demands as an ideal for the common man. There can be no enduring democracy without emotional freedom, which should be added to the four freedoms of President Roosevelt. For the man or woman emotionally free and fully developed will be easily directed toward love, rather than hate, of his fellow creatures. The need for love, like the need of political freedom, must be satisfied by a successful democracy. Was Whitman soundly prophetic in this? I think so, for in our own day the enemies of democracies have used, as the spearhead of their attack, the cult of hate.

This then is Whitman's democratic idealism. But I wish to emphasize that, while it is idealistic, it is in no sense visionary. It is the program of a man who, better than any other of our writers, knew how politics work and was himself a professional in the art and science of public opinion. It is a program most difficult of realization, but it is not visionary. There is no blueprint for a Utopia in Whitman. His ideas are flexible, often indefinite, but they are based on what became an extraordinarily wide and intuitive knowledge of the heart of the common people, and it may well be true that only along the path he indicates can democracy succeed. One remembers that the real visionaries of the twenties of this century were not the idealists, but the supposedly hard-headed industrialists, financiers, and politicians who have been proved by the depression and the war to have been dreamers, whose fantasies of progress were not even good dreams, and emphatically did not come true. It may well be that Whitman's prophetic optimism for democracy is as well founded and well directed as his prophetic pessimism has already proved itself to be in these distressing years.

3

And yet it would be unfair to Whitman not to note that his passionate faith in democracy is mystical as well as practical. It is clear now that he was one of the great rebels of the nineteenth century. He did not rebel against the science which made that century famous. He rebelled against the gross and premature materialism which resulted from the supposed discovery that man and nature were both superior mechanisms, subject like dead matter to measurement and complete explanation by physical and chemical laws. We are aware now that this is not true, even of inert matter, but we are still in the downward swing away from religion and faith which has been responsible for so much in the cynical present. Whitman, never a dogmatist, was in rebellion against all this. Science, for him, was the great hope of the future, but it was ultimately a mysticism, as it is to most of the physicists today. Democracy, for him, was also ultimately a religion, based upon the spiritual worth of the individual soul, upon what he called identity, which lay beyond analysis and had to be accepted by faith. It is this faith which gives passion to his prophecies, and this faith which may very possibly account for the truth of his intuitions.

There is much of it in 'Democratic Vistas,' but Whitman felt that he could convey his full message only to the imagination and by means of the noble indirection of poetry. The constant emphasis of the 'Vistas' (as in his Preface of 1855) is upon the not-to-be-exaggerated need for a 'literatus,' as he so quaintly calls him, who has the art to transmit the vision, the ideals, the 'eidólons,' without which the democratic nation, like any other nation, eventually perishes.

This is a job for literature. It is a task performed magnificently in the past by the great Greeks for their republic, by the great Hebrews for their ecclesiastical state, by the Dantes, the Shakespeares for an age still thinking in terms of feudalism. 'Ye powerful and resplendent ones! Ye were in your atmosphere grown not for America, but rather for her foes, the feudal and the old — while our genius is democratic and modern. Yet could ye, indeed, but breathe your breath of life into our New World's nostrils — not to enslave us, as now but, for our needs, to breed a spirit like your own.' Instead of which, the word of the modern poet is 'culture' — 'genteel, pistareen, paste-pot' culture, distributed by Americans whose inspiration comes entirely from abroad, who run errands for a culture outmoded at home, inapplicable here.

And Walt Whitman himself has more to offer than can be found in the shrewd, hard, eloquent, and epigrammatic 'Vistas.' The reader should pass on from this tract for the times to a noble poem, *Passage to India*, written in the same year, a poem which contains, so Walt said, more of himself than any other. *Passage to India* begins with joy in material progress. In 1869, the Suez Canal had been opened to join Europe to Asia, and in the same year our transcontinental railroad had linked the Atlantic with the Pacific. Now there could be free movement and easy contact between the ancient lands where our imagination had been formed and the New World where man's long probation might end in a new society more hopeful than any yet seen.

The works of engineers were a new step in the adventure which Columbus and Vasco da Gama and other pioneers had begun. Their attempts at passage to India were symbolic of human aspiration, as India itself was symbolic. This restless seeking was in the nature of humankind and the cause of its progress. It was an evolution of the eager, crescent mind irrepressibly pushing toward a liberation from ignorance, doubt, fear, and superstition. Not a Darwinian evolution, conditioned by necessity and circumstance, but rather a Hegelian evolution, dependent upon an idea, which is to say, upon will and hope and love:

Away O soul! hoist instantly the anchor!
Cut the hawsers — haul out — shake out every sail!
Have we not stood here like trees in the ground long enough?
Have we not grovel'd here long enough, eating and drinking like mere
    brutes?
Have we not darken'd and daz'd ourselves with books long enough?
Sail forth — steer for the deep waters only.

Alfred Tennyson's Ulysses, in the poem written a score of years earlier, sailed west toward the Americas to satisfy his Puritan desire for achievement, and in the spirit of the empire builders, Whitman's soul, his 'actual me,' as he called it, sails east to complete the rondure of the world, the wedding of the various races, the welding of the lands. Its spirit is internationalist. For men were to learn in this passage to India that they were all the younger brothers of God, potentially equal among themselves, potentially a brotherhood. Thus, as always with Whitman, the ultimate values are to be spiritual and represent the only divinity he knows by personal knowledge, the divine in man.[3]

Readers of 'Democratic Vistas' and this noble poem will never be content again with easy generalizations about Whitman's idealistic optimism. His vision of democracy as the guardian of personality, the nurse of individual growth, seems overconfident until one discovers how much more he knew of the danger and diseases of democracy than even the ablest of his critics. Politics and economics are for him only means for preserving the essential freedoms, and here he differs sharply from his admirers among left-wing moderns, who have vainly tried to pin their labels on his book. You cannot make a silk purse out of a sow's ear. If democracy grows hoggish, it is no longer important that its government is democratic. Neither a congress nor a constitution makes a democracy, but only the nature of the individuals in the state. These are his warnings; but his faith in democracy is still more important. 'To be a voter with the rest is not so much . . . but to become an enfranchised man, . . . to stand stark without humiliation, and equal with the rest; to have the road cleared to commence the grand experiment, whose end (perhaps requiring several generations) may be the forming of a full-grown man or woman — that *is* something.' Because in modern times only such an achievement can 'ballast' and make secure a state worth living in, worth fighting for.

CHAPTER XXV

'Shut not your doors to me proud libraries'

For Whitman, the years from the end of the Civil War to his paralysis and departure from Washington were memorable for his first notable success in giving his book to the world at large. Yet his success in England, now to be recorded, did not seem to him as important at the time as when, a decade later, sick, much poorer, still unaccepted by his countrymen, he recalled again and again, and with a defiant satisfaction, his capture of strong minds and influential men abroad.

He was still living too intensely, still too creative in the sixties and early seventies, to regard any success but the greatest, and that at home, as definitive.[1] These years in personal friendships, in unaccustomed (and short-lived) prosperity, in opportunities for his own work, were successful. If he was not recognized in the United States as the 'literatus' he believed himself to be, he was becoming well known, at least by name, and was respected for his unselfish services in the war. His contacts were increasingly extensive, and among friends of position who felt honored by his visits. He writes to Pete Doyle of lavish hospitality at the house of Congressman Thomas Davis in Providence; when he went to New York it was often as a guest. And if I am right in my theory that the secret story with a long tail, that was to last all night and which never did get told to his old-age intimates, had its origin in Washington days, then he may have known satisfying love. And certainly he experienced not only distrust and despair, but also renewed confidence and hope for democracy, as the sordid and fanatical battle of Reconstruction dragged through on Capitol Hill.

He lived then, as he always had, with such inner fire that his life itself seemed worth while, book or no book. Traubel asked him the question once, "'Suppose the whole damned thing went up in smoke, Walt: would you consider your life a failure?" He cried out at once with intense feeling: "Not a bit of it.... No life is a failure. I have done the work: I have thrown my life into the work:... — my single simple life: putting it up for what it was worth: into the book — pouring it into the book: honestly, without stint, giving the book all, all, all: why should I call it a failure? why? why? I don't think a man can be so easily wrecked as that."' [2]

Nor did he fail in these climactic years of the 'Leaves' to push hard to give his poems every chance in his own country. In 1867, he got the 'Leaves' printed in a new edition, not markedly changed. In the same year, the first book about him, 'Notes on Walt Whitman as Poet and Person,' by his friend John Burroughs, was published, but probably little read. In 1871, he rearranged the 'Leaves,' adding 'Drum-Taps' and the Lincoln poems, with *Passage to India* as a supplement, printing again from new stereotype plates. I say published. These poems were not truly published. They were privately printed, and distributed in any way he found possible, and there was no good way except selling them himself. Even bibliography can sometimes be dramatic. To anyone familiar with the publishing trade, the poster inserted in an 1871 edition has a melancholy interest:

Walt Whitman's Books

Leaves of Grass Complete..........$3.00 [red-penciled from what seems to have been $3.50]
Passage to India...................$1.00
Democratic Vistas.................$ .75
Can be obtained of the author at Washington, D.C.

Other addresses are given, J. S. Redfield, the printer of Fulton Street, New York, significantly described elsewhere as 'upstairs,' B. F. Felt of New York, Philip Solomon, Washington, and (with bravado) Trübner, London. We know from Walt's later complaint that he was constantly cheated by his depositaries. What he depended upon, and was to depend upon chiefly, until 1881 at least, was mail order. He had been his own printer, now he was his own publisher. What that means to a writer seeking a hearing any professional knows.

2

It was different in England. Copies of the first edition of the 'Leaves' are said to have got to a bookseller, James Grindrod of Sunderland in England, who seems to have bought up remainders for auction.[3] John Camden Hotten, who was later to become Whitman's publisher in England (and also, according to Walt, his pirate), imported others, perhaps of the 1860 edition. As a result, by the later 1860's Whitman became known to a few readers there, but these of weight and substance. Frederick W. H. Myers, essayist, poet, and psychical researcher, was one, who passed on his interest to John Addington Symonds, author of 'The Renaissance in Italy.' Tennyson became one of Whitman's readers, and Swinburne, who first overpraised Walt, then denied him the name of poet. Most important, however, was the seed of enthusiasm which fell on the rich ground of the minds of the two Rossettis, Dante Gabriel and William Michael. It was William Rossetti, scholar and critic, who had published the famous magazine, *The Germ* — where *The Blessed Damozel* appeared — which was the germ, indeed, of the Pre-Raphaelite movement, and much besides. Rossetti, himself an intellectual revolutionary, and convinced republican, was a discriminating man of letters, later to become biographer of Shelley, Blake, and his brother Dante Gabriel, a very different sponsor from the ardent but erratic O'Connor or the still simple and naïve John Burroughs. Rossetti published in *The Chronicle*, an 'organ of advanced Catholic views,' a criticism of the 'Leaves' which, though judicious, asserted that Whitman's achievement was the most impressive of his period. This review was copied in the American papers, always willing to print anything favorable said by an Englishman about an American book.

Rossetti's really important service followed upon Hotten's suggestion that he edit a volume of selections from the 'Leaves,' including the original Preface of 1855. The book was published in 1868, and went far and wide in England and on the Continent. It gave Whitman a standing in Great Britain which he had not yet got in America. It made him accessible there. These 'Selections' omitted all poems objectionable to what Rossetti called the 'squeamishness' of the times, and liable to the strict English censorship of sexual references. But while dropping about half of the 'Leaves' for this or other reasons, they did contain most of the fine poems. From this time on in England, word-of-mouth, that most powerful force in book distribution, began for the 'Leaves,' and among circles both influential and progressive. Madox Brown lent his copy to Mrs. Alexander Gilchrist, widow of the biographer of William Blake, with momentous personal results for Walt later. Her enthusiastic comments were printed in *The Boston Radical*. Edward Dowden, a scholar of Trinity College, Dublin, later distinguished for his work on Shakespeare, praised Whitman in *The Westminster Review* of 1871, and became Walt's friend for life. Moncure D. Conway, who had known Walt at home since 1855, and was now in England, had already written of the 'Leaves' in *The Fortnightly Review*, and was busy with young English writers to bring Whitman to attention and publication when the 'Selections' were arranged for. In a year or two Whitman was being read in the universities, by the London critics, and by readers who were impatient of Victorian controls. There were attacks, of course, but internationally (if not nationally) Whitman's reputation as an outstanding poet of the New World was made.

It sounds like the familiar story of an American reputation made abroad, like Irving's, or Melville's. The analogy is incomplete. Whitman gained fame abroad, and, directly or indirectly, a substantial amount of money, but his difficulties at home were increased rather than swept away. He was pleased and grateful, yet he was right in feeling that the problem of how to establish the 'Leaves' had not been solved. Why had he found no such sponsoring in his own country?

The question raises important distinctions between the two nations and can be answered only by considering the whole problem as to why this author of *the* 'American poem,' as Emerson prophetically called the first 'Leaves,' failed, until our day, to get a standing in American literature, and an audience beyond the temperamentally predisposed reader. The answer is triple. He was not rightly known in his own country, because he was not adequately published here until our own times. He was not adequately published because he refused to compromise and permit expurgation or omission of his poems. His reputation as a poet of importance recognized by readers whose say-so carried real weight was made in England rather than in America, because, frankly, and in the last analysis, he was too native, too American for the taste of critics and scholars on this side of the water who still thought that the American, and American literature, should be in a state of becoming more European, more British, not less so.

The reader of the interesting correspondence between Whitman and Rossetti will see clearly why Rossetti proposed selections only, and the removal from the Preface of 1855 of a few such objectionable words as 'onanist' and 'father-stuff,' but not so clearly why Whitman consented to these changes in England, while refusing omissions for his homeland, which might well have hastened the spread of his reputation here by thirty years.

Rossetti's appeal for such a permission was well reasoned, and Whitman's reply, written without any of his usual quirks and qualifications, was candid and direct.[4] He would not authorize anything that could be called an expurgated edition; on the other hand, if the 'Selections' were under way, he would raise no objection. He would not take the responsibility for deprecating, even by indirection, any poem of his, though he was willing to say that some, if they were rewritten, would have a different cast, and he had already removed a few objectionable words from his text.

In later life Walt was not so sure he had been right in making even this much concession, and he was not at all satisfied with Rossetti's classification of the poems that were published. It is important to understand why he felt so. Still more, why the simple and honest expedient of Hotten's and Rossetti's was not immediately adopted for the American public. The 'Selections' did for Whitman in England what Arnold's selections from Wordsworth had done for that poet, once regarded, though for different reasons, as unreadable. Would not the printing of an American 'Selections' have accomplished the same most desirable purposes here? Whitman would not permit it. He never did permit it. And it is questionable whether if he had, it would have come to the same success.

The British intellectuals had already begun that revolt against laissez-faire materialism which has never ceased up to our own times. England, thanks to their efforts, was, in the twentieth century, to be a score of years ahead of America in projects of social reform. Even Tennyson in *Locksley Hall*, years earlier, had forecast some of the aspirations of *Passage to India*. Carlyle, in his narrow and obstinate way, Ruskin in his attacks on the soul-destruction of industrialism, Pater in his mellifluous nostalgias, Arnold with his sweetness and light, the Pre-Raphaelites with their democratizing of art — all were inclined toward a new order, all were dissatisfied with Victorianism. I do not forget that equivalent movements were sweeping across America in the decades before the cataclysm of the Civil War and the demoralization that followed the westward capture of a continent. But the point for the sixties and seventies is this: that for the English progressives, a radical abroad, a social radical, a sexual radical, a radical in democracy, such as Whitman, had an appeal, even if, like Carlyle, they thought him a rough blusterer. He had an appeal precisely because he was not British, because in Whitman's case he could be supposed to represent the laboratory of democracy in a new rough world. There virtue was supposed to be savage, and so did not offend, and there not the amenities, or culture, or even thinking was to be expected, but lessons from the primitive, examples of human nature released. America was a continent, so they thought, where, by the accident of geography, the common man, whose plight in England had been made so desperate by industrialism, had been put on his own, and clearly done remarkable things, the vulgarity and brashness of which need not too much concern the parent race.

And so English cultivated circles were predisposed to accept eccentricity, wildness, bad manners, contradiction, and Westernism generally in the American artist. They were delighted by the pioneers of Bret Harte, not seeing that they were sentimentalized; they were tricked by the sham primitiveness of Joachim Miller. They liked Mark Twain precisely for the barbaric exaggerations which shocked Boston. It would be slanderous to say that it was Walt Whitman's buffalo hair, his democratic effusiveness, his lack of literary manners, his shouts for a democracy of firemen, farm-hands, and pioneers, that attracted such men as the Rossettis. They felt in his poems the wise seer, the tender lover, and something new and vigorous and hopeful beneath the clatter of the erratic poems. But for the 'Selections,' and their readers, this romantic interest in democratic primitiveness was a great help. And thanks to Rosetti's pruning, these readers did not encounter either the sexual radicalism or the lapses in taste and in art that prejudiced American critics. And to read Walt without prejudice was inevitably to admit his size, if not his success.

As for Walt, and in spite of his later qualms, there was no real compromise in permitting the emasculation of the 'Leaves' for England. His poems were written for the world perhaps, but, in the majority of instances, not about the world or England. They were about America. At home, they stood or fell, so he thought, as a whole. 'Leaves of Grass,' he was to say in *A Backward Glance O'er Travel'd Roads*, had been an attempt to put a human being in the latter half of the nineteenth century, in America, freely, fully and truly on record. To yield to prejudice and emasculate this American picture was to deny its value as a national ideal. Let the English read him piecemeal, if they wished, as an introduction to his study of a complete democratic nationality. At home, it must be all or nothing. That was the way his mind worked.

He felt, and rightly, that literary America was against him. He must stand up to his country's critics or be defeated, no matter what his success abroad. Lowell was reported to have said to a visitor from England bearing a letter of introduction to Walt, 'Do you know who Walt Whitman is? Why — Walt Whitman is a rowdy, a New York tough, a loafer, a frequenter of low places — friend of cab drivers.'[5] 'In my own country, so far,' Whitman wrote to Conway in 1868, 'from the press, and from authoritative quarters, I have received but one long tirade of impudence, mockery, and scurrilous jeers. Only since the English recognition have the skies here lighted up a little.'[6]

He may very well have remembered the review of his 1856 edition in *The Christian Examiner* of Boston, which gathered into one blast the distress of the prudish and the anger of the godly. The 'Leaves,' which the reviewer hoped had died in 1855, had sprouted fresh and must be spoken of as they deserve:

'For here is not a question of literary opinion principally, but the very essence of religion and morality . . . impious and obscene . . . one of its worst disgraces . . . an impertinence toward the English language; and in point of sentiment, an affront upon the recognized morality of respectable people. Both its language and its thought seem to have just broken out of Bedlam . . . the most ridiculous swell of self-applause . . . he will accept nothing which all cannot have in the same terms. . . . These quotations are made with cautious delicacy . . . he has no objection to any person, unless they wear good clothes, or keep themselves tidy . . . this foul work.'

3

It was not fair to say that everyone was against him. He had plenty of kind and discriminating notices in the press, even excluding those written by himself. He had already passionate adherents, men and women who had no doubt of his essential greatness, and often too little doubt that he was in every way a superman. Yet the powers that be were either arrayed against him, or indifferent or wavering.

The truth is that there was a fundamental antagonism between what he was trying to do and what the intellectuals at home thought ought to be done by American writers. So, naturally, the English recognition hurt as well as helped. Even with friends

like Bayard Taylor and Curtis, there was an irritant in the
'Leaves' which worked into their skin. The book simply was not
what the British thought it to be. Howells, who had been so
enthusiastic about Whitman the man, set down in his reminiscences that Whitman's work did not seem to him 'so valuable
in its effect as in intention.' He was a 'liberating force ... but
liberty is never anything but a means, and what Whitman
achieved was a means not an end, in what must be called his
verse.' This is what liberal Boston thought in later years. In
the sixties, Lowell, even if misquoted in the passage above, was
inclined to be contemptuous. Norton, who worshipped at the
shrine of Ruskin and Carlyle, and sent Lowell's essays to Fitz-
gerald as the best that was being done in criticism, found the
democratic barbarian preposterous, if fascinating. As for New
York, which had become by the seventies, as it has since remained, the arbiter of the fate of current books, there his own
successors in the journalist-critic profession were undoubtedly
determined to keep him down. There was a real antagonism,
because his American opponents had a real reason — apart
from the prejudices of literary taste — for trying to keep Walt
in his place. What modern readers of Whitman too easily forget
is that the 'culture' he attacked so witheringly in 'Democratic
Vistas,' and the 'refinement,' which was a password in American
literature of the latter nineteenth century, had sound historical
reasons for a vigorous support. Not so much can be said for
the 'genteel,' which was merely an American exaggeration of
refinement. Whitman's most earnest antagonists were the
honest and honorable intellectuals who were trying to civilize
the United States. His most violent and fanatical enemies were
the self-appointed guardians of the 'genteel.'

The four terrible years of our Civil War, succeeding a decade
of vicious compromise and repressed passion, had been disrup-
tive of American life. Morals, social codes, manners, idealisms,
the very organization of society, North as well as South, were
torn and dented when the war was over. The reaction into
sentimental romance as an escape from the past and the present
in the South is well known, and shaped literature of and about

the South for half a century. But what is not sufficiently understood is what demoralization, what license, what disillusion and cynicism came back from the war. Wealth moved into hands not accustomed to the amenities; with the rapid extension of transportation westward, populations changed their habitat, leaving their stabilities behind them; in the East, a predatory race for money and power brought on the era of the millionaires, who were often just thieves and gamblers; the West beyond the Mississippi became all frontier. The frontier was never a pretty place in spite of the pretty books about it. Not only the daring energies of Whitman's pioneers went there, but all the dissolute instincts let loose from the bonds of a too rigid morality. It is a saying in Connecticut that for every man who went West to get rich, another went to escape from the severity of Connecticut manners. And now millions of young men, released from four years of dirt, danger, and disease, drifted out to start life over again, with the war as their background. In St. Louis in the late sixties, at the saloons, scalps made from the private parts of Indian women were being boastfully exhibited.[7] East and West, the tone of American society — though not its vitality or energy or, indeed, its essential long-term idealism — was lowered. The sexual morality of the trapper, the financial code of the gambler, the manners of the army camp or the frontier town, seemed to be flooding back across the country. Church, school, and literature were too stiff or too feeble to counter this widespread upheaval of the instincts after the wildness of war and in a country rich in opportunities for indulgence. It was only, as Whitman saw, by regarding the evil as a part of the shaping force of energies set loose that a moralist could understand how the American future might develop new *mores* fit for a vigorous democratic state, expansive in body but expansive also in soul.

He was right. This uncontrolled energy was to prove a factor of greatness; refinement was only its brake. Yet this new barbarism did not so appear to what, for convenience, I shall call the intellectual classes. To them, if they were scholars or literati, or educators, or the clergy, it seemed that there was real danger of a destruction or degeneration of that precious European culture which we had brought to the New World. A century earlier many a white American, man or woman, stepped off or was carried away to the freedoms of the Indian country, and never willingly came back. So now, this rough and tough America, disorganized, brutish after war, greedy for the senses, greedy for power, impatient of restraint, seemed likely to drag us all back to a democratic anarchy. The pious and the worthy had some justification for their fears; the thing was possible, and without the increasing mobility of transportation might conceivably have happened.

Naturally, therefore, the refiners, who seldom analyzed the ultimate cause of their dislike or distrust of Whitman, were determined to bring about a restoration of culture, by which was meant the European tradition of the humanities, and an increase of refinement, by which they usually meant good manners according to the code of an English gentleman. They were inclined to disregard the new needs of a democracy building a continent, for freedom from convention and the ideals of a more creative and applicable culture. Thus the impulse of the writers who, in an overpowering majority, belonged with the would-be civilizers was swung away from realism, away from portraiture of the rawness and vigor of the New World, away from satire, toward romance, toward the elegant, the elevating, the refined. Shut your eyes, the novelists and poets seemed to say, to the crudities of this country, enjoy its local color, but consider especially what we might all be like if our manners and education were better. So it went until Dreiser in the next generation was capable of shocking his public by descriptions that now seem as much melodrama as naturalism. Even the honest realist, Howells, upholds a kindly respectability as the desideratum for American society. Henry James went abroad to find themes worth writing about. Mark Twain, who really knew his America, makes savage satire in his greatest book subordinate to an idyllic trip down the Mississippi, and scores of competent authors, who wrote the kind of books called for by readers who were endeavoring to civilize themselves into gentility, need not now be mentioned because no one remembers their names. At the same time, the magazines, ever the chief reading stock for the United States, went in for manners wholesale, and with Philadelphia, Boston, and New York as fashion centres, promoted refinement in dress, conversation, cooking, religion, and male and female relations in the farthest mining camps of the West.

I could cite scores of instances of this crusade for culture which was so damaging to Whitman's success. I shall choose, however, only one, but that from the noblest refiner of them all, written before he sought subtlety in the interworld of international society. In 1865, when he was only twenty-two, Henry James reviewed 'Drum-Taps' in the first volume of *The Nation*. He may have had before him only the first issue, without the major Lincoln poems, but this volume did contain *Pioneers! O Pioneers!* And he seems to have read, or read in, the previous 'Leaves,' since it would be difficult, even for a conservative critic to find what he called 'wanton eccentricities' which seem 'monstrous' in the restraint of 'Drum-Taps.' It is a searching, caustic, somewhat condescending review, in which everything is reasonably true except James's account of Walt Whitman's emotions, which, as he was incapable of feeling them himself, he naturally could not describe. 'It is not enough to be vigorous,' he says. Whitman's work is the 'effort of an essentially prosaic mind to lift itself by a prolonged muscular strain, into poetry.' The poet 'must forget himself in his idea.' 'If the idea which possesses you is the idea of your country's greatness, then you are a national poet and not otherwise.' Whitman, James said, never grasped that idea. He never understood that 'this democratic, liberty-loving American populace, this stern and war-tried people, is a great civilizer. It is devoted to refinement.' Alas, Mr. James, it was devoted to nothing of the kind, and that was perhaps the chief reason that you went abroad to be successful, and Walt Whitman stayed at home to wage unequal battle for a democracy that did not expurgate the rough and tough, the simple and the common, from its ideals.

4

While I have oversimplified this picture, I have not exaggerated it, and Walt was the victim. He was the victim too of the 'genteel,' which was just one aspect of the plaster of refinement then being applied so liberally to the façades of the new rich everywhere. The almost pathological modesty of expression in polite society and polite literature in the seventies and eighties was worse than the narrowest moralism of New England in the forties and fifties, because it was less sincere.

Unfortunately, the true issue between Whitman and his American opponents was seldom joined, because his enemies were shocked by his language, and found that the charge of 'indecency' was the easiest way to stop his progress. It was not the indecency of the camps and the frontier, of course; it was worse, it was obscenity (their favorite word) creeping in by the back door of literature and soiling the parlor table with words that refined society had agreed should be at least kept out of print. Words, too, used in an apocalyptic fashion as by a revivalist preacher. Even as President Dwight of Yale at the turn of the century had been sure that the infidel Jefferson intended to deliver the somewhat suppressed maidens of Connecticut to a kind of legal prostitution, so these guardians of the hearth and home (ex-Bohemians some of them and none too particular in their private lives) never got beyond the elementary idea that the man who counselled fullness of sexual relations could only be an advocate of that 'free love' which was the sophisticated version of what was happening only too freely all along and across the frontier.

And they were equally angry when they read (probably like Harlan, skippingly) Whitman's boisterous praises of 'savage virtue,' of rough simplicity, of the superior virtues of instinctive common man. This America was their own republic, with a bad reputation already for its manners, vulgarity, and complete freedom of the more violent instincts. Whitman, they thought, was trying to make it worse. And, indeed, his fondness for exaggeration did lead him to make his country even tougher, louder, more virile, commoner, more contemptuous of refinement, than was really the case.

It must be added for the New York coteries, and for the aca-

demic groups, who, with their descendants, were to pooh-pooh
his importance for two more generations, that Whitman made
them uncomfortable for still more damaging reasons. There was
in the latter third of the nineteenth century, as one sees now,
and particularly among the writers, a lack of vitality, and a
tendency toward a merely genteel competence which, by the
end of the century, had made the United States the happy
home of light essays, light romance, and still lighter verse. This
could not be said of the real men-of-letters of the period — of
Howells, of Henry Adams — but nothing can be more certain
than that these powerful writers — and particularly Adams —
felt a sense of divorce, which in Adams's case was an unhappy
sense, from the whole area of American life. Adams blamed
America and not his Boston upbringing, but the fact remained.

For men feeling as all these did — and particularly the little
ones — too much praise of Whitman seemed an insult to their
country. The praise, like Whitman himself, was definitely a
challenge to authors who were trying to make their country
more decent, more respectable, more respectful of culture and
good manners, by giving it only what was decent, respectable,
and cultivated to read.

As if all this were not enough, the very style of the man acted
as an abrasive upon the intellectuals of his generation. He wrote
poetry that was not recognizable as verse, and prose that often
seemed to be trying to be poetry. This latter third of the century
was one of those periods common in the arts, when the forms
of literature seem to be set, when even poetasters become competent in the general patterns, and a new diction, a heretical
rhythm, or whatever calls itself poetry or music or painting, and
is not any of these by accepted standards, is upsetting to the
point of pain. Kipling gave pain in his day; so did the dissonances
of modern music and the non-representational experiments of
painting and sculpture. But no writer in our time has given as
much pain to the orthodox reader as did the style of Whitman.
That is a tribute to his originality, though chargeable also to his
willingness to write badly when his genius was asleep. What was

this style of Whitman? The answer must wait for another chapter.

As for Walt himself in this discussion, which seems to have got a long way from the 'Selections,' but has not, he was well aware of the issues at stake though he would have phrased them differently, with less concern for refinement, some misunderstanding of culture, and a powerful defence of the American's ability to do his own working up from rowdyism into a virile democracy.

And he stood fast on his own ground: 'I am large, I contain multitudes.' 'Who takes me, must take me whole.' All had to be told, or the testimony would not be true. An editor may deplore the imperfect sequence, the wasteful prodigality, the uneven quality, and the expansive excesses of the 'Leaves,' but a biographer must add that in no other way could Whitman have made his book — nor was he capable of altering his Intentions in order to make it completely successful as literature in his own time — or any time.

CHAPTER XXVI

'Old, poor, and paralyzed, I thank thee'

In the evening of January 23, 1873, sitting in the library of the Treasury, reading before a pleasant open fire a novel by Bulwer-Lytton, Whitman suddenly felt unwell; got home unaided, but in great discomfort. When he awoke in the morning, his left arm and leg were paralyzed. He felt sure he would recover, and indeed did get out again soon and as far as his office. Yet the letter in shaky pencilling to his mother, telling of his attack, must, to his own eyes as he wrote it, have seemed ominous for the future.[1] From that night on, he might have said on almost any day, as in 1891: 'I realize perfectly well that definition Epictetus gives of the living personality and body, "A corpse dragging a soul hither and thither."'

He was not to be a corpse for nearly twenty years, nor a crippled soul, but only a slowed-up mind, yet with the loss of his vigor some essential quality soon drained from his intellect. His mind works freely, first in good years, then on good days, up to the verge of death, and at the moment of physical disaster his imagination seems not to have felt the blow to the body. But the creativeness is soon gone. From 1875 on, all that is significant in Whitman's writing is referential to or repetitive of the earlier 'Leaves.' Lines he writes of power and beauty, makes incisive, penetrating remarks. But his poems are only a filling in of the chinks of his life work, or are captions for what has been done before. The essential 'Leaves,' except for rearrangement and these plasterings and annotations, is, if not finished, essentially concluded.

By May of 1873 he was discouraged enough to draw up a rather pathetic will.[2] His gold watch he left to his mother; his portrait, by Walter Libby, he gives to his brother Jeff, whose wife, 'Mat,' Walt's close friend, had died in February. Apparently he had nothing else he wished to specify, though there must have been some cash and books. It is clear that his copyrights did not seem to him then to have a realizable value.

Thoroughly miserable, he set off in May of this year for a vacation in Camden, where George, now an inspector of pipes, was residing in a good house on Stevens Street. Old Mrs. Whitman, who was living with her son and taking care of poor Eddie, was ill, and on the twenty-third of May, while Walt was at home, she died. In a few months he had lost his own health permanently, his hope of a steady income, his dear sister-in-law, and his mother. The last blow was probably the hardest. Louisa Whitman through life had been Walt's background of love and the security of love. She was his stability, a world of affection to which he never had to adjust himself, where, never understood as a poet, he was always and completely accepted as the son who would and could do no wrong.

Sick again after this shock, he settled down with George, comfortably provided for on an upper floor. In 1874, his job in the Treasury, which had been filled by a substitute, was (quite rightly) taken from him. It is not surprising that again and again in later years, he refers to the mid-seventies as the worst, the lowest, the most hopeless period of his life.

However, as so often happens with men at the end of a creative career, and especially with writers whose work has been intensely personal, the vision of himself wrecked before his work was done revived his energies for a poem which reads like the last aria of the tenor in a tragic opera. It must have been written after his recovery from his second breakdown following his mother's death, and was published in *Harper's Magazine* in March of 1874. By now his ego had made terms with his cosmos, and he dramatized a historical Columbus while writing symbolically of himself:

> A batter'd, wreck'd old man,
> Thrown on this savage shore, far, far from home, ...
> Sore, stiff with many toils, sicken'd and nigh to death, ...

Haply I may not live another day;
I cannot rest O God, I cannot eat or drink or sleep,
Till I put forth myself, my prayer, once more to Thee, ...

Thou knowest my years entire, my life,
My long and crowded life of active work, not adoration merely; ...
Intentions, purports, aspirations mine, leaving results to Thee.

O I am sure they really came from Thee,
The urge, the ardor, the unconquerable will,
The potent, felt, interior command, stronger than words, ...

By me and these the work so far accomplish'd,
By me earth's elder cloy'd and stifled lands uncloy'd, unloos'd, ...

The end I know not, it is all in Thee,
Or small or great I know not — haply what broad fields, what lands,
Haply the brutish measureless human undergrowth I know,
Transplanted there may rise to stature, knowledge worthy Thee, ...

Old, poor, and paralyzed, I thank Thee.

This *Prayer of Columbus* [3] is the poetic autobiography of a soul reconciled to death, and, in the face of death, uncertain and humble in achievement and hope. Tennysonian in music, it is Whitman at his finest in controlled rhythm and in the expression of indomitable optimism. The same year he repeated the theme in the *Song of the Redwood Tree*, only now he is surer of the future. The vast tree crashes down after its 'great patient rugged joys,' after grandly filling its time (as he had tried to do) with Nature's calm content and with tacit huge delight. Its space is left for a superber race, long predicted. Is it a dream, he asks in a third poem of this climactic year, *Song of the Universal*, that out of even the frauds of men and states, good may come? Is this faith a dream? To lack it is to dream of failure. This was his valedictory, and even in the *Song of the Universal* the stiffening and flattening of his so flexible mind begins to be apparent. His personal story as seer and poet is nearly finished, but of the life of the man and his books there is still much to say.

2

I do not intend to follow in close detail the events of the decades after 1874 except to correct some misconceptions, to describe one curious experience, new for him and moving, and to put in order the essential narrative. Only one major objective was left to Whitman in life after his powers began to fail, and everything he did with energy from now on had reference to what his friend Kennedy called somewhat extravagantly, yet with a large kernel of truth, the fight of a book for the world.[4]

He was not destitute, as has been often stated, not uncared for, except for a very brief period later on, never rightly an object of pity, unless as a man only in his fifties whose magnificent mind and body were shaken by physical disaster. A letter to Pete Doyle describes his outer circumstances fairly enough:[5]

'322 Stevens St., Camden, N.J. Wednesday forenoon, June 18, [1873]   Dear Pete — It has been a good move of me coming here, as I am pleasantly situated, have two rooms on 2d floor, with north and south windows, so I can have the breeze through — I can have what I wish in the grub line, have plenty of good strawberries — and my brother and sister [George had married] are very kind — It is very quiet, and I feel like going in for getting well — There is not much change so far — but I feel comparatively comfortable since I have been here — and better satisfied — My brother is full of work (inspecting pipe manufactured here at the foundries for water works and sewers in Northern cities) — he is in splendid health — a great stout fellow — weighs more than I do — he is building a handsome new house here, to be done latter part of August.' But five weeks later he changes his tone. 'Half a block tires me. Pete, my darling son, I still think I shall weather it but time only can show — Mother's death is on my mind yet, time does not lift the cloud from me at all.'

He was lonely in Camden, found no intimate acquaintances, longed for the companionship of Washington, the friendly presence and magnetism he needed. By June of 1874, he began to feel that things were steadily growing worse. Then he rallied. From his savings he bought in this year a cheap lot, hoping to build a little house for himself. In 1875, a trickle of energy commenced to flow. He was setting up type for his 1876 edition. In 1876, now expecting to remain in Camden, he began his summerings on Timber Creek, which flows into the Delaware on the New Jersey side a few miles below Camden, traversing the pleasant farming country which Swedes and Quakers had settled before the coming of William Penn. He stayed near Whitehorse, on the road to Atlantic City, in a charming old farmhouse tenanted by the George Strafford family. As usual, it was the wife, Mrs. Strafford, to whom he became an especial friend. On the shore of a secluded pool, he spent long hours of quiet meditation, went mud-bathing in an old mud pit, enjoyed sun-bathing in the nudity he had once written about so flauntingly. Gradually he recovered to a partial lameness only. By the turn of the mid-eighties, he was at worst a slightly crippled old man, able to put together reminiscences from his notebooks, and add new poetry. No one, he said, gave a damn for his prose, which is too harsh. But it is secondary writing. The poetry declined from his best. His creative vigor never returned.

Pathetic stories are told of the seemingly old man, crawling about Camden or Philadelphia now and later, selling his 'Leaves' from a basket on his arm. This is nonsense. He never lacked support in these years. The basket, of course, was for delivery of such books as were ordered from near-by. It was by purchase from him personally that the few copies of the 'Leaves' in circulation were being bought. A memorandum scribbled in a notebook of this time, now in the Yale Library, tells how a copy of the 'Leaves' is to be left for R. H. Eaton at a shop on the northwest corner of Front and Market Streets, just across the Camden Ferry. One can see him hobbling up the slope from the ferry, the book or books in a basket on his free arm. Everyone carried, at one time or another, baskets in Philadelphia in those days, for marketing or the like.

What troubled him was not destitution. There was never real danger of that — but dependency — his earning capacity, he feared, was nearly over. The bard of the buffalo hair was caught by the leg in the house of his kin, who were fond of him, but made nothing of his poetry — could not, and did not, talk his language except in terms of affection and simplicity. It was a tough fate for a rambler across the earth, and an intellectual Bohemian. How to escape the body of this death? There seemed to be no way. Later, friends and admirers were to seek and find him, but at this time what more than anything lifted his depression and blew the airs of life through his mind again, were the vacations on the borders of Timber Creek, which are described at length, and sometimes very beautifully, in 'Specimen Days.'

Yet in spite of the attempts of his chroniclers to add these descriptions to the long series of fine nature books in American literature, his records are more interesting as biography than as nature study. Nature for Walt was very different from Emerson's powerful goddess, still more different from the animated nature his friend Burroughs wrote about with charm and accuracy, or the world of shape and form and action with which Thoreau was obsessed. Nature for Walt was an extension of his own ego, serving it as the sun and air served his lame body. He does not get outside of himself to see birds and flowers, they come into his interior life, leaving their personalities (and often their names) behind. When the birds speak in his poetry, it is very definitely Walt singing. Their identity is with phases of his own imagination, not with themselves.

Through the latter 1870's Walt continued to improve both in health and spirits. The loneliness of Camden was broken by new friendships, such as a close and rewarding relationship with J. H. Johnston, a jeweller of New York and a personality. Walt had helped him to resolve some of his difficulties when faith in his youthful orthodoxies broke down. With Johnston and his wife and children, whom he came to love, he stayed for a month at a time, and was able to renew happily many of his New York memories. There was also the beginning of the steady flow of visitors which was to relieve (and sometimes weary) his old age. The engaging English radical, Edward Carpenter, who wrote 'Towards Democracy' and has left reminiscences of Walt, was one. There was also Doctor Richard M. Bucke, the Canadian alienist, who became his first real biographer, and was responsible for a good deal of theorizing about Whitman's spiritual states, but whose book is still the chief source for Whitman's early life.

Whitman began to travel now (usually by invitation), as he would have so much liked to do earlier. He went to St. Louis and Colorado in 1879 with Colonel John W. Forney, whose Old Settlers of Kansas Committee had invited him to read from his poetry at the Kansas Quarter-Centennial.[6] On the way back from the Rockies, he stayed with Jeff in St. Louis, but was ill there. He visited John Burroughs in his picturesque 'Slabsides' at Esopus, travelled up the Saguenay with Doctor Bucke, returned at least once to Washington, and spent a profitable two or three months in Boston in 1881, seeing an edition through the press. While there, he visited Concord, talked of Thoreau with the survivors of the great Concord coterie (increasingly, as Whitman grew older, Thoreau impressed his imagination), and saw for the last time Emerson, now near his end, yet still speaking a word or phrase where needed, and always with a smile — 'the old clear-peering aspect quite the same.'[7] At the house of Quincy A. Shaw, he was shown for the first time Millet's pictures, and, recognizing a genius akin to his own, studied them with the deepest interest and referred to them often later. Hitherto painting had meant story-telling to Whitman.

It was on April 14, 1879, that he delivered for the first time his lecture on Lincoln, repeated frequently, and later made an occasion for laudatory tribute to him, and a substantial increase in his scanty income. By 1886 and 1887 he was realizing as much as six to seven hundred dollars from each reading, with such hearers as Mark Twain, Stedman, John Hay, General Sherman, Andrew Carnegie, and even Lowell. In the late seventies he had become a well-known but still questionable public character, like an old politician on his way to the name of statesman. As Curtis said of him about this time, he was an object of general curiosity. The laity honored him because he looked as if he should be honored. The inner circle of his devotees, 'the hot little prophets,' as Bliss Perry called them, felt some divinity in him and did not hesitate to say so. But it cannot be said that either in the 1870's or the 1880's, Whitman's place among the great in poetry had been adequately or even inadequately recognized, and of this the poet was aware.

It will be noted that this brief summary of Whitman's life and activities from 1873 to the early eighties has a retrospective and a finishing-off quality, which, indeed, is my intention in summarizing so briefly. The details are easily available in other books and in Walt's own 'Specimen Days.' I believe this to be the right perspective. The true history of Whitman from 1874 on is of his book and the best background is the final and most intimate glimpse of his personality, which we get from Traubel's records in the late 1880's. There is an important symbolic record of these years in the many photographs of the aging poet, some magnificent, leonine, with a slow-burning vitality, though in others and especially the profile views, where the beard does not so much conceal the features, he looks like a worn old man nearly burnt out. One rather absurd picture with an artificial butterfly clamped to one finger, he used as a frontispiece to the 1881 edition. Walt was both the powerful rememberer and interpreter of himself and his times, and the worn-out, weary, vivid, defeated, yet still hopeful artist, depending upon when you saw him. His work was done, except for mopping up. But his fight was by no means over; indeed, its most sensational episode came in the eighties.

CHAPTER XXVII

'Ah you foes that in conflict have overcome me'

A LL THROUGH these discouraging years, Whitman's determination to win a hearing for his writing was unfaltering.
After the edition of the 'Leaves' in 1867, with its annexes, and
'Democratic Vistas' and *Passage to India* in the same year of
1871, came 'After All Not to Create Only,' also in 1871. This
was his tribute to the great American Institute's exhibition of
'Current Inventions, Science, Patriotism,' and was read there by
invitation. Editions of the 'Leaves,' not much changed, were
printed in both 1871 and 1872. In 1872 he wrote, and delivered
at Dartmouth College, *As a Strong Bird on Pinions Free*, invited
there by the students who are said, on gossiping authority, to
have hoped to stir up their professors. Neither they nor the
verses were particularly successful. A volume of 1872, with this
poem as title-piece, contained, however, Whitman's fine tribute
to France, which had just gone down in defeat before a ruthless
Prussia. Whitman had leaned toward the Germans at the beginning of this war. It was from their philosophy that, at second
and third hand, he had drawn strength for his own innate Transcendentalism.[1] Yet he quickly swung to the side of the van-
quished French, recording, in a note to 'Democratic Vistas,'
the ominous warning of Prussian absolutism after Napoleon had
surrendered and Paris still held out: 'His Majesty refuses to treat
on any terms, with a government risen out of Democracy.'[2]
'Let us note the words,' he says, 'and not forget them ... the
only vast, emotional, real affinity of America is with the course
of Popular Government.' So spoke Woodrow Wilson a half-
century later, so Franklin D. Roosevelt.

In 1875 he published, himself, *Memoranda of the War*, which later went into 'Specimen Days.' In 1876, again publishing himself, he brought out the Centennial edition of his works, in two volumes, to synchronize with the epoch-making exhibition in Philadelphia, which did so much to set the United States in world currents again after the isolationism of a westward-expanding half-century and the Civil War.

2

Unhappily, just when he most needed encouragement, a misapprehension of his poverty stirred up again the now tender consciences and the perennial sensitiveness to comments from abroad of his American critics. Robert Buchanan, who had praised him before with reservations, wrote letters to *The London Daily News* inspired by an article in *The West Jersey Press*, which may have been written by Walt, and which said of the 'Leaves' that 'the determined denial, disgust and scorn of orthodox American authors, publishers, and editors, and in a pecuniary and worldly sense, have certainly wrecked the life of their author.' [3] Buchanan described the destitution of a great American poet, neglected by his countrymen, attacked America and American authors violently, and asked for aid. Walt's old acquaintance Conway, resident in England, replied, denying that Walt was in danger of starving, and so a controversy began, well aired first in England and then in America. Now, Walt was underestimated and opposed by his contemporaries in America for reasons stated before, but his financial distresses were not the fault of his country. He had freely chosen to write unsalable books. And for nearly ten years he had been supported by the government, quite as much on account of his reputation and past services as for the good but not hard work he did in his various departments. Nor was he without cash, or in danger of anything except dependency upon a family where he had always paid his way, and of which, in tougher times, he had been one of the chief supports. There was, as he said, 'a great rattling of dry bones over there and here... about my poverty.'

So he wrote to Buchanan that he was right in principle, but not as to the facts of destitution.[4] He himself was living comfortably with George and paying 'just the same as at an inn.' His savings had about given out but some money was coming in from the new editions. He would gladly accept more help, but it should be through the sale of a subscription edition (which Buchanan had mentioned). Alfred Austin's remark in the course of the discussion, 'While we talk, he starves,' was absurd.

The result in England was a subscription edition promoted by Rossetti, with a most generous response from such men as Lord Houghton, Edward Carpenter, Tennyson, Ruskin, Edmund Gosse, George Saintsbury, G. H. Lewis, E. J. A. Balfour, many of whom oversubscribed. Buchanan, who had written the famous 'The Fleshly School of Literature,' attacking Dante Gabriel Rossetti, risked his own reputation in defending Walt's. He disapproved of his sexual references but believed in his philosophy.

The home-grown pundits and the literary columnists had another grievance. So far it had been safe enough for casual reviewers to regard Walt as a wild man, a freak, or a crackpot, and for the more important critics to damn him with qualified praise, as a phenomenon of unrestrained democracy whose language they deplored. His English reception had already ruffled these enemies and part friends, who believed that the British enthusiasm was for a roughness and a toughness which foreigners liked to think was characteristic of the United States. The English, so they thought, enjoyed Walt's bawling for virility and the freedoms of the West, which sounded to many of the cultivated in Boston and New York like shouts for free whisky in a saloon full of tipplers. But now we were being called a prudish, unappreciative country that starved its great men. Naturally, there was a reaction.

Whitman had the same opportunity, said George William Curtis, as Bryant and Longfellow.[5] There was no conspiracy against him. Unfriendly editorials, later stated by O'Connor to have been written by Bayard Taylor, once Walt's friend, appeared in *The New York Tribune* of the same year. He was not, the editorials implied, quite so original as the English thought. When the 1881 edition appeared, someone on *The Tribune*, probably William Winter, the dramatic critic, was sure that as a poet Whitman had been overestimated.[6] Winter, if it was Winter, had been one of Whitman's associates at Pfaff's. 'A young Longfellow,' Walt had called him, which was taken as a sneer; 'Weeping Willie' was his later nickname because of the lachrymose obituaries he wrote. He was a sound, but reactionary, and eventually a petrified, critic of the drama. In the review, the 'Leaves' were described as a 'slop-bucket.' As for Walt, 'that he is a poet most of us frankly admit,' but he still takes his trousers off in public. It is art in its last degradation. Whitman resented the reservations of the editorials more than the review. Taylor had been his admirer. Willy Winter he had always despised.

This exchange of brickbats and bouquets made one thing seem probable, that the opposition to the 'Leaves of Grass' in this genteel age of our culture was growing, not decreasing, and that a definite attempt was being made by leaders in the critical world to put brakes on Whitman's slow advance toward general recognition. His friends were sure of this, so sure that Kennedy, in his 'The Fight of a Book for the World,' prints in contrasting paragraphs lists, which Walt must have helped to prepare before his death, of 'Whole-hearted Accepters,' and 'Bitter and Relentless Foes and Vilifiers.'[7] Among the vilifiers is a group of names very often mentioned by Walt himself, as belonging to a cabal or conspiracy against his reputation. It was not a conspiracy, but these men did belong to a coterie, which, to an outsider, can be quite as harmful as a cabal, especially when its members can influence both the word-of-mouth and word-in-print which so strongly affect the rise and fall of fame.

Edgar Fawcett was one, a rich Columbia graduate, who published in his time thirty-five novels, all conventional, poor plays, and good satiric verse. Richard Henry Stoddard, once called the literary arbiter of New York, was another. A poet of slender talent, he was book reviewer of *The New York World* from 1860 to 1870, from 1880 literary editor of *The Mail and Express*. His home, after 1870, was a literary salon. Hating Bohemians, he was a good man, narrow, erudite, and at the end frustrated. As a type he was antagonistic to all Whitman stood for. William Winter was still another. One notes that he was next-door neighbor to Curtis on Staten Island.

In a second category, were Bayard Taylor, a deserter from the cause of Whitman's reputation, and Richard Watson Gilder, the kindly gentleman of impeccable taste who, through *The Century Magazine* in its great period, ruled American poetry for many years. And Stedman and Curtis and Bryant. These men were, or had been, his friends, and he was grateful to them, but always their praise was half-hearted, always they made reservations which to Whitman were as serious as condemnation. He was, in his own opinion, touched with greatness or a failure, and greatness they would not admit.

Now that Boston had yielded to New York as the publishing center of the country, such men, with others more casually mentioned, did heavily influence the fate of current books and reputations, as far as critics and commentators could control it. They were the 'refiners' who dominated the taste of the seventies, eighties, and nineties, as the Bostonians, notably Lowell, had dominated before. And they were, most of them, friends and constant associates, the importance of which will be obvious to those who know how sales and reputation are made. At this time, if there was a literary broadcasting station in New York for verbal opinion, it was certainly The Century Association, a club which was much more of a literary place of might then than now, whose frequent gatherings of the editorial and literary celebrities of the metropolis were famous and have been commemorated on canvas as well as by pen.[8] Bryant, whom Whitman so much admired, but who was 'cold' to him after the appearance of the first 'Leaves' in 1855, was a distinguished member till his death in 1878. Gilder, Stedman, Taylor, and Lowell were members, and so were Fawcett, Stoddard, and Curtis. They must have sat in at many an evening gathering whose verdicts would be reflected in the literary journals, as happens now in less Victorian environments. And Weeping Willie must have often joined the group, though apparently never a member of the club.[9]

The outspoken O'Connor, whose information must have come from Walt, tells how the friends of the 'Leaves' felt about this club and another in 1876:[10] 'They go to their scratch-my-back club, which is called "The Century," and their tickle-my-elbow club, which is called "The Lotos,"[11] and they read each other their little essays and their less verses; and they call each other gods and geniuses, and they concoct their epigrams and epithets, and arrange who shall be written up, and who down, and police Parnassus generally.' The rest of the letter is an attack upon Bayard Taylor direct. It is not surprising that the supposedly complete library of American poetry in *The Century* had, in the middle 1920's, no copy of the 'Leaves of Grass.'

Thus Whitman's angry suspicions cannot be called just writer's paranoia. It was the genteel age that he was encountering in its most respectable American club, and in his own New York. An outsider now by circumstance, always an outsider socially and in character and performance, helpless in Camden, he saw his poetical work essentially finished, yet still condemned because it was not respectable. That he was on the main line, and the others close to a dead-end, is proved by the drift downward below the surface of literary history of all that genteel, refining group, except Bryant, who, of course, was much more than a refiner. Winter in his old age refused to accept the new realism of the American drama, and his reviews became 'unintelligible' to the oncoming generation. Gilder, one of the most generous minds of our critical tradition, has come to be fatally associated with the age of 'magazine verse' which preceded the poetic renaissance of the early twentieth century. One has only to consult Stedman's anthologies to see how definitely, and one can say, permanently, our sense of values in American literature has changed from his. Fawcett and Stoddard are forgotten. Bayard Taylor, whose ambitions were as great as Whitman's, is well-nigh forgotten, too.

And it seems most probable that these men, and the genteel reviewers elsewhere, did succeed in holding back Whitman's recognition in this country as a great if faulty poet in a time of small men of culture. They are not excusable as were the critics of the mid-fifties, for now his mature work was before them. With the assistance of literary professors from the colleges, they may have delayed his acceptance by twenty years. Even in 1899, Thomas Wentworth Higginson, last of the Boston arbiters, old style, could assert in his reminiscent 'Contemporaries' that Whitman's verse did not have poetic rhythm, and that Sidney Lanier was a more heroic character and a greater genius. Higginson had discovered Emily Dickinson, but Emily, in spite of her self-revelations, never took off her skirts in the presence of Boston, and The Century — either magazine or club.

It was not until 1881 that the axe of censorship finally fell, and then, fortunately, it did more harm to an eminent publisher than to Whitman.

In 1881 the great Boston publisher, James R. Osgood, midwife for most of the Boston immortals, decided (so it would seem) that the wild poet of democracy had become sufficiently respectable since his appearance in Boston as a Lincoln lecturer to merit a speculation. After some discussion, it was agreed that the 'Leaves of Grass' should be published without expurgation under this august imprint. Walt, as has been recorded, went to Boston for a second publishing of his book, which now had become his life, and the edition was issued. 'Until now,' said *The Tribune*, reviewing the book on November 19, 'it cannot be said that his verses have ever been published at all.' A handsome sale had begun, two thousand, so Walt's friend Johnson was told, when the New England Society for the Suppression of Vice persuaded the district attorney, Oliver Stevens, to suggest that the book should be suppressed in order to avoid action. Quotations had been supplied him by agents, with whom, according to O'Connor, the so long to be notorious Anthony Comstock was in collaboration. According to Doctor Bucke's account, a number of lines, and the poems *A Woman Waits for Me*, *The Dalliance of the Eagles*, and *To a Common Prostitute*, were used as a basis for the charge of dangerous indecency. It was, of course, easy to pick out a line here and there from the 'Leaves' which was frank to indecency, yet certainly not obscene, but the poems chosen as an excuse for suppression are amazing, even for Boston, where it would seem that even in 1881 eagles might mate without danger to the morals of Back Bay. The amazement grows when one learns that a little later the official mind consented to be satisfied if *To a Common Prostitute* and *A Woman Waits for Me* were removed from the text. The latter is the poem in which Whitman states:

Without shame the man I like knows and avows the deliciousness of his sex,
Without shame the woman I like knows and avows hers.

There was no question of 'free love,' a red rag for the genteel age, for the symbolic Walt asserts that he will be 'the robust husband of such women':

They are not one jot less than I am,
They are tann'd in the face by shining suns and blowing winds, . . .
They know how to swim, row, ride, wrestle, shoot, run, strike, retreat, advance, resist, defend themselves,

which sounds like one of those girls' camps whose popularity began, I believe, among respectable Boston families.

It is true that the seminal is characteristically mentioned more often than necessary in this poem, though clearly made symbolical (and a little ridiculous):

I pour the stuff to start sons and daughters fit for these States.

Nevertheless, Mr. Stevens, the district attorney, seems, in this instance, to have been willing to let the book go on if these poems and the mention of the essential processes of reproduction should be omitted.

As for *To a Common Prostitute*, first published in 1860, the emphasis in that superb little poem falls upon the fine lines:

Not till the sun excludes you do I exclude you.

And it seems probable from the context that the appointment for which she was to wait and make herself 'patient and perfect' was as symbolic as Christ's words to Mary Magdalene, which the Society for the Suppression of Vice must have forgotten.

Osgood could have asked for a jury trial. Instead, he took to cover, not wishing to risk the high respectability of his firm.

The edition was called off before prosecution was undertaken. Yet the episode, if indicative of the strength of the prudish-genteel forces, whose final defeat in the realm of literature did not come till the famous case of Joyce's 'Ulysses' in the 1930's, had its fortunate aspects for Whitman. After their long estrangement, O'Connor flew to his defence. Osgood released the plates for the accrued royalties of five hundred dollars, and the book was taken over by a more courageous, if less famous, publisher, in a more liberal city, Rees, Welsh and Company, of Philadelphia, whose business was shortly assumed by David McKay, described by Whitman as 'young-blooded, careful, wide-awake, vital.' [12] With the brevet of the Boston Society, which (as so often) was a response to vitality rather than to true indecency, the new edition in its new home yielded Whitman thirteen hundred dollars, more money probably than he had earned before by his pen alone in all his life. Two first editions sold, according to Walt, in one day.

3

Vitality, not sexuality, not indecency, was the true word for Whitman's own work. And one extraordinary episode, an outcome of his English reputation, was in itself the finest testimony to the vitality of his poems of love and the magnetism of one of the great souls of the nineteenth century.

No woman had written about the 'Leaves' (though many must have read it) since the unstable and sentimental Fanny Fern in the 1850's. This could scarcely have happened if Walt had published in the 1830's or the 1840's when feminism was mounting and new philosophies of all kinds, including ideas as to sexual relations, were sprouting like crops from New England to the Mississippi. But by the time the first 'Leaves' began to get around, the age of refinement and gentility was under way, and the outspoken, revolutionary women were too busy with Abolition and, later, the war, to crusade for sexual equality. It was not until 1869 (so far as I know) that Walt found a woman reader who was intelligent, high-charged with idealism and passion, and willing to speak her mind. Anne Gilchrist was one of those social and spiritual revolutionists who have been so loosely and inadequately called Pre-Raphaelites. Her husband, an art critic, was engaged at the time of his death upon a life of that early revolutionary, the poet, William Blake. She finished the book and published it.

Mysticism, literary radicalism, spiritual sensuousness were in her environment. She had been happy with her husband, but he had not aroused a nature which was both passionate and intellectual — a dangerous combination. Through Madox Brown, her friend, she came to read, in 1869, Rossetti's 'Selections' from Whitman, afterward the whole of the 'Leaves.' It entered into the very fibre of her being, and she responded with a lengthy letter, which was put into article form and finally published in 1870, as *A Woman's Estimate of Walt Whitman* in Joseph B. Marvin's *Boston Radical.* Whitman read this perceptive analysis of his emotional purposes with deep satisfaction. Here was an understanding he had not got, could not get from the women he cherished — the Prices, the Nellie O'Connors, who loved him, and accepted (and excused) the ardors of the 'Leaves' for his sake. He was not, at first, particularly concerned with the author, except that she was a woman, highly intelligent, and entirely understanding of his message to love. But through Rossetti he soon learned of her identity, and sent a copy of the 1871 edition 'for *the lady*.' That was as far as it went.

But with '*the lady*' it went much further, and soon became her story, not Walt's, and can be read in her letters. If I give the narrative little space, it is because the drama (almost melodrama) was really hers, not his.[13] Yet what happened illustrates better than any other incident in his life the difference between Walt of the 'Leaves' and Walt the man. She fell in love with the poet's projection of himself, not knowing that in the effort of creation his love had already become universal and impersonal.

Mrs. Gilchrist is described as not being beautiful. Yet her picture suggests a quality of passionate emotion in eyes and mouth that must have made her more attractive than many handsomer women. There is force and strength but no angularity or repression in her figure and face. The reading of the 'Leaves' was for her a 'new birth of the soul.' But there was a rebirth, or perhaps a first birth, of more than her soul. It must have been an embarrassing surprise to Walt when, in response to his gift of the new edition, he got a letter from overseas saying that she can wait, but 'nothing in life or death can tear out of my heart the passionate belief that one day I shall hear that voice say to me "My Mate."' It is cruel to quote her lines without full context, and I do so, not to make fun of the unprompted ardors of a splendid woman, but to illustrate the emotional force of poems which were still being derided in America.

Whitman waited until November of 1871 to answer, hoping as he said for 'a sort of Sabbath, or holy day apart to itself, under serene & propitious influences — confident that I could then write you a letter which would do you good, & me too. But I must at least show, without further delay, that I am not insensible to your love. I too send you my love. And do you feel no disappointment because I now write but briefly. My book is my best letter, my response, my truest explanation of all. In it I have put my body & spirit. You understand this better & fuller & clearer than anyone else. And I too fully & clearly understand the loving & womanly letter it has evoked. Enough that there surely exists between us so beautiful & delicate a relation, accepted by both of us with joy.' [14]

It was the best he could do — indeed beautifully done, with sincerity and a tact which those who know Whitman only by report would not expect. But of course it was not enough. She was, naturally, disappointed. But so intense was her reaction to the man she felt in the 'Leaves' that she was neither deterred nor discouraged. Two years later, after she knew of his paralysis, although probably not of its severity, she was still writing: 'Perhaps if my hand were in yours, dear Walt, you would get along faster.' 'Dearer and sweeter' that lot than to have been his bride in the 'full flush and glory of your youth.' She could not live if she did not believe he would say sometime, 'Come, my Darling.' 'Try me for this life,' she urges. She was still young enough to give him a 'perfect child.'

Well, she did live on, and, indeed, in 1876, against Whitman's express advice, with the excuse of a medical education for her daughter and experience for her artist son, she crossed to America and settled in Philadelphia, where she stayed for three years. It is a tribute to Walt, and also to her, that she became neither wife, nor lover, of the crippled man, but his closest woman friend, with whom he spent countless hours.

Perhaps he would have been wise to marry her, for he needed care and comfort badly. I think not. The old Bohemian was too settled in freedom, too regardless of comfort, too indifferent to security. She nourished his thinking, but it is probable that she was too intense for long continuance with a mind that liked to think its own thoughts. And if she was passionate, she was also an intellectual. Walt may have bluffed about his fondness for the roughs and his own democratic simplicity. Yet nothing can be more obvious than that his deepest affections were aroused by simple, uncomplicated people. If he was ever in love, it was surely with such a woman; if he had children, it was surely by such a woman. Anne Gilchrist could offer him everything except what he got from Pete Doyle, or perhaps some willing predecessor or successor of 'Number 16.' And from such perturbations he had been trying to escape.

She was his dear friend, but the 'savage virtue' he projected into his ideal of womankind was a different quality from culture, no matter how passionate. The poet writes from experience but uses his experience to create types themselves creative for the future. It is questionable (if he is really creative) whether he ever finds them at his own level of time. Anne Gilchrist was set afire by induced electricity, but she was not his type, and it is probable that she knew it within five minutes after she had first seen and talked with him.

4

To think of Whitman as looking like a broken man in this decade is wrong. He seems to have given the impression to those who visited him and those he visited of a vigorous old man, peaceful, quiet, and powerful where his visitors had expected to find him exhausted, nervous, and noisily complaining or asserting his ego. George took him buggy-riding. There were the Gilchrists to visit, later the Pearsall Smiths. There were long days when he sat on the driver's stool in the Philadelphia horsecars from Camden to the Centennial Buildings and back. Only in his later reminiscences do we discover how broken he felt inside, broken by hope deferred of success for his book as much as, and probably more than, by disease. He was writing extensively, preparing his books, such as 'Specimen Days,' and 'Collect,' which, with 'November Boughs,' were to serve as his memoirs; writing also many of the new verses that appeared in later editions of the 'Leaves.' But all of it, except for an occasional group of lines, was just that — verse. It was November with him. He was saying good-bye to his fancy. Yet the full significance of what he had stood for in the century was only just becoming apparent — even to him.

CHAPTER XXVIII

'I hear America singing'

I HAVE left until this late chapter a question which vexed Whitman's contemporaries even more than his so-called obscenity. I have left it till now because what seemed his insolent break away from orthodox rhyme and metre no longer shocks a generation familiar with all kinds (and usually bad kinds) of free verse. And also because our concern is not now with his rebellion against the verse forms of his time, but rather with what he did with the rhythms of his language, and was it successful, and if so, why? He had startled the conventional in 1855 with poetry which they felt, and sometimes rightly, was a kind of exhibitionism. But by the sixties and seventies he knew not only what he wanted to do, but how to do it successfully. He had perfected (though he did not always live up to) his style.

In no way does Whitman better show his deep affiliation with the American Transcendentalists than in his method of composition. Like Emerson, like Thoreau, he set down on stray papers or in his notebooks, lines, projects (often vast ones), isolated paragraphs, themes.[1] On them his imagination brooded. In poetry, he seems to have written a line or two at a time, carrying with him always packets of stitched paper, on which he jotted his inspiration.[2] So did Thoreau, copying his observations or his epigrams into his journal later. Whitman worked slowly on these lines or passages, fitting them into larger unities, often moving them from poem to poem. He believed that he thought by flashes from the inner light. Then, rewriting, reshaping, he finally got a form for his inspiration. After this, usually, he stopped lest an artificial polish destroy the freshness and validity of what had seemed inspiration from the source. This is pure Transcendentalism in contrast to the build-up toward an ideal of sound and metre practised by most poets — Tennyson, for example. The result, of course, was often to leave crudities to which an obstinate man clung because the verse came to him that way. Yet it is a great error to suppose that there was no ideal form in Whitman's mind. The difference was merely that it was subjective to what he heard in his imagination, not objective to the familiar rules and customs of poetry.

So much has been written — analysis, abuse, praise, satire, and pedantry — upon Walt Whitman's verse, that I am most desirous to explain what he tried to do and what he did as simply as is possible without oversimplification. Nor is what follows a technical interlude in a biography, meant to be skipped, for this man was definitely trying to make what he regarded as a new civilization articulate. And for that purpose he believed that he had to find a new language of emotional communication — by which he meant, of course, a style which belonged to this new civilization and which was capable of suggesting as well as saying what was novel, or hitherto unexpressed, in democracy. Clearly it must be a style closer to the emotional speech used by and familiar to the average man in America than the standard literary prose and standard poetry of the native literature which Whitman believed, and rightly, were still dependent heavily upon English models.

What was this style to be? Walt's attempts to write regular verse in his youth [3] were not impressive, and showed only that he knew the rules of writing, and could be competently, if not outstandingly, orthodox. We know from his own statement in 'Good-Bye My Fancy' that, when real poetry began to surge in him, he spent some time (it must have been several years) learning how to get rid of the conventions of standard poetry. 'I had great trouble in leaving out the stock poetical touches — but succeeded at last.' [4]

The reference here does not seem to be to rhyme or rhythm, but to figures of speech, forms of address, diction. Yet a curious phrase in one of his early notes, put rhythm in it, shows that he was concerned with more than vocabulary. Whitman was trying to escape from the trite and stale, and to make a new style that he could feel was his own.

But no one invents a style (except perhaps a Gertrude Stein) any more than one invents a tennis racket. A writer uses some familiar rhythm and diction at the beginning which shapes itself to his mind as he conceives. Gradually the borrowed style becomes his own and automatically responds to the lift of his imagination. When the idea pushes upon utterance, there is a way of speaking ready for it which is elastic, variable, flowing with the thought, a personal pattern — the man's style.

2

With what did Whitman begin? It is certain that he did not begin with the platitudinous verse he imitated in his earliest poetry, for the first recorded lines of the *Song of Myself* are in a different poetic language. It would be in accord with his ambition to become the American bard, if one could say that, like Robert Frost, he learned his rhythms and his idiom from the everyday speech of his country. That is simply not true. Phrases were taken from the talk about him, sometimes whole lines, but you cannot reconstruct the way of talking of the en-masse of the American nineteenth century from Walt Whitman's poetry. He wanted a style which would let in the wide freedoms of America, in which he could express with emotional fervor, sex, sweat, ships, gross occupations, common passions, a free and uncontrolled people. Rhyme and metre did not do it, or at least he could not make them do it. The familiar rhythms he heard about him in everyday speech did not do it, or at least he never tried to make a style of them.

Walt's prose as one reads it in his familiar letters is obviously written as he talked. It has no style in the literary sense of adaptiveness to great themes, but is beautiful in its simplicity. His editorial prose is workmanlike and expressive, but not distinguished. His poetical prose, when he speaks from his inner self, is much more than this. It is epigrammatic, often really poetical, sometimes magnificent. But usually it is a style of oratory, broken by asides and interpolations, complex, ejaculatory, easy to quote from but hard to read. When he wrote this poetic, exhortatory prose, and also when he wrote in the poetical forms to which it is closely related, he was terribly in earnest. He wrote such prose and such verse only when he was strongly moved, and with a rhythm entirely different from his leisurely speech as recorded in conversation and in his letters. It is significant that he could not remember his own poetry well enough to quote it accurately in calm talk with his friends. Walt, in truth, was very much like the Quakers of his youth, who had a definite diction and a style (bad singsong usually) when they were moved by the inner voice, which was utterly different from their usual speech.

These rhythms in both poetic prose and in poetry, these rhythms of passion, mysticism, exaltation, of deep emotion whether religious or not, were, in their ultimate source, the rhythms of the English Bible. This was natural in a country where simple people, like his family, usually had only one book, and all the people were nourished upon, or at least were familiar with, the sound of that book. I do not say that Whitman's poetical style is imitated from Job or Isaiah. If there is imitation, it is much more of the style of the revivalist or the Quaker preacher who shaped his own words to the Bible rhythms which sang in his head. The point to be emphasized is that free rhythms, in no tight pattern, yet able to lift and discharge imagination (which is the function of poetry), were natural, inescapable for the American masses. Free verse of the Biblical kind was their *emotionalized* speech. A self-educated Wordsworth endeavoring to escape from the frozen poetic diction of the eighteenth century might have drawn his rhythms, as he did his vocabulary, from the folk around him in their exalted moods. But Wordsworth wrote about simple people, was not one of them, and did not try to be. He wrote in a stratified society, Walt in a fluid one, where, to a prophetic soul, it was the masses not the classes that needed a poetry. And the basic poetry of the American masses was the Bible.

3

Walt's second main source was Shakespeare, whose work he knew passionately, especially the historical plays. Yet this influence was not from Shakespeare the dramatist, or Shakespeare the artificer of subtle and magnificent blank verse, or Shakespeare the lyricist. What he seems to have spouted on beaches and bus tops were the great speeches, oratorical, eloquent, of the plays, and from them he borrowed the complex rhetoric of the seventeenth century, itself based on classic examples taken from the highly stylized languages of Latin and Greek oratory. And this influence from the practice of all the languages of the Renaissance was reinforced by the translations from Homer he read extensively, especially Buckley's,[5] which was his favorite. The rhythms were his own, his vocabulary was much simpler and more colloquial and experimental than that of the contemporary spouters and gushers in pulpit and rostrum. But the syntax and general rhetorical effect, as of long compounded sentences, devised to throw up to the light a series of more or less parallel clauses, show that if Whitman had not been a poet he would have tried to become an orator, a declaimer of the now old-fashioned breed which owed more to Demosthenes, Homer, Vergil, Cicero, as they read them in translation or in the original, than to the grammar and rhetoric of their own tongue.

And, of course, we know by multitudinous reference that he did want to be an orator. That if he could not make the people read the 'Leaves' he hoped somehow, someday, to make them listen to him — and trained for it, and analyzed the techniques of facial expression and gesture as well as of words. I put Shakespeare first in the influences pushing him in this direction only because the really great oratory he had heard, and heard constantly, was the declamation of the race of Shakespearian actors, dominating the stage in his youth. A quiet, slow speaker, with a sweet, but rather high voice, he probably never would have succeeded even if the opportunity had been given him. There is no record of his having impressed a large audience, except (in his

Lincoln lectures) as a picturesque figure with something to say. He did not have what it takes.

But if any doubt the presence of the declamatory rhetoric of the Renaissance in Whitman, let him read *Give Me the Splendid Silent Sun*, with its structure as elaborate and as balanced as a passage in 'Paradise Lost' or the first strophe of *Out of the Cradle Endlessly Rocking*, or (for prose sentences) 'Democratic Vistas.' [6]

The influence of this rhetorical tradition upon the technique of the 'Leaves' is, of course, very great. The writer bred in it feels that the reader must be *spoken* to direct, must be aroused. Not for nothing had Whitman seen, night after night, a crowded theatre moved to tears and shouts by such rhetoric. His poems — hundreds of them — and especially his addresses and his catalogues are composed for cumulative effect. Their typical structure usually resembles a speech, still more a sermon.[7] They begin with a text, usually the memorable line of the title, of which dozens have passed into quotation and many have become titles for books. This line is explained, expanded, expounded, repeated, fulfilled, like 'To be or not to be' in Hamlet's soliloquy — and that is the poem, unless lyric passages intersperse. By Whitman's day this method had passed out of literature into the folk expression of preachers and exhorters, but he in his reading and hearing went to the source. He brings it back into literature with fresh rhythms and a fresher vocabulary just as it was becoming old-style, and trite.

Only by understanding that Walt always thought of himself as chanting when he wrote, and as using his voice, even his facial expressions, is it possible to understand his prosody and read him aright, whether in prose or verse. In prose, this declamatory style is often intolerable — a series of parentheses, asides, and recurrences — as for example this rather terrible sentence: 'The purpose of democracy — supplanting old belief in the necessary absoluteness of establish'd dynastic rulership, temporal, ecclesiastical, and scholastic, as furnishing the only security against chaos, crime, and ignorance — is, through many transmigrations, and amid endless ridicules, arguments, and ostensible failures, to illustrate, at all hazards, this doctrine or theory that man, properly train'd in sanest, highest freedom, may and must become a law, and series of laws, unto himself, surrounding and providing for, not only his own personal control, but all his relations to other individuals, and to the State; and that, while other theories, as in the past histories of nations, have proved wise enough, and indispensable perhaps for their conditions, *this*, as matters now stand in our civilized world, is the only scheme worth working from, as warranting results like those of Nature's laws, reliable, when once establish'd, to carry on themselves.' [8] Yet even this pseudo seventeenth-century monstrosity when read aloud, dropping or raising the voice for each subordinate clause, and emphasizing the parentheses by a look at the audience, is readily intelligible.

In poetry, music helped; indeed, opera is one of Whitman's major sources of influence. Passionately fond of music, he knew next to nothing about its essential structure, and in spite of incomparably greater opportunities, he was almost as ignorant as Emerson and quite as naïve as Thoreau. About musical diction, about the production of tone, about the quality of instruments, particularly that prime instrument, the human voice, he knew much and was acutely critical. Yet his description of pure music, of a septette of Beethoven for example, is invariably what musicians call 'literary.' It was not the composition of a symphony but the effect upon his fancy of the sounds, which he recorded in his criticisms.

Opera, however, especially Italian opera, was his specialty. Opera of all kinds (Wagner's operas possibly excepted) is, I suppose, a mixed or impure artistic form. The composition of the whole is determined by the story, and the music is only an accompaniment to the action, not a carrier for the action itself. Whitman's ideal for opera was even more literary, less musical, than the facts. He liked 'heart music' rather than 'art music' [9] and thought true American opera would be a play interspersed with songs. An opera, for him, was so much recitative, that is, rhythmic language where the music emphasized the rhythm. This was interspersed by lyrics in which the emotion rises to poetry released in song, and climaxed by pure declamation where both words and music are oratorical. Here, of course, is the precise pattern of the most lyrical of his poems. A perfect example is *Out of the Cradle Endlessly Rocking*, which consists of recitative in which are inserted pure lyric passages in a different rhythm and set in italics.

In this brief résumé of the source of the Whitman style, I have omitted any reference to contemporary books, and I think rightly. Whitman, so far as I know, never made the absurd claim of inventing free verse. If there were others, like Martin F. Tupper, practising it in his day, their methods have little resemblance to his. He picked up free verse as naturally from oratory based upon the Bible, and from the Bible itself, as a child picks up slang. What he sought was a rhythmic method suited to his purpose, and that he got, and, after hard labor, perfected.

4

What is the Whitman style? Its originality is obvious from the innumerable imitations, none of which are successful except in parody, a sign of distinctive style. And still more from his influence upon others, for his name as a maker of poets has been stamped upon at least three continents, including his own.

Style, one of the most elusive of terms, is the end-product of four controls — over rhythm, over sound, over vocabulary, over the composition of the whole. And these controls have only two objectives, which are to suffuse expression with the personality of the writer and to adapt the medium to his theme. A writer can make an adequate statement without style; he cannot, without style, transmit the full context of his imagination. Nonsense can have its style, falsity can have style, but fortunately false or nonsensical people seldom achieve it.

If Whitman's verse sometimes fails to be poetry, it is not because he has scrapped both metre and regularly recurrent rhymes. Poetry is no more dependent upon metre than upon rhyme. If he writes rhythmic prose when he is supposed to be writing poetry, it is because his imagination at the moment is prosaic.

All poets, including the best, have occasionally put prose into the forms of verse. The question with Whitman is, how, and by what devices, or in what medium, did he turn his imagination, when it was poetical, into poetry? For poetry stays unexpressed, even if written as such, until the language lifts to the level of the poetic emotion.

The chief medium of poetic thought is rhythm, for rhythm is man's instinctive response to emotion. Through elaborate analysis it is always possible to indicate how orthodox poetry by subtle variants from a fixed metrical pattern, such as the five-stress iambic line, achieves this response to a burning thought. But no poet writes from analysis. Perhaps the most subtle and skilful prosodist in modern literature was William Butler Yeats, yet in Mr. Hone's recent biography he is quoted as saying that he knew nothing whatsoever of prosody, could not understand it, wrote entirely by ear. So did Whitman. And in his free verse even analysis cannot follow Whitman, because the movements of his rhythm are in large patterns, like brush strokes on a mural, easy to feel, impossible to reduce (like a metrical line) to a formula. A writer of free verse who does not avail himself of metre and rhyme must insure his continuity and secure his unity by a felt and characteristic style, as must, indeed, the writer of literary prose, who has the same problem. The question, then, with Whitman's verse is not his metrics, which are rudimentary. Try to read Whitman as you read Bryant, Tennyson, Milton (which is what his contemporaries did, and most unliterary readers still do) and you are baffled, thrown off the track, grounded at the beginning. The solution of his continuity and his unity is in his style.

But, of course, this style has its controls, like any poetic style. In rhythm, Whitman's control is far looser than the orthodox continuity of metre. In sound, he is, if anything, tighter than the orthodox. In vocabulary, he is freer. In composition (at his best), he can be as rigorous as a sonneteer. I ask the reader's patience while I point out a few of his stylistic qualities, assuring him that they must be recognized if Whitman's book, which was so much himself, is to be read with pleasure and intelligence.

In rhythm, even the most casual reader must have recognized Whitman's fondness for a stress and movement not usually dominant in English verse. Longfellow chose the trochaic measure for his *Hiawatha* in order to mark with a certain strangeness his epic of a savage race. Mrs. Whitman, it will be remembered, thought that it was not poetry, not any more than Walt's. English is a prevailingly iambic language. In couplets, as well as in blank verse, our ear takes most easily (and words most readily adapt themselves) to the iambic flow, the stress *after* the unaccented syllable, not before. The troche has been used as a variant to avoid monotony, not usually as dominant in the music. A typical English line is:

> The world is too much with us, late and soon,

not

> By the shores of Gitche Gumee,
> By the shining Big-Sea-Water.

But Walt, either because of his obstinate desire for a new music for a new world, or because his taste ran that way, is prevailingly trochaic. Or perhaps it was because the emphasis, the deadly earnestness, the orator's insistence with which he wrote, led him to bang down the stress with the first word:

> Out of the cradle endlessly rocking

Or see the innumerable lines that begin with an emphatic *I*, *You*, *How*, *On*.

There is still another rhythmic peculiarity in his style which gives it more continuity, and indeed more regularity, than is apparent to the over-refining analyist. His long lines split up typically into a prefatory unit of three or four stresses, followed by a natural break or caesura, and then by a second member, usually shorter. There is no formula, yet the constant reader of Whitman begins to feel for a passage of seven stresses as a place of recurrence. Thus, regarded as style, his lines swing on a point of balance, which is the caesura, and the shift of that balance, one way and another, provides an endless variety without loss of a large unity in the poetic style. It is a dangerous practice — breaks down easily into the flatness of plain prose, enables the poet to pad in with what phrases occur to him, is effective only when his sensitive ear is aware of the whole pattern. Yet this is Whitman's own style, so much so that already he has imitators in many languages. He must have felt himself the dangers of this loose movement, for it will be noted that, in his longer poems, he has key lines, often identical in words, always in rhythm, to which he returns like a conductor beating a measure. He was never so lawless as to lose that sense of recurrence in movement which rhythm essentially is.

As for sound, Whitman maintained that he threw rhyme, which is recurrent sound, overboard as an artificial principle not suitable for the literature of a free people. Actually, he did nothing of the sort. He got rid of the convention of the use of identical vowels with different consonants at set places, so that a pattern should be emphasized; but he kept the principle whenever he needed it to keep his sprawling texture from tearing apart. There is no regular rhyme in Whitman, except in a few poems such as his popular *O Captain! My Captain!*, which owes its success to its subject, Lincoln, and still more to a form which children and unpoetical adults immediately identify as poetry. But Walt (and many a poet after him) when he needed rhyme, used it in its so-called impure form of assonance, a recurrence of like, but not identical, vowel sounds. Or he used pure rhyme not in any regular pattern, but set within the line when the ear needed a repetition of sound to keep continuity. Rhyme for him is like the painter's recurrent curves that help harmony in a composition. Note in these lines the repeated present participle in *ing* used with the effect of rhyme:

The love in the heart long pent, now loose, now at last tumultuously bursting,
The aria's meaning, the ears, the soul, swiftly depositing,
The strange tears down the cheeks coursing,
The colloquy there, the trio, each uttering,
The undertone, the savage old mother incessantly crying,
To the boy's soul's questions sullenly timing, some drown'd secret hissing,
To the outsetting bard.[10]

Far more difficult to describe is Whitman's use of the sounds of words as a color to his style to make it characteristic. Such color is easily observable in most conscious stylists — Tennyson's superb use of long *o*'s and *oo*'s, Stevenson's too artificial play with consonants, Sterne's slipping sweetness, our own Hemingway's blows of brutal-sounding words. Whitman, I think, was never facile, and seldom excellent, here. He has gorgeous lines, such as the many which describe the hiss and moan and loneliness of the sea. But he has many others which, for all their expressiveness, hurt the ear, when they do not reveal positive vulgarity, which he mistakes for forcefulness. I think when he said he never polished his verses, that this is what he may have meant. Like many an honest man of the people, whose education in esthetics has come late, he did not like refinement, and sounds in style (unlike its rhythm) are definitely a refinement which comes usually from a refined memory of the best. When Walt said something beautifully, as he often did, he liked to follow it with raucous sounds, like a man who covers up his own emotion with a harsh laugh. Can a more consonant-tangled line be written than —

Does it meet modern discoveries, calibres, facts, face to face?

Much the same thing may be said of Whitman's vocabulary. There is an attempt here also to avoid prettiness by discord (as in modern music), which is an earmark and helps to stamp his style as his own. Although he spent endless time writing and thinking about words, he never got them under complete control, and often he misused, and sometimes misunderstood them. Frequently he got the perfect word — as a great man should:

As your ranks, your immortal ranks, return, return from the battles,...
As those slanted bayonets, whole forests of them appearing in the distance,
    approach and pass on, returning homeward,
Moving with steady motion, swaying to and fro to the right and left,
Evenly, lightly rising and falling while the steps keep time.[11]

But, and especially when his poetry descended into prose, and often after a magnificent passage, he lets whatever came into his mind stand, even though it is as incongruous as a bandanna handkerchief in the tail of a dress coat. There was a defiance here, a pose, a challenge from one of the roughs, a definite lack of taste of which he was uneasily aware. For it is clear that he was tossing in his colloquialisms and rough words and flat words to remind the reader that after all he was a man of the people and refused to think too carefully of how to speak his inspiration. And, of course, his colloquial words, like 'cute' for acute, which get so tiresome, belong in the same category. And still more fatally his ignorantly borrowed words, like *allons* and *feuillage* and *respondez*, where he was both making a play as the universal democrat writing for all lands, and trying to impress the reader with the breadth of his experience.

Yet all this is part of his style. It is unfair to quote Whitman without exhibiting some of it, for whether you like it or not, whether it holds him back again and again from absolute excellence, as it certainly does, it is his brand, and there is no true Whitman without these liabilities to bad knowledge and bad taste. You might as well try to present that great stylist, Sir John Falstaff, without his obscenity, or that mediocre but most pleasing stylist, Washington Irving, without his platitudes.

Yet curiously enough, in an essay called 'An American Primer,'[12] he made an important critical contribution to the nature of the word, which may be compared to some of the statements in the modern science of semantics. A word is a power, he says, and, properly used, a *thing*, and has life of its own. Words are alive, hence America must develop its own language. A characteristic word once used in a poem is then exhausted. One single name belongs to a single place only. 'To me each word . . . has its own meaning, and does not stand for anything but itself — and there are not two words the same any more than there are two persons the same.' 'The Morning has its words, and the Evening has its words.' It is quite possible that we are too close to the vocabularies of the books in which we have been educated to judge finally Whitman's diction. And yet I feel sure myself, that here, as elsewhere, the 'Leaves' was still imperfect: its diction was in a state of becoming, experimental not finished.

5

When Whitman said in his first notebook that the poet who had a message for the New World would and must find a language for it, he meant, of course, a style that would take up new meanings and communicate them. I have been describing some of the tricks of his trade, devices for making his poems continuities, and wholes in which he could incarnate himself until the poem became like his handshake or his kiss. As it is precisely the rambling free verse of many of Walt's long poems that has given him a bad reputation for formlessness, we must consider more closely how he tried (often with brilliant success) to weave into a harmonic unity those line-by-line compositions so lengthily built up from his little scraps of paper which recorded the multitudinous things his mind contained. It was difficult for him, and sometimes it was impossible, to control and make stylistically unified the whole of a long poem.

It was easy for the man to write epigrams. Sometimes, I think that Walt will eventually be remembered for a few poems, and many passages, which are really epigrams. But a personality does not freely speak through an epigram, and even less a man trying to represent his kind. The instant you go beyond oracular statement, such as 'I sit and look out,' or 'To think of time,' the problem of attention is urgent. There you are, chanting, and the reader must know that what he reads is a single, separate chant with beginning, middle, and end. (This is impossible with some of Whitman's poems, but even so you can see him trying.) It is the problem of all literary expression, and especially of poetry, where the attention required is intense. If you insist on contradicting yourself because you contain multitudes, if you borrow the unexpected technique of opera, if you discard the old props of the poetic stage, the effort has to be considerable or the poem breaks down into a sprawl. With Whitman it was considerable. He knew (and this is what his critics have failed to emphasize) that if you break the old rules, you must make new ones, or the whole simply disintegrates into its parts.

In many brief poems and in a few long ones his control of the entire unity was complete. What experience lay behind the elegy, *Out of the Cradle Endlessly Rocking*, we shall never know. But this much is sure, that it is a reminiscence of youth or childhood, made poignant perhaps by some recent loss and sorrow. It is a reminiscence [13] of yearning, unsatisfied love, perhaps the uncontrolled passionate emotion of a sensitive boy pressing upon experience and finding no release or return in the inadequacy of his companionships, his friendships, and his loves. It is a reminiscence of a boy's discovery that the only surcease for desire is in the peace of death. And for this poem the symbols are the mocking-bird longing for its dead mate, and the sea answering with the strong and delicious word, death. The poem dates from 1859, and was first published in *The Saturday Press*. I shall quote only the first strophes for a study of his style:

Out of the cradle endlessly rocking,
Out of the mocking-bird's throat, the musical shuttle,
Out of the Ninth-month midnight,
Over the sterile sands and the fields beyond, where the child leaving his bed
    wander'd alone, bareheaded, barefoot,
Down from the shower'd halo,
Up from the mystic play of shadows twining and twisting as if they were
    alive,
Out from the patches of briers and blackberries,
From the memories of the bird that chanted to me,
From your memories sad brother, from the fitful risings and fallings I heard,
From under that yellow half-moon late-risen and swollen as if with tears,
From those beginning notes of yearning and love there in the mist,
From the thousand responses of my heart never to cease,
From the myriad thence-arous'd words,
From the word stronger and more delicious than any,
From such as now they start the scene revisiting,
As a flock, twittering, rising, or overhead passing,
Borne hither, ere all eludes me, hurriedly,
A man, yet by these tears a little boy again,
Throwing myself on the sand, confronting the waves,
I, chanter of pains and joys, uniter of here and hereafter,
Taking all hints to use them, but swiftly leaping beyond them,
A reminiscence sing.

Once Paumanok,
When the lilac-scent was in the air and Fifth-month grass was growing,
Up this seashore in some briers,

Two feather'd guests from Alabama, two together,
And their nest, and four light-green eggs spotted with brown,
And every day the he-bird to and fro near at hand,
And every day the she-bird crouch'd on her nest, silent, with bright eyes,
And every day I, a curious boy, never too close, never disturbing them,
Cautiously peering, absorbing, translating.

The first stanza, admittedly beautiful, perfect in its flow, is an admirable example of how Whitman achieved a unifying style by definite methods of harmonizing expression which he chose in place of the familiarities of rhyme and metre.

First of all is what may be named perpendicular alliteration. Note the first word chosen for each line until the continuity of the pattern has been established: *out, out, out, over, down, up, out, from, from, from, from, from, from, from, from.* Next is interior alliteration, the repetition of the same consonant sound within the lines: here *m*, and *n*. Reading through one finds: *endlessly, mocking-bird, musical, Ninth-month, midnight, sands, and, beyond, wander'd, alone, down, from, mystic, twining, from, from, memories, chanted, me, from, memories, from, risings, fallings, from, under, moon, risen, swollen, from, beginnings, notes, yearning, in, mist, from, responses, my, never, from, myriad, thence, from, more, any, from, now, scene, rising, borne, me, man, again, myself, sand, confronting, chanter, pains, uniter, and, hints, them, them, reminiscence.*

And there is still a further alliterative (and rhyming) chain in the present participles — *rocking, mocking, leaving, twining, twisting, risings, fallings, beginning, yearning, revisiting, rising, passing, throwing, confronting, taking, leaping.*

More subtly, but with an equal effect of unity and continuity, is the nature of the line beginnings. They are pointing words; *out, over, down, up, from.* And the emphasis of position upon them is such as to make the movement of the poetry trochaic: '*Out of the, down from the.*' One must read *from* your memories, *from* those beginning, no matter what a futile scansion of the line into the supposed, but in English non-existent, 'feet' would indicate.

Thus the music and the continuity of style in this poem is established. So that the second stanza, beginning 'Once Paumanok, when the lilac-scent was in the air,' can pick up the *ins* and *ons*, and the participles with *growing*, and the pointing words with *up*, and the perpendicular alliteration with a new series: *and, and, and, and;* the internal alliteration with *every day, every day, every day,* and the trochaic feel of the measure with the emphasis upon *once, and, when, two, every,* and *cautiously.*

And thus, in a rhythmic and aural continuity, a poetic idea is expanded into a movement of verse. Nor should one fail to note the syntactical structure borrowed from oratorical rhetoric. The first stanza is all one sentence of balanced clauses, with its meaning suspended to the last word. This rhetorical characteristic of Whitman's style is again a device for unity, successful here, but often not successful. Periods, it may be said, usually appear in Walt's writing only when the breath is just about to give out!

I shall leave to the reader, if he is interested, the following-through of these devices to set the style and keep continuity in the rest of this perfectly composed poem, noting only, in the recitative, that the *m's* continue (surely the reason for bringing the *m*ocking-bird from Alabama).

Finally, the structure of the whole poem is as outstanding as the structure of a good essay. Its composition is complete, and the roman type and the italics indicate it. We have an introduction in recitative, a lyric beginning 'Shine! shine! shine!' a continuing narrative, a lyric 'Blow! blow! blow!' a meditation in recitative, a lyric 'Soothe! soothe! soothe!' in which the song is that of the boy's past but the love seems to be of the present as the intensity of the sexual imagery suggests, the waves embracing, lapping, the moon heavy with love, the sea pushing madly on the land. Here the purely lyric passages end with 'The aria sinking.' Whitman is conscious this time of the pattern of opera, and uses its vocabulary. The bird is identified in his fancy with a pure soprano reaching for the last tremulous notes, 'We two together no more.' And as in opera, the recitative again takes up the action, and so on to an elegy in which hopeless love is assuaged by the reconciliations of death.

I do not wish to labor this principle of unity in Whitman's style, and for this reason I make no attempt here to enter into

subtler devices by which the intuitive poet gave form to his poetry
of democracy which he thought must be freed from every shackle
of convention. What he did, of course, was to try, as an innovator
must, to find new binding forms for his chants — knowing well
that even anarchy must have form if it is to be expressed. And
where he failed, his poems crumble into a mass of lines — precisely as where his conventional contemporaries failed (Tennyson
sometimes, Longfellow often), their poems become mere petrifi-
cations of words, held together by the silica of their techniques.
The careful reader of the 'Leaves' will find that Whitman seldom
failed in execution, but only in inspiration. When he thinks and
feels prose, the structure loosens, weakens, gaps appear where
there is only statement and no harmony, long catalogues are held
together by a weak system of monotonous alliteration, or rhythmic similarity. But always, even when feeble, there is style.

6

To broaden the base of this description, and suggest the scope
of the art of this supposedly lawless craftsman, I must at least
refer to one other poem, if only because, in addition to the devices listed above, it shows a Wagnerian appreciation of the use
of theme. Wagner was unintelligible to Whitman's ear when he
heard his music in old age. He had been conditioned by Italian
opera. Yet he had already used in language Wagner's musical
device of a meaningful theme which united sound and sense and
helped to compose the whole. The poem, which the reader will
find as the *Prelude* to 'Drum-Taps,' describes New York rising to
meet the first crisis of the Civil War. Eighteen hundred and
sixty-one was the date of the experience, and probably of the
verses. New York has thrown off the costumes of peace, all are
in arms, it is to be an arm'd nation. Whitman's style must rise
to the pitch of his emotion. It needs the emphasis of a drum-
beat, the recurrence of a thematic word. Rhythm and alliteration and assonance are not enough:

> Manhattan arming,
> To the drum-taps prompt,
> The young men falling in and arming.

The theme is 'arm'd.' And like a roulade increasing with each tap the momentum of the poem, the word is varied and repeated: the mechanics *arming*. *Arm'd! arm'd!* is the cry everywhere, an *arm'd* race is advancing; to *arms*, and *arm*. The theme word holds the ear, beating the poem into a resonant unity.

Surely enough has been said in these paragraphs to prove that Walt Whitman, at least after the middle fifties, was no wild man of wild verse, no posturing bard endeavoring to get attention by eccentricity, but a new master in the craft of words. Even after three-quarters of a century, this does not seem to be realized by the general reader, nor by many academic critics. The first has not learned how to read him, being in this respect like contemporary audiences in the first reactions to Beethoven or Wagner. The second have preferred to cite Whitman's failures, and have applied measuring rods of use and wont to a prosody never meant to be measured in this way. Whitman himself felt humble beside such a consummate artist as Tennyson, but only because he was well aware that he was not always an artist, and that it would be bards of the future who would refine his new idiom into fool-proof patterns which lesser men could use. They might or might not be poets. He was one — in his best moments — and a man of magnitude always.

The moral of this chapter for the reader is simple. When you read Whitman, think of the Bible first, and of Longfellow not at all. Read him aloud if possible. Read him as if he were speaking (or chanting). Forget your prejudices in poetry, if any, and try to feel his style. Then your mind will be open to genuine appreciation without sacrificing the power to discriminate between failure and success.

CHAPTER XXIX

'Who learns my lesson complete?'

WILLARD GIBBS, Herman Melville, and Walt Whitman, so says Muriel Rukeyser in a biography [1] of the great mathematical physicist, were the three great American rebels against the complacent and dangerous certainties of the nineteenth century. And Henry Adams, the seeker, was their prophet, although it was only the work of Gibbs that he knew and questioned painfully for some unity below the anarchy of so-called progress. I shall not enter into Miss Rukeyser's complex and perhaps too ambitious argument, but draw from it and develop an analogy which is of great help in understanding the defeat, slowly turning into success, of Walt Whitman.

No two men, no two methods of approach to universal problems, could seem to be more different than Whitman with his 'Leaves' and Gibbs with his exact and beautiful mathematical thinking. Willard Gibbs, his figure erect and dignified, his face brooding and reticent, as I used to see him often on the streets of New Haven, was the antithesis of the bushy Whitman, rolling his elephantine gait, waving to the bus drivers, usually chanting some song or another to himself, jolly, exhibitionistic, but with piercing eyes. One man worked with the excessively difficult behavior of matter under the control of force. The other, with the apparent disorder of life itself. It was the job of Gibbs to find the laws which explained and could be used to control the multitudinous phenomena of nature. It was the ambition of Whitman to create patterns of human life in which a new age might find inspiration for history in the making. Gibbs was master of his methodology, Whitman was not always a master of his art. Yet, with less intellectual ability, he had the harder, and probably the more important task. Gibbs's success in his work, so far as he pursued it, was absolute, Whitman's relative.

Both men, to use Miss Rukeyser's phrase, created creativity. That will certainly be Willard Gibbs's ultimate claim to greatness, and Whitman would have been well satisfied with such a definition of his service to mankind. Gibbs's formulas will be absorbed in others more comprehensive. Whitman, as is the way with art, has a better chance of survival for his achievement, because of poems which do not merely stimulate, but, as with the individual human being, are life and personality in themselves. The urge, the order, the unconquerable will of these so disparate men came from a like cause, which Whitman called God, and Gibbs, the reticent Congregationalist, was content to name a desire to find a system in the universe.

As for science, its rapid advance in the nineteenth century had raised more questions than it answered. Nature was being rapidly brought under physical control. Yet its phenomena, with each application of theory to practice, became not simpler but more complex and less calculable. New formulas in physics and chemistry fanned invention like winds on a prairie fire, increasing man's power until Progress became the word of the century. These formulas were soon to prove, under analysis, to be only experimental generalizations. Nevertheless, their success spread an insidious materialism which proposed soon to make life itself a formula. Typical of their progress was the social theory of Karl Marx, who believed that history itself could be explained by economic law. All unities of past thinking about our world were disintegrating, though in the excitement of scientific discovery and the progress in the arts of life, this crumbling of the cements of society was deplored only by conservatives, who themselves had little new to offer an industrial age.

Gibbs set for himself two guiding maxims — that the whole was simpler than its parts, and that physical phenomena, no matter how diverse, were all subject to fundamental laws. He knew no more of the essential nature of matter than his contemporaries, who were still concerned with molecules and atoms. His task was to find a method of predicting the behavior of matter *whatever* its ultimate nature might be. He developed the analysis of forces, he laid down the principles governing the behavior of substances in mixtures. Upon his principles, the laws of thermodynamics, metallurgy, the mathematics of radio-activity were based. The second World War is being fought with many by-products of Gibbs's theorizing. While his colleagues were busy with diversity by experiment, he had sought unity in design. Although he never entered a laboratory, a thousand laboratories operate because of him.

Naturally he knew nothing of Whitman, and Whitman would have bogged down in the first line of any one of his formulas. Yet the relation between the new applications of science and the state of society in the nineteenth century was obvious, at least to Whitman. And the efforts of the two men, each aware of the disintegration of traditional theory and each trying to find some new unity of truth, are obviously parallel.

Whitman grew up in the Great Expansion of the thirties, the forties, the fifties. His first stimulus was from the ideologies of that fertile period — most fertile in America — where thousands of active minds, and a few great ones such as Emerson's, were rejoicing in the breakdown of old dogmatisms and the breakup of social crystallizations which had been clamping the spirit of man. And at the same time these seekers were trying to find some new unity of meaning for an expanding revolutionary society, at its strongest in a new continent. Like so many Americans of that age, and far more than most of the writers and scholars, Whitman's 'robust mind' was impressed by the achievement of science:

> Hurrah for positive science! long live exact demonstration! ...
> Gentlemen, to you the first honors always! [2]

He was keenly aware that the sudden increase in productivity beginning with the industrial revolution, itself a product of applied science, made democracy as we know it today possible everywhere, and a bright hope in a new continent where, freed from the grip of privilege and given new instruments for subduing nature, the common man, the en-masse, had its great opportunity of all the ages.

Yet in spite of the work of the eighteenth century in formulating new political institutions, there was no law, no new ideal, for such unpredicted mingling and altering of populations as resulted from immigration into a new world and the creation of democratic opportunity. Democracy, impure as yet, and given new powers, was a new mixture, a mixture so full of dynamic possibility that society everywhere in the Western world, though most of all in America, was evidently in the midst of rapid and incalculable change. Reaction chained the turbulence in Europe, but the chains broke. The Civil War here bled democracy white, but the vast resources of the continent set the forces of individualism on their way again in an orgy of material success in which the dangers of the new social mixture became only too apparent. By the twentieth century, applied science had outrun its controls and was seized by reaction for its own purposes. Democracy became static, like the complacent theories of the nineteenth-century chemists and physicists, and the world blew up in war. To comprehend imaginatively, to provide emotional guidance, to set ideals and discover some spiritual law for the individuals in this new social mixture, was Whitman's deeply conscious and lifelong wish.

By comparison with Gibbs, Whitman may seem to the modern mind, which has fed on and perhaps been debilitated by technology, a weak instrument. The nineteenth-century disorder, which Santayana also saw and from the Catholic point of view, seemed to the majority of that century to be not disorder at all but progress toward a Utopia of comfort in a peaceful world. Whitman did not think clearly, his idealisms were as vague as they were vigorous. The inadequacy of his knowledge of history, and the cloudiness of his philosophy, led him to rely first on his own experience and his own ego. But he was powerful there, drawing the strengths of his new country into himself, and he could confidently dramatize the new democrat in his own person (though not always accurately) and demand what he himself as representative man needed in order to find meaning and unity in the new social mixture caused by democracy. The whole, he, too, thought, must be simpler than its parts. The whole was his dramatized self, which he did know and was not afraid to expose in every hidden fibre. His need was for full self-development, limited only by the law of love. His need was for a unity of body and soul, physical and spiritual, bound together in an inseparable continuity of life and death.

But he could expect no immediate success. A physicist like Gibbs could escape from the rule of *ought* into the search for *is*, while remaining orthodox in his morals and his religion. He worked in regions of discovery where no one of the earlier cosmologies was adequate to explain what now could be proved to be happening in the universe. No prejudices, no faiths were able to resist indefinitely the demonstrable facts of the law of thermodynamics or even of the evolution of species. Hence the opposition to the scientist soon came to be from passive ignorance rather than from active denial. Without being conscious of what he was doing, the scientist could spread a crass materialism throughout civilized society, so long as he continued to pay lip service to the vested interests of the church and education.

Not so indeed with the poet (or indeed with the sociologists and psychologists) who worked with the values and the nature of human experience. Whitman's democratic dream, which needed centuries and continents to prove itself, was not likely, and did not have to be, more than sixty per cent right, since it was an ideal which might make history, but would certainly be reshaped itself as time marched on. Nevertheless, his audacity, his egoism, his challenge to the prudish, his assumptions of prophetic inspiration were all attacks upon current values of living, and therefore ran head on into prejudice. A society instinctively sure that to be bigger, wealthier, more powerful, more comfortable was the true, if not the whole, duty of man, would not easily stand for such doctrine as his from a maker of eccentric verse who had neither the traditional right to reform of a prophet in the days of Israel, nor the otherworldliness of a saint. He ran head on into commercialism, into imperialism, into refinement, into nationalism. And since he spoke for a new social mixture which so far had been really tested only in politics, and since he spoke too symbolically for the masses to understand, and seldom with enough appearance of art to capture the unfriendly imagination of the literate, he failed, or often thought he had failed. 'Democracy,' he had said in "Democratic Vistas," . . . is a great word, whose history, I suppose, remains unwritten, because that history has yet to be enacted.' He might have added, has yet to be enacted in economics, in sex relations, in education, in religion, as well as in politics. Therefore all his eloquence was as nothing in its immediate effect by comparison with Gibbs's modest push. This was inevitable, the nineteenth century being what it was, Whitman being what he was, human life being the intricate complex of elements it is, only a few of which we understand. But it was not the end of the story.

2

All these considerations, though differently seen and phrased, were in Whitman's mind in the last of his creative years in Washington and in his long reminiscent period afterward. He wrestled with opponents to his faith in poems such as *Chanting the Square Deific* (1865–66), that attempt to reconcile evil and good, death and life, body and spirit; in *Eidôlons* (1876), the poem of ideals; in *Passage to India* (1868), where the eager self-development he called for is spiritualized.

'Who learns my lesson complete?' he had asked in 1855,[3] and answers, as he was still to answer at the end:

> It is no lesson — . . .
> The great laws take and effuse without argument,
> I am of the same style, for I am their friend.

If, on the whole, he was right, and the materialism as well as the social orthodoxy of the nineteenth century was wrong, it was because he was trying to write the biography of a new type of man and a new mixture of society. 'Put in thy chants,' said the seer of the poem *Eidôlons*:

No more the puzzling hour nor day, nor segments, parts, put in,
Put first before the rest as light for all and entrance-song of all, that of
eidôlons.

Eidôlons (not a happy word), by which he means the phantom

ideal of becoming, the whole toward which all segments point. The dim beginning, the rounding of the circle, the old urge, the present, the tendency to shape the things to come, all make and are made by ideals which, through the mediation of poetry, can create a new type of man. Take the Transcendental out of his language and it states very simply Whitman's purpose, which was to fuse all his experience into a moral, physical, spiritual unity of significance for his beloved democracy. And thus he opposes directly the centrifugal forces set loose by applied science and scientific materialism, which, while the geographical world was drawing together, were destroying its last spiritual unities, so that when the ideological conflicts of the twentieth century burst, even the moral concepts of the great cultures were found to be split into incompatible beliefs. As Gibbs sought laws to end the confusion of science, so Whitman tried to create a new human unity by imagining a completely democratized man.

And an inseparable part of this unity was death. Immortality, as the church had described it, was one of the continuities which the materialism of the nineteenth century had weakened as an item of accepted belief. Death for an increasing number of the skeptical became the end, not a part of being. Whitman's imaginative brooding upon death, observable even in his youth, was a corollary to his even stronger obsession with bodily vigor and health. And also he was a lonely and sensitive man, out of joint with his hopes, for whom the 'strong and delicious' idea of death meant an end to yearning. But as he grew older the meaning deepened and took a surer place in his cosmic scheme, as part of one law for the body and the soul. He had offended at least one of his critics by what seemed the flippancy of the close of the *Song of Myself*:

> I bequeath myself to the dirt to grow from the grass I love,
> If you want me again look for me under your boot-soles.

That was written in perfect health. After forty, and a first experience with wounds, disease, and death for others, and weakness and a shaken body for oneself, a man does not speak so cheerfully of dirt and the grave. In death he seeks, as in life, comfort and continuity.

Whitman had begun characteristically with the hope that the identity of the simple, separate person was being strengthened in order to persist beyond the tomb:

Something long preparing and formless is arrived and form'd in you,
You are henceforth secure, whatever comes or goes....

And I have dream'd that the purpose and essence of the known life, the
     transient,
Is to form and decide identity for the unknown life, the permanent.[4]

This was in 1855, and in 1861–1862, he wrote:

When shows break up what but One's-Self is sure?[5]

But his full desire is apparent when this egoism of personal immortality lessens with the nearer contemplation of death. He wishes to bring these phenomena of birth, life, and death under one law. It can only be a law intuitively arrived at, a feat of the imagination. But it must satisfy both the lovers of life and the mystics. It must bring death, which the crude materialist had come to suppose was only a stopping of a machine, into the unity of human values again, where it had always belonged in the great religions and mythologies. The 'simple, separate person' was not, so he felt passionately, like a hoop, which is inert matter before its brief roll through space and inert matter afterward. Whether the identity of the individual remained after death came to seem not so important as the continuity of the life of the soul. An immortality of spiritual energy, which he calls joy, is to follow release from the bonds of time and space. 'Darest thou now O Soul,' he wrote in 1868,[6]

Walk out with me toward the unknown region,
Where neither ground is for the feet nor any path to follow?

There is 'no map ... nor voice ... nor face ... all is a blank before us.' The thinking is not clear, indeed it is not thinking at all but a passionate symbolism drawn from an inner certainty. Sometimes it is 'Ones-self' that is sure, sometimes merely an assurance that the dynamism of life goes on in the grass under your boot-sole. What he offers as testimony is his faith that death and what comes after is part of the unity of experience.[7]

Both mathematician and poet were under compulsion to formulate some unity beneath the confused mechanical phenomena of the progressive century, which, without such a faith, might be heading (indeed, was heading) for disintegration and a moral chaos made disastrous by the material forces let loose. Parts become anarchical, once we have lost a meaning for the whole. 'Is only matter triumphant?' Whitman asked of his complacent century in 1860, and answered eight years later, not as a historian or philosopher, but as a poet, in a poem inspired by confident intuition:

At the last, tenderly,
From the walls of the powerful fortress'd house,
From the clasp of the knitted locks, from the keep of the well-closed doors,
Let me be wafted.

Let me glide noiselessly forth;
With the key of softness unlock the locks — with a whisper,
Set ope the doors O soul.

Tenderly — be not impatient,
(Strong is your hold O mortal flesh,
Strong is your hold O love).[8]

CHAPTER XXX

'Who touches this touches a man'

GEORGE WHITMAN, who continued to prosper, decided to leave Camden and build for himself in Burlington, a little way up the river. But for Walt, the easy access to Philadelphia from Camden, where he could go to visit friends, and the convenience of Camden for friends and hero-worshippers, was a strong argument for staying behind. He had saved up money — quite a little by now — and his old independence seemed possible again. So he bought for himself in March of 1884, a little house on Mickle Street near the railroads and the river. Here he could sit out on the steps if he wanted to, like everyone else in suburban Philadelphia, or be secluded among his books and papers in a big bed-sitting room on the second floor.

Sitting there perhaps, 'in the early candle-light of old age — I and my book — casting backward glances over our travel'd road,'[1] Walt composed a definition of his life work, describing his intentions which at the time of the writing had been so often unconscious. Of this I have already quoted a part.

A grateful legatee of the past, a born child of the New World, he had wished to present himself as a personality of the nineteenth century. He had hoped to prove that the democratic average of America was eligible for the grandest and the best. He had intended to offer, not a dead level of humanity, but rather a myriad of fully developed individuals as the purpose of democracy. The 'Leaves,' he felt as he looked backward, could not possibly have been fashioned from any other era than the nineteenth century nor in any other land than democratic America.[2]

It was an epic conception, too ambitious for complete success, even for a man of fewer idiosyncrasies and greater scholarship. One lifetime was not long enough. Himself he might reveal more fully than men are usually revealed, at least the aspects of self he chose for revealing, but his New World, his democracy, that was a different and more difficult problem. This nineteenth century of his was, as we now see, transitional to an unusual degree. Science and industrialism were just beginning a world transformation. Democracy, even in America, was but just beginning to be tested. The New World experiment, which seemed to him (and was) of such transcendent importance, was still in its prefatory and formative chapters. Gibbs might devise elegant and definitive formulas for physical processes which needed an accurate methodology to control. But the impact of science upon human nature, and the mixture of classes which was democracy, could not yet be studied by logic, or, except as a process, be grasped by the imagination. The effort of an American writer to give form to the formless was sure to be difficult and likely to be unsuccessful. And yet the nineteenth was in many respects truly the American century, infinitely worthy to be made articulate.

Herman Melville, feeling more strongly than most of his contemporaries the moral anarchy of society so visible in America, made the attempt to describe what he saw, and was driven into symbolism — successful only in 'Moby Dick,' and there (like Whitman) with spill-overs into incoherence and repetition. Thoreau, whose attention was fixed on the new scientific thinking, spent half his lifetime trying to reconcile nature with spiritual significance, and left a great book unassembled in his Journals, because he could not see what could be its conclusion. Thomas Wolfe, coming into the twentieth century from a nineteenth-century environment, and trying, like Whitman, to give a free, full, and true record of a personality in contact with democratic experience, could write only one endless — and shapeless — novel, terminated artificially by his death. Not until his last chapters did he begin the search for some spiritual unity which was Whitman's quest from the beginning. Our statesmen had organized democratic politics, our industrialists and empire builders had organized (and exploited) an American democracy. But the imagination could be only intuitive, tentative, and prophetic about essential democracy and culture. It was too early for a 'Leaves of Grass,' if that book was to stand for our modern times as Dante stood for the Middle Ages.

Who could penetrate, who could unify the multitudinous individuals of this explosive democracy, stating ideals for it which were not just methods of organization, discerning in it human types which the imagination could grasp? Whitman was no analytic philosopher. His ideals of self-development, his pantheistic religion, and his sense of a directing purpose behind democracy were all fluid. They had seeped in, early in life, from many sources, like spring water, and they were flowing out with a change only in purity, in intensity, in volume, and direction. Yet his imagination was involved with the rapidly changing society about him. He believed there was a unity of evolutionary democratic experience — and found it by exploring and exploiting himself.

Thus he separated consciously his artistic personality from the great artists who had been able to detach themselves from the mature civilizations in which they lived — the heroic in the Homeric age, the feudal in the Middle Ages, the aristocratic in the Renaissance, the pseudo-classic and politically formative in the eighteenth century — from Homer, Dante, Shakespeare, Pope. This is what he meant by saying so often that the 'Leaves' was not to be regarded as literature. It was evidence. These great men had been able to give at least an illusion of completeness, and had made their ages intelligible as stepping-stones leading across chaos, and toward the unknown destination of the human race. Whitman chose — had to choose — to represent rather than memorialize his rapidly changing time. He never emerged from the swirl of experience, except as a prophet pointing toward the future; and he hoped to record the quality of the nineteenth century by chanting the appearances of the New World in terms of his own faith and desire.

Therefore the 'Leaves' had to be psychology and sociology as well as poetry (the modern terms of course are ours not his). There was to be testimony as well as inspiration. This is why he packs into his book all the facts and feelings which interest him, stuffing it with his own reactions to his America many times repeated, with bits of American history in picture form, with self-interviews, with the behaviorism [3] of the democratic public, and with great statistical catalogues of characteristic activities. All this is held together by his fluid philosophy of self-development, inspired by a mystic sense of leadership, and given harmony by his style. Thus the 'Leaves' became, not so much a composite poem as a source-book for the American imagination, fiery with the vast hopes of democracy, aflutter with the winds of American expansion, yet essentially an anthology of his own poetic emotions.

Continually, from 1860 on, he arranged and rearranged the 'Leaves,' hoping always to give it a symphonic unity — a message as a whole, that would be simpler than the diverse lessons of its parts. Yet if one studies the various editions, including that of 1892 which was to be final for posterity in the order of its poems, it is clear that he failed. The unity remained himself. Who touched this book, touched a man everywhere, Walt Whitman. But who reads the 'Leaves' entire finds no unity of composition as in an epic or a great picture. It is more like an encyclopedia, organized with care for groupings and emphasis. To change the figure, it is no Parthenon or medieval cathedral, but does resemble one of those great national or international expositions which always aroused Whitman's enthusiasm. Faith in progress, that philosophy of the nineteenth century, backed those great shows. Yet there was another purpose — and particularly in America — which was to exhibit to the people the possibilities of their future. In some great hall, or a set of rambling buildings, there were assembled machines, food, instruments of family life, pictures, engineering, and also there was oratory, music, prayer, which urged the sweaty multitudes of the common people looking at the products of their energy to be as good as their machines, as vital as their continent. The 'Leaves of Grass' is such an exposition, rich in description, lyric and evocative with chants.

But the more Whitman arranged and rearranged the 'Leaves,' the more improbable seemed complete success. Even if it had been possible to compose a life lived in a century of dynamic change into a harmony, it was not possible for Walt. He was, as Thoreau would have said, cluttered in his own traps. Like most self-educated men, he took all knowledge for his province, ingorged without discrimination, and disgorged without much selection. His Freudian-Proustian attempt to make a complete record of a personality was as unintegrated as a set of case histories. Furthermore, he had the Transcendentalist's dislike of omitting anything that might have been inspired, even though the poem showed no inspiration. And to make disorder worse, he broke the chronological order of his poems in order to fill out his groupings, mixing styles of his various periods, flaming youth and weary age, authentic poetry and prosaic repetition. No one but a Whitman specialist ever reads the 'Leaves' from cover to cover. No one should. (Incidentally, no one but a specialist should read the later poems of Wordsworth, or the inferior plays of Shakespeare.)

2

In his old age, Walt sometimes said that the significance of his book as a whole was a secret, sometimes that he did not understand it himself. But he perfectly understood what he had accomplished in his lifetime, and in the 'Leaves,' and this is the directive for those who wish to read and absorb Whitman.

Viewed not as a shifting arrangement of poems, but as twenty years of vital creation, the confusion resolves itself into a series of chants appealing to the responsible guardians of democratic man.

The Song of Myself is Whitman's own inner life made dramatic, lyric, descriptive, and symbolic, with expanding America in the background. From it could be deduced by a creative mind all the book of which it is the overture but not the summary. It is youthful, egregious, defiant, with raucous chords of egoism smashed down on the keys in the attempt to get attention, and full of unresolved mysticism, suppressed sexuality, and a vague philosophy. Here is the naked Walt, flaunting his vigor, determined that the New World shall recognize its rich rank blood as the conditioner of soul in democratic man.

The strong poems that immediately follow in time continue the vigors and egoisms of the *Song of Myself*, and expand its interplay of apparent and spiritual reality. Read *Salut au Monde, Crossing Brooklyn Ferry, Song of the Answerer, Song of the Broad-Axe, A Song of the Rolling Earth.*

Next, the sexual suppressions of the *Song of Myself* and the partial release of *The Body Electric*, burst into the dramatic lyrics of *Children of Adam* and *Calamus*.

It is 1860 now. Passion and pride have reacted into disillusion and depression. Here are the bitter poems, some of them omitted from later editions, and here the nostalgic odes of remembered love and joy. The rank ego is sublimated into mystical ecstasy, or into love of life blended with death in a unity of acceptance. Whitman retires into his real self, which is not the same as the brash, projected ego of the poems of the mid-fifties. Read *Respondez* (written by 1856 but presaging the mood), and *I Sit and Look Out*, and afterward *I Ebb'd With the Ocean of Life*, and *Out of the Cradle Endlessly Rocking*.

Then the war and 'Drum-Taps.' His roots go deeper into the common ground. After all, he had been right about democracy. The people are sound, vigorous, and sweet, especially the young. It is not necessary to bare a hairy chest and flex the biceps against the old systems and repressions. Enfranchise the individual wholly, and virility will take care of itself. Millions are like Whitman, only less vocal, and they are asking to be led. Lincoln, a prudent idealist and a leader of the people, becomes his archetype for a new kind of hero, sprung from the common ground and to be loved rather than worshipped.

After the war, begins the stirring end of a great productive century. It is the age of the machine, of science triumphant. But its theme-song, 'progress,' may be spiritualized, may be used to make better men, more ardent love, stronger souls. He writes *Passage to India*.

At last, physical collapse, a clouded brain, a sense of failure, the continuing hope that others will carry on and win. The great poems conclude with the tragic notes of *The Prayer of Columbus*, and the optimism of *The Song of the Redwood Tree*.

No book, no organization of his poems, conveying this ring-by-ring growth, yet in itself a living tree, could have been made by Walt. The products and by-products and débris of his biography of America and autobiography of himself lay about in piles like the manuscripts and letters in his Mickle Street rooms. The best he could do was to sweep them together, divide them into groups, and hope that they would tell their own story. Which they do.

3

Even the most conservative have at last agreed that the best of the 'Leaves' is poetry, and much of it great poetry. Is it also history? Does it project, as Whitman hoped, the essential reality of nineteenth-century America? And is it prophecy? Nearly a century of that future of which Walt was always talking has been unveiled since he began to find his true tongue and write. We have enough perspective to say how far his challenge has been met.

Of course, as a realistic picture of men and women going about their business in the mid-nineteenth century, the 'Leaves' has very little verisimilitude. No such society of hearty, spiritualized men and healthy, ardent women as he depicts existed, though his descriptions of occupations, environment, and character are usually accurate enough. His rough and loving en-masse, and his deeply emotionalized individuals, are as romantic as Poe's fantastic creations, or the crew of Melville's ship. As sociology, as behaviorism, the 'Leaves' has little value. There is more realism in one of Whitman's letters to his mother from the Washington hospitals than in all his 'Leaves.' The America he described was in his own imagination, which was awash with a crisscross of waves coming up from his subconscious and in from the active life he saw, or fancied, in his expanding nation.

If Whitman was writing history at all, it was ideological history, like Karl Marx's or Fanny Wright's or Fourier's. He realized, like his master Emerson, the immense energies released in the New World by the breakdown of the old systems, and the opportunities for new ideas in a new and rich continent. Emerson offered his kind of future for those able to take it and lead in it.

Whitman, magnificent animal that he was in his youth, broadened the invitation to include the full-blooded physical energies of a still pioneering society, the phallic urges of the men, the fertility of the women, in a land where seeds sown for the future might sprout unbelievably. Both were preachers of the potential, not historians of the actual present.

And yet, whatever may be said for Emerson as a historian (and of course, much can be said), Walt Whitman and his book are, from another point of view, of immense historical importance. Though he idealized the nineteenth century out of easy recognition, the nineteenth century produced in Walt Whitman a fact and a vital reality. He may not have been representative, but he was symbolic of its expansiveness, its moral conflicts, its essential quality of continuous revolution, its struggle for fraternity, its large hopes. And though, more than he knew, he spoke for himself, he was certainly the nineteenth century speaking. If not the Time Spirit, he assuredly was one of its instruments. One of its prophets might be a truer phrase, and a prophet particularly in his insistence that democracy must take over the virtues and vigors and vitalities once reserved for the aristocracy, and now in danger of disappearing among decadent societies.

In many ways the wisest and soundest of all nineteenth-century historians was the great Swiss, Jacob Burckhardt. In his 'Force and Freedom: Reflections on History,' he defines the poet's part. 'Poetry seeks the supreme expressions of humanity and embodies them in ideal figures which incorporate human passion. . . . It reveals to man the secrets which he has within him and which, without poetry, would never find a voice. . . . This is achieved because the poet is himself suffering.' Great poets are great, he continues, when they are the most important witnesses of the spirit of their age. They do not have to be accepted by their times in order to have this importance. The relevance of all this to Whitman's peculiar service to the history of the imagination is obvious.

4

It is difficult to write about Walt Whitman without becoming

Transcendental and declamatory. He was always so himself when his genius was active. Even in private life he had no small talk. Yet he was not like those Harvard intellectuals whom Santayana describes as constantly applying fundamental principles to trivialities. Nothing, no matter how slight or mean, if it was human, was trivial to Walt. This does not encourage a sense of humor, either in him, or in his critics, or in his biographers. It is easy to make him seem ridiculous when he describes the ideal democrat as looking extraordinarily like his bearded self, or insists upon going naked in the woods. It is not so easy to deal with his excesses by gentle irony as Max Beerbohm has done in his cartoon, where a pudgy Walt in stocking-feet and on tiptoe, his trousers hitched to his paunch by red suspenders, urges a bored and sleepy bird of freedom to soar. (See Plate XIII in this book.) And yet the laughter at Whitman's eccentricities stops in the throat. There are better sources of mirth than the tensity and overseriousness of the great. Those who made fun of Adolf Hitler — in many respects Whitman's antithesis in world history — paid for their fun.[4] Those who laugh at Walt's egoisms are justified, but sooner or later a little unhappy about their mirth.

It has proved tempting for many to make fun of Whitman's untidy, exuberant, contradictory, and overambitious attempt to write a Bible for a democracy that had only begun to make its own history. But if it is true, as Walt himself said, that 'he is wisest who has the most caution,' it is true, as he also said, that 'he only wins who goes far enough.'[5] His poems, having deeply affected modern literatures, are passing into public consciousness, though not so much through the 'Leaves' as a whole as by lines, by passages, and by superb chants. For individuals everywhere they have provided the materials for a new Sacrament. No one who understands Whitman's deep religiosity will think that the word exaggerates his intention, or is blasphemously used. He offered his own self-revelations, and the powerful confessions of a man whose inner life was incredibly rich though he lived only on common ground. He offered a passionate faith in the possibilities of human nature set free by the growth of the individual. He offered love — not in the abstract, but as a function of a healthy, beautiful body, which the common man might possess as certainly as the aristocrat. It was a love spiritualized by mind. He himself was alive and sensitive in one of the ages of change, when the human race leaps forward toward a new order which may prove disaster or a new creation. And he said (in effect): Take, eat, drink, this is the imperfect but deeply felt body of my experience, and this is the blood of my faith. Do this in fulfilment of what I hope for the future:

> Dear friend whoever you are take this kiss, . . .
> Remember my words, I may again return, . . .
> I am as one disembodied, triumphant, dead.[6]

CHAPTER XXXI

'Good-bye my fancy'

AND SO, on March 26, 1884, he settled on Mickle Street, in the little house, now a Walt Whitman memorial, excellently kept. It is not far from the Delaware, with its shimmering mists and ferry bells and whistles, which pleased the old man, for ferries, while he could still move about easily, were his chief recreation. Mickle Street in his day was attractive, tree-lined, a pleasant workman's street. Now it is in a factory slum, with broken pavements, and looks like many decadent regions of the Philadelphia area. The house itself is good. Built in the 1840's, it is narrow and flush with adjoining houses, with a clapboarded front, coarse moulding over the doorway, and good woodwork and stairway inside. The stairs are steep, a difficult descent for the feeble man when visitors were in the parlor. Later on, he lived almost entirely in the big front room of the second floor, well proportioned and lit, with plenty of floor as well as wall room for his letters and manuscripts, and his few favorite books. There was a wood stove in front of the closed fireplace, a big double bed opposite, his capacious chairs set round, a chest, and personal pictures on the wall. It was a good prison.

He shared the house at first with a laborer's family, and seems to have got into a rather sad condition. Then, just as he had found the Prices and Nellie O'Connor as substitutes for his mother, he discovered Mrs. Mary Davis, widow of a sailor, who took pity on his evident inability to keep himself and his own house. She was persuaded to move in on the basis of shared expenses. It was, on the whole, an excellent arrangement, although

Mrs. Davis seems to have expected more for the future than had occurred to Walt. He had never been an easy person in the home — and now, having, for the first time, money laid by, he became a little miserly, as old people will. She paid more than her share. Later, he had a man nurse, a dog, a canary, a parrot; but neither Mrs. Davis, the animals, nor the birds provided company for Walt. He needed friends, and fortunately many came to visit him.

His friends bought him in 1885 a horse and buggy which he drove too fast, and kept too long, one evening in 1888, on the open river shore, with a serious relapse following. Nevertheless, he got about for Lincoln lectures which brought in good returns, and for visits with his friends, who made his own birthday a time of celebration. Helped by Traubel, he brought out 'November Boughs' in 1881; the eighth edition of his poems, and third of his complete works, in 1888–1889; 'Good-Bye My Fancy,' with new poems, in 1891; and the ninth edition of the 'Leaves' in 1892, the year of his death. It was a noble operation of mopping up.

Not only friends came, but visitors from far away of all grades of distinction and lack of it. Even in Camden he was to have the rewards, and pay the penalty, of both fame and notoriety. These pilgrims to a poet's home were most of them like-minded disciples, such as Doctor John Johnston, representing an English group of admirers, who wrote about his visit. Most surprising perhaps was Oscar Wilde, whose conversation with Walt seems to have been amicable in spite of the extreme of 'culture' which he then was propagandizing. Most surprising literary incident was the offer of Sir Edwin Arnold, author of the 'Light of Asia,' a popularization of Buddhism, to quote any poem from the 'Leaves' that Whitman would name.

Many other visitors came out of curiosity; and some of the 'plain people,' who knew him not as a poet, but only as a good man. Not so many as one would have expected from the literary circles of the United States, and surprisingly few from the universities. It still required some courage in the orthodox, or the merely respectable, to enter Whitman's area of free speech. Although, now that he was a chained lion, his literary contemporaries freely contributed both money and good words when asked for them, even Colonel Robert Ingersoll, the golden-tongued agnostic, had to be persuaded to read the 'Leaves' before he dropped his prejudices and became one of Whitman's staunchest defenders. He gave a benefit lecture once which brought in $839 to Walt; but in their conversations he never shook Whitman's deep religiosity. I am told by John Erskine, who has made a novel from Whitman's life, that even as late as the early 1900's, Professor Trent of Columbia, a specialist in American literary history, warned him against attending a meeting of Whitman's friends to celebrate his growing fame. They and he were still regarded by the respectable as a group of intellectual Communists might be today.

More constant and significant were the frequent visits of friends who were also his companions. O'Connor was dead, John Burroughs lived far away and came but seldom. Pete Doyle was overawed by the company he found in Mickle Street. Doctor Bucke came when he could. For the family, George was often there. The high-hearted daughter of a Quaker manufacturer, Mary Whitall Smith, insisted upon calling on Whitman, and made him her friend, and a visitor at their Spruce Street house in Philadelphia, where he used to carol cheerfully in the morning, locked in the single bathroom, while the family waited a turn. Pearsall Smith, whose critical essays are among the most discriminating of our time, joined his sister in friendship, though not in whole-hearted admiration.

Photographers kept soliciting a chance to make Walt's portrait. At one time, both Herbert Gilchrist, son of Whitman's friend, and Sidney Morse were at work upon his fine head, the one painting, the other modelling. If it had not been for his bad health, and annoyance at the still active opposition to his book, these might have been pleasant years.

There was an inner circle of these friends, and of this Horace Traubel was the hub. The Traubels were a German-Jewish family kin to the parents of Alfred Einstein. Horace Traubel himself was a socialist by faith, a hero-worshipper by nature, with a talent for friendly service. When Traubel was a Camden youth he was attracted to the poet, and became, in the latter 1880's, not so much the Boswell of Whitman (which was his ambition) as the Pepys of his slightest word and action. In these years, he was Walt's almost nightly visitor and companion. For him the old man raked over piles of letters on the floor, or searched for them in the old chest, giving him invaluable records of his past without which a biography would be incomplete. As they gossiped, Traubel, standing behind his chair, or in the hallway, took down the talk in a short hand of his own invention, which he expanded afterward. Three volumes of these journal notes, covering eighteen months in 1888 and 1889, have already been published, and many more pages, recording later years, and not yet translated, remain. In this, Traubel did inestimable service to Whitman's later biographers, and I have drawn freely from the stores in these volumes throughout this book. His transcripts are, as might be expected, colored by his own personality and his desire to make of Walt a socialist like himself; and it has been charged that the frequent 'damns' and 'hells' are his own contribution, Walt having been unusually clean and careful in his speech. Yet read with a consciousness that this is Whitman seen through a colored glass, the student will be rewarded by a moving portrait of his last days, and invaluable memoirs of his creative years.

But only a quarter-man is presented in Traubel's book. It was a paralytic, with frequently clouded brain that appears there, and though some of his buoyancy and all of his courage remained, he was reticent as to many aspects of his past, and there were areas of his mind that Traubel never touched, or did not understand. To all of the Camden circle, Walt seems to have appeared as an old revolutionary still fronting the enemy. Whitman the poet does not often enter these pages, nor was it Whitman the poet that Traubel and the rest were really interested in. Perhaps that fire had died down. Perhaps no friends at any time could have broken through his resolve never to seem literary. Whatever the cause, Walt, in this, the only full record of his talk, seems incredibly different from the spokesman in *Out of the Cradle Endlessly Rocking*, or *When Lilacs Last in the Door Yard Bloom'd*, or even *Crossing Brooklyn Ferry*. The prophet often speaks, the ex-editor (though he said little of his editing) more often still. But the poet is silent.

I may be unjust to the devoted friends who kept him talking about public affairs and the controversies of the past, and who seem to have read the 'Leaves' more as doctrine than as poetry. It is probable that Whitman's real poetry came from such depths of his being that no one at any time made contact with the profundities of his nature except through his book. He says so more than once, and it must have been true.

Horace Traubel's services, whatever his deficiencies as a reporter, were invaluable to the almost helpless Whitman. He made it possible for him to go on with the laborious process of publication, he brought into the house the familiar, trivial life of outdoors which Whitman always sniffed so keenly. He kept his mind stirring, and encouraged him to talk endlessly of himself. Indeed, it is overconsideration which makes 'Walt Whitman in Camden' tiresome — as are the books of so many of Walt's admirers. Traubel was infected by the indiscriminate unselectivity which was the lifelong disease of the poet. Everything goes into the record, as everything went into the 'Leaves' or 'Specimen Days.'

Traubel's sister was married to an able lawyer and booklover, Thomas B. Harned, and with their friends a new home circle was established for Whitman. J. H. Johnston, the New York jeweller, was often with them. Kennedy, too, was at work in Philadelphia for a while, and made his bonds closer. Thomas Donaldson, a business man and a good story-teller, became one of the group, and he, too, wrote reminiscences. Not so familiar, but welcome, were Talcott Williams, the Philadelphia journalist, who became the first head of the Columbia School of Journalism, Horace Howard Furness, editor of the great Variorum Shakespeare, himself also an eccentric, and the afterward famous William Osler, who advised as to Whitman's health.

What will occur to the reader of Traubel, however, is that Whitman in his old age, when he had become a landmark in literature, ran true to form in his companionships. Those with him most were neither writers nor intellectuals by profession, nor from the laboring class, but typical figures of American town life, whose chief interests were practical, not esthetic or philosophical. Even Traubel's intellectual interests ran on a narrow path. Celebrities might visit Mickle Street, or disciples like his farmer convert from the South, or a liberal clergyman, or an old Quaker, but his good companions were undistinguished except by their affection for him, and not different from such men and women as might have been drawn together in any sizable community in the nation. Perhaps he liked the easy superiority of his innate genius; but they never questioned him much as to his art, which was probably what he wanted. He knew that they would fight for his reputation after he was gone, and gave them the ammunition, but trusted more to his book, in which he was right. They and the other friends were the last of the joys of life he clung to, and he made for them one of the best of his old-age poems:

After the supper and talk — after the day is done,
As a friend from friends his final withdrawal prolonging,
Good-bye and Good-bye with emotional lips repeating, . . .
E'en at the exit-door turning — charges superfluous calling back — e'en
    as he descends the steps, . . .
Soon to be lost for aye in the darkness — loth, O so loth to depart!
Garrulous to the very last.

Indeed with these good friends of his departing days, the slow-spoken, reticent Walt did become garrulous — a tribute to them.

2

Walt in his last decade lived in the past, except for the excitement of some review of his new editions, or the petty incidents of publishing. He was only briefly pleased or angered by the political doings of the country, or views of the larger world. When he was really stirred, it was because some incident reminded him of his persecutors — the Stoddards, the Winters, the Harlans — or when his mind turned back to the sick and wounded soldiers in the hospitals. Then he would dig out some old letter from a soldier boy and let it be read while tears came to his eyes. Yet what he talked about in his past was always vital. His life of day to day, his 'perturbations,' the 'smutch'd deeds,' if any, seldom floated to the surface except by indirection. It was his experience as a revolutionary in the good old cause and in the new cause of sexual vitality that he impressed upon his friends. That was what he wanted them to remember.

Whitman's financial troubles, which seem to have increased in the first years in Mickle Street, were soon relieved, if indeed they were not caused by his desire to save. From writing contributed irregularly to *The New York Herald* for years and well paid for, from occasional poems sold, and from sales of his books, he had a reasonable income and considerable reserves, which were increased by a subscription raised for him in London in 1886, by the proceeds of his Lincoln lectures, and from another friendly fund of eight hundred dollars subscribed in America to get him a cottage in the country, a project which soon became impracticable. The aging man, for the first time in his life, was close with his money, paid his publishing bills unwillingly, stinted Mrs. Davis,[1] and allowed (without too much questioning) his friends to pay expenses for his illness which he could have handled himself. He was secretive about his resources. The truth was that he was establishing a fund to take care of Eddie after his death, leave gifts to his friends, and complete the monumental vault he was building in a Camden cemetery.

He has been unjustly criticized for this ostentation, as it has been called. The tomb was to be for the Whitman family, his last sign of the deep affection he had always felt for his close kin. Its design was taken from a drawing by William Blake, and the total bill (said to have been more than twenty-five hundred dollars) was an unhappy surprise to everyone but the contractor, who cheated Whitman while he was alive, and was properly handled by Harned (who paid part of what was paid) after the poet's death. Walt's last will,[2] which is not the one reproduced by Traubel, disposed of the unexpected sum of six thousand dollars including the Mickle Street property, in addition to his copyrights and personal belongings.

He had been in no real need of money from his friends, but depended on their love, the more so since for many years he was in almost constant distress of body, nearly died in 1888, and was only half alive for the four years remaining to him. The quite unnecessary autopsy after his death showed a terrifying complex of diseases ravaging his once magnificent body — not only paralysis but widespread tuberculosis, and wasteage of vital organs. Only his immense vitality had made him last so long. He suffered from insistent headaches and abdominal distress. One of his last poems (1888) is pathetic:

> As I sit writing here, sick and grown old,
> Not my least burden is that dulness of the years, querilities, ...
> May filter in my daily songs.

Walt Whitman died quietly, and with apologies for the length of his dying, his hand in Traubel's, on March 26 of 1892.

The will, made in 1892, is the sensible disposition of a man whose grasp upon practical affairs, except where they concerned his own enrichment, was always prudent and sound. Doctor Bucke, Harned, and Traubel were his executors, and they divided in what seems to have been a rather haphazard fashion the masses of notes, clippings, manuscripts of all kinds in his house on Mickle Street. While, with real concern for his reputation, they authorized a so-called complete edition of his work, with a biography, bibliography, and commentaries (published in 1902), the original confusion has never been entirely cleared up, and students of Whitman must consult many supplementary volumes.

At the funeral by the vault built from Blake's impressive drawing were many true friends, and a concourse of the people, drawn, it would seem, chiefly by curiosity, for Whitman had become a feature in Camden news. There was an elaborate and rather rhetorical program of tributes, which were, however, heartfelt and sincere. He would, I think, have approved of his funeral. He liked oratory, he liked appreciation, he exaggerated the importance of any claims for his greatness made by his friends and contemporaries. He would have liked to talk of it afterward. 'Did you hear what Ingersoll said?' 'I wish O'Connor could have been there.' He liked crowds of the common people, too, and he would have found in this one some man or woman whose face was electric for him, from that time no stranger, even if never seen again. To all such and his closer friends he had said his farewell years before:

> Dear friend whoever you are take this kiss, . . .
> I feel like one who has done work for the day to retire awhile, . . .
> I love you, I depart from materials.
> *So long!*

3

Thus departed the symbolic man of the nineteenth century. Not its representative man, but certainly he who made its inner, unconscious life, its bent for the future, most articulate. The century was closing when he died. Its cycle was over, its forces were already passing into new tensions and balances. In six years more his country ended its three-quarters of a century of isolationism and plunged into an egregious foreign war. Power, generated by the vast energies of expansion, was shaping a new and different world. Science was becoming a commodity. The little cloud no bigger than a man's hand on the horizon threatening democracy had no longer its prophet to warn us. In America, poetry was imitative or trivial. In England, Rudyard Kipling, another great maker of chants (and far more singable songs), was celebrating, not the future of democracy, but the glories of an empire whose end, as empire, was near at hand. The 'Leaves' were already fluttering abroad, in many languages, gaining disciples, yet, like Emerson's essays, more often stirring imaginations to new and original achievements. But Whitman, the buffalo-headed wild man, the rather admirable old freak, the vulgar sexualist, about whom there had been so much talk, was safely dead — so must have thought — so did think — many a refined and respectable editor and critic of the nineties.

The judgment was premature. 'Liberty, let others despair of thee, But I never despair of thee,' Walt had written in his prime. He never despaired of an understanding audience somewhere, sometime, and he was right. Centuries do not die, they live on in their consequences. And so it was to be with him.

4

The personality of Walt Whitman is elusive. Even though he speaks so often and so much of 'personalism,' even when his gait, his clothes, his face, his voice have been described at length, still the man's inner individuality escapes from the record. We fail to fetch him. The delusively simple and affectionate Walt of the letters and of his own autobiographies is easy to grasp, but for that 'essential me' of which he was always writing, there seems to be no sharp-angled core of individual being.

With many writers of genius, the personality, like the style, becomes more and more a definite, definable entity as you read and study. With some, like Henry Thoreau, it is clearly the most important aspect of the man as artist; more important, in a literary sense, than his ideas. Thoreau was God's spy in Concord, and every bird and flower and every river or forest thought took on his mind's color and became part of his inner life.

But Walt Whitman was not that kind of genius at all. He has no core in which experience is assimilated. He is more like a funnel for the sensations and the wandering ideas of his world. They flow in, they flow out, channelled toward democracy, made articulate by his style. When he has phrased them, they become, as he says — himself. He is a powerful voice responding to the stimulus of inspiration. Desires burn through him, he speaks with the tongue of the angels, or shouts for the en-masse; but as a personality — like Doctor Johnson, like Oliver Wendell Holmes, like Chaucer, like Thoreau — he escapes into words.

John Keats understood this occasional attribute of genius. After talking with Brown and Dilke one day, 'It struck me,' he said, 'what quality went to form a Man of Achievement, and which Shakespeare possessed so enormously — I mean *Negative Capability*, that is, when a man is capable of being in uncertainties, mysteries, doubts, without any irritable reaching after fact and reason. Coleridge, for instance, would let go by a fine isolated verisimilitude caught from the Penetralium of mystery, from being incapable of remaining content with half-knowledge. . . .

With a great poet the sense of Beauty overcomes every other consideration, or rather obliterates all consideration.' [3]

It was not beauty, as Keats understood beauty, that was always, or even often, Whitman's consideration. His negative capability was a power to absorb into the imagination a new democratic world whose beauty was strange, unfamiliar, often dissonant; and his poetry was not halted by attempts to analyze fine isolated verisimilitudes discovered by intuition.

Intent upon a task not yet amenable to fact and reason, he was like the Hebrew prophets who had no private life that mattered. He might be compared to Gabriel in that great American folk play, 'The Green Pastures'; a simple fellow, but he could blow the Last Trump! He belongs with Homer, who seems to have been content to make immortal the memories and faiths of an age, not with Euripides or Plato. He resembled Washington rather than Jefferson. He was the actor who makes Hamlet live, not Hamlet himself.

How great a man for the American nineteenth century was Whitman by comparison with these famous names, is not the question. I am saying here merely that 'missing me one place, search another' holds for his personality, and the search may be long. What he had was something greater than personality, though at a risk which all oracles, whether of Delphi or of Brooklyn, must take when, losing themselves in inspiration, they become prophetic, or vacuous, or sometimes both. Yet though it is difficult to grasp and hold and be sure of Walt Whitman's personality, it is impossible today to escape his voice. Wherever he is waiting, we seem to have caught up, and we tune to his wave easily. For this generation he is intelligible and dynamic. We accept, as the nineteenth century would not, his confident assertion: 'I speak the pass-word primeval, I give the sign of democracy.'

THE END

Notes

CHAPTER II

1. From the Bucke MSS. Notes for a catalogue of the sale at the American Art Association in 1936, by E. F. Hannaburgh.
2. 'The Complete Writings of Walt Whitman' (New York and London: G. P. Putnam's Sons, 1902), I, 30.
3. *Ibid.*, I, 31.
4. 'The Complete Writings,' *Specimen Days*, IV, 12, and Bucke MSS., *op. cit.*
5. *Ibid.*, IV, 8.
6. Bucke MSS., *op. cit.*
7. 'The Complete Writings,' *There Was a Child Went Forth*, II, 137.
8. Horace Traubel, 'With Walt Whitman in Camden' (Boston: Small, Maynard and Company, 1906; New York: D. Appleton and Company, 1908; New York: Mitchell Kennerly, 1914), II, 41.
9. MS. in Yale Library.
10. Traubel, 'W. W. in C.,' I, 322.
11. He was said to have been a Quaker, like his wife, but there were some strange fellow travellers in that sect. Certainly, he was a friend of the great Quaker, Elias Hicks.
12. 'The Complete Writings,' *Specimen Days*, IV, 10.
13. Bucke MSS., *op. cit.*
14. There is perhaps a physiological reason, to be discussed later, for his rounded, almost feminine muscles.
15. 'In Re Walt Whitman,' Edited by his Literary Executors, Horace L. Traubel, Richard Maurice Bucke, Thomas B. Harned (Philadelphia: David McKay, 1893), pp. 196, 198.

CHAPTER III

1. 'The Complete Writings,' *There Was a Child Went Forth*, II, 135 ff.
2. *Ibid.*, *Out of the Cradle Endlessly Rocking*, II, 11–12.
3. *Ibid.*, *Beginning My Studies*, I, 9–10.
4. *Ibid.*, *Specimen Days*, IV, 4, note.
5. 'The Uncollected Poetry and Prose of Walt Whitman,' Collected and Edited by Emory Holloway (New York: Doubleday Page and Company, 1921), I, xxvi, note.
6. 'The Complete Writings,' IV, 17.
7. Doctor Bucke says he worked for a doctor also. As errand boy for the Clarkes, he used to take messages across the river to Aaron Burr.

8. MS. in Library of Congress.
9. He was at 'Worthington's,' presumably a printer, in the summer of 1832. 'Uncoll.,' II, 86, autobiographical note.
10. Bucke MSS., *op. cit.*
11. 'The Complete Writings,' *Specimen Days*, IV, 22–23.
12. *Ibid.*, *Specimen Days*, IV, 19.
13. Traubel, 'W. W. in C.,' II, 241–242.
14. MS. in Library of Congress, Cit. Catel.
15. 'Uncoll.,' II, 86.
16. 'The Complete Writings,' *Specimen Days*, IV, 24–25.
17. *Ibid.*, IV, 25.
18. *Ibid.*, VI, 192.
19. 'Uncoll.,' I, xxx.
20. His brother George was one of the scholars. He said Walt had the reputation of being a good teacher. 'In Re.,' p. 33 ff.
21. See particularly 'Whitman's Teaching at Smithtown, 1837–1838,' by Katherine Molinoff, New York, 1941.
22. *Desk of a Schoolmaster, Sundown Papers.* From 'Uncoll.,' I, 32 ff.
23. 'The Complete Writings,' *Specimen Days*, IV, 20.
24. 'Uncoll.,' I, xxxiv, note.
25. 'An Unpublished Whitman Manuscript: The Record Book of the Smithtown Debating Society, 1837–1838,' New York, 1941.
26. See a letter from Mary, his sister, in Greenport, December 23, 1883, now in the Yale Library. 'I do not suppose I should ever know anything about the family if it was not for you as I never get a letter from any of them.'
27. 'In Re.,' p. 35.
28. See extracts from unpublished manuscripts in a review by Clifton Joseph Furness in *American Literature*, January, 1942, for a view of the family as it was later in Walt's life. Edward became half-witted after early illness.

CHAPTER IV

1. 'The Complete Writings,' *Song of Myself*, I, 108. This famous line must have been inspired by Emerson's *Self-Reliance* (1841). See The Centenary Edition, II, 57, second paragraph.
2. *Sundown Papers, No. 7.* From *The Long Island Democrat*, September 29, 1840. 'Uncoll.,' I, 37 ff.
3. 'The Complete Writings,' II, 36.
4. See *Song of Myself*, 'The Complete Writings,' I, 62, and the original text of the first edition, *ibid.*, III, 109, for his use and then omission of 'one of the roughs.'
5. In 1890, in a manuscript note now in the Yale Library, he de-

scribes himself as 'perceptibly Quaker.' In 'W. W. in C.,' II, 19, he said to Traubel: 'When I was a young fellow up on the Long Island shore I seriously debated whether I was not by spiritual bent a Quaker? — whether if not one I should not become one? — But ... I was never made to live inside a fence.'

6. Traubel, 'W. W. in C.,' II, 114.
7. *Ibid.*, III, 192.
8. He was disowned by what came to be called the Orthodox Friends, in 1828.
9. Note, for example, the poem *A Child's Amaze*, quoted above.

CHAPTER V

1. Reminiscences in the Camden, N.J. *Press*. Cited by Bliss Perry, 'Walt Whitman, His Life and Work' (New York: Houghton Mifflin Company, 1906), pp. 17–18.
2. George Whitman, in 'In Re.,' stated that he was co-proprietor, but he was only twelve at the time.
3. See a letter to T. G. Bergen. 'Walt Whitman, Complete Poetry and Selected Prose and Letters.' Edited by Emory Holloway (London: The Nonesuch Press, 1938), p. 883.
4. 'Uncoll.,' II, 15.
5. MS. in the Yale Library. See also 'Whitman,' Edited by E. Holloway, p. 883.
6. 'W. W. in C.,' I, 467.
7. See for particularly horrible examples, 'The Half-Breed and Other Stories,' edited by Thomas Ollive Mabbott (New York, 1927).
8. The American poet, J. G. Percival, was leading much the same double life in his successful popular poetry and his unpublished experiments, which were some of them of high originality.
9. 'Uncoll.,' II, 87 ff.
10. *Idem.*
11. Cited by Bliss Perry, 'Whitman,' pp. 22–23 and note.
12. See Walt Whitman, 'The Gathering of the Forces' (New York and London: G. P. Putnam's Sons, 1920), Edited by Cleveland Rogers and John Black, II, 113 ff. This portrait is certainly some years earlier than the 1854 daguerreotype.
13. 'Uncoll.,' I, 114–117.
14. *Ibid.*, II, 88.
15. See 'The Gathering of the Forces,' *passim.*
16. *Ibid.*, p. xlix.
17. Emory Holloway, 'Whitman, An Interpretation in Narrative,' (New York and London: Alfred A. Knopf, 1926), pp. 5–6.

18. 'I Sit and Look Out,' Edited by Emory Holloway and Vernolian Schwartz (New York: Columbia University Press, 1932), pp. 33–34. Written on January 30, 1858.

19. Bernard De Voto, 'The Year of Decision, 1846' (New York: Little Brown and Company, 1943). The quotation in this book was condensed before publication.

CHAPTER VI

1. Dr. Richard Maurice Bucke, 'Walt Whitman' (Philadelphia: David McKay, 1883), p. 67.

2. See *The Democratic Review*, November, 1841. Noted also by Jean Catel, 'Walt Whitman, La Naissance du Poète' (Montpellier: Causse, Graille et Castelnau, 1929).

3. Taken from editorials in 'The Gathering of the Forces,' *passim*.

CHAPTER VII

1. 'In Re.,' p. 311.

2. See Plate IV in this book. If the later photograph of Walt in Plate VI is correctly dated, which I doubt, it shows an easy Bohemianism. But though he marked this picture himself as of 1849, it looks more like 1859. Such errors were not uncommon in his old-age datings.

3. 'The Complete Writings,' *Give Me the Splendid Silent Sun*, II, 78–79.

4. *Ibid.*, IV, 20–24.

5. *Ibid.*, VI, 185 ff.

6. Clifton Joseph Furness, 'Walt Whitman's Workshop' (Cambridge: Harvard University Press, 1928), p. 202.

7. 'The Complete Writings,' IV, 287–288.

8. 'The Complete Writings,' IX.

9. 'Uncoll.,' I, 125 ff.

10. See also Furness, 'W. W.'s Workshop,' p. 196.

11. See Cleveland Rogers, 'Walt Whitman the Politician,' from *The Literary Review* of *The New York Evening Post*, September 22, 1923.

12. Bucke MSS., *op. cit.*, contain a speech for the campaign of 1848, to be delivered at Groton, against the extension of slavery.

13. See 'Writers in Crisis; the American Novel between Two Wars' (Boston, 1942), by Maxwell David Geismar.

CHAPTER VIII

1. See Camden, New Jersey *Courier*, 1st No. Cited by Bliss Perry, 'Whitman,' pp. 41–42.

2. See 'I Sit and Look Out,' p. 5. Quotation from *The Eagle*. This, however, is not to be relied on for its details.
3. 'The Complete Writings,' IX, 201, 217, 218, etc.
4. 'Uncoll.,' I, 225.
5. Jeff wrote home, 'Walter . . . already has quite a sum, as soon as he gets a thousand dollars he is coming North.' Bucke MSS., *op. cit.*
6. See 'Uncoll.,' I, 26, 27.
7. See 'Whitman,' Edited by Emory Holloway, pp. 505, 506. Later called *Europe*.

CHAPTER IX

1. The date is not certain. In a 'Remembrance Copy' of his book in the Yale Library, Whitman states to John Swinton that his friend, Gabriel Harrison, in Fulton Street, Brooklyn, took the daguerreotype one hot day in August, 1855. This is evidently an error, since the edition with a drawing made from the picture was published in July. Whitman probably meant 1854.
2. The so-called 1849 photograph of Walt in rough, flowing clothing and with grizzled hair and beard, certainly represents him as he usually dressed in his Bohemian days of the fifties, whatever its actual date, as contemporary descriptions of the man indicate. I believe it to be later than 1856, probably of 1859.
3. Bucke MSS., *op. cit.* 'July 31, 1852 — Mr. Scofield owes W. W. for 11 days work. Aug. 21 — Made full week the past week (Scofield owes for 23½ days, $26.42).'
4. 'In Re.,' p. 35.
5. 'Uncoll.,' II, 88, note 8.

CHAPTER X

1. These four are published entire, the rest in extracts by Holloway in 'Uncoll.,' II. The originals are in the Library of Congress.
2. 'The Complete Writings,' IX, 3. 'My poems when complete should be a *unity*, in the same sense that the earth is, or . . . that a perfect musical composition is.' This is a note probably made in the early 1850's.
3. So he states. His biographers have misread him.
4. Written before 1855.
5. See 'The Complete Writings,' and Furness, 'W. W.'s Workshop.'

CHAPTER XI

1. 'New York Dissected,' Edited by Emory Holloway and Ralph Adimari (New York: Rufus Rockwell Wilson, 1938), p. 24.

2. Traubel, 'W. W. in C.,' I, 92.
3. 'Carte de visite' was commonly used at this time to describe a small portrait photograph.
4. 'Uncoll.,' II, 91.
5. My quotations are from the poem as finally revised. The refinements and omissions and additions made after 1855 did not change the poem essentially.
6. 'The Complete Writings,' V, 192.
7. *Ibid.*, III, 56–57.
8. *Ibid.*, III, 65.
9. See *Song of Myself*.
10. *Idem.*, I, 78.

CHAPTER XII

1. *Song of Myself*.
2. Traubel, 'W. W. in C.,' III, 515.
3. *Ibid.*, I, 111. He was inclined to include Hawthorne but 'not surely.'
4. *The Tribune* on July 23, 1855, had published a sympathetic review of the 'Leaves,' possibly by Dana himself.
5. The current anti-alien party.
6. See Kenneth Murdock, 'A Leaf of Grass from Shady Hill,' 1928.
7. It is interesting to note that *The New York Times* review (reprinted by Whitman in his 'Leaves of Grass Imprints' of 1860) was held up for some months, and published when the second edition appeared. The rather extensive abuse in the first part of the review gives way to such phrases as 'brave stuff' and an 'electric attraction.'

CHAPTER XIII

1. See 'I Sit and Look Out,' *passim*.
2. Holloway, *op. cit.*, comes to this conclusion.
3. See 'Uncoll.,' II, 91, note.
4. See 'I Sit and Look Out,' p. 92.
5. Traubel, 'W. W. in C.,' II, 486.
6. Furness, 'W. W.'s Workshop,' pp. 85–113.
7. *Ibid.*, p. 100 and p. 93. See page 164 of this book for the later expansion of this attack.
8. *Ibid.*, p. 113.
9. 'New York Dissected,' p. 12.

CHAPTER XIV

1. If I am right in believing that the picture in Plate VI of this book, dated 1849–1850, by Walt himself years later, is actually of the late 1850's, here is an excellent representation of Walt the hearty and healthy man-about-town.
2. 'The Complete Writings,' *Good-Bye, My Fancy*, VII, 57.
3. MS. in the Yale Library. Whitman had distinguished predecessors in the practice of reviewing himself anonymously, notably Sir Walter Scott and Erasmus.
4. By 'cuteness' Walt always means 'acuteness.'
5. See 'I Sit and Look Out,' p. 12.
6. This painting is now in the possession of Miss Bertha Johnston of Brooklyn, daughter of his old friend, J. H. Johnston.
7. I am told that it was suspended and revived for the same reason — need of cash.
8. William Dean Howells, 'Literary Friends and Acquaintances' (New York and London: Harper and Brothers, 1900), p. 70.
9. *Ibid.*, p. 74.
10. 'Uncoll.,' II, 91.
11. *Ibid.*, II, 92 ff.
12. In the Congressional Library.
13. See 'Whitman,' Edited by E. Holloway, pp. 927–928.
14. See *A War-Time Letter*, 'Uncoll.,' II, 21–26, and 'Whitman,' Edited by E. Holloway, pp. 895–900, pp. 915–917, pp. 923–925; also a statement on p. 1099, showing that some of these meetings were at Pfaff's.
15. Hugo Fritsch, called by Walt, Fritschy, son of the Austrian consul-general. He went to the opera with Walt.

CHAPTER XV

1. In the original draft of Thoreau's letter to Blake, now in the Middlebury College Library (see page 151 of this book), Thoreau had written of his talk with Whitman, 'In his apologizing account of the matter he had made the printing of E.'s letter seem a simple thing — and to some extent throws the burden of it — if there is any, on the writer.' See Viola C. White, *The New England Quarterly*, vol. 8, 263.
2. Ralph L. Rusk, 'The Letters of Ralph Waldo Emerson' (New York: Columbia University Press, 1939), IV, 530, and V, 86.
3. Editor of *The Free Inquirer*, friend of Lafayette.
4. Henry Seidel Canby, 'Thoreau' (Boston: Houghton Mifflin Company, 1939), p. 413.

5. Moncure Daniel Conway, liberal clergyman, editor of the works of Thomas Paine, and friend of the Concord group, also visited Whitman in 1855 and again in 1857. See his 'Autobiography' (Boston and New York: Houghton Mifflin Company, 1904), I, 215–219, and *The Fortnightly Review*, VI, 538.

6. See 'The Journals of Bronson Alcott,' Edited by Odell Shepard (Boston: Little, Brown and Company, 1938), p. 290.

7. Later called *Brooklyn Ferry*.

8. See 'The Writings of Henry David Thoreau,' Edited by F. B. Sanborn (Boston and New York: Houghton Mifflin Company, 1906), VI, 291, 295–296.

9. See Traubel, 'W. W. in C.,' I, 212–213.

10. He entered the first edition, and second (which Walt gave him in 1856), as accessories to his library as of 1858. He was in New York in 1858.

11. Traubel, 'W. W. in C.,' III, 354.

12. *Ibid.*, III, 374–375.

13. *Ibid.*, III, 318, 319.

14. *Ibid.*, II, 354, and Rusk, 'Emerson,' V, 53.

15. John Burroughs, 'Whitman, A Study' (Boston and New York: Houghton Mifflin Company, 1896), p. 50.

16. Clara Barrus, 'Whitman and Burroughs, Comrades' (Boston and New York: Houghton Mifflin Company, 1931), p. 64. From Burroughs' Journal.

17. Traubel, 'W. W. in C.,' I, 61.

18. *Ibid.*, II, 69. 'But I got my roots stronger in the earth — master would not do any more.'

19. Edward Carpenter, 'My Days and Dreams' (London: George Allen and Unwin Ltd., 1916), p. 88.

20. Traubel, 'W. W. in C.,' I, 61.

21. MS. in the Yale Library.

22. 'Her book about Epicurus was daily food to me: I kept it about me for years.' Traubel, 'W. W. in C.,' II, 445.

CHAPTER XVI

1. 'The Complete Writings,' *Democratic Vistas*, V, 86, 87. Written 1868.

2. *Ibid.*, V, 151 ff.

3. *Ibid.*, V, 152–154. The earlier document was drawn upon for this later invective.

4. 'I Sit and Look Out,' p. 87. From *The Brooklyn Times*, May 14, 1857.

5. 'The Complete Writings,' III, 312–316.
6. *Ibid.*, II, 34.

CHAPTER XVII

1. 'Whitman,' Edited by E. Holloway, p. 885.
2. See his review of 'Drum Taps' and the 'Leaves' in *The Galaxy* of 1866.
3. William Sloane Kennedy, 'The Fight of a Book for the World' (Massachusetts: The Stonecroft Press, 1926), p. 243, says that over ten thousand copies of these pirated 'Leaves' were sold over a period of years.
4. 'My Own Story' (Boston and New York: Houghton Mifflin Company, 1903), p. 362.
5. 'The Complete Writings,' *Specimen Days*, V, 26–27.
6. *Ibid.*, V, 265 ff.
7. *Ibid.*, III, 255. *So Long.* Text of the 1860 version.
8. *Ibid.*, III, 91. Original version.
9. Published by *The Saturday Press* in 1859.
10. Note that the first line is from *As I Ebb'd with the Ocean of Life*, while the second is from the first version of *Out of the Cradle Endlessly Rocking*. (See 'The Complete Writings,' III, 187).
11. See 'I Sit and Look Out,' p. 10.
12. See also page 119 of this book.
13. 'The Complete Writings,' *Specimen Days*, IV, 29.
14. *Ibid.*, IV, 31, 35.

CHAPTER XVIII

1. Whitman's chart is interesting. He used it, of course, to strengthen his own self-estimate. See 'In Re.,' p. 25. '"Phrenological notes on W. Whitman," by L. N. Fowler, July, 1849. — size of head, 23 inches. Leading traits appear to be Friendship, Sympathy, Sublimity, and Self-Esteem, and markedly among its combinations the dangerous faults of Indolence, a tendency to the pleasures of voluptuousness and Alimentiveness, and a certain reckless swing of animal will.' There follows a chart of Whitman's bumps marked on a scale of 1–7.
2. *The Dalliance of the Eagles*, 1880, a magnificent picture which offended some of the prudish, is scarcely an exception.
3. Whitman's unpublished letters in the Congressional Library are illuminating as to this general situation.
4. 'The Complete Writings,' IX, 39, written in 1855 or 1856.

5. Canby, 'Thoreau,' p. 127.
6. See the account of this woman in a quotation to be found in the Furness review, note 29, chap. III.
7. 'Whitman,' Edited by E. Holloway, p. 1052 ff.
8. *Ibid.*, p. 1052.
9. *Ibid.*, p. 1056.
10. There are eleven references to this 'tail' in the conversations of Traubel's books, and in one of them he speaks of himself as 'Not too much of a bachelor, either, if you knew it all!' (II, 328, and see also II, 425.) Usually it is a period of time, not an incident, to which he seems to refer. I should like to be convinced of the validity of what might be a most interesting story, but I fear Walt was playing the cat with his friendly mice.
11. The number 16 is written in over the erasure of an initial. The number 164, with probably the same reference, is inscribed over a dash which indicated a blank. An ingenious but entirely unconvincing theory that these numbers referred only to Walt's phrenological chart has been advanced by Professor Edward Hungerford in an article 'Walt Whitman and his Chart of Bumps.' See *American Literature*, 1931.

CHAPTER XIX

1. 'The Complete Writings,' VIII, 7.
2. *Ibid.*, VIII, 51–54.
3. 'Whitman,' Edited by E. Holloway, pp. 935–936.
4. See Traubel, 'W. W. in C.,' III, 299 for Whitman's definition of the word.
5. See 'Uncoll.,' II, 96 and note.
6. 'Whitman,' Edited by E. Holloway, p. 1052.
7. I follow, in some respects, Catel, *op. cit.*, in this conclusion.
8. 'The Complete Writings,' *Song of Myself*, I, 63.
9. *Ibid.*, *Calamus*, I, 160.

CHAPTER XX

1. Traubel, 'W. W. in C.,' I, 13.
2. *Idem.*, 'The Negro was not the chief thing: the chief thing was to stick together.'
3. See 'Whitman,' Edited by E. Holloway, p. 934. Perhaps Whitman means he drilled, perhaps enlisted. He certainly did not go to the front.
4. Bucke, 'Whitman,' p. 104.

5. From *Drum-Taps*, 'The Complete Writings,' II, 77.
6. See Kennedy, *op. cit.*, p. 243.
7. For Whitman's attitude toward war, see Traubel, 'W. W. in C.,' III, 293. It has been suggested that Traubel did some strengthening of his own in this passage, probably supplied the 'God damns.' However, it is clear that this is a hysterical outburst, and certain that Whitman, like Sherman, whom he quotes, hated war *as such*, but certain also that he did not hate *all wars*.
8. 'The Complete Writings,' *The Wound-Dresser*, VII, 77.
9. *Ibid.*, VII, 218.
10. Charles I. Glicksberg, 'Walt Whitman and the Civil War' (Philadelphia: University of Pennsylvania Press, 1933), p. 28.
11. *Ibid.*, p. 29.

CHAPTER XXI

1. See 'The Complete Writings,' *The Wound-Dresser*, VII. I have excerpted from these letters and articles so as to give a narrative of Whitman's typical hospital experiences.
2. Christian Commission delegates did not nurse or give medicine. They supplied 'personal service.'
3. 'The Complete Writings,' I, 89.
4. He seems to have enrolled at first with the Christian Commissioners as a volunteer, but soon found that his methods were too individualistic for them, and that he could do best on his own. He had a copy of their book of instructions and two of their circulars which speak of three hundred 'gentlemen of the highest respectability,' who were distributing books and food among sick and wounded. See MS. in the Yale Library. Also 'Abraham Lincoln and Walt Whitman' (Indianapolis: The Bobbs-Merrill Company, 1928), by William E. Barton. Barton's estimate of the nature and cause of Walt's services is prejudiced.
5. Traubel, 'W. W. in C.,' III, 77.
6. A rather absurd attempt has been made to minimize Whitman's services and possible damage to health, by showing that he spent usually his evenings and not all of them in the hospitals. You can tell little about wine by the time it takes to pour a glassful.
7. 'Whitman,' Edited by E. Holloway, p. 914.
8. 'The Complete Writings,' VII, 198.
9. *Ibid.*, VII, 119.
10. Furness, 'W. W.'s Workshop,' p. 127 ff.
11. 'The Complete Writings,' *Drum-Taps*, II, 91.

CHAPTER XXII

1. 'The Complete Writings,' IV, 140.
2. He proposed in the Autumn of 1863 for the Christmas trade, 'Memoranda of a Year: 1863,' calling it 'an ardent book ... full of these tremendous days ... full of the blood and vitality of the American people. A book gestated amid the ocean life and cosmopolitanism of New York. Nationality and Freedom & Real Democracy — such is the new volume.' This was to be the blurb. He goes on with a draft of a letter saying that it is to be something more than hospital sketches — a French 'memoire,' dealing with the President, Seward, army organization, etc. It is to sell for 35 cents and be out by mid or the 20th of November. (MS., Yale Library.) This sounds like a combination of some of the 'Drum-Taps' with the material which appeared in 1875 on, as 'Memoranda of the War' and later in 'Specimen Days,' and other notes.
3. 'Whitman,' Edited by E. Holloway, pp. 949–950.
4. Recently reissued.
5. 'The Complete Writings,' *A Sight in Camp in the Daybreak Gray and Dim*, II, 71.
6. *Ibid.*, *A March in the Ranks Hard-Prest, and the Road Unknown*, II, 69.
7. *Ibid.*, II, 97.
8. *Ibid.*, *Specimen Days*, IV, 71–72, 120.
9. Glicksberg, 'W. W. and the Civil War,' p. 173 ff., has a discussion of Barton's (*op. cit.*) comment upon Van Rensselaer's letter. Barton's attempt to show it is a fraud is not very convincing.
10. *Ibid.*, p. 138.
11. 'The Complete Writings,' II, 108.
12. *Ibid.*, IV, 87–89.
13. *Ibid.*, *To a Stranger*, I, 153.
14. Though irrelevant to the theme of the poem, an ornithological note should be recorded here. Whatever this bird was, it was not the hermit-thrush, which Burroughs, in Washington, told Walt was the finest American singer. The hermit-thrush does breed and sing on Long Island, though normally it is a mountain bird. (See R. C. Murphy, American Museum of Natural History pamphlets, *Conservation, IV, p. 51*.) But its song is not 'reedy' as Whitman describes it, nor is it patterned in brief repetitions, like 'praise, praise, praise,' or 'with joy, with joy,' 'in the day, in the night, to all, to each.' It is shy, as he says, and gray-brown, as Burroughs probably told him. Either the thrasher's or the catbird's song conforms to Whitman's rhythms, and of course the mocking-bird's, if we can suppose another arrival of this

2. September 19, 1870. The note is added to an 1871 edition of the 'Vistas.'
3. Holloway, 'Whitman,' pp. 288, 289.
4. Traubel, 'W. W. in C.,' I, 369, 370.
5. *Harper's Magazine*, June, 1876.
6. His remarks in his 'Old Friends' of 1909 have much the same salty sarcasm. Taylor, of course, had died in 1878.
7. Kennedy, 'The Fight of a Book,' pp. 287–288.
8. See a picture of a Saturday night in the early nineties in the possession of the Century Club.
9. Some of these men do not appear in the present club directory, since they resigned before their death.
10. Clara Barrus, 'Whitman and Burroughs, Comrades,' p. 129.
11. The Lotos was less literary, but at least one of Walt's enemies, Whitelaw A. Reid, was a member.
12. Traubel, 'W. W. in C.,' II, 175.
13. For a lengthy treatment see Francis Winwar's 'American Giant: Walt Whitman and his Times' (New York and London: Harper and Brothers, 1941). For Mrs. Gilchrist's letters, see 'The Letters of Anne Gilchrist and Walt Whitman,' Edited by Thomas B. Harned (New York: Doubleday, Doran and Company, 1918).
14. 'Whitman,' Edited by E. Holloway, p. 998.

CHAPTER XXVIII

1. See 'The Complete Writings,' vols. IX, X.
2. See Harrison S. Morris, 'Walt Whitman; a brief biography with reminiscences' (Cambridge: Harvard University Press, 1929).
3. Nor are his too regular poems in 'Drum Taps' among his best.
4. 'The Complete Writings,' VII, 641.
5. Theodore Alois Buckley's translation, dating 1849–1853, is a literal prose version.
6. Thoreau, a much greater artist in prose than Whitman, is capable of such rhetorical Renaissance sentences. In both cases the flow of the long sentence floats and displays the epigram.
7. See also Jean Catel, 'Rhythme et Langage dans la 1re Edition des "Leaves of Grass" (1855)' (Montpellier, 1930), with reference to the structure.
8. 'The Complete Writings,' *Democratic Vistas*, V, 69–70.
9. 'The Gathering of the Forces,' II, 346 ff.
10. 'The Complete Writings,' *Out of the Cradle Endlessly Rocking*, II, 12.
11. *Ibid.*, II, 90.

12. First printed in 1904.
13. The poem was first called *A Child's Reminiscence.*

CHAPTER XXIX

1. See Muriel Ruckeyser, 'Willard Gibbs, American Genius' (New York: Doubleday, Doran and Company, 1942), *passim.*
2. 'The Complete Writings,' *Song of Myself,* I, 61.
3. *Ibid., Who Learns My Lesson Complete?,* II, 168.
4. *Ibid., To Think of Time,* II, 217 ff.
5. *Ibid., Quicksand Years,* II, 228.
6. *Ibid., Darest Thou O Soul,* II, 221.
7. See also an unpublished manuscript called 'Immortality and Democracy' in the Rollins College Library, and many references in Traubel's 'Walt Whitman, in Camden.'
8. 'The Complete Writings,' *The Last Invocation,* II, 233.

CHAPTER XXX

1. 'The Complete Writings,' III, 41 ff. The title of the preface to the 1888 edition of the 'Leaves' is *A Backward Glance O'er Travel'd Roads.*
2. An interesting addition is to be found in an interview in St. Louis in 1879. See note 6, chapter XXVI of this book: 'The whole tendency of poetry has been toward refinement. I myself have been ambitious to do something entirely different from that. . . . I have felt that was not worthy of America. Something more vigorous, *al fresco* was needed. . . . I determined from the beginning to put a whole living man in the expression of a poem, without wincing.'
3. Whitman does use 'behavior' in this modern sense.
4. Whitman had the same theory of a super 'race' as Hitler's, but an utterly different practice and hope. All men freely developing were to belong to his 'race.' He was the militant Quaker who proposed to make all the world friends. Hitler was the fanatical and cynical hater of men and exploiter of the weaknesses of human nature.
5. 'Whitman,' Edited by E. Holloway, p. 525.
6. 'The Complete Writings,' II, 290.

CHAPTER XXXI

1. She had to sue the executors after his death to get what the jury felt was her due share in the estate.
2. See Kennedy, 'The Fight of a Book,' p. 287.
3. 'Letters of John Keats,' Edited by Sidney Colvin (London: The Macmillan Company, 1928), p. 48.

A Selective Bibliography

BIBLIOGRAPHIES

Allen, Gay Wilson, 'Twenty-Five Years of Walt Whitman Bibliography, 1918–1942.' Boston: The F. W. Faxon Company, rev. ed., 1943.

Furness, Clifton Joseph, and Saunders, Henry S. A complete bibliography of Whitman is ready for publication.

Goldsmith, Alfred F., and Wells, Carolyn, 'A Concise Bibliography of the Works of Walt Whitman.' Boston and New York: Houghton Mifflin Company, 1922.

THE WORKS OF WALT WHITMAN

'Franklin Evans; Or the Inebriate.' Original Temperance Novel. Published as an extra to *The New World*. New York: November, 1842. (Pamphlet form.) See Emory Holloway, 'Uncollected Poetry and Prose.'

'Voices From the Press.' A Collection of Essays, Sketches, and Poems. Edited by James J. Brenton. New York: Charles B. Norton, 1850. Contains 'The Tomb Blossoms' reprinted from *The Democratic Review*.

'Leaves of Grass.' Brooklyn, New York, 1855. *First Edition.*

'Leaves of Grass.' Brooklyn, New York, 1856. *Second Edition.* Quotation from Emerson's letter: 'I greet you at the beginning of a great career. R. W. Emerson,' on backstrip.

'Leaves of Grass.' *Imprints.* American and European Criticisms of 'Leaves of Grass.' Boston: Thayer and Eldridge, 1860.

'Leaves of Grass.' Boston: Thayer and Eldridge, 1860–61. *Third Edition.*

'Walt Whitman's Drum Taps.' New York, 1865. Second edition contains the Lincoln poems.

'Leaves of Grass.' New York, 1867. *Fourth Edition.*

'Poems by Walt Whitman.' Selected and Edited by William Michael Rossetti. London: John Camden Hotten, 1868.

'Leaves of Grass.' Washington, D.C., 1871. *Fifth Edition.*

'After All Not to Create Only.' Recited by Walt Whitman on Invitation of Managers American Institute, On Opening Their 40th Annual Exhibition. New York, noon, September 7th, 1871. Boston: Roberts Brothers, 1871.

'Democratic Vistas.' Memoranda. Washington, D.C., 1871. (Pamphlet form.)

'Passage to India.' 'Leaves of Grass.' Washington, D.C., 1871. (Pamphlet form.)

'As a Strong Bird on Pinions Free and Other Poems.' Washington, D.C., 1872.

'Memoranda of the War.' *Author's Publication.* Camden, New Jersey, 1875–76. On Cover: 'Walt Whitman's Memoranda of the War. Written on the Spot in 1863–65.'

'Leaves of Grass.' Nine-Line Poem beginning 'Come, Said My Soul.' Author's autograph in ink on title-page. *Author's Edition,* with portraits from Life. Camden, New Jersey, 1876. *Sixth Edition.*

'Two Rivulets, including Democratic Vistas, Centennial Songs, and Passage to India.' *Author's Edition.* Camden, New Jersey, 1876. The 1876 'Leaves' and 'Two Rivulets' were sold by Whitman as a complete edition and called the *Centennial Edition.*

'The Poetry of the Future.' First printed in *The North American Review,* February, 1881. (Pamphlet form.)

'Leaves of Grass.' Boston: James R. Osgood and Company, 1881–82. *Seventh Edition.*

'Leaves of Grass.' *Author's Copyright Edition.* London: David Bogue, 1881.

'Leaves of Grass.' Preface to the original edition. London: Trubner and Company, 1881.

'Leaves of Grass.' Nine-Line Poem beginning 'Come, Said My Soul,' signed with author's autograph in ink. *Author's Edition.* Camden, New Jersey, 1882. *Eighth Edition.*

'Leaves of Grass.' Philadelphia: Rees, Welsh and Company, 1882. *Ninth Edition.*

'Specimen Days and Collect.' Philadelphia: Rees, Welsh and Company, 1882–83. Companion volume to the 1882 'Leaves.'

'Obsequies of Red Jacket.' Volume III of Transactions of the Buffalo Historical Society. Published by order of the Society. Buffalo, 1885. Contains 'Red Jacket, an Impromptu,' by Walt Whitman.

'Specimen Days in America.' Newly revised by the author, with fresh preface and additional note. London: Walter Scott, 1887.

'November Boughs.' Philadelphia: David McKay, 1888.

'Democratic Vistas, and Other Papers.' Published by arrangement with the author. London: Walter Scott, 1888.

'Complete Poems and Prose of Walt Whitman, 1855–1888.' Authenticated and Personal. (Handled by Walt Whitman.) Portraits from life. Autograph. *Tenth Edition.*

'Leaves of Grass.' With Sands at Seventy and a Backward Glance o'er Travel'd Roads. May 31, 1889. Special Edition of the 'Leaves.' *Eleventh Edition.*

'Good-Bye, My Fancy.' *2d Annex to Leaves of Grass.* Philadelphia: David McKay, 1891.

'Leaves of Grass.' Including 'Sands at Seventy.' 1st Annex, Good-Bye, My Fancy; 2d Annex, A Backward Glance o'er Travel'd Roads, and Portrait from Life. (Nine-Line Poem, facsimile signature of the author.) Philadelphia: David McKay, 1891–92. *Twelfth Edition.*

'Complete Prose Works.' Philadelphia: David McKay, 1892. Companion volume to the 1892 'Leaves.'

'In Re Walt Whitman.' Edited by his Literary Executors, Horace L. Traubel, Richard Maurice Bucke, Thomas B. Harned. Published by the Editors through David McKay, Philadelphia, 1893.

'Calamus.' A Series of Letters Written during the Years 1868–1880. By Walt Whitman to a Young Friend (Peter Doyle). Edited with an introduction by Richard Maurice Bucke, M.D., one of Whitman's Literary Executors. Boston: Laurnes Maynard, 1897.

'The Wound Dresser.' A Series of Letters Written from the Hospitals in Washington during the War of Rebellion. Edited by Richard Maurice Bucke, M.D., one of Whitman's literary executors. Boston: Small, Maynard and Company, 1898.

'Notes and Fragments.' Edited by Dr. Richard Maurice Bucke, One of His Literary Executors. 'Waifs From the Deep Cast High and Dry,' 'Leaves of Grass,' printed for private distribution only. 1899.

'Letters Written By Walt Whitman to His Mother From 1866 to 1872.' Together with Certain Papers Prepared from Material now First Utilized. Edited by Thomas B. Harned, one of Whitman's Literary Executors. New York and London: G. P. Putnam's Sons, 1902.

'The Complete Writings of Walt Whitman.' Issued under the editorial supervision of his Literary Executors, Richard Maurice Bucke, Thomas B. Harned, and Horace L. Traubel. With additional bibliographical and critical material by Oscar Lovell Triggs, Ph.D. New York and London: G. P. Putnam's Sons, 1902. 10 vols.

'Walt Whitman's Diary in Canada.' With Extracts from other of his Diaries and Literary Note-Books. Edited by William Sloane Kennedy. Boston: Small, Maynard and Company, 1904.

'An American Primer.' With Facsimiles of the Original Manuscript. Edited by Horace Traubel. Boston: Small, Maynard and Company, 1904.

'The Letters of Anne Gilchrist and Walt Whitman.' Edited by Thomas B. Harned. New York: Doubleday, Doran and Company, 1918.

'The Gathering of the Forces.' Editorials, Essays, Literary and Dramatic Reviews and other material Written by Walt Whitman as Editor of the Brooklyn Daily Eagle in 1846 and 1847. Edited by Cleveland Rogers and John Black. With a foreword and a Sketch of Whitman's Life and Work During Two Unknown Years. New York and London: G. P. Putnam's Sons, 1920. 2 vols.

'The Uncollected Poetry and Prose of Walt Whitman.' Much of Which Has Been But Recently Discovered with Various Early Manuscripts Now First Published. Collected and Edited by Emory Holloway. New York: Doubleday, Doran and Company, 1921. 2 vols.

'Pictures.' An Unpublished Poem by Walt Whitman. With an Introduction and Notes by Emory Holloway. New York: The Pine House, 1927.

'The Half-Breed and Other Stories.' Edited by Thomas Ollive Mabbott. New York, 1927.

'Walt Whitman's Workshop.' Edited by Clifton Joseph Furness. Cambridge: Harvard University Press, 1928.

'I Sit and Look Out.' Editorials from the Brooklyn Daily Times. Selected and Edited by Emory Holloway and Vernolian Schwartz. New York: Columbia University Press, 1932.

'New York Dissected.' A Sheaf of Recently Discovered Newspaper Articles by the author of 'Leaves of Grass.' Introduction and Notes by Emory Holloway and Ralph Adimari. New York: Rufus Rockwell Wilson, Inc., 1936.

'Walt Whitman, Complete Poetry and Selected Prose and Letters.' Edited by Emory Holloway. London: The Nonesuch Press.

'Leaves of Grass.' Edited by Emory Holloway. New York: E. P. Dutton and Company. Everyman's Library. (Forthcoming.)

BIOGRAPHY AND CRITICISM

Allen, Gay Wilson, 'A Walt Whitman Handbook.' Chicago: Packard and Company (to be issued in 1943 or 1944).

Arvin, Newton, 'Whitman.' New York: The Macmillan Company, 1938.

Barrus, Clara, 'Whitman and Burroughs, Comrades.' Boston and New York: Houghton Mifflin Company, 1931.

Bazalgette, Léon, 'Le Poème-Évangile de Walt Whitman.' Paris: Mercure de France, 1921.

Binns, Henry Bryan, 'A Life of Walt Whitman.' New York: E. P. Dutton and Company, 1905.

Bucke, Dr. Richard Maurice, 'Walt Whitman.' Philadelphia: David McKay, 1883.

Burroughs, John, 'Notes on Walt Whitman as Poet and Person.' New York: American News Company, 1867. Revised Edition in 1871.

Burroughs, John, 'Whitman, A Study.' Boston and New York: Houghton Mifflin Company, 1896.

Canby, Henry Seidel, 'Classic Americans: A Study of Eminent American Writers from Irving to Whitman.' New York: Harcourt Brace and Company, 1931.

Catel, Jean, 'Rhythme et Langage dans la Ire Edition des "Leaves of Grass" (1855).' Montpellier: Causse, Graille et Castelnau, 1930.

Catel, Jean, 'Walt Whitman, La Naissance du Poète.' Montpellier: Causse, Graille et Castelnau, 1929.

Deutsch, Babette, 'Walt Whitman, Builder for America.' New York: Julian Messner Inc., 1941.

Fausset, Hugh L'Anson, 'Walt Whitman: Poet of Democracy.' New Haven: Yale University Press, 1942.

Furness, Clifton Joseph, 'Walt Whitman's Workshop.' Cambridge: Harvard University Press, 1928.

Glicksberg, Charles I., 'Walt Whitman and the Civil War.' A Collection of Original Articles and Manuscripts. Philadelphia: University of Pennsylvania Press, 1933.

Holloway, Emory, 'Whitman, An Interpretation in Narrative.' New York and London: Alfred A. Knopf, 1926.

'In Re Walt Whitman.' Edited by his Literary Executors, Horace L. Traubel, Richard Maurice Bucke, Thomas B. Harned. Published by the Editors through David McKay, Philadelphia, 1893.

Kennedy, William Sloane, 'The Fight of a Book for the World.' Massachusetts: The Stonecroft Press, 1926.

Kennedy, William Sloane, 'Reminiscences of Walt Whitman. With Extracts from His Letters and Remarks on His Writings.' Paisley and London: Alexander Gardner, 1896.

Matthiesen, F. O., 'American Renaissance.' New York: Oxford University Press, 1941

Morris, Harrison S., 'Walt Whitman; a Brief Biography with Reminiscences.' Boston, 1929.

Perry, Bliss, 'Walt Whitman, His Life and Work.' New York: Houghton Mifflin Company, 1906.

Schyberg, Frederik, 'Walt Whitman.' Köbenhavn, Gyldendal, 1933. (Valuable for its discussion of Whitman's European parallels and influences.)

Traubel, Horace, 'With Walt Whitman in Camden.' Vol. I, Boston: Small, Maynard and Company, 1906. Vol. II, New York: D. Appleton and Company, 1908. Vol. III, New York: Mitchell Kennerly, 1914.

'The Uncollected Poetry and Prose of Walt Whitman.' Collected and Edited by Emory Holloway. New York: Doubleday, Doran and Company, 1921. 2 vols.

Winwar, Francis, 'American Giant: Walt Whitman and his Times.' New York and London: Harper and Brothers, 1941.

(See Notes to this volume for other references to books and articles about Walt Whitman.)

INDEX

〰〰〰